D1482488

The
House of the Arrow

Books by A. E. W. MASON

The
House of the Arrow

By
A. E. W. MASON

Carroll & Graf Publishers, Inc.
New York

First Carroll & Graf edition 1984.

Carroll & Graf Publishers, Inc.
260 Fifth Avenue
New York, N.Y. 10001

ISBN: 0-88184-066-1

Manufactured in the United States of America

CONTENTS

v

Contents

THE HOUSE OF THE ARROW

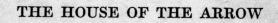

CHAPTER ONE: *Letters of Mark*

MESSRS. FROBISHER & HASLITT, the solicitors on the east side of Russell Square, counted amongst their clients a great many who had undertakings established in France; and the firm was very proud of this branch of its business.

"It gives us a place in history," Mr. Jeremy Haslitt used to say. "For it dates from the year 1806, when Mr. James Frobisher, then our very energetic senior partner, organised the escape of hundreds of British subjects who were detained in France by the edict of the first Napoleon. The firm received the thanks of His Majesty's Government and has been fortunate enough to retain the connection thus made. I look after that side of our affairs myself."

Mr. Haslitt's daily batch of letters, therefore, contained as a rule a fair number bearing the dark-blue stamp of France upon their envelopes. On this morning of early April, however, there was only one. It was addressed in a spidery, uncontrolled hand with which Mr. Haslitt was unfamiliar. But it bore the postmark of Dijon, and Mr. Haslitt tore it open rather quickly. He had a client in Dijon, a widow, Mrs. Harlowe, of whose health he had had bad reports. The letter was certainly written from her house, La Maison Grenelle, but not by her. He turned to the signature.

"Waberski?" he said, with a frown. "Boris Waberski?" And then, as he identified his correspondent, "Oh, yes, yes."

He sat down in his chair and read. The first part of the letter was merely flowers and compliments, but halfway down the second page its object was made clear as

9

glass. It was five hundred pounds. Old Mr. Haslitt smiled and read on, keeping up, whilst he read, a one-sided conversation with the writer.

"I have a great necessity of that money," wrote Boris, "and——"

"I am quite sure of that," said Mr. Haslitt.

"My beloved sister, Jeanne-Marie——" the letter continued.

"Sister-in-law," Mr. Haslitt corrected.

"——cannot live for long, in spite of all the care and attention I give to her," Boris Waberski went on. "She has left me, as no doubt you know, a large share of her fortune. Already, then, it is mine—yes? One may say so and be favourably understood. We must look at the facts with the eyes. Expedite me, then, by the recommended post a little of what is mine and agree my distinguished salutations."

Haslitt's smile became a broad grin. He had in one of his tin boxes a copy of the will of Jeanne-Marie Harlowe drawn up in due form by her French notary at Dijon, by which every farthing she possessed was bequeathed without condition to her husband's niece and adopted daughter, Betty Harlowe. Jeremy Haslitt almost destroyed that letter. He folded it; his fingers twitched at it; there was already actually a tear at the edges of the sheets when he changed his mind.

"No," he said to himself. "No! With the Boris Waberskis one never knows," and he locked the letter away on a ledge of his private safe.

He was very glad that he had when three weeks later he read, in the obituary column of *The Times,* the announcement of Mrs. Harlowe's death, and received a big card with a very deep black border in the French style from Betty Harlowe inviting him to the funeral at Dijon. The invitation was merely formal. He could hardly have reached Dijon in time for the ceremony had he started off that instant. He contented himself with writing a few lines of sincere condolence to the girl, and a letter to the

French notary in which he placed the services of the firm at Betty's disposal. Then he waited.

"I shall hear again from little Boris," he said, and he heard within the week. The handwriting was more spidery and uncontrolled than ever; hysteria and indignation had played havoc with Waberski's English; also he had doubled his demand.

"It is outside belief," he wrote. "Nothing has she left to her so attentive brother. There is something here I do not much like. It must be one thousand pounds now, by the recommended post. 'You have always had the world against you, my poor Boris,' she say with the tears all big in her dear eyes. 'But I make all right for you in my will.' And now nothing! I speak, of course, to my niece—ah, that hard one! She snap her the fingers at me! Is that a behaviour? One thousand pounds, mister! Otherwise there will be awkwardnesses! Yes! People do not snap them the fingers at Boris Waberski without the payment. So one thousand pounds by the recommended post or awkwardnesses"; and this time Boris Waberski did not invite Mr. Haslitt to agree any salutations, distinguished or otherwise, but simply signed his name with a straggling pen which shot all over the sheet.

Mr. Haslitt did not smile over this letter. He rubbed the palms of his hands softly together.

"Then we shall have to make some awkwardnesses too," he said hastily, and he locked this second letter away with the first. But Mr. Haslitt found it a little difficult to settle to his work. There was that girl out there in the big house at Dijon and no one of her race near her! He got up from his chair abruptly and crossed the corridor to the offices of his junior partner.

"Jim, you were at Monte Carlo this winter," he said.

"For a week," answered Jim Frobisher.

"I think I asked you to call on a client of ours who has a villa there—Mrs. Harlowe."

Jim Frobisher nodded. "I did. But Mrs. Harlowe was ill. There was a niece, but she was out."

"You saw no one, then?" Jeremy Haslitt asked.

"No, that's wrong," Jim corrected. "I saw a strange creature who came to the door to make Mrs. Harlowe's excuses—a Russian."

"Boris Waberski," said Mr. Haslitt.

"That's the name."

Mr. Haslitt sat down in a chair.

"Tell me about him, Jim."

Jim Frobisher stared at nothing for a few moments. He was a young man of twenty-six who had only during this last year succeeded to his partnership. Though quick enough when action was imperative, he was naturally deliberate in his estimates of other people's characters; and a certain awe he had of old Jeremy Haslitt doubled that natural deliberation in any matters of the firm's business. He answered at length.

"He is a tall, shambling fellow with a shock of grey hair standing up like wires above a narrow forehead and a pair of wild eyes. He mabe me think of a marionette whose limbs have not been properly strung. I should imagine that he was rather extravagant and emotional. He kept twitching at his moustache with very long, tobacco-stained fingers. The sort of man who might go off at the deep end at any moment."

Mr. Haslitt smiled.

"That's just what I thought."

"Is he giving you any trouble?" asked Jim.

"Not yet," said Mr. Haslitt. "But Mrs. Harlowe is dead, and I think it very likely that he will. Did he play at the tables?"

"Yes, rather high," said Jim. "I suppose that he lived on Mrs. Harlowe."

"I suppose so," said Mr. Haslitt, and he sat for a little while in silence. Then: "It's a pity you didn't see Betty Harlowe. I stopped at Dijon once on my way to the South of France five years ago when Simon Harlowe, the husband, was alive. Betty was then a long-legged slip of a girl in black silk stockings with a pale, clear face and

12

dark hair and big eyes—rather beautiful." Mr. Haslitt moved in his chair uncomfortably. That old house with its great garden of chestnuts and sycamores and that girl alone in it with an aggrieved and half-crazed man thinking out awkwardnesses for her—Mr. Haslitt did not like the picture!

"Jim," he said suddenly, "could you arrange your work so that you could get away at short notice, if it becomes advisable?"

Jim looked up in surprise. Excursions and alarms, as the old stage directions have it, were not recognised as a rule by the firm of Frobisher & Haslitt. If its furniture was dingy, its methods were stately; clients might be urgent, but haste and hurry were words for which the firm had no use. No doubt, somewhere round the corner, there would be an attorney who understood them. Yet here was Mr. Haslitt himself, with his white hair and his curious round face, half-babyish, half-supremely intelligent, actually advocating that his junior partner should be prepared to skip to the Continent at a word.

"No doubt I could," said Jim, and Mr. Haslitt looked him over with approbation.

Jim Frobisher had an unusual quality of which his acquaintances, even his friends, knew only the outward signs. He was a solitary person. Very few people up till now had mattered to him at all, and even those he could do without. It was his passion to feel that his life and the means of his life did not depend upon the purchased skill of other people; and he had spent the spare months of his life in the fulfilment of his passion. A half-decked sailing-boat which one man could handle, an ice-axe, a rifle, an inexhaustible volume or two like *The Ring and the Book*—these with the stars and his own thoughts had been his companions on many lonely expeditions; and in consequence he had acquired a queer little look of aloofness which made him at once noticeable amongst his fellows. A misleading look, since it encouraged a confidence for which there might not be suffi-

cient justification. It was just this look which persuaded
Mr. Haslitt now. "This is the very man to deal with
creatures like Boris Waberski," he thought, but he did
not say so aloud.

What he did say was:

"It may not be necessary after all. Betty Harlowe has
a French lawyer. No doubt he is adequate. Besides"—
and he smiled as he recollected a phrase in Waberski's
second letter—"Betty seems very capable of looking after
herself. We shall see."

He went back to his own office, and for a week he heard
no more from Dijon. His anxiety, indeed, was almost
forgotten when suddenly startling news arrived and by the
most unexpected channel.

Jim Frobisher brought it. He broke into Mr. Haslitt's
office at the sacred moment when the senior partner was
dictating to a clerk the answers to his morning letters.

"Sir!" cried Jim, and stopped short at the sight of the
clerk. Mr. Haslitt took a quick look at his young partner's face and said:

"We will resume these answers, Godfrey, later on."

The clerk took his shorthand notebook out of the room,
and Mr. Haslitt turned to Jim Frobisher.

"Now, what's your bad news, Jim?"

Jim blurted it out.

"Waberski accuses Betty Harlowe of murder."

"What!"

Mr. Haslitt sprang to his feet. Jim Frobisher could
not have said whether incredulity or anger had the upper
hand with the old man, the one so creased his forehead,
the other so blazed in his eyes.

"Little Betty Harlowe!" he said in a wondering voice.

"Yes. Waberski has laid a formal charge with the
Prefect of Police at Dijon. He accuses Betty of poison-
ing Mrs. Harlowe on the night of April the twenty-
seventh."

"But Betty's not arrested?" Mr. Haslitt exclaimed.

"No, but she's under surveillance."

Mr. Haslitt sat heavily down in his arm-chair at his table. Extravagant! Uncontrolled! These were very mild epithets for Boris Waberski. Here was a devilish malignity at work in the rogue, a passion for revenge just as mean as could be imagined.

"How do you know all this, Jim?" he asked suddenly.

"I have had a letter this morning from Dijon."

"You?" exclaimed Mr. Haslitt, and the question caught hold of Jim Frobisher and plunged him too among perplexities. In the first shock of the news, the monstrous fact of the accusation had driven everything else out of his head. Now he asked himself why, after all, had the news come to him and not to the partner who had the Harlowe estate in his charge.

"Yes, it is strange," he replied. "And here's another queer thing. The letter doesn't come from Betty Harlowe, but from a friend, a companion of hers, Ann Upcott."

Mr. Haslitt was a little relieved.

"Betty had a friend with her, then? That's a good thing." He reached out his hand across the table. "Let me read the letter, Jim."

Frobisher had been carrying it in his hand, and he gave it now to Jeremy Haslitt. It was a letter of many sheets, and Jeremy let the edges slip and flicker under the ball of his thumb.

"Have I got to read all this?" he said ruefully, and he set himself to his task. Boris Waberski had first of all accused Betty to her face. Betty had contemptuously refused to answer the charge, and Waberski had gone straight off to the Prefect of Police. He had returned in an hour's time, wildly gesticulating and talking aloud to himself. He had actually asked Ann Upcott to back him up. Then he had packed his bags and retired to an hotel in the town. The story was set out in detail, with quotations from Waberski's violent, crazy talk; and as the old man read, Jim Frobisher became more and more uneasy, more and more troubled.

He was sitting by the tall, broad window which looked out upon the square, expecting some explosion of wrath and contempt. But he saw anxiety peep out of Mr. Haslitt's face and stay there as he read. More than once he stopped altogether in his reading, like a man seeking to remember or perhaps to discover.

"But the whole thing's as clear as daylight," Jim said to himself impatiently. And yet—and yet—Mr. Haslitt had sat in that arm-chair during the better part of the day, during the better part of thirty years. How many men and women during those years had crossed the roadway below this window and crept into this quiet oblong room with their grievances, their calamities, their confessions? And had passed out again, each one contributing his little to complete the old man's knowledge and sharpen the edge of his wit? Then, if Mr. Haslitt was troubled, there was something in that letter, or some mission from it, which he himself in his novitiate had overlooked. He began to read it over again in his mind to the best of his recollection, but he had not got far before Mr. Haslitt put the letter down.

"Surely, sir," cried Jim, "it's an obvious case of blackmail."

Mr. Haslitt awoke with a little shake of his shoulders. "Blackmail? Oh! that of course, Jim."

Mr. Haslitt got up and unlocked his safe. He took from it the two Waberski letters and brought them across the room to Jim.

"Here's the evidence, as damning as any one could wish."

Jim read the letters through and uttered a little cry of delight.

"The rogue has delivered himself over to us."

"Yes," said Mr. Haslitt.

But to him, at all events, that was not enough; he was still looking through the lines of the letter for something beyond, which he could not find.

"Then what's troubling you?" asked Frobisher.

16

Mr. Haslitt took his stand upon the worn hearthrug with his back towards the fire.

"This, Jim," and he began to expound. "In ninety-five of these cases out of a hundred, there is something else, something behind the actual charge, which isn't mentioned, but on which the blackmailer is really banking. As a rule it's some shameful little secret, some blot on the family honour, which any sort of public trial would bring to light. And there must be something of that kind here. The more preposterous Waberski's accusation is, the more certain it is that he knows something to the discredit of the Harlowe name, which any Harlowe would wish to keep dark. Only, I haven't an idea what the wretched thing can be!"

"It might be some trifle," Jim suggested, "which a crazy person like Waberski would exaggerate."

"Yes," Mr. Haslitt agreed. "That happens. A man brooding over imagined wrongs, and flighty and extravagant besides—yes, that might well be, Jim."

Jeremy Haslitt spoke in a more cheerful voice.

"Let us see exactly what we do know of the family," he said, and he pulled up a chair to face Jim Frobisher and the window. But he had not yet sat down in it, when there came a discreet knock upon the door, and a clerk entered to announce a visitor.

"Not yet," said Mr. Haslitt before the name of the visitor had been mentioned.

"Very good, sir," said the clerk, and he retired. The firm of Frobisher & Haslitt conducted its business in that way. It was the real thing as a firm of solicitors, and clients who didn't like its methods were very welcome to take their affairs to the attorney round the corner. Just as people who go to the real thing in the line of tailors must put up with the particular style in which he cuts their clothes.

Mr. Haslitt turned back to Jim.

"Let us see what we know," he said, and he sat down in the chair.

"SIMON HARLOWE," he began, "was the owner of the famous Clos du Prince vineyards on the Côte-d'Or to the east of Dijon. He had an estate in Norfolk, this big house, the Maison Grenelle in Dijon, and a villa at Monte Carlo. But he spent most of his time in Dijon, where at the age of forty-five he married a French lady, Jeanne-Marie Raviart. There was, I believe, quite a little romance about the affair. Jeanne-Marie was married and separated from her husband, and Simon Harlowe waited, I think, for ten years until the husband Raviart died."

Jim Frobisher moved quickly and Mr. Haslitt, who seemed to be reading off this history in the pattern of the carpet, looked up.

"Yes, I see what you mean," he said, replying to Jim's movement. "Yes, there might have been some sort of affair between those two before they were free to marry. But nowadays, my dear Jim! Opinion takes a more human view than it did in my youth. Besides, don't you see, this little secret, to be of any value to Boris Waberski, must be near enough to Betty Harlowe—I don't say to affect her if published, but to make Waberski think that she would hate to have it published. Now Betty Harlowe doesn't come into the picture at all until two years after Simon and Jeanne-Marie were married, when it became clear that they were not likely to have any children. No, the love-affairs of Simon Harlowe are sufficiently remote for us to leave them aside."

Jim Frobisher accepted the demolition of his idea with a flush of shame.

"I was a fool to think of it," he said.

"Not a bit," replied Mr. Haslitt cheerfully. "Let us

look at every possibility. That's the only way which will
help us to get a glimpse of the truth. I resume, then.
Simon Harlowe was a collector. Yes, he had a passion
for collecting and a very catholic one. His one sitting-
room at the Maison Grenelle was a perfect treasure-house,
not only of beautiful things, but of out-of-the-way things
too. He liked to live amongst them and do his work
amongst them. His married life did not last long. For
he died five years ago at the age of fifty-one."

Mr. Haslitt's eyes once more searched for recollections
amongst the convolutions of the carpet.

"That's really about all I know of him. He was a
pleasant fellow enough, but not very sociable. No, there's
nothing to light a candle for us there, I am afraid."

Mr. Haslitt turned his thoughts to the widow.

"Jeanne-Marie Harlowe," he said. "It's extraordinary
how little I know about her, now I come to count it up.
Natural too, though. For she sold the Norfolk estate
and has since passed her whole time between Monte Carlo
and Dijon and—oh, yes—a little summer-house on the
Côte-d'Or amongst her vineyards."

"She was left rich, I suppose?" Frobisher asked.

"Very well off, at all events," Mr. Haslitt replied.
"The Clos du Prince Burgundy has a fine reputation, but
there's not a great deal of it."

"Did she come to England ever?"

"Never," said Mr. Haslitt. "She was content, it
seems, with Dijon, though to my mind the smaller provincial towns of France are dull enough to make one
scream. However, she was used to it, and then her heart
began to trouble her, and for the last two years she has
been an invalid. There's nothing to help us there." And
Mr. Haslitt looked across to Jim for confirmation.

"Nothing," said Jim.

"Then we are only left the child Betty Harlowe and—
oh, yes, your correspondent, your voluminous correspondent, Ann Upcott. Who is she, Jim? Where did she
spring from? How does she find herself in the Maison

Grenelle? Come, confess, young man," and Mr. Haslitt archly looked at his junior partner. "Why should Boris Waberski expect her support?"

Jim Frobisher threw his arms wide.

"I haven't an idea," he said. "I have never seen her. I have never heard of her. I never knew of her existence until that letter came this morning with her name signed at the end of it."

Mr. Haslitt started up. He crossed the room to his table and, fixing his folding glasses on the bridge of his nose, he bent over the letter.

"But she writes to you, Jim," he objected. " 'Dear Mr. Frobisher,' she writes. She doesn't address the firm at all"; and he waited, looking at Jim, expecting him to withdraw this denial.

Jim, however, only shook his head.

"It's the most bewildering thing," he replied. "I can't make head or tail of it"; and Mr. Haslitt could not doubt now that he spoke the truth, so utterly and frankly baffled the young man was. "Why should Ann Upcott write to me? I have been asking myself that question for the last half-hour. And why didn't Betty Harlowe write to you, who have had her affairs in your care?"

"Ah!"

That last question helped Mr. Haslitt to an explanation. His face took a livelier expression.

"The answer to that is in Waberski's, the second letter. Betty—she snap her fingers at his awkwardnesses. She doesn't take the charge seriously. She will have left it to the French notary to dispose of it. Yes—I think that makes Ann Upcott's letter to you intelligible, too. The ceremonies of the Law in a foreign country would frighten a stranger, as this girl is apparently, more than they would Betty Harlowe, who has lived for four years in the midst of them. So she writes to the first name in the title of the firm, and writes to him as a man. That's it, Jim," and the old man rubbed his hands together in his satisfaction.

"A girl in terror wouldn't get any comfort out of writing to an abstraction. She wants to know that she's in touch with a real person. So she writes, 'Dear Mr. Frobisher.' That's it! You can take my word for it."

Mr. Haslitt walked back to his chair. But he did not sit down in it; he stood with his hands in his pockets, looking out of the window over Frobisher's head.

"But that doesn't bring us any nearer to finding out what is Boris Waberski's strong suit, does it? We haven't a clue to it," he said ruefully.

To both of the men, indeed, Mr. Haslitt's flat, unilluminated narrative of facts, without a glimpse into the characters of any of the participants in the little drama, seemed the most unhelpful thing. Yet the whole truth was written there—the truth not only of Waberski's move, but of all the strange terrors and mysteries into which the younger of the two men was now to be plunged. Jim Frobisher was to recognise that, when, shaken to the soul, he resumed his work in the office. For it was interrupted now.

Mr. Haslitt, looking out of the window over his partner's head, saw a telegraph-boy come swinging across the square and hesitate in the roadway below.

"I expect that's a telegram for us," he said, with the hopeful anticipation people in trouble have that something from outside will happen and set them right.

Jim turned round quickly. The boy was still upon the pavement examining the numbers of the houses.

"We ought to have a brass plate upon the door," said Jim with a touch of impatience; and Mr. Haslitt's eyebrows rose half the height of his forehead towards his thick white hair. He was really distressed by the Waberski incident, but this suggestion, and from a partner in the firm, shocked him like a sacrilege.

"My dear boy, what are you thinking of?" he expostulated. "I hope I am not one of those obstinate old fogies who refuse to march with the times. We have had, as you know, a telephone instrument recently installed in the

21

junior clerks' office. I believe that I myself proposed it. But a brass plate upon the door! My dear Jim! Let us leave that to Harley Street and Southampton Row! But I see that telegram is for us."

The tiny Mercury with the shako and red cord to his uniform made up his mind and disappeared into the hall below. The telegram was brought upstairs and Mr. Haslitt tore it open. He stared at it blankly for a few seconds, then without a word, but with a very anxious look in his eyes, he handed it to Jim Frobisher.

Jim Frobisher read:

> *Please, please, send some one to help me at once. The Prefect of Police has called in Hanaud, a great detective of the Sûreté in Paris. They must think me guilty.—Betty Harlowe.*

The telegram fluttered from Jim's fingers to the floor. It was like a cry for help at night coming from a great distance.

"I must go, sir, by the night boat," he said.

"To be sure!" said Mr. Haslitt a little absently.

Jim, however, had enthusiasm enough for both. His chivalry was fired, as is the way with lonely men, by the picture his imagination drew. The little girl, Betty Harlowe! What age was she? Twenty-one! Not a day more. She had been wandering with all the proud indifference of her sex and youth, until suddenly she found her feet caught in some trap set by a traitor, and looked about her; and terror came and with it a wild cry for help.

"Girls never notice danger signals," he said. "No, they walk blindly into the very heart of catastrophe." Who could tell what links of false and cunning evidence Boris Waberski had been hammering away at in the dark, to slip swiftly at the right moment over her wrist and ankle? And with that question he was seized with a great discouragement.

"We know very little of Criminal Procedure, even in our own country, in this office," he said regretfully.

"Happily," said Mr. Haslitt with some tartness. With him it was the Firm first and last. Messrs. Frobisher & Haslitt never went in to the Criminal Courts. Litigation, indeed, even of the purest kind was frowned upon. It is true there was a small special staff, under the leadership of an old managing clerk, tucked away upon an upper floor, like an unpresentable relation in a great house, which did a little of that kind of work. But it only did it for hereditary clients, and then as a favour.

"However," said Mr. Haslitt as he noticed Jim's discomfort, "I haven't a doubt, my boy, that you will be equal to whatever is wanted. But remember, there's something at the back of this which we here don't know."

Jim shifted his position rather abruptly. This cry of the old man was becoming parrot-like—a phrase, a formula. Jim was thinking of the girl in Dijon and hearing her piteous cry for help. She was not "snapping her the fingers" now.

"It's a matter of common sense," Mr. Haslitt insisted. "Take a comparison. Bath, for instance, would never call in Scotland Yard over a case of this kind. There would have to be the certainty of a crime first, and then grave doubt as to who was the criminal. This is a case for an autopsy and the doctors. If they call in this man Hanaud"—and he stopped.

He picked the telegram up from the floor and read it through again.

"Yes—Hanaud," he repeated, his face clouding and growing bright and clouding again like a man catching at and just missing a very elusive recollection. He gave up the pursuit in the end. "Well, Jim, you had better take the two letters of Waberski, and Ann Upcott's three-volume novel, and Betty's telegram"—he gathered the papers together and enclosed them in a long envelope—"and I shall expect you back again with a smiling face in

23

a very few days. I should like to see our little Boris when he is asked to explain those letters."

Mr. Haslitt gave the envelope to Jim and rang his bell.

"There is some one waiting to see me, I think," he said to the clerk who answered it.

The clerk named a great landowner, who had been kicking his heels during the last half-hour in an undusted waiting-room with a few mouldy old Law books in a battered glass case to keep him company.

"You can show him in now," said Mr. Haslitt as Jim retired to his own office; and when the great landowner entered, he merely welcomed him with a reproach.

"You didn't make an appointment, did you?" he said.

But all through that interview, though his advice was just the precise, clear advice for which the firm was quietly famous, Mr. Haslitt's mind was still playing hide-and-seek with a memory, catching glimpses of the fringes of its skirt as it gleamed and vanished.

"Memory is a woman," he said to himself. "If I don't run after her she will come of her own accord."

But he was in the common case of men with women: he could not but run after her. Towards the end of the interview, however, his shoulders and head moved with a little jerk, and he wrote a word down on a slip of paper. As soon as his client had gone, he wrote a note and sent it off by a messenger who had orders to wait for an answer. The messenger returned within the hour and Mr. Haslitt hurried to Jim Frobisher's office.

Jim had just finished handing over his affairs to various clerks and was locking up the drawers of his desk.

"Jim, I have remembered where I have heard the name of this man Hanaud before. You have met Julius Ricardo? He's one of our clients."

"Yes," said Frobisher. "I remember him—a rather finnicking person in Grosvenor Square."

"That's the man. He's a friend of Hanaud and absurdly proud of the friendship. He and Hanaud were somehow mixed up in a rather scandalous crime some time ago—at Aix-les-Bains, I think. Well, Ricardo will give you a letter of introduction to him, and tell you something about him, if you will go round to Grosvenor Square at five this afternoon."

"Capital!" said Jim Frobisher.

He kept the appointment, and was told how he must expect to be awed at one moment, leaped upon unpleasantly at the next, ridiculed at a third, and treated with great courtesy and friendship at the fourth. Jim discounted Mr. Ricardo's enthusiasm, but he got the letter and crossed the Channel that night. On the journey it occurred to him that if Hanaud was a man of such high mark, he would not be free, even at an urgent call, to pack his bags and leave for the provinces in an instant. Jim broke his journey, therefore, at Paris, and in the course of the morning found his way to the Direction of the Sûreté on the Quai d'Horloge just behind the Palais de Justice.

"Monsieur Hanaud?" he asked eagerly, and the porter took his card and his letter of introduction. The great man was still in Paris, then, he thought with relief. He was taken to a long dark corridor, lit with electric globes even on that bright morning of early summer. There he rubbed elbows with malefactors and gendarmes for half an hour whilst his confidence in himself ebbed away. Then a bell rang and a policeman in plain clothes went up to him. One side of the corridor was lined with a row of doors.

"It is for you, sir," said the policeman, and he led Frobisher to one of the doors and opened it, and stood aside. Frobisher straightened his shoulders and marched in.

CHAPTER THREE: *Servants of Chance*

FROBISHER found himself at one end of an oblong room. Opposite to him a couple of windows looked across the shining river to the big Théâtre du Chatelet. On his left hand was a great table with a few neatly arranged piles of papers, at which a big, rather heavily-built man was sitting. Frobisher looked at that man as a novice in a duelling field might look at the master swordsman whom he was committed to fight; with a little shock of surprise that after all he appeared to be just like other men. Hanaud, on his side, could not have been said to have looked at Frobisher at all; yet when he spoke it was obvious that somehow he had looked and to very good purpose. He rose with a little bow and apologised.

"I have kept you waiting, Mr. Frobisher. My dear friend Mr. Ricardo did not mention your object in his letter. I had the idea that you came with the usual wish to see something of the underworld. Now that I see you, I recognise your wish is more serious."

Hanaud was a man of middle age with a head of thick dark hair, and the round face and shaven chin of a comedian. A pair of remarkably light eyes under rather heavy lids alone gave a significance to him, at all events when seen for the first time in a mood of good-will. He pointed to a chair.

"Will you take a seat? I will tell you, Mr. Frobisher, I have a very soft place in my heart for Mr. Ricardo, and a friend of his—— These are words, however. What can I do?"

Jim Frobisher laid down his hat and stick upon a side table and took the chair in front of Hanaud's table.

"I am partner in a firm of lawyers which looks after

the English interests of a family in Dijon," he said, and he saw all life and expression smoothed out of Hanaud's face. A moment ago he had been in the company of a genial and friendly companion; now he was looking at a Chinaman.

"Yes?" said Hanaud.

"The family has the name of Harlowe," Jim continued.

"Oho!" said Hanaud.

The ejaculation had no surprise in it, and hardly any interest. Jim, however, persisted.

"And the surviving member of it, a girl of twenty, Betty Harlowe, has been charged with murder by a Russian who is connected with the family by marriage—Boris Waberski."

"Aha!" said Hanaud. "And why do you come to me, Mr. Frobisher?"

Jim stared at the detective. The reason of his coming was obvious.

And yet—he was no longer sure of his ground. Hanaud had pulled open a drawer in his table and was beginning to put away in it one of his files.

"Yes?" he said, as who should say, "I am listening."

"Well, perhaps I am under a mistake," said Jim. "But my firm has been informed that you, Monsieur Hanaud, are in charge of the case," he said, and Hanaud's movements were at once arrested. He sat with the file poised on the palm of his hand as though he was weighing it, extraordinarily still; and Jim had a swift impression that he was more than disconcerted. Then Hanaud put the file into the drawer and closed the drawer softly. As softly he spoke, but in a sleek voice which to Frobisher's ears had a note in it which was actually alarming.

"So you have been informed of that, Mr. Frobisher! And in London! And—yes—this is only Wednesday! News travels very quickly nowadays, to be sure! Well, your firm has been correctly informed. I congratulate you. The first point is scored by you."

Jim Frobisher was quick to seize upon that word. He

had thought out upon his journey in what spirit he might most usefully approach the detective. Hanaud's bitter little remark gave him the very opening which he needed.

"But, Monsieur Hanaud, I don't take that point of view at all," he argued earnestly. "I am happy to believe that there is going to be no antagonism between us. For, if there were, I should assuredly get the worst of it. No! I am certain that the one wish you have in this matter is to get at the truth. Whilst my wish is that you should just look upon me as a very second-rate colleague who by good fortune can give you a little help."

A smile flickered across Hanaud's face and restored it to some of its geniality.

"It has always been a good rule to lay it on with a trowel," he observed. "Now, what kind of help, Mr. Frobisher?"

"This kind of help, Monsieur Hanaud. Two letters from Boris Waberski demanding money, the second one with threats. Both were received by my firm before he brought this charge, and both of course remain unanswered."

He took the letters from the long envelope and handed them across the table to Hanaud, who read them through slowly, mentally translating the phrases into French as he read. Frobisher watched his face for some expression of relief or satisfaction. But to his utter disappointment no such change came; and it was with a deprecating and almost regretful air that Hanaud turned to him in the end.

"Yes—no doubt these two letters have a certain importance. But we mustn't exaggerate it. The case is very difficult."

"Difficult!" cried Jim in exasperation. He seemed to be hammering and hammering in vain against some thick wall of stupidity. Yet this man in front of him wasn't stupid.

"I can't understand it!" he exclaimed. "Here's the clearest instance of blackmail that I can imagine——"

"Blackmail's an ugly word, Mr. Frobisher," Hanaud warned him.

"And blackmail's an ugly thing," said Jim. "Come, Monsieur Hanaud, Boris Waberski lives in France. You will know something about him. You will have a dossier."

Hanaud pounced upon the word with a little whoop of delight, his face broke into smiles, he shook a forefinger gleefully at his visitor.

"Ah, ah, ah, ah! A dossier! Yes, I was waiting for that word! The great legend of the dossiers! You have that charming belief too, Mr. Frobisher. France and her dossiers! Yes. If her coal-mines fail her, she can always keep warm by burning her dossiers! The moment you land for the first time at Calais—boum! your dossier begins, eh? You travel to Paris—so! You dine at the Ritz Hotel—so! Afterwards you go where you ought not to go—so-o-o! And you go back late to the hotel very uncomfortable because you are quite sure that somewhere in the still night six little officials with black beards and green-shaded lamps are writing it all down in your dossier. But—wait!"

He suddenly rose from his chair with his finger to his lips, and his eyes opened wide. Never was a man so mysterious, so important in his mystery. He stole on tiptoe, with a lightness of step amazing in so bulky a man, to the door. Noiselessly and very slowly, with an alert, bright eye cocked at Frobisher like a bird's, he turned the handle. Then he jerked the door swiftly inwards towards him. It was the classic detection of the eavesdropper, seen in a hundred comedies and farces; and carried out with so excellent a mimicry that Jim, even in this office of the Sûreté, almost expected to see a flustered chambermaid sprawl heavily forward on her knees. He saw nothing, however, but a grimy corridor lit with artificial light in which men were patiently waiting. Hanaud closed the door again, with an air of intense relief.

"The Prime Minister has not overheard us. We are

safe," he hissed, and he crept back to Frobisher's side. He stooped and whispered in the ear of that bewildered man:

"I can tell you about those dossiers. They are for nine-tenths the gossip of the *concièrge* translated into the language of a policeman who thinks that everybody had better be in prison. Thus, the *concièrge* says: 'This Mr. Frobisher—on Tuesday he came home at one in the morning and on Thursday at three in fancy dress'; and in the policeman's report it becomes, 'Mr. Frobisher is of a loose and excessive life.' And that goes into your dossier—yes, my friend, just so! But here in the Sûreté—never breathe a word of it, or you ruin me!—here we are like your Miss Betty Harlowe, 'we snap us the fingers at those dossiers.'"

Jim Frobisher's mind was of the deliberate order. To change from one mood to another required a progression of ideas. He hardly knew for the moment whether he was upon his head or his heels. A minute ago Hanaud had been the grave agent of Justice; without a hint he had leaped to buffoonery, and with a huge enjoyment. He had become half urchin, half clown. Jim could almost hear the bells of his cap still tinkling. He simply stared, and Hanaud with a rueful smile resumed his seat.

"If we work together at Dijon, Monsieur Frobisher," he said with whimsical regret, "I shall not enjoy myself as I did with my dear little friend Mr. Ricardo at Aix. No, indeed! Had I made this little pantomime for him, he would have sat with the eyes popping out of his head. He would have whispered, 'The Prime Minister comes in the morning to spy outside your door—oh!' and he would have been thrilled to the marrow of his bones. But you—you look at me all cold and stony, and you say to yourself, 'This Hanaud, he is a comic!'"

"No," said Jim earnestly, and Hanaud interrupted the protest with a laugh.

"It does not matter."

"I am glad," said Jim. "For you just now said something which I am very anxious you should not withdraw. You held me out a hope that we should work together." Hanaud leaned forward with his elbows on his desk.

"Listen," he said genially. "You have been frank and loyal with me. So I relieve your mind. This Waberski affair—the Prefect at Dijon does not take it very seriously; neither do I here. It is, of course, a charge of murder, and that has to be examined with care."

"Of course."

"And equally, of course, there is some little thing behind it," Hanaud continued, surprising Frobisher with the very words which Mr. Haslitt had used the day before, though the one spoke in English and the other in French. "As a lawyer you will know that. Some little unpleasant fact which is best kept to ourselves. But it is a simple affair, and with these two letters you have brought me, simpler than ever. We shall ask Waberski to explain these letters and some other things too, if he can. He is a type, that Boris Waberski! The body of Madame Harlowe will be exhumed to-day and the evidence of the doctors taken, and afterwards, no doubt, the case will be dismissed and you can deal with Waberski as you please."

"And that little secret?" asked Jim.

Hanaud shrugged his shoulders.

"No doubt it will come to light. But what does that matter if it only comes to light in the office of the examining magistrate, and does not pass beyond the door?"

"Nothing at all," Jim agreed.

"You will see. We are not so alarming after all, and your little client can put her pretty head upon the pillow without any fear that an injustice will be done to her."

"Thank you, Monsieur Hanaud!" Jim Frobisher cried warmly. He was conscious of so great a relief that he himself was surprised by it. He had been quite captured by his pity for that unknown girl in the big house, set upon by a crazy rascal and with no champion but another girl of her own years. "Yes, this is good news to me."

But he had hardly finished speaking before a doubt crept into his mind as to the sincerity of the man sitting opposite to him. Jim did not mean to be played and landed like a silly fish, however inexperienced he might be. He looked at Hanaud and wondered. Was this present geniality of his any less assumed than his other moods? Jim was unsettled in his estimate of the detective. One moment a judge, and rather implacable, now an urchin, now a friend! Which was travesty and which truth? Luckily there was a test question which Mr. Haslitt had put only yesterday as he looked out from the window across Russell Square. Jim now repeated it.

"The affair is simple, you say?"

"Of the simplest."

"Then how comes it, Monsieur Hanaud, that the examining judge at Dijon still finds it necessary to call in to his assistance one of the chiefs of the Sûreté of Paris?"

The question was obviously expected, and no less obviously difficult to answer. Hanaud nodded his head once or twice.

"Yes," he said, and again "Yes," like a man in doubt. He looked at Jim with appraising eyes. Then with a rush, "I shall tell you everything, and when I have told you, you will give me your word that you will not betray my confidence to any one in this world. For this is serious."

Jim could not doubt Hanaud's sincerity at this moment, nor his friendliness. They shone in the man like a strong flame.

"I give you my word now," he said, and he reached out his hand across the table. Hanaud shook it. "I can talk to you freely, then," he answered, and he produced a little blue bundle of very black cigarettes. "You shall smoke."

The two men lit their cigarettes and through the blue cloud Hanaud explained:

"I go really to Dijon on quite another matter. This Waberski affair, it is a pretence! The examining judge who calls me in—see, now, you have a phrase for him,"

32

and Hanaud proudly dropped into English more or less. "He excuse his face! Yes, that is your expressive idiom. He excuse his face, and you will see, my friend, that it needs a lot of excusing, that face of his, yes. Now listen! I get hot when I think of that examining judge."

He wiped his forehead with his handkerchief and, setting his sentence in order, resumed in French.

"The little towns, my friend, where life is not very gay and people have the time to be interested in the affairs of their neighbours, have their own crimes, and perhaps the most pernicious of them all is the crime of anonymous letters. Suddenly out of a clear sky they will come like a pestilence, full of vile charges difficult to refute and —who knows?—sometimes perhaps true. For a while these abominations flow into the letter-boxes and not a word is said. If money is demanded, money is paid. If it is only sheer wickedness which drives that unknown pen, those who are lashed by it none the less hold their tongues. But each one begins to suspect his neighbour. The social life of the town is poisoned. A great canopy of terror hangs over it, until the postman's knock, a thing so welcome in the sane life of every day, becomes a thing to shiver at, and in the end dreadful things happen."

So grave and quiet was the tone which Hanaud used that Jim himself shivered, even in this room whence he could see the sunlight sparkling on the river and hear the pleasant murmur of the Paris streets. Above that murmur he heard the sharp knock of the postman upon the door. He saw a white face grow whiter and still eyes grow haggard with despair.

"Such a plague has descended upon Dijon," Hanaud continued. "For more than a year it has raged. The police would not apply to Paris for help. No, they did not need help, they would solve this pretty problem for themselves. Yes, but the letters go on and the citizens complain. The police say, 'Hush! The examining magistrate, he has a clue. Give him time!' But the letters still go on. Then after a year comes this godsend

of the Waberski affair. At once the Prefect of Police
and the magistrate put their heads together. 'We will
send for Hanaud over this simple affair, and he will find
for us the author of the anonymous letters. We will
send for him very privately, and if any one recognises
him in the street and cries "There is Hanaud," we can say
he is investigating the Waberski affair. Thus the writer
of the letters will not be alarmed and we—we excuse our
faces.' Yes," concluded Hanaud heatedly, "but they
should have sent for me a year ago. They have lost a
year."

"And during that year the dreadful things have happened?" asked Jim.

Hanaud nodded angrily.

"An old, lonely man who lunches at the hotel and takes
his coffee at the Grande Taverne and does no harm to any
one, he flings himself in front of the Mediterranean express and is cut to pieces. A pair of lovers shoot themselves in the Forêt des Moissonières. A young girl comes
home from a ball; she says good night to her friends gaily
on the doorstep of her house, and in the morning she is
found hanging in her ball dress from a rivet in the wall
of her bedroom, whilst in the hearth there are the burnt
fragments of one of these letters. How many had she
received, that poor girl, before this last one drove her to
this madness? Ah, the magistrate. Did I not tell you?
He has need to excuse his face."

Hanaud opened a drawer in his desk and took from it
a green cover.

"See, here are two of those precious letters," and removing two typewritten sheets from the cover he handed
them to Frobisher. "Yes," he added, as he saw the dis-
gust on the reader's face, "those do not make a nice sauce
for your breakfast, do they?"

"They are abominable," said Jim. "I wouldn't have
believed——" he broke off with a little cry. "One moment, Monsieur Hanaud!" He bent his head again over
the sheets of paper, comparing them, scrutinising each

sentence. No, there were only the two errors which he
had noticed at once. But what errors they were! To
any one, at all events, with eyes to see and some luck in
the matter of experience. Why, they limited the area of
search at once!

"Monsieur Hanaud, I can give you some more help,"
he cried enthusiastically. He did not notice the broad
grin of delight which suddenly transfigured the detective's
face. "Help which may lead you very quickly to the
writer of these letters."

"You can?" Hanaud exclaimed. "Give it to me, my
young friend. Do not keep me shaking in excitement.
And do not—oh! do not tell me that you have discovered
that the letters were typed upon a Corona machine. For
that we know already."

Jim Frobisher flushed scarlet. That is just what he
had noticed with so much pride in his perspicuity. Where
the text of a sentence required a capital D, there were instead the two noughts with the diagonal line separating
them (thus, %), which are the symbol of "per cent.";
and where there should have been a capital S lower down
the page, there was the capital S with the transverse lines
which stands for dollars. Jim was familiar with the
Corona machine himself, and he had remembered that if
one used by error the stop for figures, instead of the stop
for capital letters, those two mistakes would result. He
realised now, with Hanaud's delighted face in front of
him—Hanaud was the urchin now—that the Sûreté was
certain not to have overlooked those two indications even
if the magistrate at Dijon had; and in a moment he began
to laugh too.

"Well, I fairly asked for it, didn't I?" he said as he
handed the letter back. "I said a wise thing to you,
Monsieur, when I held it fortunate that we were not to be
on opposite sides."

Hanaud's face lost its urchin look.

"Don't make too much of me, my friend, lest you be
disappointed," he said in all seriousness. "We are the

servants of Chance, the very best of us. Our skill is to seize quickly the hem of her skirt, when it flashes for the fraction of a second before our eyes."

He replaced the two anonymous letters in the green cover and laid it again in the drawer. Then he gathered together the two letters which Boris Waberski had written and gave them back to Jim Frobisher.

"You will want these to produce at Dijon. You will go there to-day?"

"This afternoon."

"Good!" said Hanaud. "I shall take the night express."

"I can wait for that," said Jim. But Hanaud shook his head.

"It is better that we should not go together, nor stay at the same hotel. It will very quickly be known in Dijon that you are the English lawyer of Miss Harlowe, and those in your company will be marked men too. By the way, how were you informed in London that I, Hanaud, had been put in charge of this case?"

"We had a telegram," replied Jim.

"Yes? And from whom? I am curious!"

"From Miss Harlowe."

For a moment Hanaud was for the second time in that interview quite disconcerted. Of that Jim Frobisher could have no doubt. He sat for so long a time, his cigarette half-way to his lips, a man turned into stone. Then he laughed rather bitterly, with his eyes alertly turned on Jim.

"Do you know what I am doing, Monsieur Frobisher?" he asked. "I am putting to myself a riddle. Answer it if you can! What is the strongest passion in the world? Avarice? Love? Hatred? None of these things. It is the passion of one public official to take a great big club and hit his brother official on the back of the head. It is arranged that I shall go secretly to Dijon so that I may have some little chance of success. Good! On Saturday it is so arranged, and already on Monday my colleagues have so spread the news that Miss Harlowe can telegraph it to you on Tuesday morning. But that is kind, eh? May I please see the telegram?"

Frobisher took it from the long envelope and handed it to Hanaud, who received it with a curious eagerness and opened it out on the table in front of them. He read it very slowly, so slowly that Jim wondered whether he too heard through the lines of the telegram, as through the receiver of a telephone, the same piteous cry for help which he himself had heard. Indeed, when Hanaud raised his face all the bitterness had gone from it.

"The poor little girl, she is afraid now, eh? The slender fingers, they do not snap themselves any longer, eh? Well, in a few days we make all right for her."

"Yes," said Jim stoutly.

"Meanwhile I tear this, do I not?" and Hanaud held up the telegraph form. "It mentions my name. It will be safe with you, no doubt, but it serves no purpose. Everything which is torn up here is burnt in the evening. It is for you to say," and he dangled the telegram before Jim Frobisher's eyes.

"By all means," said Jim, and Hanaud tore the telegram across. Then he placed the torn pieces together and tore them through once again and dropped them into his waste-paper basket. "So! That is done!" he said. "Now tell me! There is another young English girl in the Maison Grenelle."

"Ann Upcott," said Jim with a nod.

"Yes, tell me about her."

Jim made the same reply to Hanaud which he had made to Mr. Haslitt.

"I have never seen her in my life. I never heard of her until yesterday."

But whereas Mr. Haslitt had received the answer with amazement, Hanaud accepted it without comment.

"Then we shall both make the acquaintance of that young lady at Dijon," he said with a smile, and he rose from his chair.

Jim Frobisher had a feeling that the interview which had begun badly and moved on to cordiality was turning back upon itself and ending not too well. He was conscious of a subtle difference in Hanaud's manner, not a diminution in his friendliness, but—Jim could find nothing but Hanaud's own phrase to define the change. He seemed to have caught the hem of the skirt of Chance as it flickered for a second within his range of vision. But when it had flickered Jim could not even conjecture.

He picked up his hat and stick. Hanaud was already at the door with his hand upon the knob.

"Good-bye, Monsieur Frobisher, and I thank you sincerely for your visit."

"I shall see you in Dijon," said Jim.

"Surely," Hanaud agreed with a smile. "On many occasions. In the office, perhaps, of the examining magistrate. No doubt in the Maison Grenelle."

But Jim was not satisfied. It was a real collaboration which Hanaud had appeared a few minutes ago not merely to accept, but even to look forward to. Now, on the contrary, he was evading it.

"But if we are to work together?" Jim suggested.

"You might want to reach me quickly," Hanaud continued. "Yes. And I might want to reach you, if not so quickly, still very secretly. Yes." He turned the question over in his mind. "You will stay at the Maison Grenelle, I suppose?"

"No," said Jim, and he drew a little comfort from Hanaud's little start of disappointment. "There will be no need for that," he explained. "Boris Waberski can attempt nothing more. Those two girls will be safe enough."

"That's true," Hanaud agreed. "You will go, then, to the big hotel in the Place Darcy. For me I shall stay in one that is more obscure, and not under my own name. Whatever chance of secrecy is still left for me, that I shall cling to."

He did not volunteer the name of the obscure hotel or

the name under which he proposed to masquerade, and Jim was careful not to inquire. Hanaud stood with his hand upon the knob of the door and his eyes thoughtfully resting upon Frobisher's face.

"I will trust you with a little trick of mine," he said, and a smile warmed and lit his face to good humour. "Do you like the pictures? No—yes? For me, I adore them. Wherever I go I snatch an hour for the cinema. I behold wonderful things and I behold them in the dark—so that while I watch I can talk quietly with a friend, and when the lights go up we are both gone, and only our empty bocks are left to show where we were sitting. The cinemas—yes! With their audiences which constantly change and new people coming in who sit plump down upon your lap because they cannot see an inch beyond their noses, the cinemas are useful, I tell you. But you will not betray my little secret?"

He ended with a laugh. Jim Frobisher's spirits were quite revived by this renewal of Hanaud's confidence. He felt with a curious elation that he had travelled a long way from the sedate dignities of Russell Square. He could not project in his mind any picture of Messrs. Frobisher & Haslitt meeting a client in a dark corner of a cinema theatre off the Marylebone Road. Such manœuvres were not amongst the firm's methods, and Jim began to find the change exhilarating. Perhaps, after all, Messrs. Frobisher & Haslitt were a little musty, he reflected. They missed—and he coined a phrase, he, Jim Frobisher! . . . they missed the ozone of police-work.

"Of course I'll keep your secret," he said with a thrill in his voice. "I should never have thought of so capital a meeting-place."

"Good," said Hanaud. "Then at nine o'clock each night, unless there is something serious to prevent me, I shall be sitting in the big hall of the Grande Taverne. The Grande Taverne is at the corner across the square from the railway station. You can't mistake it. I shall be on the left-hand side of the hall and close up to the

screen and at the edge near the billiard-room. Don't look
for me when the lights are raised, and if I am talking to
any one else, you will avoid me like poison. Is that understood?"

"Quite," Jim returned.

"And you have now two secrets of mine to keep."
Hanaud's face lost its smile. In some strange way it
seemed to sharpen, the light-coloured eyes became very
still and grave. "That also is understood, Monsieur Frobisher," he said. "For I begin to think that we may both
of us see strange things before we leave Dijon again for
Paris."

The moment of gravity passed. With a bow he held
open the door. But Jim Frobisher, as he passed out into
the corridor, was once again convinced that at some definite point in the interview Hanaud had at all events
caught a glimpse of the flickering skirts of Chance, even
if he had not grasped them in his hands.

CHAPTER FOUR: *Betty Harlowe*

JIM FROBISHER reached Dijon that night at an hour too late for any visit, but at half-past nine on the next morning he turned with a thrill of excitement into the little street of Charles-Robert. This street was bordered upon one side, throughout its length, by a high garden wall above which great sycamores and chestnut trees rustled friendlily in a stir of wind. Towards the farther mouth of the street the wall was broken, first by the end of a house with a florid observation-window of the Renaissance period which overhung the footway; and again a little farther on by a pair of elaborate tall iron gates. Before these gates Jim came to a standstill. He gazed into the courtyard of the Maison Grenelle, and as he gazed his excitement died away and he felt a trifle ashamed of it. There seemed so little cause for excitement.

It was a hot, quiet, cloudless morning. On the left-hand side of the court women-servants were busy in front of a row of offices; at the end Jim caught glimpses of a chauffeur moving between a couple of cars in a garage, and heard him whistling gaily as he moved; on the right stretched the big house, its steep slate roof marked out gaily with huge diamond patterns of bright yellow, taking in the sunlight through all its open windows. The hall door under the horizontal glass fan stood open. One of the iron gates, too, was ajar. Even the *sergent-de-ville* in his white trousers out in the small street here seemed to be sheltering from the sun in the shadow of the high wall rather than exercising any real vigilance. It was impossible to believe, with all this pleasant evidence of normal life, that any threat was on that house or upon any of its inhabitants.

"And indeed there is no threat," Jim reflected. "I have Hanaud's word for it."

He pushed the gate open and crossed to the front door. An old serving-man informed him that Mademoiselle Harlowe did not receive, but he took Jim's card nevertheless, and knocked upon a door on the right of the big square hall. As he knocked, he opened the door; and from his position in the hall Jim looked right through a library to a window at the end and saw two figures silhouetted against the window, a man and a girl. The man was protesting, rather extravagantly both in word and gesture, to Jim's Britannic mind, the girl laughing—a clear, ringing laugh, with just a touch of cruelty, at the man's protestations. Jim even caught a word or two of the protest spoken in French, but with a curiously metallic accent.

"I have been your slave too long," the man cried, and he girl became aware that the door was open and that the old man stood inside of it with a card upon a silver salver. She came quickly forward and took the card. Jim heard the cry of pleasure, and the girl came running out into the hall.

"You!" she exclaimed, her eyes shining. "I had no right to expect you so soon. Oh, thank you!" and she gave him both her hands.

Jim did not need her words to recognise in her the "little girl" of Mr. Haslitt's description. Little in actual height Betty Harlowe certainly was not, but she was such a slender trifle of a girl that the epithet seemed in place. Her hair was dark brown in colour, with a hint of copper where the light caught it, parted on one side and very neatly dressed about her small head. The broad forehead and oval face were of a clear pallor and made vivid the fresh scarlet of her lips; and the large pupils of her grey eyes gave to her a look which was at once haunting and wistful. As she held out her hands in a warm gratitude and seized his, she seemed to him a creature of delicate flame and fragile as fair china. She looked him over with one swift comprehensive glance and breathed a little sigh of relief.

"I shall give you all my troubles to carry from now on," she said, with a smile.

"To be sure. That's what I am here for," he answered. "But don't take me for anything very choice and particular."

Betty laughed again and, holding him by the sleeve, drew him into the library.

"Monsieur Espinosa," she said, presenting the stranger to Jim. "He is from Cataluna, but he spends so much of his life in Dijon that we claim him as a citizen."

The Catalan bowed and showed a fine set of strong white teeth.

"Yes, I have the honour to represent a great Spanish firm of wine-growers. We buy the wines here to mix with our better brands, and we sell wine here to mix with their cheaper ones."

"You mustn't give your trade secrets away to me," Jim replied shortly. He disliked Espinosa on sight, as they say, and he was at no very great pains to conceal his dislike. Espinosa was altogether too brilliant a personage. He was a big, broad-shouldered man with black shining hair and black shining eyes, a florid complexion, a curled moustache, and gleaming rings upon his fingers.

"Mr. Frobisher has come from London to see me on quite different business," Betty interposed.

"Yes?" said the Catalan a little defiantly, as though he meant to hold his ground.

"Yes," replied Betty, and she held out her hand to him. Espinosa raised it reluctantly to his lips and kissed it.

"I shall see you when you return," said Betty, and she walked to the door.

"If I go away," Espinosa replied stubbornly. "It is not certain, Mademoiselle Betty, that I shall go"; and with a ceremonious bow to Jim he walked out of the room; but not so quickly but that Betty glanced swiftly from one man to the other with keen comparing eyes, and Jim detected the glance. She closed the door and turned back to Jim with a friendly little grimace which somehow put him in a good humour. He was being compared to another man to his advantage, and however modest one may be, such a comparison promotes a pleasant warmth.

"More trouble, Miss Harlowe," he said with a smile, "but this time the sort of trouble which you must expect for a good many years to come."

He moved towards her, and they met at one of the two side windows which looked out upon the courtyard. Betty sat down in the window-seat.

"I really ought to be grateful to him," she said, "for he made me laugh. And it seems to me ages since I laughed"; she looked out of the window and her eyes suddenly filled with tears.

"Oh! don't, please," cried Jim in a voice of trouble.

The smile trembled once more on Betty's lips deliciously.

"I won't," she replied.

"I was so glad to hear you laugh," he continued, "after your unhappy telegram to my partner and before I told you my good news."

Betty looked up at him eagerly.

"Good news?"

Jim Frobisher took once more from his long envelope the two letters which Waberski had sent to his firm and handed them to Betty.

"Read them," he said, "and notice the dates."

Betty glanced at the handwriting.

"From Monsieur Boris," she cried, and she settled down in the window-seat to study them. In her short black frock with her slim legs in their black silk stockings extended and her feet crossed, and her head and white neck bent over the sheets of Waberski's letters, she looked to Jim like a girl fresh from school. She was quick enough, however, to appreciate the value of the letters.

"Of course I always knew that it was money that Monsieur Boris wanted," she said. "And when my aunt's will was read and I found that everything had been left to me, I made up my mind to consult you and make some arrangement for him."

"There was no obligation upon you," Jim protested. "He wasn't really a relation at all. He married Mrs. Harlowe's sister, that's all."

"I know," replied Betty, and she laughed. "He always objected to me because I would call him 'Monsieur Boris' instead of 'uncle.' But I meant to do something nevertheless. Only he gave me no time. He bullied me first of all, and I do hate being bullied—don't you, Mr. Frobisher?"

"I do."

Betty looked at the letters again.

"That's when I snapped me the fingers at him, I suppose," she continued, with a little gurgle of delight in the phrase. "Afterwards he brought this horrible charge against me, and to have suggested any arrangement would have been to plead guilty."

"You were quite right. It would indeed," Jim agreed cordially.

Up to this moment, a suspicion had been lurking at the back of Jim Frobisher's mind that this girl had been a trifle hard in her treatment of Boris Waberski. He was a sponger, a wastrel, with no real claim upon her, it was true. On the other hand, he had no means of livelihood, and Mrs. Harlowe, from whom Betty drew her fortune, had been content to endure and support him. Now, however, the suspicion was laid, the little blemish upon the girl removed and by her own frankness.

"Then it is all over," Betty said, handing back the letters to Jim with a sigh of relief. Then she smiled ruefully—"But just for a little while I was really frightened," she confessed. "You see, I was sent for and questioned by the examining magistrate. Oh! I wasn't frightened by the questions, but by him, the man. I've no doubt it's his business to look severe, but I couldn't help thinking that if any one looked as terrifically severe as he did, it must be because he hadn't any brains and wanted you not to know. And people without brains are always dangerous, aren't they?"

"Yes, that wasn't encouraging," Jim agreed.

"Then he forbade me to use a motor-car, as if he expected me to run away. And to crown everything, when I came away from the Palais de Justice, I met some friends outside who gave me a long list of people who had been condemned and only found to be innocent when it was too late."

Jim stared at her.

"The brutes!" he cried.

"Well, we have all got friends like that," Betty returned philosophically. "Mine, however, were particularly odious. For they actually discussed, as a reason of course, why I should engage the very best advocate, whether, since Mrs. Harlowe had adopted me, the charge couldn't be made one of matricide. In which case there could be no pardon, and I must go to the guillotine with a black veil over my head and naked feet." She saw horror and indignation in Jim Frobisher's face and she reached out a hand to him.

"Yes. Malice in the provinces is apt to be a little blunt, though"—and she lifted a slim foot in a shining slipper and contemplated it whimsically—"I don't imagine that, given the circumstances, I should be bothering my head much as to whether I was wearing my best shoes and stockings or none at all."

"I never heard of so abominable a suggestion," cried Jim.

"You can imagine, at all events, that I came home a little rattled," continued Betty, "and why I sent off that silly panicky telegram. I would have recalled it when I rose to the surface again. But it was then too late. The telegram had——"

She broke off abruptly with a little rise of inflexion and a sharp indraw of her breath.

"Who is that?" she asked in a changed voice. She

had been speaking quietly and slowly, with an almost humorous appreciation of the causes of her fear. Now her question was uttered quickly and anxiety was predominant in her voice. "Yes, who is that?" she repeated.

A big, heavily built man sauntering past the great iron gates had suddenly whipped into the courtyard. A fraction of a second before he was an idler strolling along the path, now he was already disappearing under the big glass fan of the porch.

"It's Hanaud," Jim replied, and Betty rose to her feet as though a spring in her had been released, and stood swaying.

"You have nothing to fear from Hanaud," Jim Frobisher reassured her. "I have shown him those two letters of Waberski. From first to last he is your friend. Listen. This is what he said to me only yesterday in Paris."

"Yesterday, in Paris?" Betty asked suddenly.

"Yes, I called upon him at the Sûreté. These were his words. I remembered them particularly so that I could repeat them to you just as they were spoken. 'Your little client can lay her pretty head upon her pillow confident that no injustice will be done to her.'"

The bell of the front door shrilled through the house as Jim finished.

"Then why is he in Dijon? Why is he at the door now?" Betty asked stubbornly.

But that was the one question which Jim must not answer. He had received a confidence from Hanaud. He had pledged his word not to betray it. For a little while longer Betty must believe that Waberski's accusation against her was the true reason of Hanaud's presence in Dijon, and not merely an excuse for it.

"Hanaud acts under orders," Jim returned. "He is here because he was bidden to come"; and to his relief the answer sufficed. In truth, Betty's thoughts were diverted to some problem to which he had not the key.

"So you called upon Monsieur Hanaud in Paris," she

said, with a warm smile. "You have forgotten nothing which could help me." She laid a hand upon the sill of the open window. "I hope that he felt all the flattery of my panic-stricken telegram to London."

"He was simply regretful that you should have been so distressed."

"So you showed him the telegram?"

"And he destroyed it. It was my excuse for calling upon him with the letters."

Betty sat down again on the window-seat and lifted a finger for silence. Outside the door voices were speaking. Then the door was opened and the old man-servant entered. He carried this time no card upon a salver, but he was obviously impressed and a trifle flustered.

"Mademoiselle," he began, and Betty interrupted him. All trace of anxiety had gone from her manner. She was once more mistress of herself.

"I know, Gaston. Show Monsieur Hanaud in at once."

But Monsieur Hanaud was already in. He bowed with a pleasant ceremony to Betty Harlowe and shook hands cordially with Jim Frobisher.

"I was delighted as I came through the court, Mademoiselle, to see that my friend here was already with you. For he will have told you that I am not, after all, the ogre of the fairy-books."

"But you never looked up at the windows once," cried Betty in perplexity.

Hanaud smiled gaily.

"Mademoiselle, it is in the technique of my trade never to look up at windows and yet to know what is going on behind them. With your permission?" And he laid his hat and cane upon a big writing-table in the middle of the room.

"**B**UT we cannot see even through the widest of windows," Hanaud continued, "what happened behind them a fortnight ago. In those cases, Mademoiselle, we have to make ourselves the nuisance and ask the questions."

"I am ready to answer you," returned Betty quietly.

"Oh, of that—not a doubt," Hanaud cried genially. "Is it permitted to me to seat myself? Yes?"

Betty jumped up, the pallor of her face flushed to pink.

"I beg your pardon. Of course, Monsieur Hanaud."

That little omission in her manners alone showed Jim Frobisher that she was nervous. But for it, he would have credited her with a self-command almost unnatural in her years.

"It is nothing," said Hanaud with a smile. "After all, we are—the gentlest of us—disturbing guests." He took a chair from the side of the table and drew it up close so that he faced Betty. But whatever advantage was to be gained from the positions he yielded to her. For the light from the window fell in all its morning strength upon his face, whilst hers was turned to the interior of the room.

"So!" he said as he sat down. "Mademoiselle, I will first give you a plan of our simple procedure, as at present I see it. The body of Madame Harlowe was exhumed the night before last in the presence of your notary."

Betty moved suddenly with a little shiver of revolt.

"I know," he continued quickly. "These necessities are distressing. But we do Madame Harlowe no hurt, and we have to think of the living one, you, Miss Betty Harlowe, and make sure that no suspicion shall rest upon you—no, not even amongst your most loyal friends.

Isn't that so? Well, next, I put my questions to you here. Then we wait for the analyst's report. Then the Examining Magistrate will no doubt make you his compliments, and I, Hanaud, will, if I am lucky, carry back with me to that dull Paris, a signed portrait of the beautiful Miss Harlowe against my heart."

"And that will be all?" cried Betty, clasping her hands together in her gratitude.

"For you, Mademoiselle, yes. But for our little Boris —no!" Hanaud grinned with a mischievous anticipation. "I look forward to half an hour with that broken-kneed one. I shall talk to him and I shall not be dignified—no, not at all. I shall take care, too, that my good friend Monsieur Frobisher is not present. He would take from me all my enjoyment. He would look at me all prim like my maiden aunt and he would say to himself, 'Shocking! Oh, that comic! What a fellow! He is not proper.' No, and I shall not be proper. But, on the other hand, I will laugh all the way from Dijon to Paris."

Monsieur Hanaud had indeed begun to laugh already and Betty suddenly joined in with him. Hers was a clear, ringing laugh of enjoyment, and Jim fancied himself once more in the hall hearing that laughter come pealing through the open door.

"Ah, that is good!" exclaimed Hanaud. "You can laugh, Mademoiselle, even at my foolishnesses. You must keep Monsieur Frobisher here in Dijon and not let him return to London until he too has learnt that divinest of the arts."

Hanaud hitched his chair a little nearer, and a most uncomfortable image sprang at once into Jim Frobisher's mind. Just so, with light words and little jokes squeezed out to tenuity, did doctors hitch up their chairs to the bedsides of patients in a dangerous case. It took quite a few minutes of Hanaud's questions before that image entirely vanished from his thoughts.

"Good!" said Hanaud. "Now let us to business and get the facts all clear and ordered!"

"Yes," Jim agreed, and he too hitched his chair a little closer. It was curious, he reflected, how little he did know of the actual facts of the case.

"Now tell me, Mademoiselle! Madame Harlowe died, so far as we know, quite peacefully in her bed during the night."

"Yes," replied Betty.

"During the night of April the 27th?"

"Yes."

"She slept alone in her room that night?"

"Yes, Monsieur."

"That was her rule?"

"Yes."

"I understand Madame Harlowe's heart had given her trouble for some time."

"She had been an invalid for three years."

"And there was a trained nurse always in the house?"

"Yes."

Hanaud nodded.

"Now tell me, Mademoiselle, where did this nurse sleep? Next door to Madame?"

"No. A bedroom had been fitted up for her on the same floor but at the end of the passage."

"And how far away was this bedroom?"

"There were two rooms separating it from my aunt's."

"Large rooms?"

"Yes," Betty explained. "These rooms are on the ground-floor, and are what you would call reception-rooms. But, since Madame's heart made the stairs dangerous for her, some of them were fitted up especially for her use."

"Yes, I see," said Hanaud. "Two big reception-rooms between, eh? And the walls of the house are thick. It is not difficult to see that it was not built in these days. I ask you this, Mademoiselle. Would a cry from Madame

Harlowe at night, when all the house was silent, be heard in the nurse's room?"

"I am very sure that it would not," Betty returned. "But there was a bell by Madame's bed which rang in the nurse's room. She had hardly to lift her arm to press the button."

"Ah!" said Hanaud. "A bell specially fitted up?"

"Yes."

"And the button within reach of the fingers. Yes. That is all very well, if one does not faint, Mademoiselle. But suppose one does! Then the bell is not very useful. Was there no room nearer which could have been set aside for the nurse?"

"There was one next to my aunt's room, Monsieur Hanaud, with a communicating door."

Hanaud was puzzled and sat back in his chair. Jim Frobisher thought the time had come for him to interpose. He had been growing more and more restless as the catechism progressed. He could not see any reason why Betty, however readily and easily she answered, should be needlessly pestered.

"Surely, Monsieur Hanaud," he said, "it would save a deal of time if we paid a visit to these rooms and saw them for ourselves."

Hanaud swung round like a thing on a swivel. Admiration beamed in his eyes. He gazed at his junior colleague in wonder.

"But what an idea!" he cried enthusiastically. "What a fine idea! How ingenious! How difficult to conceive! And it is you, Monsieur Frobisher, who have thought of it! I make you my distinguished compliments!" Then all his enthusiasm declined into lassitude. "But what a pity!"

Hanaud waited intently for Jim to ask for an explanation of that sigh, but Jim simply got red in the face and refused to oblige. He had obviously made an asinine suggestion and was being rallied for it in front of the beautiful Betty Harlowe, who looked to him for her salvation; and on the whole he thought Hanaud to be a rather insufferable person as he sat there brightly watching for some second inanity. Hanaud in the end had to explain.

"We should have visited those rooms before now, Monsieur Frobisher. But the Commissaire of Police has sealed them up and without his presence we must not break the seals."

An almost imperceptible movement was made by Betty Harlowe in the window; an almost imperceptible smile flickered for the space of a lightning-flash upon her lips; and Jim saw Hanaud stiffen like a watch-dog when he hears a sound at night.

"You are amused, Mademoiselle?" he asked sharply.

"On the contrary, Monsieur."

And the smile reappeared upon her face and was seen to be what it was, pure wistfulness. "I had a hope those great seals with their linen bands across the doors were all now to be removed. It is fanciful, no doubt, but I have a horror of them. They seem to me like an interdict upon the house."

Hanaud's manner changed in an instant.

"That I can very well understand, Mademoiselle," he said, "and I will make it my business to see that those seals are broken. Indeed, there was no great use in affixing them, since they were only affixed when the charge was brought and ten days after Madame Harlowe died." He turned to Jim. "But we in France are all tied up in red tape, too. However, the question at which I am driving does not depend upon any aspect of the rooms. It is this, Mademoiselle," and he turned back to Betty.

"Madame Harlowe was an invalid with a nurse in constant attendance. How is it that the nurse did not sleep in that suitable room with the communicating-door? Why must she be where she could hear no cry, no sudden call?"

Betty nodded her head. Here was a question which demanded an answer. She leaned forward, choosing her words with care.

"Yes, but for that, Monsieur, you must understand something of Madame my aunt and put yourself for a moment in her place. She would have it so. She was, as you say, an invalid. For three years she had not gone beyond the garden except in a private saloon once a year to Monte Carlo. But she would not admit her malady. No, she was in her mind strong and a fighter. She was going to get well, it was always a question of a few weeks with her, and a nurse in her uniform always near with the door open, as though she were in the last stages of illness—that distressed her." Betty paused and went on again. "Of course, when she had some critical attack, the nurse was moved. I myself gave the order. But as soon as the attack subsided, the nurse must go. Madame would not endure it."

Jim understood that speech. Its very sincerity gave him a glimpse of the dead woman, made him appreciate her tough vitality. She would not give in. She did not want the paraphernalia of malady always about her. No, she would sleep in her own room, and by herself, like other women of her age. Yes, Jim understood that and believed every word that Betty spoke. Only—only—she was keeping something back. It was that which troubled him. What she said was true, but there was more to be said. There had been hesitation in Betty's speech, too nice a choice of words and then suddenly a little rush of phrases to cover up the hesitations. He looked at Hanaud, who was sitting without a movement and with his eyes fixed upon Betty's face, demanding more from her by his very impassivity. They were both, Jim felt sure, upon the edge of that little secret which, according to Haslitt as to Hanaud was always at the back of such wild charges as Waberski brought—the little shameful family secret which must be buried deep from the world's eyes. And while Jim was pondering upon this explanation of Betty's manner, he was suddenly startled out of his wits by a passionate cry which broke from her lips.

"Why do you look at me like that?" she cried to Hanaud, her eyes suddenly ablaze in her white face and her lips shaking. Her voice rose to a challenge.

"Do you disbelieve me, Monsieur Hanaud?"

Hanaud raised his hands in protest. He leaned back in his chair. The vigilance of his eyes, of his whole attitude, was relaxed.

"I beg your pardon, Mademoiselle," he said with a good deal of self-reproach. "I do not disbelieve you. I was listening with both my ears to what you said, so that I might never again have to trouble you with my questions. But I should have remembered, what I forgot, that for a number of days you have been living under a heavy strain. My manner was at fault."

The small tornado of passion passed. Betty sank back in the corner of the window-seat, her head resting against the side of the sash and her face a little upturned.

"You are really very considerate, Monsieur Hanaud," she returned. "It is I who should beg your pardon. For I was behaving like a hysterical schoolgirl. Will you go on with your questions?"

"Yes," Hanaud replied gently. "It is better that we finish with them now. Let us come back to the night of the twenty-seventh!"

"Yes, Monsieur."

"Madame was in her usual health that night—neither better nor worse."

"If anything a little better," returned Betty.

"So that you did not hesitate to go on that evening to a dance given by some friends of yours?"

Jim started. So Betty was actually out of the house on that fatal night. Here was a new point in her favour. "A dance!" he cried, and Hanaud lifted his hand.

"If you please, Monsieur Frobisher!" he said. "Let Mademoiselle speak!"

"I did not hesitate," Betty explained. "The life of the household had to go on normally. It would never have done for me to do unusual things. Madame was quick to notice. I think that although she would not admit that she was dangerously ill, at the bottom of her mind she suspected that she was; and one had to be careful not to alarm her."

"By such acts, for instance, as staying away from a dance to which she knew that you had meant to go?" said Hanaud. "Yes, Mademoiselle. I quite understand that."

He cocked his head at Jim Frobisher, and added with a smile, "Ah, you did not know that, Monsieur Frobisher. No, nor our friend Boris Waberski, I think. Or he would hardly have rushed to the Prefect of Police in such a hurry. Yes, Mademoiselle was dancing with her friends on this night when she is supposed to be committing the most monstrous of crimes. By the way, Mademoiselle, where was Boris Waberski on the night of the 27th?"

"He was away," returned Betty. "He went away on the 25th to fish for trout at a village on the River Ouche, and he did not come back until the morning of the 28th."

"Exactly," said Hanaud. "What a type that fellow! Let us hope he had a better landing-net for his trout than the one he prepared so hastily for Mademoiselle Harlowe. Otherwise his three days' sport cannot have amounted to much."

His laugh and his words called up a faint smile upon Betty's face and then he swept back to his questions.

"So you went to a dance, Mademoiselle. Where?"

"At the house of Monsieur de Pouillac on the Boulevard Thiers."

"And at what hour did you go?"

"I left this house at five minutes to nine."

"You are sure of the hour?"

"Quite," said Betty.

"Did you see Madame Harlowe before you went?"

"Yes," Betty answered. "I went to her room just before I left. She took her dinner in bed, as she often did. I was wearing for the dance a new frock which I had bought this winter at Monte Carlo, and I went to her room to show her how I looked in it."

"Was Madame alone?"

"No; the nurse was with her."

And upon that Hanaud smiled with a great appearance of cunning.

"I knew that, Mademoiselle," he declared with a friendly grin. "See, I set a little trap for you. For I have here the evidence of the nurse herself, Jeanne Baudin."

He took out from his pocket a sheet of paper upon which a paragraph was typed. "Yes, the examining magistrate sent for her and took her statement."

"I didn't know that," said Betty. "Jeanne left us the day of the funeral and went home. I have not seen her since."

She nodded at Hanaud once or twice with a little smile of appreciation.

"I would not like to be a person with a secret to hide from you, Monsieur Hanaud," she said admiringly. "I do not think that I should be able to hide it for long."

Hanaud expanded under the flattery like a novice, and, to Jim Frobisher's thinking, rather like a very vulgar novice.

"You are wise, Mademoiselle," he exclaimed. "For, after all, I am Hanaud. There is only one," and he thumped his chest and beamed delightedly. "Heavens, these are politenesses! Let us get on. This is what the nurse declared," and he read aloud from his sheet of paper:

"Mademoiselle came to the bedroom, so that Madame might admire her in her new frock of silver tissue and her silver slippers. Mademoiselle arranged the pillows and saw that Madame had her favourite books and her drink beside the bed. Then she wished her good night, and with her pretty frock rustling and gleaming, she tripped out of the room. As soon as the door was closed, Madame said to me——" and Hanaud broke off abruptly. "But that does not matter," he said in a hurry.

Suddenly and sharply Betty leaned forward.

"Does it not, Monsieur?" she asked, her eyes fixed upon his face, and the blood mounting slowly into her pale cheeks.

"No," said Hanaud, and he began to fold the sheet of paper.

"What does the nurse report that Madame said to her about me, as soon as the door was closed?" Betty asked, measuring out her words with a slow insistence. "Come, Monsieur! I have a right to know," and she held out her hand for the paper.

"You shall judge for yourself that it was of no importance," said Hanaud. "Listen!" and once more he read.

"Madame said to me, looking at her clock, 'It is well that Mademoiselle has gone early. For Dijon is not Paris, and unless you go in time there are no partners for you to dance with.' It was then ten minutes to nine."

With a smile Hanaud gave the paper into Betty's hand; and she bent her head over it swiftly, as though she doubted whether what he had recited was really written on that sheet, as if she rather trembled to think what Mrs. Harlowe had said of her after she had gone from the room. She took only a second or two to glance over the page, but when she handed it back to him, her manner was quite changed.

"Thank you," she said with a note of bitterness, and her deep eyes gleamed with resentment. Jim understood the change and sympathised with it. Hanaud had spoken of setting a trap when he had set none. For there was no conceivable reason why she should hesitate to admit that she had seen Mrs. Harlowe in the presence of the nurse, and wished her good night before she went to the party. But he had set a real trap a minute afterwards and into that Betty had straightway stumbled. He had tricked her into admitting a dread that Mrs. Harlowe might have spoken of her in disparagement or even in horror after she had left the bedroom.

"You must know, Monsieur Hanaud," she explained

very coldly, "that women are not always very generous to one another, and sometimes have not the imagination —how shall I put it?—to visualise the possible consequences of things they may say with merely the intention to hurt and do a little harm. Jeanne Baudin and I were, so far as I ever knew, good friends, but one is never sure, and when you folded up her statement in a hurry I was naturally very anxious to hear the rest of it."

"Yes, I agree," Jim intervened. "It did look as if the nurse might have added something malevolent, which could neither be proved nor disproved."

"It was a misunderstanding, Mademoiselle," Hanaud replied in a voice of apology. "We will take care that there shall not be any other." He looked over the nurse's statement again.

"It is said here that you saw that Madame had her favourite books and her drink beside the bed. That is true."

"Yes, Monsieur."

"What was that drink?"

"A glass of lemonade."

"It was placed on a table, I suppose, ready for her every night?"

"Every night."

"And there was no narcotic dissolved in it?"

"None," Betty replied. "If Mrs. Harlowe was restless, the nurse would give an opium pill and very occasionally a slight injection of morphia."

"But that was not done on this night?"

"Not to my knowledge. If it was done, it was done after my departure."

"Very well," said Hanaud, and he folded the paper and put it away in his pocket. "That is finished with. We have you now out of the house at five minutes to nine in the evening, and Madame in her bed with her health no worse than usual."

"Yes."

"Good!" Hanaud changed his attitude. "Now let us

go over your evening, Mademoiselle! I take it that you stayed at the house of M. de Pouillac until you returned home."

"Yes."

"You remember with whom you danced? If it was necessary, could you give me a list of your partners?"

She rose and, crossing to the writing table, sat down in front of it. She drew a sheet of paper towards her and took up a pencil. Pausing now and again to jog her memory with the blunt end of the pencil at her lips, she wrote down a list of names.

"These are all, I think," she said, handing the list to Hanaud. He put it in his pocket.

"Thank you!" He was all contentment now. Although his questions followed without hesitation, one upon the other, it seemed to Jim that he was receiving just the answers which he expected. He had the air of a man engaged upon an inevitable formality and anxious to get it completely accomplished, rather than of one pressing keenly a strict investigation.

"Now, Mademoiselle, at what hour did you arrive home?"

"At twenty minutes past one."

"You are sure of that exact time? You looked at your watch? Or at the clock in the hall? Or what? How are you sure that you reached the Maison Grenelle exactly at twenty minutes past one?"

Hanaud hitched his chair a little more forward, but he had not to wait a second for the answer.

"There is no clock in the hall and I had no watch with me," Betty replied. "I don't like those wrist-watches which some girls wear. I hate things round my wrists," and she shook her arm impatiently, as though she imagined the constriction of a bracelet. "And I did not put my watch in my hand-bag because I am so liable to leave that behind. So I had nothing to tell me the time when I reached home. I was not sure that I had not kept Georges

60

—the chauffeur—out a little later than he cared for. So I made him my excuse, explaining that I didn't really know how late I was."

"I see. It was Georges who told you the time at the actual moment of your arrival?"

"Yes."

"And Georges is no doubt the chauffeur whom I saw at work as I crossed the courtyard?"

"Yes. He told me that he was glad to see me have a little gaiety, and he took out his watch and showed it to me with a laugh."

"This happened at the front door, or at those big iron gates, Mademoiselle?" Hanaud asked.

"At the front door. There is no lodge-keeper and the gates are left open when any one is out."

"And how did you get into the house?"

"I used my latch-key."

"Good! All this is very clear."

Betty, however, was not mollified by Hanaud's satisfaction with her replies. Although she answered him without delay, her answers were given mutinously. Jim began to be a little troubled. She should have met Hanaud half-way; she was imprudently petulant.

"She'll make an enemy of this man before she has done," he reflected uneasily. But he glanced at the detective and was relieved. For Hanaud was watching her with a smile which would have disarmed any less offended young lady—a smile half friendliness and half amusement. Jim took a turn upon himself.

"After all," he argued, "this very imprudence pleads for her better than any calculation. The guilty don't behave like that." And he waited for the next stage in the examination with an easy mind.

"Now we have got you back home and within the Maison Grenelle before half past one in the morning," resumed Hanaud. "What did you do then?"

"I went straight upstairs to my bedroom," said Betty.

"Was your maid waiting up for you, Mademoiselle?"

"No; I had told her that I should be late and that I could undress myself."

"You are considerate, Mademoiselle. No wonder that your servants were pleased that you should have a little gaiety."

Even that advance did not appease the offended girl.

"Yes?" she asked with a sort of silky sweetness which was more hostile than any acid rejoinder. But it did not stir Hanaud to any resentment.

"When, then, did you first hear of Madame Harlowe's death?" was asked.

"The next morning my maid Francine came running into my room at seven o'clock. The nurse Jeanne had just discovered it. I slipped on my dressing-gown and ran downstairs. As soon as I saw that it was true, I rang up the two doctors who were in the habit of attending here."

"Did you notice the glass of lemonade?"

"Yes. It was empty."

"Your maid is still with you?"

"Yes—Francine Rollard. She is at your disposal."

Hanaud shrugged his shoulders and smiled doubtfully.

"That, if it is necessary at all, can come later. We have the story of your movements now from you, Mademoiselle, and that is what is important."

He rose from his chair.

"I have been, I am afraid, a very troublesome person, Mademoiselle Harlowe," he said with a bow. "But it is very necessary for your own sake that no obscurities should be left for the world's suspicions to play with. And we are very close to the end of this ordeal."

Jim had nursed a hope the moment Hanaud rose that this wearing interview had already ended. Betty, for her part, was indifferent.

"That is for you to say, Monsieur," she said implacably.

"Just two points then, and I think, upon reflection,

you will understand that I have asked you no question which is unfair."

Betty bowed.

"Your two points, Monsieur."

"First, then. You inherit, I believe, the whole fortune of Madame?"

"Yes."

"Did you expect to inherit it all? Did you know of her will?"

"No. I expected that a good deal of the money would be left to Monsieur Boris. But I don't remember that she ever told me so. I expected it, because Monsieur Boris so continually repeated that it was so."

"No doubt," said Hanaud lightly. "As to yourself, was Madame generous to you during her life?"

The hard look disappeared from Betty's face. It softened to sorrow and regret.

"Very," she answered in a low voice. "I had one thousand pounds a year as a regular allowance, and a thousand pounds goes a long way in Dijon. Besides, if I wanted more, I had only to ask for it."

Betty's voice broke in a sob suddenly and Hanaud turned away with a delicacy for which Jim was not prepared. He began to look at the books upon the shelves, that she might have time to control her sorrow, taking down one here, one there, and speaking of them in a casual tone.

"It is easy to see that this was the library of Monsieur Simon Harlowe," he said, and was suddenly brought to a stop. For the door was thrown open and a girl broke into the room.

"Betty," she began, and stood staring from one to another of Betty's visitors.

"Ann, this is Monsieur Hanaud," said Betty with a careless wave of her hand, and Ann went white as a sheet.

Ann! Then this girl was Ann Upcott, thought Jim Frobisher, the girl who had written to him, the girl, all

63

acquaintanceship with whom he had twice denied, and he had sat side by side with her, he had even spoken to her. She swept across the room to him.

"So you have come!" she cried. "But I knew that you would!"

Jim was conscious of a mist of shining yellow hair, a pair of sapphire eyes, and of a face impertinently lovely and most delicate in its colour.

"Of course I have come," he said feebly, and Hanaud looked on with a smile. He had an eye on Betty Harlowe, and the smile said as clearly as words could say, "That young man is going to have a deal of trouble before he gets out of Dijon."

CHAPTER SIX: *Jim Changes His Lodging*

THE library was a big oblong room with two tall windows looking into the court, and the observation window thrown out at the end over the footway of the street. A door in the inner wall close to this window led to a room behind, and a big open fire-place faced the windows on the court. For the rest, the walls were lined with high book-shelves filled with books, except for a vacant space here and there where a volume had been removed. Hanaud put back in its place the book which he had been holding in his hand.

"One can easily see that this is the library of Simon Harlowe, the collector," he said. "I have always thought that if one only had the time to study and compare the books which a man buys and reads, one would more surely get the truth of him than in any other way. But alas! one never has the time." He turned towards Jim Frobisher regretfully. "Come and stand with me, Monsieur Frobisher. For even a glance at the backs of them tells one something."

Jim took his place by Hanaud's side.

"Look, here is a book on Old English Gold Plate, and another—pronounce that title for me, if you please."

Jim read the title of the book on which Hanaud's finger was placed.

"Marks and Monograms on Pottery and Porcelain."

Hanaud repeated the inscription and moved along. From a shelf at the level of his breast and just to the left of the window in which Betty was sitting, he took a large, thinnish volume in a paper cover, and turned over the plates. It was a brochure upon Battersea Enamel.

"There should be a second volume," said Jim Frobisher

65

with a glance at the bookshelf. It was the idlest of remarks. He was not paying any attention to the paper-covered book upon Battersea Enamel. For he was really engaged in speculating why Hanaud had called him to his side. Was it on the chance that he might detect some swift look of understanding as it was exchanged by the two girls, some sign that they were in a collusion? If so, he was to be disappointed. For though Betty and Ann were now free from Hanaud's vigilant eye, neither of them moved, neither of them signalled to the other. Hanaud, however, seemed entirely interested in his book. He answered Jim's suggestion.

"Yes, one would suppose that there were a second volume. But this is complete," he said, and he put back the book in its place. There was room next to it for another quarto book, so long as it was no thicker, and Hanaud rested his finger in the vacant place on the shelf, with his thoughts clearly far away.

Betty recalled him to his surroundings.

"Monsieur Hanaud," she said in her quiet voice from her seat in the window, "there was a second point, you said, on which you would like to ask me a question."

"Yes, Mademoiselle, I had not forgotten it."

He turned with a curiously swift movement and stood so that he had both girls in front of him, Betty on his left in the window, Ann Upcott standing a little apart upon his right, gazing at him with a look of awe.

"Have you, Mademoiselle," he asked, "been pestered, since Boris Waberski brought his accusation, with any of these anonymous letters which seem to be flying about Dijon?"

"I have received one," answered Betty, and Ann Upcott raised her eyebrows in surprise. "It came on Sunday morning. It was very slanderous, of course, and I should have taken no notice of it but for one thing. It told me that you, Monsieur Hanaud, were coming from Paris to take up the case."

"Oho!" said Hanaud softly. "And you received this

letter on the Sunday morning? Can you show it to me, Mademoiselle?"

Betty shook her head.

"No, Monsieur."

Hanaud smiled.

"Of course not. You destroyed it, as such letter should be destroyed."

"No, I didn't," Betty answered. "I kept it. I put it away in a drawer of my writing-table in my own sitting-room. But that room is sealed up, Monsieur Hanaud. The letter is in the drawer still."

Hanaud received the statement with a frank satisfaction.

"It cannot run away, then, Mademoiselle," he said contentedly. But the contentment passed. "So the Commissaire of Police actually sealed up your private sitting-room. That, to be sure, was going a little far."

Betty shrugged her shoulders.

"It was mine, you see, where I keep my private things. And after all I was accused!" she said bitterly; but Ann Upcott was not satisfied to leave the matter there. She drew a step nearer to Betty and then looked at Hanaud.

"But that is not all the truth," she said. "Betty's room belongs to that suite of rooms in which Madame Harlowe's bedroom was arranged. It is the last room of the suite opening on to the hall, and for that reason, as the Commissaire said with an apology, it was necessary to seal it up with the others."

"I thank you, Mademoiselle," said Hanaud with a smile. "Yes, that of course softens his action." He looked whimsically at Betty in the window-seat. "It has been my misfortune, I am afraid, to offend Mademoiselle Harlowe. Will you help me to get all these troublesome dates now clear? Madame Harlowe was buried, I understand, on the Saturday morning twelve days ago!"

"Yes, Monsieur," said Ann Upcott.

"And after the funeral, on your return to this house, the notary opened and read the will?"

"Yes, Monsieur."

"And in Boris Waberski's presence?"

"Yes."

"Then exactly a week later, on Saturday, the seventh of May, he goes off quickly to the Prefecture of Police?"

"Yes."

"And on Sunday morning by the post comes the anonymous letter?"

Hanaud turned away to Betty, who bowed her head in answer.

"And a little later on the same morning comes the Commissaire, who seals the doors."

"At eleven o'clock, to be exact," replied Ann Upcott.

Hanaud bowed low.

"You are both wonderful young ladies. You notice the precise hour at which things happen. It is a rare gift, and very useful to people like myself."

Ann Upcott had been growing easier and easier in her manner with each answer that she gave. Now she could laugh outright.

"I do, at all events, Monsieur Hanaud," she said. "But alas! I was born to be an old maid. A chair out of place, a book disarranged, a clock not keeping time, or even a pin on the carpet—I cannot bear these things. I notice them at once and I must put them straight. Yes, it was precisely eleven o'clock when the Commissaire of Police rang the bell."

"Did he search the rooms before he sealed them?" Hanaud asked.

"No. We both of us thought his negligence strange," Ann replied, "until he informed us that the Examining Magistrate wanted everything left just as it was."

Hanaud laughed genially.

"That was on my account," he explained. "Who could tell what wonderful things Hanaud might not discover with his magnifying glass when he arrived from Paris? What fatal fingerprints! Oh! Ho! ho! What scraps of burnt letter! Ah! Ha! ha! But I tell you, Mademoi-

selle, that if a crime has been committed in this house,
even Hanaud would not expect to make any startling
discoveries in rooms which had been open to the whole
household for a fortnight since the crime. However,"
and he moved towards the door, "since I am here
now——"

Betty was upon her feet like a flash of lightning.
Hanaud stopped and swung round upon her, swiftly, with
his eyes very challenging and hard.

"You are going to break those seals now?" she asked
with a curious breathlessness. "Then may I come with
you—please, please! It is I who am accused. I have a
right to be present," and her voice rose into an earnest
cry.

"Calm yourself, Mademoiselle," Hanaud returned
gently. "No advantage will be taken of you. I am going to break no seals. That, as I have told you, is the
right of the Commissaire, who is a magistrate, and he
will not move until the medical analysis is ready. No,
what I was going to propose was that Mademoiselle
here," and he pointed to Ann, "should show me the outside of those reception-rooms and the rest of the house."

"Of course," said Betty, and she sat down again in the
window-seat.

"Thank you," said Hanaud. He turned back to Ann
Upcott. "Shall we go? And as we go, will you tell me
what you think of Boris Waberski?"

"He has some nerve. I can tell you that, Monsieur
Hanaud," Ann cried. "He actually came back to this
house after he had lodged his charge, and asked me to
support him"; and she passed out of the room in front of
Hanaud.

Jim Frobisher followed the couple to the door and
closed it behind them. The last few minutes had set his
mind altogether at rest. The author of the anonymous
letters was the detective's real quarry. His manner had
quite changed when putting his questions about them.
The flamboyancies and the indifference, even his amuse-

ment at Betty's ill-humour had quite disappeared. He had got to business watchfully, quietly. Jim came back into the room. He took his cigarette-case from his pocket and opened it.

"May I smoke?" he asked. As he turned to Betty for permission, a fresh shock brought his thoughts and words alike to a standstill. She was staring at him with panic naked in her eyes and her face set like a tragic mask.

"He believes me guilty," she whispered.

"No," said Jim, and he went to her side. But she would not listen.

"He does. I am sure of it. Don't you see that he was bound to? He was sent from Paris. He has his reputation to think of. He must have his victim before he returns."

Jim was sorely tempted to break his word. He had only to tell the real cause which had fetched Hanaud out of Paris and Betty's distress was gone. But he could not. Every tradition of his life strove to keep him silent. He dared not even tell her that this charge against her was only an excuse. She must live in anxiety for a little while longer. He laid his hand gently upon her shoulder.

"Betty, don't believe that!" he said, with a consciousness of how weak that phrase was compared with the statement he could have made. "I was watching Hanaud, listening to him. I am sure that he already knew the answers to the questions he was asking you. Why, he even knew that Simon Harlowe had a passion for collecting, though not a word had been said of it. He was asking questions to see how you would answer them, setting now and then a little trap, as he admitted——"

"Yes," said Betty in trembling voice, "all the time he was setting traps."

"And every answer that you gave, even your manner in giving them," Jim continued stoutly, "more and more made clear your innocence."

"To him?" asked Betty.

"Yes, to him. I am sure of it."

Betty Harlowe caught at his arm and held it in both her hands. She leaned her head against it. Through the sleeve of his coat he felt the velvet of her cheek.

"Thank you," she whispered. "Thank you, Jim," and as she pronounced the name she smiled. She was thanking him not so much for the stout confidence of his words, as for the comfort which the touch of him gave to her.

"Very likely I am making too much of little things," she went on. "Very likely I am ungenerous, too, to Monsieur Hanaud. But he lives amidst crimes and criminals. He must be so used to seeing people condemned and passing out of sight into blackness and horrors, that one more or less, whether innocent or guilty, going that way, wouldn't seem to matter very much."

"Yes, Betty, I think that is a little unjust," Jim Frobisher remarked gently.

"Very well, I take it back," she said, and she let his arm go. "All the same, Jim, I am looking to you, not to him," and she laughed with an appealing tremor in the laugh which took his heart by storm.

"Luckily," said he, "you don't have to look to any one," and he had hardly finished the sentence before Ann Upcott came back alone into the room. She was about Betty's height and Betty's age and had the same sort of boyish slenderness and carriage which marks the girls of this generation. But in other respects, even to the colour of her clothes, she was as dissimilar as one girl can be from another. She was dressed in white from her coat to her shoes, and she wore a big gold hat so that one was almost at a loss to know where her hat ended and her hair began.

"And Monsieur Hanaud?" Betty asked.

"He is prowling about by himself," she replied. "I showed him all the rooms and who used them, and he said that he would have a look at them and sent me back to you."

"Did he break the seals on the reception-rooms?" Betty Harlowe asked.

"Oh, no," said Ann. "Why, he told us that he couldn't do that without the Commissaire."

"Yes, he told us that," Betty remarked dryly. "But I was wondering whether he meant what he told us."

"Oh, I don't think Monsieur Hanaud's alarming," said Ann. She gave Jim Frobisher the impression that at any moment she might call him a dear old thing. She had quite got over the first little shock which the announcement of his presence had caused her. "Besides," and she sat down by the side of Betty in the window-seat and looked with the frankest confidence at Jim—"besides, we can feel safe now, anyway."

Jim Frobisher threw up his hands in despair. That queer look of aloofness had played him false with Ann Upcott now, as it had already done with Betty. If these two girls had called on him for help when a sudden squall found them in an open sailing-boat with the sheet of the sail made fast, or on the ice-slope of a mountain, or with a rhinoceros lumbering towards them out of some forest of the Nile, he would not have shrunk from their trust. But this was quite a different matter. They were calmly pitting him against Hanaud.

"You were safe before," he exclaimed. "Hanaud is not your enemy, and as for me, I have neither experience nor natural gifts for this sort of work"—and he broke off with a groan. For both the girls were watching him with a smile of complete disbelief.

"Good heavens, they think that I am being astute," he reflected, "and the more I confess my incapacity the astuter they'll take me to be." He gave up all arguments. "Of course I am absolutely at your service," he said.

"Thank you," said Betty. "You will bring your luggage from your hotel and stay here, won't you?"

Jim was tempted to accept that invitation. But, on the one hand, he might wish to see Hanaud at the Grande Taverne; or Hanaud might wish to see him, and secrecy was to be the condition of such meetings. It was better that he should keep his freedom of movement complete.

"I won't put you to so much trouble, Betty," he replied. "There's no reason in the world that I should. A call over the telephone and in five minutes I am at your side."

Betty Harlowe seemed in doubt to press her invitation or not.

"It looks a little inhospitable in me," she began, and the door opened, and Hanaud entered the room.

"I left my hat and stick here," he said. He picked m up and bowed to the girls.

"You have seen everything, Monsieur Hanaud?" Betty asked.

"Everything, Mademoiselle. I shall not trouble you again until the report of the analysis is in my hands. I wish you a good morning."

Betty slipped off the window-seat and accompanied him out into the hall. It appeared to Jim Frobisher that she was seeking to make some amends for her ill-humour; and when he heard her voice he thought to detect in it some note of apology.

"I shall be very glad if you will let me know the sense of that report as soon as possible," she pleaded. "You, better than any one, will understand that this is a difficult hour for me."

"I understand very well, Mademoiselle," Hanaud answered gravely. "I will see to it that the hour is not prolonged."

Jim, watching them through the doorway, as they stood together in the sunlit hall, felt ever so slight a touch upon his arm. He wheeled about quickly. Ann Upcott was at his side with all the liveliness and even the delicate colour gone from her face, and a wild and desperate appeal in her eyes.

"You will come and stay here? Oh, please!" she whispered.

"I have just refused," he answered. "You heard me."

"I know," she went on, the words stumbling over one another from her lips. "But take back your refusal. Do!

73

Oh, I am frightened out of my wits. I don't understand anything. I am terrified!" And she clasped her hands together in supplication. Jim had never seen fear so stark, no, not even in Betty's eyes a few minutes ago. It robbed her exquisite face of all its beauty, and made it in a second, haggard and old. But before he could answer, a stick clattered loudly upon the pavement of the hall and startled them both like the crack of a pistol.

Jim looked through the doorway. Hanaud was stooping to pick up his cane. Betty made a dive for it, but Hanaud already had it in his hands.

"I thank you, Mademoiselle, but I can still touch my toes. Every morning I do it five times in my pyjamas," and with a laugh he ran down the couple of steps into the courtyard and with that curiously quick saunter of his was out into the street of Charles-Robert in a moment. When Jim turned again to Ann Upcott, the fear had gone from her face so completely that he could hardly believe his eyes.

"Betty, he is going to stay," she cried gaily.

"So I inferred," replied Betty with a curious smile as she came back into the room.

CHAPTER SEVEN: *Exit Waberski*

JIM FROBISHER neither saw nor heard any more of Hanaud that day. He fetched his luggage away from the hotel and spent the evening with Betty Harlowe and Ann Upcott at the Maison Grenelle. They took their coffee after dinner in the garden behind the house, descending to it by a short flight of stone steps from a great door at the back of the hall. And by some sort of unspoken compact they avoided all mention of Waberski's charge. They had nothing to do but to wait now for the analyst's report. But the long line of high, shuttered windows just above their heads, the windows of the reception-rooms, forbade them to forget the subject, and their conversation perpetually dwindled down into long silences. It was cool out here in the dark garden, cool and very still; so that the bustle of a bird amongst the leaves of the sycamores startled them and the rare footsteps of a passer-by in the little street of Charles-Robert rang out as though they would wake a dreaming city. Jim noticed that once or twice Ann Upcott leaned swiftly forward and stared across the dark lawns and glimmering paths to the great screen of tall trees, as if her eyes had detected a movement amongst their stems. But on each occasion she said nothing and with an almost inaudible sigh sank back in her chair.

"Is there a door into the garden from the street?" Frobisher asked, and Betty answered him.

"No. There is a passage at the end of the house under the reception-rooms from the courtyard which the gardeners use. The only other entrance is through the hall behind us. This old house was built in days when your house really was your castle and the fewer the entrances, the more safely you slept."

The clocks of that city of Clocks clashed out the hour of eleven, throwing the sounds of their strokes backwards and forwards above the pinnacles and roof-tops in a sort of rivalry. Betty rose to her feet.

"There's a day gone, at all events," she said, and Ann Upcott agreed with a breath of relief. To Jim it seemed a pitiful thing that these two girls, to whom each day should be a succession of sparkling hours all too short, must be rejoicing quietly, almost gratefully, that another of them had passed.

"It should be the last of the bad days," he said, and Betty turned swiftly towards him, her great eyes shining in the darkness.

"Good night, Jim," she said, her voice ever so slightly lingering like a caress upon his name and she held out her hand. "It's terribly dull for you, but we are not unselfish enough to let you go. You see, we are shunned just now—oh, it's natural! To have you with us means a great deal. For one thing," and there came a little lilt in her voice, "I shall sleep to-night." She ran up the steps and stood for a moment against the light from the hall. "A long-legged slip of a girl, in black silk stockings"—thus Mr. Haslitt had spoken of her as she was five years ago, and the description fitted her still.

"Good night, Betty," said Jim, and Ann Upcott ran past him up the steps and waved her hand.

"Good night," said Jim, and with a little twist of her shoulders Ann followed Betty. She came back, however. She was wearing a little white frock of *crêpe de Chine* with white stockings and satin shoes, and she gleamed at the head of the steps like a slender thing of silver.

"You'll bolt the door when you come in, won't you?" she pleaded with a curious anxiety considering the height of the strong walls about the garden

"I will," said Jim, and he wondered why in all this business Ann Upcott stood out as a note of fear. It was high time indeed, that the long line of windows was thrown open and the interdict raised from the house and its inmates. Jim Frobisher paced the quiet garden in the darkness with a prayer at his heart that that time would come to-morrow. In Betty's room above the reception-rooms the light was still burning behind the latticed shutters of the windows, in spite of her confidence that she would sleep—yes, and in Ann Upcott's room too, at the end of the house towards the street. A fury against Boris Waberski flamed up in him.

It was late before he himself went into the house and barred the door, later still before he fell asleep. But once asleep, he slept soundly, and when he waked, it was to find his shutters thrown wide to the sunlight, his coffee cold by his bedside, and Gaston, the old servant, in the room.

"Monsieur Hanaud asked me to tell you he was in the library," he said.

Jim was out of bed in an instant.

"Already? What is the time, Gaston?"

"Nine o'clock. I have prepared Monsieur's bath." He removed the tray from the table by the bed. "I will bring some fresh coffee."

"Thank you! And will you please tell Monsieur Hanaud that I will not be long."

"Certainly, Monsieur."

Jim took his coffee while he dressed and hurried down to the library, where he found Hanaud seated at the big writing-table in the middle of the room, with a newspaper spread out over the blotting-pad and placidly reading the news. He spoke quickly enough, however, the moment Jim appeared.

"So you left your hotel in the Place Darcy, after all, eh, my friend? The exquisite Miss Upcott! She had but to sigh out a little prayer and clasp her hands together, and it was done. Yes, I saw it all from the hall. What it is to be young! You have those two letters which Waberski wrote your firm?"

"Yes," said Jim. He did not think it necessary to explain that though the prayer was Ann Upcott's, it was the thought of Betty which had brought him to the Maison Grenelle.

"Good! I have sent for him," said Hanaud.

"To come to this house?"

"I am expecting him now."

"That's capital," cried Jim. "I shall meet him, then! The damned rogue! I shouldn't wonder if I thumped him," and he clenched his fist and shook it in a joyous anticipation.

"I doubt if that would be so helpful as you think. No, I beg of you to place yourself in my hands this morning, Monsieur Frobisher," Hanaud interposed soberly. "If you confront Waberski at once with those two letters, at once his accusation breaks down. He will withdraw it. He will excuse himself. He will burst into a torrent of complaints and reproaches. And I shall get nothing out of him. That I do not want."

"But what is there to be got?" Jim asked impatiently.

"Something perhaps. Perhaps nothing," the detective returned with a shrug of the shoulders. "I have a second mission in Dijon, as I told you in Paris."

"The anonymous letters?"

"Yes. You were present yesterday when Mademoiselle Harlowe told me how she learned that I was summoned from Paris upon this case. It was not, after all, any of my colleagues here who spread the news. It is even now unknown that I am here. No, it was the writer of the letters. And in so difficult a matter I can afford to neglect no clue. Did Waberski know that I was going to be sent for? Did he hear that at the Prefecture when he lodged his charge on the Saturday or from the examining magistrate on the same day? And if he did, to whom did he talk between the time when he saw the magistrate and the time when letters must be posted if they are to be delivered on the Sunday morning? These are questions I must have the answer to, and if we at once administer the knock-out with your letters, I shall not get them. I must lead him on with friendliness. You see that."

Jim very reluctantly did. He had longed to see Hanaud dealing with Waberski in the most outrageous of his moods, pouncing and tearing and trampling with the gibes of a schoolboy and the improprieties of the gutter. Hanaud indeed had promised him as much. But he found him now all for restraint and sobriety and more concerned apparently with the authorship of the anonymous letters than with the righting of Betty Harlowe. Jim felt that he had been defrauded.

"But I am to meet this man," he said. "That must not be forgotten."

"And it shall not be," Hanaud assured him. He led him over to the door in the inner wall close to the observation window and opened it.

"See! If you will please to wait in here," and as the disappointment deepened on Jim's face, he added, "Oh, I do not ask you to shut the door. No. Bring up a chair to it—so! And keep the door ajar so! Then you will see and hear and yet not be seen. You are content? Not very. You would prefer to be on the stage the whole time like an actor. Yes, we all do. But, at all events, you do not throw up your part," and with a friendly grin he turned back to the table.

A shuffling step which merged into the next step with a curiously slovenly sound rose from the courtyard.

"It was time we made our little arrangements," said Hanaud in an undertone. "For here comes our hero from the Steppes."

Jim popped his head through the doorway.

"Monsieur Hanaud!" he whispered excitedly. "Monsieur Hanaud! It cannot be wise to leave those windows open on the courtyard. For if we can hear a footstep so loudly in this room, anything said in this room will be easily overheard in the court."

"But how true that is!" Hanaud replied in the same

voice and struck his forehead with his fist in anger at his folly. "But what are we to do? The day is so hot. This room will be an oven. The ladies and Waberski will all faint. Besides, I have an officer in plain clothes already stationed in the court to see that it is kept empty. Yes, we will risk it."

Jim drew back.

"That man doesn't welcome advice from any one," he said indignantly, but he said it only to himself; and almost before he had finished, the bell rang. A few seconds afterwards Gaston entered.

"Monsieur Boris," he said.

"Yes," said Hanaud with a nod. "And will you tell the ladies that we are ready?"

Boris Waberski, a long, round-shouldered man with bent knees and clumsy feet, dressed in black and holding a soft black felt hat in his hand, shambled quickly into the room and stopped dead at the sight of Hanaud. Hanaud bowed and Waberski returned the bow; and then the two men stood looking at one another—Hanaud all geniality and smiles, Waberski a rather grotesque figure of uneasiness like one of those many grim caricatures carved by the imagination of the Middle Ages on the columns of the churches of Dijon. He blinked in perplexity at the detective and with his long, tobacco-stained fingers tortured his grey moustache.

"Will you be seated?" said Hanaud politely. "I think that the ladies will not keep us waiting."

He pointed towards a chair in front of the writing-table but on his left hand and opposite to the door.

"I don't understand," said Waberski doubtfully. "I received a message. I understood that the Examining Magistrate had sent for me."

"I am his agent," said Hanaud. "I am——" and he stopped. "Yes?"

Boris Waberski stared.

"I said nothing."

"I beg your pardon. I am—Hanaud."

He shot the name out quickly, but he was answered by no start, nor by any sign of recognition.

"Hanaud?" Waberski shook his head. "That no doubt should be sufficient to enlighten me," he said with a smile, "but it is better to be frank—it doesn't."

"Hanaud of the Sûreté of Paris."

And upon Waberski's face there came slowly a look of utter consternation.

"Oh!" he said, and again "Oh!" with a lamentable look towards the door as if he was in two minds whether to make a bolt of it. Hanaud pointed again to the chair, and Waberski murmured, "Yes—to be sure," and made a little run to it and sank down.

Jim Frobisher, watching from his secret place, was certain of one thing. Boris Waberski had not written the anonymous letter to Betty nor had he contributed the information about Hanaud to the writer. He might well have been thought to have been acting ignorance of Hanaud's name, up to the moment when Hanaud explained who Hanaud was. But no longer. His consternation then was too genuine.

"You will understand, of course, that an accusation so serious as the one you have brought against Mademoiselle Harlowe demands the closest inquiry," Hanaud continued without any trace of irony, "and the Examining Magistrate in charge of the case honoured us in Paris with a request for help."

"Yes, it is very difficult," replied Boris Waberski, twisting about as if he was a martyr on red-hot plates.

But the difficulty was Waberski's, as Jim, with that distressed man in full view, was now able to appreciate. Waberski had rushed to the Prefecture when no answer came from Messrs. Frobisher & Haslitt to his letter of threats, and had brought his charge in a spirit of disappointment and rancour, with a hope no doubt that some offer of cash would be made to him and that he could withdraw it. Now he found the trained detective service of France upon his heels, asking for his proofs and evidence. This was more than he had bargained for.

"I thought," Hanaud continued easily, "that a little informal conversation between you and me and the two young ladies, without shorthand writers or secretaries, might be helpful."

"Yes, indeed," said Waberski hopefully.

"As a preliminary of course," Hanaud added dryly, "a preliminary to the more serious and now inevitable procedure."

Waberski's gleam of hopefulness was extinguished.

"To be sure," he murmured, plucking at his lean throat nervously. "Cases must proceed."

"That is what they are there for," said Hanaud sententiously; and the door of the library was pushed open. Betty came into the room with Ann Upcott immediately behind her.

"You sent for me," she began to Hanaud, and then she saw Boris Waberski. Her little head went up with a jerk, her eyes smouldered. "Monsieur Boris," she said, and again she spoke to Hanaud. "Come to take possession, I suppose?" Then she looked round the room for Jim Frobisher, and exclaimed in a sudden dismay:

"But I understood that——" and Hanaud was just in time to stop her from mentioning any name.

"All in good time, Mademoiselle," he said quickly. "Let us take things in their order."

Betty took her old place in the window-seat. Ann Upcott shut the door and sat down in a chair a little apart from the others. Hanaud folded up his newspaper and laid it aside. On the big blotting-pad which was now revealed lay one of those green files which Jim Frobisher had noticed in the office of the Sûreté. Hanaud opened it and took up the top paper. He turned briskly to Waberski.

"Monsieur, you state that on the night of the 27th of April, this girl here, Betty Harlowe, did wilfully give to

82

her adoptive mother and benefactress, Jeanne-Marie Harlowe, an overdose of a narcotic by which her death was brought about."

"Yes," said Waberski with an air of boldness, "I declare that."

"You do not specify the narcotic?"

"It was probably morphine, but I cannot be sure."

"And administered, according to you, if this summary which I hold here is correct, in the glass of lemonade which Madame Harlowe had always at her bedside."

"Yes."

Hanaud laid the sheet of foolscap down again.

"You do not charge the nurse, Jeanne Baudin, with complicity in this crime?" he asked.

"Oh, no!" Waberski exclaimed with a sort of horror, with his eyes open wide and his eyebrows running up his forehead towards his hedge of wiry hair. "I have not a suspicion of Jeanne Baudin. I pray you, Monsieur Hanaud, to be clear upon that point. There must be no injustice! No! Oh, it is well that I came here to-day! Jeanne Baudin! Listen! I would engage her to nurse me to-morrow, were my health to fail."

"One cannot say more than that," replied Hanaud with a grave sympathy. "I only asked you the question because undoubtedly Jeanne Baudin was in Madame's bedroom when Mademoiselle entered it to wish Madame good night and show off her new dancing-frock."

"Yes, I understand," said Waberski. He was growing more and more confident, so suave and friendly was this Monsieur Hanaud of the Sûreté. "But the fatal drug was slipped into that glass without a doubt when Jeanne Baudin was not looking. I do not accuse her. No! It is that hard one," and his voice began to shake and his mouth to work, "who slipped it in and then hurried off to dance till morning, whilst her victim died. It is terrible that! Yes, Monsieur Hanaud, it is terrible. My poor sister!"

"Sister-in-law."

The correction came with an acid calm from an arm-chair near the door in which Ann Upcott was reclining.

"Sister to me!" replied Waberski mournfully and he turned to Hanaud. "Monsieur, I shall never cease to reproach myself. I was away fishing in the forest. If I had stayed at home! Think of it! I ask you to——" and his voice broke.

"Yes, but you did come back, Monsieur Waberski," Hanaud said, "and this is where I am perplexed. You loved your sister. That is clear, since you cannot even think of her without tears."

"Yes, yes." Waberski shaded his eyes with his hand.

"Then why did you, loving her so dearly, wait for so long before you took any action to avenge her death? There will be some good reason not a doubt, but I have not got it." Hanaud continued, spreading out his hands. "Listen to the dates. Your dear sister dies on the night of the 27th of April. You return home on the 28th; and you do nothing, you bring no charge, you sit all quiet. She is buried on the 30th, and after that you still do nothing, you sit all quiet. It is not until one week after that you launch your accusation against Mademoiselle. Why? I beg you, Monsieur Waberski, not to look at me between the fingers, for the answer is not written on my face, and to explain this difficulty to me."

The request was made in the same pleasant, friendly voice which Hanaud had used so far and without any change of intonation. But Waberski snatched his hand away from his forehead and sat up with a flush on his face.

"I answer you at once," he exclaimed. "From the first I knew it here," and he thumped his heart with his fist, "that murder had been committed. But as yet I did not know it here," and he patted his forehead, "in my head. So I think and I think and I think. I see reasons and motives. They build themselves up. A young girl of beauty and style, but of a strange and secret character, thirsting in her heart for colour and laughter and enjoyment and the power which her beauty offers her if she will but grasp it, and yet while thirsting, very able to conceal all sign of thirst. That is the picture I give you of that hard one, Betty Harlowe."

For the first time since the interview had commenced, Betty herself showed some interest in it. Up till now she had sat without a movement, a figure of disdain in an ice-house of pride. Now she flashed into life. She leaned forward, her elbow on her crossed knee, her chin propped in her hand, her eyes on Waberski, and a smile of amusement at this analysis of herself giving life to her face. Jim Frobisher, on the other hand, behind his door felt that he was listening to blasphemies. Why did Hanaud endure it? There was information, he had said, which he wanted to get from Boris Waberski. The point on which he wanted information was settled long ago, at the very beginning of this informal session. It was as clear as daylight that Waberski had nothing to do with Betty's anonymous letter. Why, then, should Hanaud give this mountebank of a fellow a free opportunity to slander Betty Harlowe? Why should he question and question as if there were solid weight in the accusation? Why, in a word, didn't he fling open this door, allow Frobisher to produce the blackmailing letters to Mr. Haslitt, and then stand aside while Boris Waberski was put into that condition in which he would call upon the services of Jeanne Baudin? Jim indeed was furiously annoyed with Monsieur Hanaud. He explained to himself that he was disappointed.

Meanwhile, Boris Waberski, after a little nervous check when Betty had leaned forward, continued his description. "For such a one Dijon would be tiresome. It is true there was each year a month or so at Monte Carlo, just enough to give one a hint of what might be, like a cigarette to a man who wants to smoke. And then back to Dijon! Ah, Monsieur, not the Dijon of the Dukes of Burgundy, not even the Dijon of the Parliament of the States, but the Dijon of to-day, an ordinary, dull, provin-

cial town of France which keeps nothing of its former
gaieties and glory but some old rare buildings and a little
spirit of mockery. Imagine, then, Monsieur, this hard
one with a fortune and freedom within her grasp if only
she has the boldness on some night when Monsieur Boris
is out of the way to seize them! Nor is that all. For
there is an invalid in the house to whom attentions are
owed—yes, and must be given." Waberski, in a flight of
excitement checked himself and half closed his eyes, with
a little cunning nod. "For the invalid was not so easy.
No, even that dear one had her failings. Oh, yes, and we
will not forget them when the moment comes for the
extenuating pleas. No, indeed," and he flung his arm
out nobly. "I myself will be the first to urge them to the
judge of the Assizes when the verdict is given."

Betty Harlowe leaned back once more indifferent.
From an arm-chair near the door, a little gurgle of laughter broke from the lips of Ann Upcott. Even Hanaud
smiled.

"Yes, yes," he said; "but we have not got quite as far
as the Court of Assizes, Monsieur Waberski. We are
still at the point where you know it in your heart but not
in your head."

"That is so," Waberski returned briskly. "On the
seventh of May, a Saturday, I bring my accusation to the
Prefecture. Why? For, on the morning of that day I
am certain. I know it at last here too," and up went his
hand to his forehead, and he hitched himself forward on
to the edge of his chair.

"I am in the street of Gambetta, one of the small popu-
lar new streets, a street with some little shops and a reputation not of the best. At ten o'clock I am passing quickly
through that street when from a little shop a few yards
in front of me out pops that hard one, my niece."

Suddenly the whole character of that session had
changed. Jim Frobisher, though he sat apart from it,
felt the new tension, and was aware of the new expectancy. A moment ago Boris Waberski as he sat talking

and gesticulating had been a thing for ridicule, almost for outright laughter. Now, though his voice still jumped hysterically from high notes to low notes and his body jerked like a marionette's, he held the eyes of every one— every one, that is, except Betty Harlowe. He was no longer vague. He was speaking of a definite hour and a place and of a definite incident which happened there.

"Yes, in that bad little street I see her. I do not believe my senses. I step into a little narrow alley and I peep round the corner. I peep with my eyes," and Waberski pointed to them with two of his fingers as though there was something peculiarly convincing in the fact that he peeped with them and not with his elbows, "and I am sure. Then I wait until she is out of sight, and I creep forward to see what shop it is she visited in that little street of squalor. Once more I do not believe my eyes. For over the door I read the name, Jean Cladel, Herbalist."

He pronounced the name in a voice of triumph and sat back in his chair, nodding his head violently at intervals of a second. There was not a sound in the room until Hanaud's voice broke the silence.

"I don't understand," he said softly. "Who is this Jean Cladel, and why should a young lady not visit his shop?"

"I beg your pardon," Waberski replied. "You are not of Dijon. No! or you would not have asked that question. Jean Cladel has no better name than the street he very suitably lives in. Ask a Dijonnais about Jean Cladel, and you will see how he becomes silent and shrugs his shoulders as if here was a topic on which it was becoming to be silent. Better still, Monsieur Hanaud, ask at the Prefecture. Jean Cladel! Twice he has been tried for selling prohibited drugs."

Hanaud was stung at last out of his calm.

"What is that?" he cried in a sharp voice.

"Yes, twice, Monsieur. Each time he has scraped through, that is true. He has powerful friends, and witnesses have been spirited away. But he is known! Jean Cladel! Yes, Jean Cladel!"

"Jean Cladel, Herbalist of the street Gambetta," Hanaud repeated slowly. "But"—and he leaned back in an easier attitude—"you will see my difficulty, Monsieur Waberski. Ten o'clock is a public hour. It is not a likely hour for any one to choose for so imprudent a visit, even if that one were stupid."

"Yes, and so I reasoned too," Waberski interposed quickly. "As I told you, I could not believe my eyes. But I made sure—oh, there was no doubt, Monsieur Hanaud. And I thought to myself this. Crimes are discovered because criminals, even the acutest, do sooner or later some foolish thing. Isn't it so? Sometimes they are too careful; they make their proofs too perfect for an imperfect world. Sometimes they are too careless or are driven by necessity to a rash thing. But somehow a mistake is made and justice wins the game."

Hanaud smiled.

"Aha! a student of crime, Monsieur!" He turned to Betty, and it struck upon Jim Frobisher with a curious discomfort that this was the first time Hanaud had looked directly at Betty since the interview had begun.

"And what do you say to this story, Mademoiselle?"

"It is a lie," she answered quietly.

"You did not visit Jean Cladel in the street of Gambetta at ten o'clock on the morning of the 7th of May?"

"I did not, Monsieur."

Waberski smiled and twisted his moustache.

"Of course! Of course! We could not expect Mademoiselle to admit it. One fights for one's skin, eh?"

"But, after all," Hanaud interrupted, with enough savagery in his voice to check all Waberski's complacency, "let us not forget that on the 7th of May, Madame Harlowe had been dead for ten days. Why should Mademoiselle still be going to the shop of Jean Cladel?"

"To pay," said Waberski. "Oh, no doubt Jean Cladel's wares are expensive and have to be paid for more than once, Monsieur."

"By wares you mean poison," said Hanaud. "Let us be explicit."

"Yes."

"Poison which was used to murder Madame Harlowe."

"I say so," Waberski declared, folding his arms across his breast.

"Very well," said Hanaud. He took from his green file a second paper written over in a fine hand and emphasised by an official stamp. "Then what will you say, Monsieur, if I tell you that the body of Madame Harlowe has been exhumed?" Hanaud continued, and Waberski's face lost what little colour it had. He stared at Hanaud, his jaw working up and down nervously, and he did not say a word.

"And what will you say if I tell you," Hanaud continued, "that no more morphia was discovered in it than one sleeping-dose would explain and no trace at all of any other poison?"

In a complete silence Waberski took his handkerchief from his pocket and dabbed his forehead. The game was up. He had hoped to make his terms, but his bluff was called. He had not one atom of faith in his own accusation. There was but one course for him to take, and that was to withdraw his charge and plead that his affection for his sister-in-law had led him into a gross mistake. But Boris Waberski was never the man for that. He had that extra share of cunning which shipwrecks always the minor rogue. He was unwise enough to imagine that Hanaud might be bluffing too.

He drew his chair a little nearer to the table. He tittered and nodded at Hanaud confidentially.

"You say 'if I tell you,'" he said smoothly. "Yes, but you do not tell me, Monsieur Hanaud—no, not at all. On the contrary, what you say is this: 'My friend Waberski, here is a difficult matter which, if exposed, means a great scandal, and of which the issue is doubtful. There is no good in stirring the mud.'"

"Oh, I say that?" Hanaud asked, smiling pleasantly.

Waberski felt sure of his ground now.

"Yes, and more than that. You say, 'You have been badly treated, my friend Waberski, and if you will now have a little talk with that hard one your niece——' " And his chair slid back against the bookcase and he sat gaping stupidly like a man who has been shot.

Hanaud had sprung to his feet, he stood towering above the table, his face suddenly dark with passion.

"Oh, I say all that, do I?" he thundered. "I came all the way from Paris to Dijon to preside over a little bargain in a murder case! I—Hanaud! Oh! ho! ho! I'll teach you a lesson for that! Read this!" and bending forward he thrust out the paper with the official seal. "It is the report of the analysts. Take it, I tell you, and read it!"

Waberski reached out a trembling arm, afraid to venture nearer. Even when he had the paper in his hands, they shook so he could not read it. But since he had never believed in his charge that did not matter.

"Yes," he muttered, "no doubt I have made a mistake."

Hanaud caught the word up.

"Mistake! Ah, there's a fine word! I'll show you what sort of a mistake you have made. Draw up your chair to this table in front of me! So! And take a pen—so! And a sheet of paper—so! and now you write for me a letter."

"Yes, yes," Waberski agreed. All the bravado had gone from his bearing, all the insinuating slyness. He was in a quiver from head to foot. "I will write that I am sorry."

"That is not necessary," roared Hanaud. "I will see to it that you are sorry. No! You write for me what I dictate to you and in English. You are ready? Yes? Then you begin. 'Dear Sirs.' You have that?"

"Yes, yes," said Waberski, scribbling hurriedly. His head was in a whirl. He flinched as he wrote under the towering bulk of the detective. He had as yet no comprehension of the goal to which he was being led.

"Good! 'Dear Sirs,'" Hanaud repeated. "But we want a date for that letter. April 30th, eh? That will do. The day Madame Harlowe's will was read and you found you were left no money. April 30th—put it in. So! Now we go on. 'Dear Sirs, Send me at once one thousand pounds by the recommended post, or I make some awkwardnesses——'"

Waberski dropped his pen and sprang back out of his chair.

"I don't understand—I can't write that. . . . There is an error—I never meant . . ." he stammered, his hands raised as if to ward off an attack.

"Ah, you never meant the blackmail!" Hanaud cried savagely. "Ah! Ha! Ha! It is good for you that I now know that! For when, as you put it so delicately to Mademoiselle, the moment comes for the extenuating pleas, I can rise up in the Court and urge it. Yes! I will say: 'Mr. the President, though he did the blackmail, poor fellow, he never meant it. So please to give him five years more,'" and with that Hanaud swept across the room like a tornado and flung open the door behind which Frobisher was waiting.

"Come!" he said, and he led Jim into the room. "You produce the two letters he wrote to your firm, Monsieur Frobisher. Good!"

But it was not necessary to produce them. Boris Waberski had dropped into a chair and burst into tears. There was a little movement of discomfort made by every one in that room except Hanaud; and even his anger dropped. He looked at Waberski in silence.

"You make us all ashamed. You can go back to your hotel," he said shortly. "But you will not leave Dijon, Monsieur Waberski, until it is decided what steps we shall take with you."

Waberski rose to his feet and stumbled blindly to the door.

"I make my apologies," he stammered. "It is all a mistake. I am very poor . . . I meant no harm," and without looking at any one he got himself out of the room.

"That type! He at all events cannot any more think that Dijon is dull," said Hanaud, and once more he adventured on the dangerous seas of the English language. "Do you know what my friend Mister Ricardo would have said? No? I tell you. He would have said, 'That fellow! My God! What a sauce!'"

Those left in the room, Betty, Ann Upcott, and Jim Frobisher, were in a mood to welcome any excuse for laughter. The interdict upon the house was raised, the charge against Betty proved of no account, the whole bad affair was at an end. Or so it seemed. But Hanaud went quickly to the door and closed it, and when he turned back there was no laughter at all upon his face.

"Now that that man has gone," he said gravely, "I have something to tell you three which is very serious. I believe that, though Waberski does not know it, Madame Harlowe was murdered by poison in this house on the night of April the twenty-seventh."

The statement was received in a dreadful silence. Jim Frobisher stood like a man whom some calamity has stunned. Betty leaned forward in her seat with a face of horror and incredulity; and then from the arm-chair by the door where Ann Upcott was sitting there burst a loud, wild cry.

"There was some one in the house that night," she cried.

Hanaud swung round to her, his eyes blazing.

"And it is you who tell me that, Mademoiselle?" he asked in a curious, steady voice.

"Yes. It's the truth," she cried with a sort of relief in her voice, that at last a secret was out which had grown past endurance. "I am sure now. There was a stranger in the house." And though her face was white as paper, her eyes met Hanaud's without fear.

CHAPTER EIGHT: *The Book*

THE two startling declarations, one treading upon the heels of the other, set Jim Frobisher's brain whirling. Consternation and bewilderment were all jumbled together. He had no time to ask "how," for he was already asking "What next?" His first clear thought was for Betty, and as he looked at her, a sharp anger against both Hanaud and Ann Upcott seized and shook him. Why hadn't they both spoken before? Why must they speak now? Why couldn't they leave well alone?

For Betty had fallen back in the window-seat, her hands idle at her sides and her face utterly weary and distressed. Jim thought of some stricken patient who wakes in the morning to believe for a few moments that the malady was a bad dream; and then comes the stab and the cloud of pain settles down for another day. A moment ago Betty's ordeal seemed over. Now it was beginning a new phase.

"I am sorry," he said to her.

The report of the analysts was lying on the writing-table just beneath his eyes. He took it up idly. It was a trick, of course, with its seals and its signatures, a trick of Hanaud's to force Waberski to a retraction. He glanced at it, and with an exclamation began carefully to read it through from the beginning to the end. When he had finished, he raised his head and stared at Hanaud.

"But this report is genuine," he cried. "Here are the details of the tests applied and the result. There was no trace discovered of any poison."

"No trace at all," Hanaud replied. He was not in the least disturbed by the question.

"Then I don't understand why you bring the accusation or whom you accuse," Frobisher exclaimed.

"I have accused no one," said Hanaud steadily. "Let

us be clear about that! As to your other question—look!"

He took Frobisher by the elbow and led him to that bookshelf by the window before which they had stood together yesterday.

"There was an empty space here yesterday. You yourself drew my attention to it. You see that the space is filled to-day."

"Yes," said Jim.

Hanaud took down the volume which occupied the space. It was of quarto size, fairly thick and bound in a paper cover.

"Look at that," he said; and Jim Frobisher as he took it noticed with a queer little start that although Hanaud's eyes were on his face they were blank of all expression. They did not see him. Hanaud's senses were concentrated on the two girls at neither of whom he so much as glanced. He was alert to them, to any movement they might make of surprise or terror. Jim threw up his head in a sudden revolt. He was being used for another trick, as some conjurer may use a fool of a fellow whom he has persuaded out of his audience on to his platform. Jim looked at the cover of the book, and cried with enough violence to recall Hanaud's attention:

"I see nothing here to the point. It is a treatise printed by some learned society in Edinburgh."

"It is. And if you will look again, you will see that it was written by a Professor of Medicine in that University. And if you will look a third time you will see from a small inscription in ink that the copy was presented with the Professor's compliments to Mr. Simon Harlowe."

Hanaud, whilst he was speaking, went to the second of the two windows which looked upon the court and putting his head out, spoke for a little while in a low voice.

"We shall not need our sentry here any more," he said as he turned back into the room. "I have sent him upon an errand."

He went back to Jim Frobisher, who was turning over a page of the treatise here and there and was never a scrap the wiser.

"Well?" he asked.

"Strophanthus Hispidus," Jim read aloud the title of the treatise. "I can't make head or tail of it."

"Let me try!" said Hanaud, and he took the book out of Frobisher's hands. "I will show you all how I spent the half-hour whilst I was waiting for you this morning."

He sat down at the writing-table, placed the treatise on the blotting-pad in front of him and laid it open at a coloured plate.

"This is the fruit of the plant Strophanthus Hispidus, when it is ripening," he said.

The plate showed two long, tapering follicles joined together at their stems and then separating like a pair of compasses set at an acute angle. The backs of these follicles were rounded, dark in colour and speckled; the inner surfaces, however, were flat, and the curious feature of them was that, from longitudinal crevices, a number of silky white feathers protruded.

"Each of these feathers," Hanaud continued, and he looked up to find that Ann Upcott had drawn close to the table and that Betty Harlowe herself was leaning forward with a look of curiosity upon her face—"each of these feathers is attached by a fine stalk to an elliptical pod, which is the seed, and when the fruit is quite ripe and these follicles have opened so that they make a straight line, the feathers are released and the wind spreads the seed. It is wonderful, eh? See!"

Hanaud turned the pages until he came to another plate. Here a feather was represented in complete detachment from the follicle. It was outspread like a fan and was extraordinarily pretty and delicate in its texture; and from it by a stem as fine as a hair the seed hung like a jewel.

"What would you say of it, Mademoiselle?" Hanaud asked, looking up into the face of Ann Upcott with a smile. "An ornament wrought for a fine lady, by a dainty artist, eh?" and he turned the book round so that she on the opposite side of the table might the better admire the engraving.

Betty Harlowe, it seemed, was now mastered by her curiosity. Jim Frobisher, gazing down over Hanaud's shoulder at the plate and wondering uneasily whither he was being led, saw a shadow fall across the book. And there was Betty, standing by the side of her friend with the palms of her hands upon the edge of the table and her face bent over the book.

"One could wish it was an ornament, this seed of the Strophanthus Hispidus," Hanaud continued with a shake of the head. "But, alas! it is not so harmless."

He turned the book around again to himself and once more turned the pages. The smile had disappeared altogether from his face. He stopped at a third plate; and this third plate showed a row of crudely fashioned arrows with barbed heads.

Hanaud glanced up over his shoulder at Jim.

"Do you understand now the importance of this book, Monsieur Frobisher?" he asked. "No? The seeds of this plant make the famous arrow-poison of Africa. The deadliest of all the poisons since there is no antidote for it." His voice grew sombre. "The wickedest of all the poisons, since it leaves no trace."

Jim Frobisher was startled. "Is that true?" he cried.

"Yes," said Hanaud; and Betty suddenly leaned forward and pointed to the bottom of the plate.

"There is a mark there below the hilt of that arrow," she said curiously. "Yes, and a tiny note in ink."

For a moment a little gift of vision was vouchsafed to Jim Frobisher, born, no doubt, of his perplexities and trouble. A curtain was rung up in his brain. He saw no more than what was before him—the pretty group about the table in the gold of the May morning, but it was all made grim and terrible and the gold had withered to a light that was grey and deathly and cold as the grave. There were the two girls in the grace of their beauty and their youth, daintily tended, fastidiously dressed, bending their shining curls over that plate of the poison arrows like pupils at a lecture. And the man delivering the lecture, so close to them, with speech so gentle, was implacably on the trail of murder, and maybe even now looked upon one of these two girls as his quarry; was even now perhaps planning to set her in the dock of an Assize Court and send her out afterwards, carried screaming and sobbing with terror in the first grey of the morning to the hideous red engine erected during the night before the prison gates. Jim saw Hanaud the genial and friendly, as in some flawed mirror, twisted into a sinister and terrifying figure. How could he sit so close with them at the table, talk to them, point them out this and that diagram in the plates, he being human and knowing what he purposed. Jim broke in upon the lecture with a cry of exasperation.

"But this isn't a poison! This is a book about a poison. The book can't kill!"

At once Hanaud replied to him:

"Can't it?" he cried sharply. "Listen to what Mademoiselle said a minute ago. Below the hilt of this arrow marked 'Figure F,' the Professor has written a tiny note."

This particular arrow was a little different from the others in the shape of its shaft. Just below the triangular iron head the shaft expanded. It was as though the head had been fitted into a bulb; as one sees sometimes wooden penholders fine enough and tapering at the upper end, and quite thick just above the nib.

" 'See page 37,' " said Hanaud, reading the Professor's note, and he turned back the pages.

"Page 37. Here we are!"

Hanaud ran a finger half-way down the page and stopped at a word in capitals.

"Figure F."

Hanaud hitched his chair a little closer to the table; Ann Upcott moved round the end of the table that she might see the better; even Jim Frobisher found himself stooping above Hanaud's shoulder. They were all conscious of a queer tension; they were expectant like explorers on the brink of a discovery. Whilst Hanaud read the paragraph aloud, it seemed that no one breathed; and this is what he read:

" 'Figure F is the representation of a poison arrow which was lent to me by Simon Harlowe, Esq., of Blackman's, Norfolk, and the Maison Grenelle at Dijon. It was given to him by a Mr. John Carlisle, a trader on the Shiré River in the Kombé country, and is the most perfect example of a poison arrow which I have seen. The Strophanthus seed has been pounded up in water and mixed with the reddish clay used by the Kombé natives, and the compound is thickly smeared over the head of the arrow shaft and over the actual iron dart except at the point and the edges. The arrow is quite new and the compound fresh.' "

Hanaud leaned back in his chair when he had come to the end of this paragraph.

"You see, Monsieur Frobisher, the question we have to answer. Where is to-day Simon Harlowe's arrow?"

Betty looked up into Hanaud's face.

"If it is anywhere in this house, Monsieur, it should be in the locked cabinet in my sitting-room."

"Your sitting-room?" Hanaud exclaimed sharply.

"Yes. It is what we call the Treasure Room—half museum, half living-room. My uncle Simon used it, Madame too. It was their favourite room, full of curios and beautiful things. But after Simon Harlowe died Madame would never enter it. She locked the door which communicated with her dressing-room, so that she might never even in a moment of forgetfulness enter it. The room has a door into the hall. She gave the room to me."

Hanaud's forehead cleared of its wrinkles.

"I understand," he said. "And that room is sealed."

"Yes."

"Have you ever seen the arrow, Mademoiselle?"

"Not that I remember. I only looked into the cabinet once. There are some horrible things hidden away there"; and Betty shivered and shook the recollection of them from her shoulders.

"The chances are that it's not in the house at all, that it never came back to the house," Frobisher argued stubbornly. "The Professor in all probability would have kept it."

"If he could," Hanaud rejoined. "But it's out of all probability that a collector of rare things would have allowed him to keep it. No!" and he sat for a little time in a muse. "Do you know what I am wondering?" he asked at length, and then answered his own question. "I am wondering whether after all Boris Waberski was not in the street of Gambetta on the seventh of May and close, very close, to the shop of Jean Cladel the herbalist."

"Boris! Boris Waberski," cried Jim. Was he in Hanaud's eyes the criminal? After all, why not? After all, who more likely if criminal there was, since Boris Waberski thought himself an inheritor under Mrs. Harlowe's will?

"I am wondering whether he was not doing that very thing which he attributed to you, Mademoiselle Betty," Hanaud continued.

"Paying?" Betty cried.

"Paying—or making excuses for not paying, which is more probable, or recovering the poison arrow now clean of its poison, which is most probable of all."

At last Hanaud had made an end of his secrecies and reticence. His suspicion, winged like the arrow in the plate, was flying straight to this evident mark. Jim drew a breath like a man waking from a nightmare; in all of that small company a relaxation was visible; Ann Upcott drew away from the table; Betty said softly as though speaking to herself, "Monsieur Boris! Monsieur Boris! Oh, I never thought of that!" and, to Jim's admiration there was actually a note of regret in her voice.

It was audible, too, to Hanaud, since he answered with a smile:

"But you must bring yourself to think of it, Mademoiselle. After all, he was not so gentle with you that you need show him so much good will."

A slight rush of colour tinged Betty's cheeks. Jim was not quite sure that a tiny accent of irony had not pointed Hanaud's words.

"I saw him sitting here," she replied quickly, "half an hour ago—abject—in tears—a man!" She shrugged her shoulders with a gesture of distaste. "I wish him nothing worse. I was satisfied."

Hanaud smiled again with a curious amusement, an appreciation which Frobisher was quite at a loss to understand. But he had from time to time received an uneasy impression that a queer little secret duel was all this while being fought by Betty Harlowe and Hanaud underneath the smooth surface of questions and answers —a duel in which now one, now the other of the combatants got some trifling scratch. This time it seemed Betty was hurt.

"You are satisfied, Mademoiselle, but the Law is not," Hanaud returned. "Boris Waberski expected a legacy. Boris Waberski needed money immediately, as the first of the two letters which he wrote to Monsieur Frobisher's firm clearly shows. Boris Waberski had a motive." He looked from one to the other of his audience with a nod to drive the point home. "Motives, no doubt, are signposts rather difficult to read, and if one reads them amiss, they lead one very wide astray. Granted! But you must look for your signposts all the same and try to read them aright. Listen again to the Professor of Medicine in the University of Edinburgh! He is as precise as a man can be."

Hanaud's eyes fell again upon the description of Figure F in the treatise still open upon the table in front of him.

"The arrow was the best specimen of a poison arrow

which he had ever come across. The poison paste was thickly and smoothly spread over the arrow head and some inches of the shaft. The arrow was unused and the poison fresh, and these poisons retain their energy for many, many years. I tell you that if this book and this arrow were handed over to Jean Cladel, Herbalist, Jean Cladel could with ease make a solution in alcohol which injected from a hypodermic needle, would cause death within fifteen minutes and leave not one trace."

"Within fifteen minutes?" Betty asked incredulously, and from the arm-chair against the wall, where Ann Upcott had once more seated herself, there broke a startled exclamation.

"Oh!" she cried, but no one took any notice of her at all. Both Jim and Betty had their eyes fixed upon Hanaud, and he was altogether occupied in driving his argument home.

"Within fifteen minutes? How do you know?" cried Jim.

"It is written here, in the book."

"And where would Jean Cladel have learnt to handle the paste with safety, how to prepare the solution?" Jim went on.

"Here! Here! Here!" answered Hanaud, tapping with his knuckles upon the treatise. "It is all written out here—experiment after experiment made upon living animals and the action of the poison measured and registered by minutes. Oh, given a man with a working knowledge of chemicals such as Jean Cladel must possess, and the result is certain."

Betty Harlowe leaned forward again over the book and Hanaud turned it half round between them, so that both, by craning their heads, could read. He turned the pages back to the beginning and passed them quickly in review.

"See, Mademoiselle, the time tables. Strophanthus constricts the muscles of the heart like digitalis, only much more violently, much more swiftly. See the contractions of the heart noted down minute after minute, until the moment of death and all—here is the irony!—so that by means of these experiments, the poison may be transformed into a medicine and the weapon of death become an agent of life—as in good hands, it has happened." Hanaud leaned back and contemplated Betty Harlowe between his half-closed eyes. "That is wonderful, Mademoiselle. What do you think?"

Betty slowly closed the book.

"I think, Monsieur Hanaud," she said, "it is no less wonderful that you should have studied this book so thoroughly during the half-hour you waited for us here this morning."

It was Hanaud's turn to change colour. The blood mounted into his face. He was for a second or two quite disconcerted. Jim once more had a glimpse of the secret duel and rejoiced that this time it was Hanaud, the great Hanaud, who was scratched.

"The study of poisons is particularly my work," he answered shortly. "Even at the Sûreté we have to specialise nowadays," and he turned rather quickly towards Frobisher. "You are thoughtful, Monsieur?"

Jim was following out his own train of thought.

"Yes," he answered. Then he spoke to Betty.

"Boris Waberski had a latch-key, I suppose?"

"Yes," she replied.

"He took it away with him?"

"I think so."

"When are the iron gates locked?"

"It is the last thing Gaston does before he goes to bed."

Jim's satisfaction increased with every answer he received.

"You see, Monsieur Hanaud," he cried, "all this while we have been leaving out a question of importance. Who put this book back upon its shelf? And when? Yesterday at noon the space was empty. This morning it is filled. Who filled it? Last night we sat in the garden after dinner behind the house. What could have been easier than for Waberski to slip in with his latch-key at some moment when the court was empty, replace the book and slip out again unnoticed? Why——"

A gesture of Betty's brought him to a halt.

"Unnoticed? Impossible!" she said bitterly. "The police have a *sergent-de-ville* at our gates, night and day."

Hanaud shook his head.

"He is there no longer. After you were good enough to answer me so frankly yesterday morning the questions it was my duty to put to you, I had him removed at once."

"Why, that's true," Jim exclaimed joyfully. He remembered now that when he had driven up with his luggage from the hotel in the afternoon, the street of Charles-Robert had been quite empty. Betty Harlowe stood taken aback by her surprise. Then a smile made her face friendly; her eyes danced to the smile, and she dipped to the detective a little mock curtsy. But her voice was warm with gratitude.

"I thank you, Monsieur. I did not notice yesterday that the man had been removed, or I should have thanked you before. Indeed I was not looking for so much consideration at your hands. As I told my friend Jim, I believed that you went away thinking me guilty."

Hanaud raised a hand in protest. To Jim it was the flourish of the sword with which the duellist saluted at the end of the bout. The little secret combat between these two was over. Hanaud, by removing the sergeant from before the gates, had given a sign surely not only to Betty but to all Dijon that he found nothing to justify any surveillance of her goings out and comings in, or any limitations upon her freedom.

"Then you see," Jim insisted. He was still worrying at his solution of the case like a dog with a bone. "You see Waberski had the road clear for him last night."

Betty, however, would not have it. She shook her head vigorously.

"I won't believe that Monsieur Boris is guilty of so horrible a murder. More," and she turned her great eyes pleadingly upon Hanaud, "I don't believe that any murder was committed here at all. I don't want to believe it," and for a moment her voice faltered.

"After all, Monsieur Hanaud, what are you building this dreadful theory upon? That a book of my Uncle Simon was not in his library yesterday and is there to-day. We know nothing more. We don't know even whether Jean Cladel exists at all."

"We shall know that, Mademoiselle, very soon," said Hanaud, staring down at the book upon the table.

"We don't know whether the arrow is in the house, whether it ever was."

"We must make sure, Mademoiselle," said Hanaud stubbornly.

"And even if you had it now, here with the poison clinging in shreds to the shaft, you still couldn't be sure that the rest of it had been used. Here is a report, Monsieur, from the doctors. Because it says that no trace of the poison can be discovered, you can't infer that a poison was administered which leaves no trace. You never can prove it. You have nothing to go upon. It's all guesswork, and guesswork which will keep us living in a nightmare. Oh, if I thought for a moment that murder had been committed, I'd say, 'Go on, go on'! But it hasn't. Oh, it hasn't!"

Betty's voice rang with so evident a sincerity, there was so strong a passion of appeal, for peace, for an end of suspicion, for a right to forget and be forgotten, that Jim fancied no man could resist it. Indeed, Hanaud sat for a long while with his eyes bent upon the table before he answered her. But when at last he did, gently though his voice began, Jim knew at once that she had lost.

"You argue and plead very well, Mademoiselle Betty," he said. "But we have each of us our little creeds by which we live for better or for worse. Here is mine, a very humble one. I can discover extenuations in most crimes: even crimes of violence. Passion, anger, even greed! What are they but good qualities developed beyond the bounds? Things at the beginning good and since grown monstrous! So, too, in the execution. This or that habit of life makes natural this or that weapon which to us is hideous and abnormal and its mere use a sign of a dreadful depravity. Yes, I recognise these palliations. But there is one crime I never will forgive —murder by poison. And one criminal in whose pursuit I will never tire nor slacken, the Poisoner." Through the words there ran a real thrill of hatred, and though Hanaud's voice was low, and he never once raised his eyes from the table, he held the three who listened to him in a dreadful spell.

"Cowardly and secret, the poisoner has his little world at his mercy, and a fine sort of mercy he shows to be sure," he continued bitterly. "His hideous work is so easy. It just becomes a vice like drink, no more than that to the poisoner, but with a thousand times the pleasure drink can give. Like the practice of some abominable art. I tell you the truth now! Show me one victim today and the poisoner scot-free, and I'll show you another victim before the year's out. Make no mistake! Make no mistake!"

His voice rang out and died away. But the words seemed still to vibrate in the air of that room, to strike the walls and rebound from them and still be audible. Jim Frobisher, for all his slow imagination, felt that had a poisoner been present and heard them, some cry of guilt must have rent the silence and betrayed him. His heart stopped in its beats listening for a cry, though his reason told him there was no mouth in that room from which the cry could come.

Hanaud looked up at Betty when he had finished. He begged her pardon with a little flutter of his hands and a regretful smile. "You must take me, therefore, as God made me, Mademoiselle, and not blame me more than you can help for the distress I still must cause you. There was never a case more difficult. Therefore never one about which one way or the other I must be more sure."

Before Betty could reply there came a knock upon the door.

"Come in," Hanaud cried out, and a small, dark, alert man in plain clothes entered the room.

"This is Nicolas Moreau, who was keeping watch in the courtyard. I sent him some while ago upon an errand," he explained and turned again to Moreau.

"Well, Nicolas?"

Nicolas stood at attention, with his hands at the seams of his trousers, in spite of his plain clothes, and he recited rather than spoke in a perfectly expressionless official voice.

"In accordance with instructions I went to the shop of Jean Cladel. It is number seven. From the Rue Gambetta I went to the Prefecture. I verified your statement. Jean Cladel has twice appeared before the Police Correctionelle for selling forbidden drugs and has twice been acquitted owing to the absence of necessary witnesses."

"Thank you, Nicolas."

Moreau saluted, turned on his heel, and went out of the room. There followed a moment of silence, of discouragement. Hanaud looked ruefully at Betty.

"You see! I must go on. We must search in that locked cabinet of Simon Harlowe's for the poison arrow, if by chance it should be there."

"The room is sealed," Frobisher reminded him.

"We must have those seals removed," he replied, and he took his watch from his pocket and screwed up his face in grimace.

"We need Monsieur the Commissary, and Monsieur the Commissary will not be in a good humour if we disturb him now. For it is twelve o'clock, the sacred hour of luncheon. You will have observed upon the stage that Commissaries of Police are never in a good humour. It is because——" But Hanaud's audience was never to hear his explanation of this well-known fact. For he stopped with a queer jerk of his voice, his watch still dangling from his fingers upon its chain. Both Jim and Betty looked at once where he was looking. They saw Ann Upcott standing up against the wall with her hand upon the top rail of a chair to prevent herself from falling. Her eyes were closed, her whole face a mask of misery. Hanaud was at her side in a moment.

"Mademoiselle," he asked with a breathless sort of eagerness, "what is it you have to tell me?"

"It is true, then?" she whispered. "Jean Cladel exists?"

"Yes."

"And the poison arrow could have been used?" she faltered, and the next words would not be spoken, but were spoken at the last. "And death would have followed in fifteen minutes?"

"Upon my oath it is true," Hanaud insisted. "What is it you have to tell me?"

"That I could have hindered it all. I shall never forgive myself. I could have hindered the murder."

Hanaud's eyes narrowed as he watched the girl. Was he disappointed, Frobisher wondered? Did he expect quite another reply? A swift movement by Betty distracted him from these questions. He saw Betty looking across the room at them with the strangest glittering eyes he had ever seen. And then Ann Upcott drew herself away from Hanaud and stood up against the wall at her full height with her arms outstretched. She seemed to be setting herself apart as a pariah; her whole attitude and posture cried, "Stone me! I am waiting."

Hanaud put his watch into his pocket.

"Mademoiselle, we will let the Commissary eat his luncheon in peace, and we will hear your story first. But not here. In the garden under the shade of the trees." He took his handkerchief and wiped his forehead. "Indeed I too feel the heat. This room is as hot as an oven."

When Jim Frobisher looked back in after time upon the incidents of that morning, nothing stood out so vividly in his memories, no, not even the book of arrows and its plates, not Hanaud's statement of his creed, as the picture of him twirling his watch at the end of his chain, whilst it sparkled in the sunlight and he wondered whether he should break in now upon the Commissaire of Police or let him eat his luncheon in quiet. So much that was then unsuspected by them all, hung upon the exact sequence of events.

CHAPTER NINE: *The Secret*

THE garden chairs were already set out upon a lawn towards the farther end of the garden in the shadow of the great trees. Hanaud led the way towards them.

"We shall be in the cool here and with no one to overhear us but the birds," he said, and he patted and arranged the cushions in a deep arm-chair of basket work for Ann Upcott. Jim Frobisher was reminded again of the solicitude of a doctor with an invalid and again the parallel jarred upon him. But he was getting a clearer insight into the character of this implacable being. The little courtesies and attentions were not assumed. They were natural, but they would not hinder him for a moment in his pursuit. He would arrange the cushions with the swift deft hands of a nurse—yes, but he would slip the handcuffs on the wrists of his invalid, a moment afterwards, no less deftly and swiftly, if thus his duty prompted him.

"There!" he said. "Now, Mademoiselle, you are comfortable. For me, if I am permitted, I shall smoke."

He turned round to ask for permission of Betty, who with Jim had followed into the garden behind him.

"Of course," she answered; and coming forward, she sat down in another of the chairs.

Hanaud pulled out of a pocket a bright blue bundle of thin black cigarettes and lit one. Then he sat in a chair close to the two girls. Jim Frobisher stood behind Hanaud. The lawn was dappled with sunlight and cool shadows. The blackbird and the thrush were calling from bough and bush, the garden was riotous with roses and the air sweet with their perfume. It was a strange setting for the eerie story which Ann Upcott had to tell of her adventures in the darkness and silence of a night; but the very contrast seemed to make the story still more vivid.

"I did not go to Monsieur de Pouillac's Ball on the night of April the 27th," she began, and Jim started, so that Hanaud raised his hand to prevent him interrupting. He had not given a thought to where Ann Upcott had been upon that night. To Hanaud, however, the statement brought no surprise.

"You were not well?" he asked.

"It wasn't that," Ann replied. "But Betty and I had —I won't say a rule, but a sort of working arrangement which I think had been in practice ever since I came to the Maison Grenelle. We didn't encroach upon each other's independence."

The two girls had recognised from their first coming together that privacy was the very salt of companionship. Each had a sanctuary in her own sitting-room.

"I don't think Betty has ever been in mine, I only once or twice in hers," said Ann. "We had each our own friends. We didn't pester each other with questions as to where we had been and with whom. In a word, we weren't all the time shadows upon each other's heels."

"A wise rule, Mademoiselle," Hanaud agreed cordially. "A good many households are split from roof to cellar by the absence of just such a rule. The de Pouillacs then were Mademoiselle Betty's friends."

"Yes. As soon as Betty had gone," Ann resumed, "I told Gaston that he might turn off the lights and go to bed whenever he liked; and I went upstairs to my own sitting-room, which is next to my bedroom. You can see the windows from here. There!"

They were in a group facing the back of the long house across the garden. To the right of the hall stretched the line of shuttered windows, with Betty's bedroom just above. Ann pointed to the wing on the left of the hall and towards the road.

"I see. You are above the library, Mademoiselle," said Hanaud.

"Yes. I had a letter to write," Ann continued, and suddenly faltered. She had come upon some obstacle in the telling of her story which she had forgotten when she had uttered her cry in the library. She gasped. "Oh!" she murmured, and again "Oh!" in a low voice. She glanced anxiously at Betty, but she got no help from her at all. Betty was leaning forward with her elbows upon her knees and her eyes on the grass at her feet and apparently miles away in thought.

"Yes, Mademoiselle," Hanaud asked smoothly.

"It was an important letter," Ann went on again, choosing her words warily, much as yesterday at one moment in her interrogatory Betty herself had done—concealing something, too, just as Betty had done. "I had promised faithfully to write it. But the address was downstairs in Betty's room. It was the address of a doctor," and having said that, it seemed that she had cleared her obstacle, for she went on in a more easy and natural tone.

"You know what it is, Monsieur Hanaud. I had been playing tennis all the afternoon. I was pleasantly tired. There was a letter to be written with a good deal of care and the address was all the way downstairs. I said to myself that I would think out the terms of my letter first."

And here Jim Frobisher, who had been shifting impatiently from one foot to the other, broke in upon the narrative.

"But what was this letter about and to what doctor?" he asked.

Hanaud swung round almost angrily.

"Oh, please!" he cried. "These things will all come to light of themselves in their due order, if we leave them alone and keep them in our memories. Let Mademoiselle tell her story in her own way," and he was back at Ann Upcott again in a flash.

"Yes, Mademoiselle. You determined to think out the tenor of your letter."

111

A hint of a smile glimmered upon the girl's face for a second. "But it was an excuse really, an excuse to sit down in my big arm-chair, stretch out my legs and do nothing at all. You can guess what happened."

Hanaud smiled and nodded.

"You fell fast asleep. Conscience does not keep young people, who are healthy and tired, awake," he said.

"No, but it wakes up with them," Ann returned, "and upbraids at once bitterly. I woke up rather chilly, as people do who have gone to sleep in their chairs. I was wearing a little thin frock of pale blue tulle—oh, a featherweight of a frock! Yes, I was cold and my conscience was saying, 'Oh, big lazy one! And your letter? Where is it?'

"In a moment I was standing up and the next I was out of the room on the landing, and I was still half dazed with sleep. I closed my door behind me. It was just chance that I did it. The lights were all out on the staircase and in the hall below. The curtains were drawn across the windows. There was no moon that night. I was in a darkness so complete that I could not see the glimmer of my hand when I raised it close before my face."

Hanaud let the end of his cigarette drop at his feet. Betty had raised her face and was staring at Ann with her mouth parted. For all of them the garden had disappeared with its sunlight and its roses and its singing birds. They were upon that staircase with Ann Upcott in the black night. The swift changes of colour in her cheeks and of expression in her eyes—the nervous vividness of her compelled them to follow with her.

"Yes, Mademoiselle?" said Hanaud quietly.

"The darkness didn't matter to me," she went on, with an amazement at her own fearlessness, now that she knew the after-history of that evening. "I am afraid now. I wasn't then," and Jim remembered how the night before in the garden her eyes had shifted from this dark spot to that in search of an intruder. Certainly she was afraid now! Her hands were clenched tight upon the arms of her chair, her lips shook.

"I knew every tread of the stairs. My hand was on the balustrade. There was no sound. It never occurred to me that any one was awake except myself. I did not even turn on the light in the hall by the switch at the bottom of the stairs. I knew that there was a switch just inside the door of Betty's room, and that was enough. I think, too, that I didn't want to rouse anybody. At the foot of the stairs I turned right like a soldier. Exactly opposite to me across the hall was the door of Betty's room. I crossed the hall with my hands out in front of me," and Betty, as though she herself were crossing the hall, suddenly thrust both her hands out in front of her.

"Yes, one would have to do that," she said slowly. "In the dark—with nothing but space in front of one—— Yes!" and then she smiled as she saw that Hanaud's eyes were watching her curiously. "Don't you think so, Monsieur Hanaud?"

"No doubt," said he. "But let us not interrupt Mademoiselle."

"I touched the wall first," Ann resumed, "just at the angle of the corridor and the hall."

"The corridor with the windows on to the courtyard on the one side and the doors of the receptions on the other?" Hanaud asked.

"Yes."

"Were the curtains drawn across all those windows too, Mademoiselle?"

"Yes. There was not a glimmer of light anywhere. I felt my way along the wall to my right—that is, in the hall, of course, not the corridor—until my hands slipped off the surface and touched nothing. I had reached the embrasure of the doorway. I felt for the door-knob, turned it and entered the room. The light switch was in the wall at the side of the door, close to my left hand. I snapped it down. I think that I was still half asleep when I turned the light on in the treasure-room, as we called it. But the next moment I was wide awake—oh, I have never been more wide awake in my life. My fingers indeed were hardly off the switch after turning the light on, before they were back again turning the light off. But this time I eased the switch up very carefully, so that there should be no snap—no, not the tiniest sound to betray me. There was so short an interval between the two movements of my hand that I had just time to notice the clock on the top of the marquetry cabinet in the middle of the wall opposite to me, and then once more I stood in darkness, but stock still and holding my breath— a little frightened—yes, no doubt a little frightened, but more astonished than frightened. For in the inner wall of the room, at the other end, close by the window, there," —and Ann pointed to the second of those shuttered windows which stared so blankly on the garden—"the door which was always locked since Simon Harlowe's death stood open and a bright light burned beyond."

Betty Harlowe uttered a little cry.

"That door?" she exclaimed, now at last really troubled. "It stood open? How can that have been?"

Hanaud shifted his position in his chair, and asked her a question.

"On which side of the door was the key, Mademoiselle?"

"On Madame's, if the key was in the lock at all."

"Oh! You don't remember whether it was?"

"No," said Betty. "Of course both Ann and I were in and out of Madame's bedroom when she was ill, but there was a dressing-room between the bedroom and the communicating door of my room, so that we should not have noticed."

"To be sure," Hanaud agreed. "The dressing-room in which the nurse might have slept and did when Madame had a seizure. Do you remember whether the communicating door was still open or unlocked on the next morning?"

Betty frowned and reflected, and shook her head.

"I cannot remember. We were all in great trouble. There was so much to do. I did not notice."

"No. Indeed why should you?" said Hanaud. He turned back to Ann. "Before you go on with this curious story, Mademoiselle, tell me this! Was the light beyond the open door, a light in the dressing-room or in the room beyond the dressing-room, Madame Harlowe's bedroom, or didn't you notice?"

"In the far room, I think," Ann answered confidently. "There would have been more light in the treasure-room otherwise. The treasure-room is long no doubt, but where I stood I was completely in darkness. There was only this panel of yellow light in the open doorway. It lay in a band straight across the carpet and it lit up the sedan chair opposite the doorway until it all glistened like silver."

"Oho, there is a sedan chair in that museum?" said Hanaud lightly. "It will be interesting to see. So the light, Mademoiselle, came from the far room?"

"The light and—and the voices," said Ann with a quaver in her throat.

"Voices!" cried Hanaud. He sat up straight in his chair, whilst Betty Harlowe went as white as a ghost. "Voices! What is this? Did you recognise those voices?"

"One, Madame's. There was no mistaking it. It was loud and violent for a moment. Then it went off into a mumble of groans. The other voice only spoke once and very few words and very clearly. But it spoke in a whisper. There was too a sound of—movements."

"Movements!" said Hanaud sharply; and with his voice his face seemed to sharpen too. "Here's a word which does not help us much. A procession moves. So does the chair if I push it. So does my hand if I cover a mouth and stop a cry. Is it that sort of movement you mean, Mademoiselle?"

Under the stern insistence of his questions Ann Upcott suddenly weakened.

"Oh, I am afraid so," she said with a loud cry, and she clapped her hands to her face. "I never understood until this morning when you spoke of how the arrow might be used. Oh, I shall never forgive myself. I stood in the darkness, a few yards away—no more—I stood quite still and listened and just beyond the lighted doorway Madame was being killed!" She drew her hands from her face and beat upon her knees with her clenched fists in a frenzy.

"'Yes, I believe that now!' Madame cried in the hoarse, harsh voice we knew: 'Stripped, eh? Stripped to the skin!' and she laughed wildly; and then came the sound, as though—yes, it might have been that!—as though she were forced down and held, and Madame's voice died to a mumble and then silence—and then the other voice in a low clear whisper, 'That will do now.' And all the while I stood in the darkness—oh!"

"What did you do after that clear whisper reached your ears?" Hanaud commanded. "Take your hands from your face, if you please, and let me hear."

Ann Upcott obeyed him. She flung her head back with the tears streaming down her face.

"I turned," she whispered. "I went out of the room. I closed the door behind me—oh, ever so gently. I fled."

"Fled? Fled? Where to?"

"Up the stairs! To my room."

"And you rang no bell? You roused no one? You fled to your room! You hid your head under the bed-clothes like a child! Come, come, Mademoiselle!"

Hanaud broke off his savage irony to ask,

"And whose voice did you think it was that whispered so clearly, 'That will do now?' The stranger's you spoke of in the library this morning?"

"No, Monsieur," Ann replied. "I could not tell. With a whisper one voice is like another."

"But you must have given that voice an owner. To run away and hide—no one would do that."

"I thought it was Jeanne Baudin's."

And Hanaud sat back in his chair again, gazing at the girl with a look in which there was as much horror as incredulity. Jim Frobisher stood behind him ashamed of his very race. Could there be a more transparent subterfuge? If she thought that the nurse Jeanne Baudin was in the bedroom, why did she turn and fly?

"Come, Mademoiselle," said Hanaud. His voice had suddenly become gentle, almost pleading. "You will not make me believe that."

Ann Upcott turned with a helpless gesture towards Betty.

"You see!" she said.

"Yes," Betty answered. She sat in doubt for a second or two and then sprang to her feet.

"Wait!" she said, and before any one could have stopped her she was skimming half-way across the garden to the house. Jim Frobisher wondered whether Hanaud had meant to stop her and then had given up the idea as quite out of the question. Certainly he had made some small quick movement; and even now, he watched Betty's flight across the broad lawn between the roses with an inscrutable queer look.

"To run like that!" he said to Frobisher, "with a boy's nimbleness and a girl's grace! It is pretty, eh? The long slim legs that twinkle, the body that floats!" and Betty ran up the stone steps into the house.

There was a tension in Hanaud's attitude with which his light words did not agree, and he watched the blank windows of the house with expectancy. Betty, however, was hardly a minute upon her errand. She reappeared upon the steps with a largish envelope in her hand and quickly rejoined the group.

"Monsieur, we have tried to keep this back from you," she said, without bitterness but with a deep regret. "I yesterday, Ann to-day, just as we have tried for many years to keep it from all Dijon. But there is no help for it now."

She opened the envelope and, taking out a cabinet photograph, handed it to Hanaud.

"This is the portrait of Madame, my aunt, at the time of her marriage with my uncle."

It was the three-quarter length portrait of a woman, slender with the straight carriage of youth, in whose face a look of character had replaced youth's prettiness. It was a face made spiritual by suffering, the eyes shadowed and wistful, the mouth tender, and conveying even in the hard medium of a photograph some whimsical sense of humour. It made Jim Frobisher, gazing over Hanaud's shoulder, exclaim not "She was beautiful," but "I would like to have known her."

"Yes! A companion," Hanaud added.

Betty took a second photograph from the envelope.

"But this, Monsieur, is the same lady a year ago."

The second photograph had been taken at Monte Carlo, and it was difficult to believe that it was of the same woman, so tragic a change had taken place within those ten years. Hanaud held the portraits side by side. The grace, the suggestion of humour had all gone; the figure had grown broad, the features coarse and heavy; the cheeks had fattened, the lips were pendulous; and there was nothing but violence in the eyes. It was a dreadful picture of collapse.

"It is best to be precise, Mademoiselle," said Hanaud gently, "though these photographs tell their unhappy story clearly enough. Madame Harlowe, during the last years of her life, drank?"

"Since my uncle's death," Betty explained. "Her life, as very likely you know already, had been rather miserable and lonely before she married him. But she had a dream then on which to live. After Simon Harlowe died, however——" and she ended her explanation with a gesture.

"Yes," Hanaud replied, "of course, Mademoiselle, we have known, Monsieur Frobisher and I, ever since we came into this affair that there was some secret. We knew it before your reticence of yesterday or Mademoiselle Upcott's of to-day. Waberski must have known of something which you would not care to have exposed before he threatened your lawyers in London, or brought his charges against you."

"Yes, he knew and the doctors and the servants of course who were very loyal. We did our best to keep our secret but we could never be sure that we had succeeded."

A friendly smile broadened Hanaud's face.

"Well, we can make sure now and here," he said, and both the girls and Jim stared at him.

"How?" they exclaimed in an incredulous voice.

Hanaud beamed. He held them in suspense. He spread out his hands. The artist as he would have said, the mountebank as Jim Frobisher would have expressed it, had got the upper hand in him, and prepared his effect.

"By answering me one simple question," he said. "Have either of you two ladies received an anonymous letter upon the subject?"

The test took them all by surprise; yet each one of them recognised immediately that they could hardly have a better. All the secrets of the town had been exploited at one time or another by this unknown person or group of persons—all the secrets that is, except this one of Mrs. Harlowe's degradation. For Betty answered,

"No! I never received one."

"Nor I," added Ann.

"Then your secret is your secret still," said Hanaud.

"For how long now?" Betty asked quickly, and Hanaud did not answer a word. He could make no promise without being false to what he had called his creed.

"It is a pity," said Betty wistfully. "We have striven so hard, Ann and I," and she gave to the two men a glimpse of the life the two girls had led in the Maison Grenelle. "We could do very little. We had neither of us any authority. We were both of us dependent upon

Madame's generosity, and though no one could have been kinder when—when Madame was herself, she was not easy when she had—the attacks. There was too much difference in age between us and her for us really to do anything but keep guard.

"She would not brook interference; she drank alone in her bedroom; she grew violent and threatening if any one interfered. She would turn them all into the street. If she needed any help she could ring for the nurse, as indeed she sometimes, though rarely, did." It was a dreadful and wearing life as Betty Harlowe described it for the two young sentinels.

"We were utterly in despair," Betty continued. "For Madame, of course, was really ill with her heart, and we always feared some tragedy would happen. This letter which Ann was to write when I was at Monsieur de Pouillac's ball seemed our one chance. It was to a doctor in England—he called himself a doctor at all events—who advertised that he had a certain remedy which could be given without the patient's knowledge in her food and drink. Oh, I had no faith in it, but we had got to try it."

Hanaud looked round at Frobisher triumphantly.

"What did I say to you, Monsieur Frobisher, when you wanted to ask a question about this letter? You see! These things disclose themselves in their due order if you leave them alone."

The triumph went out of his voice. He rose to his feet and, bowing to Betty with an unaffected stateliness and respect, he handed her back the photographs.

"Mademoiselle, I am very sorry," he said. "It is clear that you and your friend have lived amongst difficulties which we did not suspect. And, for the secret, I shall do what I can."

Jim quite forgave him the snub which had been administered to him for the excellence of his manner towards Betty. He had a hope even that now he would forswear his creed, so that the secret might still be kept and the young sentinels receive their reward for their close watch. But Hanaud sat down again in his chair, and once more turned towards Ann Upcott. He meant to go on then. He would not leave well alone. Jim was all the more disappointed, because he could not but realise that the case was more and more clearly building itself from something unsubstantial into something solid, from a conjecture to an argument—this case against some one.

CHAPTER TEN: *The Clock upon the Cabinet*

ANN UPCOTT'S story was in the light of this new
disclosure intelligible enough. Standing in the darkness, she had heard, as she thought, Mrs. Harlowe in one
of her violent outbreaks. Then with a sense of relief she
had understood that Jeanne Baudin the nurse was with
Mrs. Harlowe, controlling and restraining her and finally
administering some sedative. She had heard the outcries
diminish and cease and a final whisper from the nurse to
her patient or even perhaps to herself, "That will do
now." Then she had turned and fled, taking care to at-
tract no attention to herself. Real cowardice had nothing
to do with her flight. The crisis was over. Her intervention, which before would only have been a provocation
to a wilder outburst on the part of Mrs. Harlowe, was
now altogether without excuse. It would once more have
aroused the invalid, and next day would have added to
the discomfort and awkwardness of life in the Maison
Grenelle. For Mrs. Harlowe sober would have known
that Ann had been a witness of one more of her dreadful
exhibitions. The best thing which Ann could do, she did,
given that her interpretation of the scene was the true one.
She ran noiselessly back in the darkness to her room.

"Yes," said Hanaud. "But you believe now that your
interpretation was not correct. You believe now that
whilst you stood in the darkness with the door open and
the light beyond, Madame Harlowe was being murdered,
coldly and cruelly murdered a few feet away from you."

Ann Upcott shivered from head to foot.

"I don't want to believe it," she cried. "It's too horrible."

"You believe now that the one who whispered 'That

will do now,' was not Jeanne Baudin," Hanaud insisted, "but some unknown person, and that the whisper was uttered after murder had been done to a third person in that room."

Ann twisted her body from this side to that; she wrung her hands.

"I am afraid of it!" she moaned.

"And what is torturing you now, Mademoiselle, is remorse that you did not step silently forward and from the darkness of the treasure-room look through that lighted doorway." He spoke with a great consideration and his insight into her distress was in its way a solace to her.

"Yes," she exclaimed eagerly. "I told you this morning I could have hindered it. I didn't understand until this morning. You see, that night something else happened"; and now indeed stark fear drew the colour from her cheeks and shone in her eyes.

"Something else?" Betty asked with a quick indraw of her breath, and she shifted her chair a little so that she might face Ann. She was wearing a black coat over a white silk shirt open at the throat, and she took her handkerchief from a side pocket of the coat and drew it across her forehead.

"Yes, Mademoiselle," Hanaud explained. "It is clear that something else happened that night to your friend, something which, taken together with our talk this morning over the book of arrows, had made her believe that murder was done." He looked at Ann. "You went then to your room?"

Ann resumed her story.

"I went to bed. I was very—what shall I say?—disturbed by Madame's outburst, as I thought it. One never knew what was going to happen in this house. It was on my nerves. For a time I tumbled from side to side in my bed. I was in a fever. Then suddenly I was asleep, sound asleep. But only for a time. I woke up and it was still pitch dark in my room. There was not a thread of light from the shutters. I turned over from my side on to my back and I stretched out my arms above my head. As God is my Judge I touched a face——" and even after all these days the terror of that moment was so vivid and fresh to her that she shuddered and a little sob broke from her lips. "A face quite close to me bending over me, in silence. I drew my hands away with a gasp. My heart was in my throat. I lay just for a second or two dumb, paralysed. Then my voice came back to me and I screamed."

It was the look of the girl as she told her story perhaps more than the words she used; but something of her terror spread like a contagion amongst her hearers. Jim Frobisher's shoulders worked uneasily. Betty with her big eyes wide open, her breath suspended, hung upon Ann's narrative. Hanaud himself said:

"You screamed? I do not wonder."

"I knew that no one could hear me and that lying down I was helpless," Ann continued. "I sprang out of bed in a panic, and now I touched no one. I was so scared out of my wits that I had lost all sense of direction. I couldn't find the switch of the electric light. I stumbled along a wall feeling with my hands. I heard myself sobbing as though I was a stranger. At last I knocked against a chest of drawers and came a little to myself. I found my way then to the switch and turned on the light. The room was empty. I tried to tell myself that I had been dreaming, but I knew that the tale wasn't true. Some one had been stealthily bending down close, oh, so close over me in the darkness. My hand that had touched the face seemed to tingle. I asked myself with a shiver, what would have happened to me if just at that moment I had not waked up? I stood and listened, but the beating of my heart filled the whole room with noise. I stole to the door and laid my ear against the panel. Oh, I could easily have believed that one after another an army was creeping on tiptoe past my door. At last I made up my mind. I flung the door open wide. For a moment I stood back from it, but once the door was open I heard nothing. I stole out to the head of the great staircase. Below me the hall was as silent as an empty church. I think that I should have heard a spider stir. I suddenly realised that the light was streaming from my room and that some of it must reach me. I cried at once, 'Who's there?' And then I ran back to my room and locked myself in. I knew that I should sleep no more that night. I ran to the windows and threw open the shutters. The night had cleared, the stars were bright in a clean black sky and there was a freshness of morning in the air. I had been, I should think, about five minutes at the window when—you know perhaps, Monsieur, how the clocks in Dijon clash out and take up the hour from one another and pass it on to the hills—all of them struck three. I stayed by the window until the morning came."

After she had finished no one spoke for a little while. Then Hanaud slowly lit another cigarette, looking now upon the ground, now into the air, anywhere except at the faces of his companions.

"So this alarming thing happened just before three o'clock in the morning?" he asked gravely. "You are very sure of that, I suppose? For, you see, it may be of the utmost importance."

"I am quite sure, Monsieur," she said.

"And you have told this story to no one until this moment?"

"To no one in the world," replied Ann. "The next morning Madame Harlowe was found dead. There were the arrangements for the funeral. Then came Monsieur Boris's accusation. There were troubles enough in the house without my adding to them. Besides, no one would have believed my story of the face in the darkness; and I didn't of course associate it then with the death of Mrs. Harlowe."

"No," Hanaud agreed. "For you believed that death to have been natural."

"Yes, and I am not sure that it wasn't natural now,"
Ann protested. "But to-day I had to tell you this story,
Monsieur Hanaud"; and she leaned forward in her chair
and claimed his attention with her eyes, her face, every
tense muscle of her body. "Because if you are right and
murder was done in this house on the twenty-seventh, I
know the exact hour when it was done."

"Ah!"

Hanaud nodded his head once or twice slowly. He
gathered up his feet beneath him. His eyes glittered very
brightly as he looked at Ann. He gave Frobisher the
queer impression of an animal crouching to spring.

"The clock upon the marquetry cabinet," he said,
"against the middle of the wall in the treasure-room.
The white face of it and the hour which leapt at you
during that fraction of a second when your fingers were
on the switch."

"Yes," said Ann with a slow and quiet emphasis. "The
hour was half-past ten."

With that statement the tension was relaxed. Betty's
tightly-clenched hand opened and her trifle of a handkerchief fluttered down on the grass. Hanaud changed
from that queer attitude of a crouching animal. Jim
Frobisher drew a great breath of relief.

"Yes, that is very important," said Hanaud.

"Important. I should think it was!" cried Jim.

For this was clear and proven to him. If murder had
been done on the night of the 27th of April, there was
just one person belonging to the household of the Maison
Grenelle who could have no share in it; and that one
person was his client, Betty Harlowe.

Betty was stooping to pick up her handkerchief when
Hanaud spoke to her; and she drew herself erect again
with a little jerk.

"Does that clock on the marquetry cabinet keep good
time, Mademoiselle?" he asked.

"Very good," she answered. "Monsieur Sabin the
watch-maker in the Rue de la Liberté has had it more

than once to clean. It is an eight-day clock. It will be going when the seals are broken this afternoon. You will see for yourself."

Hanaud, however, accepted her declaration on the spot. He rose to his feet and bowed to her with a certain formality but with a smile which redeemed it.

"At half-past ten Mademoiselle Harlowe was dancing at the house of M. de Pouillac on the Boulevard Thiers," he said. "Of that there is no doubt. Inquiries have been made. Mademoiselle did not leave that house until after one in the morning. There is evidence enough of that to convince her worst enemy, from her chauffeur and her dancing partners to M. de Pouillac's coachman, who stood at the bottom of the steps with a lantern during that evening and remembers to have held open for Mademoiselle the door of her car when she went away."

"So that's that," said Jim to himself. Betty at all events was out of the net for good. And with that certainty there came a revolution in his thoughts. Why shouldn't Hanaud's search go on? It was interesting to watch the building up of this case against an unknown criminal—a case so difficult to bring to its proper conclusion in the Court of Assize, a case of poison where there was no trace of poison, a case where out of a mass of conjectures, here and there and more and more definite facts were coming into view; just as more and more masts of ships stand up out of a tumbled sea, the nearer one approaches land. Yes, now he wanted Hanaud to go on, delving astutely, letting, in his own phrase, things disclose themselves in their due sequence. But there was one point which Hanaud had missed, which should be brought to his notice. The mouse once more, he thought with all a man's vanity in his modesty, would come to the help of the netted lion. He cleared his throat.

"Miss Ann, there is one little question I would like to ask you," he began, and Hanaud turned upon him, to his surprise, with a face of thunder.

"You wish to ask a question?" he said. "Well, Monsieur, ask it if you wish. It is your right."

His manner added, what his voice left unsaid, "and your responsibility." Jim hesitated. He could see no harm in the question he proposed to ask. It was of vital importance. Yet Hanaud stood in front of him with a lowering face, daring him to put it. Jim did not doubt any longer that Hanaud was quite aware of his point and yet for some unknown reason objected to its disclosure. Jim yielded, but not with a very good grace.

"It is nothing," he said surlily, and Hanaud at once was all cheerfulness again.

"Then we will adjourn," he said, looking at his watch. "It is nearly one o'clock. Shall we say three for the Commissary of Police? Yes? Then I shall inform him and we will meet in the library at three and"—with a little bow to Betty—"the interdict shall be raised."

"At three, then," she said gaily. She sprang up from her chair, stooped, picked up her handkerchief with a swift and supple movement, twirled upon her heel and cried, "Come along, Ann!"

The four people moved off towards the house. Betty looked back.

"You have left your gloves behind you on your chair," she said suddenly to Hanaud. Hanaud looked back.

"So I have," he said, and then in a voice of protest, "Oh, Mademoiselle!"

For Betty had already darted back and now returned dangling the gloves in her hand.

"Mademoiselle, how shall I thank you?" he asked as he took them from her. Then he cocked his head at Frobisher, who was looking a little stiff.

"Ha! ha! my young friend," he said with a grin. "You do not like that so much kindness should be shown me. No! You are looking very proper. You have the poker in the back. But ask yourself this: 'What are youth and good looks compared with Hanaud?'"

No, Jim Frobisher did not like Hanaud at all when

the urchin got the upper hand in him. And the worst of it was that he had no rejoinder. He flushed very red, but he really had no rejoinder. They walked in silence to the house, and Hanaud, picking up his hat and stick, took his leave by the courtyard and the big gates. Ann drifted into the library. Jim felt a touch upon his arm. Betty was standing beside him with a smile of amusement upon her face.

"You didn't really mind my going back for his gloves, did you?" she asked. "Say you didn't, Jim!" and the amusement softened into tenderness. "I wouldn't have done it for worlds if I had thought you'd have minded."

Jim's ill-humour vanished like mist on a summer morning.

"Mind?" he cried. "You shall pin a rose in his buttonhole if it pleases you, and all I'll say will be, 'You might do the same for me'!"

Betty laughed and gave his arm a friendly squeeze.

"We are friends again, then," she said, and the next moment she was out on the steps under the glass face of the porch. "Lunch at two, Ann!" she cried. "I must walk all the grime of this morning out of my brain."

She was too quick and elusive for Jim Frobisher. She had something of Ariel in her conception—a delicate creature of fire and spirit and air. She was across the courtyard and out of sight in the street of Charles-Robert before he had quite realised that she was going. He turned doubtfully towards the library, where Ann Upcott stood in the doorway.

"I had better follow her," he said, reaching for his hat.

Ann smiled and shook her head wisely.

"I shouldn't. I know Betty. She wants to be alone."

"Do you think so?"

"I am sure."

Jim twiddled his hat in his hands, not half as sure upon the point as she was. Ann watched him with a rather rueful smile for a little while. Then she shrugged her shoulders in a sudden exasperation.

"There is something you ought to do," she said. "You ought to let Monsieur Bex, Betty's notary here, know that the seals are to be broken this afternoon. He ought to be here. He was here when they were affixed. Besides, he has all the keys of Mrs. Harlowe's drawers and cupboards."

"That's true," Jim exclaimed. "I'll go at once."

Ann gave him Monsieur Bex's address in the Place Etienne Dolet, and from the window of the library watched him go upon his errand. She stood at the window for a long while after he had disappeared.

MONSIEUR BEX the notary came out into the hall of his house when Frobisher sent his card in to him. He was a small, brisk man with a neat pointed beard, his hair cut *en brosse* and the corner of his napkin tucked into his neck between the flaps of his collar.

Jim explained that the seals were to be removed from the rooms of the Maison Grenelle, but said nothing at all of the new developments which had begun with the discovery of the book of the arrows.

"I have had communications with Messrs. Frobisher and Haslitt," the little man exclaimed. "Everything has been as correct as it could possibly be. I am happy to meet a partner of so distinguished a firm. Yes. I will certainly present myself at three with my keys and see the end of this miserable scandal. It has been a disgrace. That young lady so delicious and so correct! And that animal of a Waberski! But we can deal with him. We have laws in France."

He gave Jim the impression that there were in his opinion no laws anywhere else, and he bowed his visitor into the street.

Jim returned by the Rue des Godrans and the main thoroughfare of the town, the street of Liberty. As he crossed the semicircle of the Place d'Armes in front of the Hôtel de Ville, he almost ran into Hanaud smoking a cigar.

"You have lunched already?" he cried.

"An affair of a quarter of an hour," said Hanaud with a wave of the hand. "And you?"

"Not until two. Miss Harlowe wanted a walk."

Hanaud smiled.

"How I understand that! The first walk after an

ordeal! The first walk of a convalescent after an operation! The first walk of a defendant found innocent of a grave charge! It must be worth taking, that walk. But console yourself, my friend, for the postponement of your luncheon. You have met me!" and he struck something of an attitude.

Now Jim had the gravest objection to anything theatrical, especially when displayed in public places, and he answered stiffly, "That is a pleasure, to be sure."

Hanaud grinned. To make Jim look "proper" was becoming to him an unfailing entertainment.

"Now I reward you," he said, though for what Jim could not imagine. "You shall come with me. At this hour, on the top of old Philippe le Bon's Terrace Tower, we shall have the world to ourselves."

He led the way into the great courtyard of the Hôtel de Ville. Behind the long wing which faced them, a square, solid tower rose a hundred and fifty feet high above the ground. With Frobisher at his heels, Hanaud climbed the three hundred and sixteen steps and emerged upon the roof into the blue and gold of a cloudless May in France. They looked eastwards, and the beauty of the scene took Frobisher's breath away. Just in front, the slender apse of Notre Dame, fine as a lady's ornament, set him wondering how in the world through all these centuries it had endured; and beyond, rich and green and wonderful, stretched the level plain with its shining streams and nestling villages.

Hanaud sat down upon a stone bench and stretched out his arm across the parapet. "Look!" he cried eagerly, proudly. "There is what I brought you here to see. Look!"

Jim looked and saw, and his face lit up. Far away on the horizon's edge, unearthly in its beauty, hung the great mass of Mont Blanc; white as silver, soft as velvet, and here and there sparkling with gold as though the flame of a fire leaped and sank.

"Oho!" said Hanaud as he watched Jim's face. "So

we have that in common. You perhaps have stood on
the top of that mountain?"

"Five times," Jim answered, with a smile made up of
many memories. "I hope to do so again."

"You are fortunate," said Hanaud a little enviously.
"For me I see him only in the distance. But even so—
if I am troubled—it is like sitting silent in the company
of a friend."

Jim Frobisher's mind strayed back over memories of
snow slope and rock ridge. It was a true phrase which
Hanaud had used. It expressed one of the many elusive,
almost incommunicable emotions which mountains did
mean to the people who had "that"—the passion for
mountains—in common. Jim glanced curiously at
Hanaud.

"You are troubled about this case, then?" he said sym-
pathetically. The distant and exquisite vision of that
soaring arc of silver and velvet set in the blue air had
brought the two men into at all events a momentary
brotherhood.

"Very," Hanaud returned slowly, without turning his
eyes from the horizon, "and for more reasons than one.
What do you yourself think of it?"

"I think, Monsieur Hanaud," Jim said dryly, "that you
do not like any one to ask any questions except yourself."

Hanaud laughed with an appreciation of the thrust.

"Yes, you wished to ask a question of the beautiful
Mademoiselle Upcott. Tell me if I have guessed aright
the question you meant to ask! It was whether the face
she touched in the darkness was the smooth face of a
woman or the face of a man."

"Yes. That was it."

It was now for Hanaud to glance curiously and quickly
at Jim. There could be no doubt of the thought which
was passing through his mind: "I must begin to give you
a little special attention, my friend." But he was careful
not to put his thoughts into words.

"I did not want that question asked," he said.

"Why?"

"Because it was unnecessary, and unnecessary questions are confusing things which had best be avoided altogether."

Jim did not believe one word of that explanation. He had too clear a recollection of the swift movement and the look with which Hanaud had checked him. Both had been unmistakably signs of alarm. Hanaud would not have been alarmed at the prospect of a question being asked, merely because the question was superfluous. There was another and, Jim was sure, a very compelling reason in Hanaud's mind. Only he could not discover it.

Besides, was the question superfluous?

"Surely," Hanaud replied. "Suppose that that young lady's hand had touched in the darkness the face of a man with its stubble, its tough skin, and the short hair of his head around it, bending down so low over hers, would not that have been the most vivid, terrifying thing to her in all the terrifying incident? Stretching out her hands carelessly above her head, she touches suddenly, unexpectedly, the face of a man? She could not have told her story at all without telling that. It would have been the unforgettable detail, the very heart of her terror. She touched the face of a man!"

Jim recognised that the reasoning was sound, but he was no nearer to the solution of his problem—why Hanaud so whole-heartedly objected to the question being asked. And then Hanaud made a quiet remark which drove it for a long time altogether out of Jim's speculations.

"Mademoiselle Ann touched the face of a woman in the darkness that night—if that night, in the darkness she touched a face at all."

Jim was utterly startled.

"You believe that she was lying to us?" he cried.

Hanaud shook a protesting hand in the air.

"I believe nothing," he said. "I am looking for a criminal."

"Ann Upcott!" Jim spoke the name in amazement.
"Ann Upcott!" Then he remembered the look of her
as she had told her story, her face convulsed with terror,
her shaking tones. "Oh, it's impossible that she was
lying. Surely no one could have so mimicked fear?"

Hanaud laughed.

"You may take this from me, my friend. All women
who are great criminals are also very artful actresses.
I never knew one who wasn't."

"Ann Upcott!" Jim Frobisher once more exclaimed,
but now with a trifle less of amazement. He was growing slowly and gradually accustomed to the idea. Still—
that girl with the radiant look of young Spring! Oh, no!

"Ann Upcott was left nothing in Mrs. Harlowe's will,"
he argued. "What could she have to gain by murder?"

"Wait, my friend! Look carefully at her story!
Analyse it. You will see—what? That it falls into two
parts." Hanaud ground the stump of his cigar beneath
his heel, offered one of his black cigarettes to Jim Frobisher and lighted one for himself. He lit it with a
sulphur match which Jim thought would never stop
fizzling, would never burst into flame.

"One part when she was alone in her bedroom—a little
story of terror and acted very effectively, but after all
any one could invent it. The other part was not so easy
to invent. The communicating door open for no reason,
the light beyond, the voice that whispered, 'That will do,'
the sound of the struggle! No, my friend, I don't believe that was invented. There were too many little details which seemed to have been lived through. The
white face of the clock and the hour leaping at her. No!
I think all that must stand. But adapt it a little. See!
This morning Waberski told us a story of the Street of
Gambetta and of Jean Cladel!"

"Yes," said Jim.

"And I asked you afterwards whether Waberski might
not be telling a true story of himself and attributing it
to Mademoiselle Harlowe?"

"Yes."

"Well, then, interpret Ann Upcott's story in the same way," continued Hanaud. "Suppose that sometime that day she had unlocked the communicating door! What more easy? Madame Harlowe was up during the daytime. Her room was empty. And that communicating door opened not into Madame's bedroom, where perhaps it might have been discovered whether it was locked or not, but into a dressing-room."

"Yes," Jim agreed.

"Well then, continue! Ann Upcott is left alone after Mademoiselle Harlowe's departure to Monsieur de Pouillac's Ball. She sends Gaston to bed. The house is all dark and asleep. Suppose then that she is joined by—some one—some one with the arrow poison all ready in the hypodermic needle. That they enter the treasure-room just as Ann Upcott described. That she turns on the light for a second whilst—some one—crosses the treasure-room and opens the door. Suppose that the voice which whispered, 'That will do now,' was the voice of Ann Upcott herself and that she whispered it across Madame Harlowe's body to the third person in that room!"

"The 'some one,'" exclaimed Jim. "But, who then? Who?"

Hanaud shrugged his shoulders. "Why not Waberski?"

"Waberski?" cried Jim with a new excitement in his voice.

"You asked me what had Ann Upcott to gain by this murder and you answered your own question. Nothing you said, Monsieur Frobisher, but did your quick answer cover the ground? Waberski—he at all events expected a fine fat legacy. What if he in return for help proposed to share that fine fat legacy with the exquisite Mademoiselle Ann. Has she no motive now? In the end what do we know of her at all except that she is the paid companion and therefore poor? Mademoiselle Ann!"; and he threw up his hands. "Where does she spring from?

How did she come into that house? Was she perhaps Waberski's friend?"—and a cry from Jim brought Hanaud to a stop.

Jim had thought of Waberski as the possible murderer if murder had been done—a murderer who, disappointed of his legacy, the profits of his murder, had carried on his villainy to blackmail and a false accusation. But he had not associated Ann Upcott with him until those moments on the Terrace Tower. Yet now memories began to crowd upon him. The letter to him, for instance. She had said that Waberski had claimed her support and ridiculed his claim. Might that letter not have been a blind and a rather cunning blind? Above all there was a scene passing vividly through his mind which was very different from the scene spread out before his eyes, a scéne of lighted rooms and a crowd about a long green table, and a fair slender girl seated at the table, who lost and lost until the whole of her little pile of banknotes was swept in by the croupier's rake, and then turned away with a high carriage but a quivering lip.

"Aha!" said Hanaud keenly. "You know something after all of Ann Upcott, my friend. What do you know?"

Jim hesitated. At one moment it did not seem fair to her that he should relate his story. Explained, it might wear so different a complexion. At another moment that it would be fairer to let her explain it. And there was Betty to consider. Yes, above all there was Betty to consider. He was in Dijon on her behalf.

"I will tell you," he said to Hanaud. "When I saw you in Paris, I told you that I had never seen Ann Upcott in all my life. I believed it. It wasn't until she danced into the library yesterday morning that I realised I had misled you. I saw Ann Upcott at the *trente et quarante* table at the Sporting Club in Monte Carlo in January of this year. I sat next to her. She was quite alone and losing her money. Nothing would go right for her. She bore herself proudly and well. The only sign I saw of distress was the tightening of her fingers about her little handbag, and a look of defiance thrown at the other players when she rose after her last coup, as though she dared them to pity her. I was on the other hand winning, and I slipped a thousand-franc note off the table on to the floor, keeping my heel firmly upon it as you can understand. And as the girl turned to move out from the crowd I stopped her. I said in English, for she was obviously of my race, 'This is yours. You have dropped it on the floor.' She gave me a smile and a little shake of the head. I think that for the moment she dared not trust her lips to speak, and in a second, of course, she was swallowed up in the crowd. I played for a little while longer. Then I too rose and as I passed the entrance to the bar on my way to get my coat, this girl rose up from one of the many little tables and spoke to me. She called me by my name. She thanked me very prettily and said that although she had lost that evening she was not really in any trouble. I doubted the truth of what she said. For she had not one ring upon any finger, not the tiniest necklace about her throat, not one ornament upon her dress or in her hair. She turned away from me at once and went back to the little table where she sat down again in the company of a man. The girl of course was Ann Upcott, the man Waberski. It was from him no doubt that she had got my name."

"Did this little episode happen before Ann Upcott became a member of the household?" Hanaud asked.

"Yes," replied Jim. "I think she joined Mrs. Harlowe and Betty at Monte Carlo. I think that she came with them back to Dijon."

"No doubt," said Hanaud. He sat for a little while in silence. Then he said softly, "That does not look so very well for Mademoiselle Ann."

Jim had to admit that it did not.

"But consider this, Monsieur Hanaud," he urged. "If Ann Upcott, which I will not believe, is mixed up in this affair, why should she of her own free will volunteer this story of what she heard upon the night of the twenty-seventh and invent that face which bent down over her in the darkness?"

"I have an idea about that," Hanaud replied. "She told us this story—when? After I had said that we must have the seals broken this afternoon and the rooms thrown open. It is possible that we may come upon something in those rooms which makes it wise for her to divert suspicion upon some other woman in the house. Jeanne Baudin, or even Mademoiselle Harlowe's maid Francine Rollard."

"But not Mademoiselle Betty," Jim interposed quickly.

"No, no!" Hanaud returned with a wave of his hand. "The clock upon the marquetry cabinet settled that. Mademoiselle Betty is out of the affair. Well, this afternoon we shall see. Meanwhile, my friend, you will be late for your luncheon."

Hanaud rose from the bench and with a last look at the magical mountain, that outpost of France, they turned towards the city.

Jim Frobisher looked down upon tiny squares green with limes and the steep gaily-patterned roofs of ancient houses. About him the fine tapering spires leapt high like lances from the slates of its many churches. A little to the south and a quarter of a mile away across the roof tops he saw the long ridge of a big house and the smoke rising from a chimney stack or two and behind it the tops of tall trees which rippled and shook the sunlight from their leaves.

"The Maison Grenelle!" he said.

There was no answer, not even the slightest movement at his side.

"Isn't it?" he asked and he turned.

Hanaud had not even heard him. He was gazing also towards the Maison Grenelle with the queerest look upon his face; a look with which Jim was familiar in some sort of association, but which for a moment or two he could not define. It was not an expression of amaze-

ment. On the other hand interest was too weak a word.
Suddenly Jim Frobisher understood and comprehension
brought with it a sense of discomfort. Hanaud's look,
very bright and watchful and more than a little inhuman,
was just the look of a good retriever dog when his master
brings out a gun.

Jim looked again at the high ridge of the house. The
slates were broken at intervals by little gabled windows,
but at none of them could he see a figure. From none of
them a signal was waved.

"What is it that you are looking at?" asked Jim in
perplexity and then with a touch of impatience. "You
see something, I'm sure."

Hanaud heard his companion at last. His face
changed in a moment, lost its rather savage vigilance, and
became the face of a buffoon.

"Of course I see something. Always I see something.
Am I not Hanaud? Ah, my friend, the responsibility of
being Hanaud! Aren't you fortunate to be without it?
Pity me! For the Hanauds must see something everywhere—even when there is nothing to see. Come!"

He bustled out of the sunlight on that high platform
into the dark turret of the staircase. The two men descended the steps and came out again into the semi-circle
of the Place d'Armes.

"Well!" said Hanaud and then "Yes," as though he
had some little thing to say and was not quite sure
whether he would say it. Then he compromised. "You
shall take a Vermouth with me before you go to your
luncheon," he said.

"I should be late if I did," Frobisher replied.

Hanaud waved the objection aside with a shake of his
outstretched forefinger.

"You have plenty of time, Monsieur. You shall take
a Vermouth with me, and you will still reach the Maison
Grenelle before Mademoiselle Harlowe. I say that,
Hanaud," he said superbly, and Jim laughed and con-
sented.

"I shall plead your vanity as my excuse when I find her and Ann Upcott half through their meal."

A café stands at the corner of the street of Liberty and the Place d'Armes, with two or three little tables set out on the pavement beneath an awning. They sat down at one of them, and over the Vermouth, Hanaud was once more upon the brink of some recommendation or statement.

"You see——" he began and then once more ran away. "So you have been five times upon the top of the Mont Blanc!" he said. "From Chamonix?"

"Once," Jim replied. "Once from the Col du Géant by the Brenva glacier. Once by the Dôme route. Once from the Brouillard glacier. And the last time by the Mont Mandit."

Hanaud listened with genuine friendliness and said:

"You tell me things which are interesting and very new to me," he said warmly. "I am grateful, Monsieur."

"On the other hand," Jim answered dryly, "you, Monsieur, tell me very little. Even what you brought me to this café to say, you are going to keep to yourself. But for my part I shall not be so churlish. I am going to tell you what I think."

"Yes?"

"I think we have missed the way."

"Oh?"

Hanaud selected a cigarette from his bundle in its bright blue wrapping.

"You will perhaps think me presumptuous in saying so."

"Not the least little bit in the world," Hanaud replied seriously. "We of the Police are liable in searching widely to overlook the truth under our noses. That is our danger. Another angle of view—there is nothing more precious. I am all attention."

Jim Frobisher drew his chair closer to the round table of iron and leaned his elbows upon it.

"I think there is one question in particular which we

must answer if we are to discover whether Mrs. Harlowe was murdered, and if so by whom."

Hanaud nodded.

"I agree," he said slowly. "But I wonder whether we have the same question in our minds."

"It is a question which we have neglected. It is this—Who put back the Professor's treatise on Sporanthus in its place upon the bookshelf in the library, between midday yesterday and this morning."

Hanaud struck another of his abominable matches, and held it in the shelter of his palm until the flame shone. He lit his cigarette and took a few puffs at it.

"No doubt that question is important," he admitted, although in rather an off-hand way. "But it is not mine. No. I think there is another more important still. I think if we could know why the door of the treasure-room, which had been locked since Simon Harlowe's death, was unlocked on the night of the twenty-seventh of April, we should be very near to the whole truth of this dark affair. But," and he flung out his hands, "that baffles me."

Jim left him sitting at the table and staring moodily upon the pavement, as if he hoped to read the answer there.

CHAPTER TWELVE: *The Breaking of the Seals*

A FEW minutes later Jim Frobisher had to admit that Hanaud guessed very luckily. He would not allow that it was more than a guess. Monsieur Hanaud might be a thorough little Mr. Know-All; but no insight, however brilliant, could inform him of so accidental a circumstance. But there the fact was. Frobisher did arrive at the Maison Grenelle, to his great discomfort, before Betty Harlowe. He had loitered with Hanaud at the café just so that this might not take place. He shrank from being alone with Ann Upcott now that he suspected her. The most he could hope to do was to conceal the reason of his trouble. The trouble itself in her presence he could not conceal. She made his case the more difficult perhaps by a rather wistful expression of sympathy.

"You are distressed," she said gently. "But surely you need not be any longer. What I said this morning was true. It was half-past ten when that dreadful whisper reached my ears. Betty was a mile away amongst her friends in a ball-room. Nothing can shake that."

"It is not on her account that I am troubled," he cried, and Ann looked at him with startled eyes.

Betty crossed the court and joined them in the hall before Ann could ask a question; and throughout their luncheon he made conversation upon indifferent subjects with rapidity, if without entertainment.

Fortunately there was no time to spare. They were still indeed smoking their cigarettes over their coffee when Gaston informed them that the Commissary of Police with his secretary was waiting in the library.

"This is Mr. Frobisher, my solicitor in London," said Betty as she presented Jim.

143

The Commissary, Monsieur Girardot, was a stout, bald, middle-aged man with a pair of folding glasses sitting upon a prominent fat nose; his secretary, Maurice Thevenet, was a tall good-looking novice in the police administration, a trifle flashy in his appearance, and in his own esteem, one would gather, rather a conqueror amongst the fair.

"I have asked Monsieur Bex, Mademoiselle's notary in Dijon, to be present," said Jim.

"That is quite in order," replied the Commissary, and Monsieur Bex was at that moment announced. He came on the very moment of three. The clock was striking as he bowed in the doorway. Everything was just as it should be. Monsieur Bex was pleased.

"With Monsieur le Commissaire's consent," he said, smiling, "we can now proceed with the final ceremonies of this affair."

"We wait for Monsieur Hanaud," said the Commissary.

"Hanaud?"

"Hanaud of the Sûreté of Paris, who has been invited by the Examining Magistrate to take charge of this case," the Commissary explained.

"Case?" cried Monsieur Bex in perplexity. "But there is no case for Hanaud to take charge of;" and Betty Harlowe drew him a little aside.

Whilst she gave the little notary some rapid summary of the incidents of the morning, Jim went out of the room into the hall in search of Hanaud. He saw him at once; but to his surprise Hanaud came forward from the back of the hall as if he had entered the house from the garden.

"I sought you in the dining-room," he said, pointing to the door of that room which certainly was at the back of the house behind the library, with its entrance behind the staircase. "We will join the others."

Hanaud was presented to Monsieur Bex.

"And this gentleman?" asked Hanaud, bowing slightly to Thevenet.

The Breaking of the Seals

"My secretary, Maurice Thevenet," said the Commissary, and in a loud undertone, "a charming youth, of an intelligence which is surprising. He will go far."

Hanaud looked at Thevenet with a friendly interest. The young recruit gazed at the great man with kindling eyes.

"This will be an opportunity for me, Monsieur Hanaud, by which, if I do not profit, I prove myself of no intelligence at all," he said with a formal modesty which quite went to the heart of Monsieur Bex.

"That is very correct," said he.

Hanaud for his part was never averse to flattery. He cocked an eye at Jim Frobisher; he shook the secretary warmly by the hand.

"Then don't hesitate to ask me questions, my young friend," he answered. "I am Hanaud now, yes. But I was once young Maurice Thevenet without, alas! his good looks."

Maurice Thevenet blushed with the most becoming diffidence.

"That is very kind," said Monsieur Bex.

"This looks like growing into a friendly little family party," Jim Frobisher thought, and he quite welcomed a "Hum" and a "Ha" from the Commissary.

He moved to the centre of the room.

"We, Girardot, Commissaire of Police, will now remove the seals," he said pompously.

He led the way from the Library across the hall and along the corridor to the wide door of Mrs. Harlowe's bedroom. He broke the seals and removed the bands. Then he took a key from the hand of his secretary and opened the door upon a shuttered room. The little company of people surged forward. Hanaud stretched out his arms and barred the way.

"Just for a moment, please!" he ordered and over his shoulder Jim Frobisher had a glimpse of the room which made him shiver.

This morning in the garden some thrill of the chase

had made him for a moment eager that Hanaud should press on, that development should follow upon development until somewhere a criminal stood exposed. Since the hour, however, which he had spent upon the Tower of the Terrace, all thought of the chase appalled him and he waited for developments in fear. This bedroom mistily lit by a few stray threads of daylight which pierced through the chinks of the shutters, cold and silent and mysterious, was for him peopled with phantoms, whose faces no one could see, who struggled dimly in the shadows. Then Hanaud and the Commissary crossed to the windows opposite, opened them and flung back the shutters. The clear bright light flooded every corner in an instant and brought to Jim Frobisher relief. The room was swept and clean, the chairs ranged against the wall, the bed flat and covered with an embroidered spread; everywhere there was order; it was as empty of suggestion as a vacant bedroom in an hotel.

Hanaud looked about him.

"Yes," he said. "This room stood open for a week after Madame's funeral. It would have been a miracle if we discovered anything which could help us."

He went to the bed, which stood with its head against the wall midway between the door and the windows. A small flat stand with a button of enamel lay upon the round table by the bed-side, and from the stand a cord ran down by the table leg and disappeared under the carpet.

"This is the bell into what was the maid's bedroom, I suppose," he said, turning towards Betty.

"Yes."

Hanaud stooped and minutely examined the cord. But there was no sign that it had ever been tampered with. He stood up again.

"Mademoiselle, will you take Monsieur Girardot into Jeanne Baudin's bedroom and close the door. I shall press this button, and you will know whether the bell rings whilst we here shall be able to assure ourselves whether sounds made in one of the rooms would be heard in the other."

"Certainly."

Betty took the Commissary of Police away, and a few seconds later those in Mrs. Harlowe's room heard a door close in the corridor.

"Will you shut our door now, if you please?" Hanaud requested.

Bex, the notary, closed it.

"Now, silence, if you please!"

Hanaud pressed the button, and not a sound answered him. He pressed it again and again with the same result. The Commissary returned to the bedroom.

"Well?" Hanaud asked.

"It rang twice," said the Commissary.

Hanaud shrugged his shoulders with a laugh.

"And an electric bell has a shrill, penetrating sound," he cried. "Name of a name, but they built good houses when the Maison Grenelle was built! Are the cupboards and drawers open?"

He tried one and found it locked. Monsieur Bex came forward.

"All the drawers were locked on the morning when Madame Harlowe's death was discovered. Mademoiselle Harlowe herself locked them in my presence and handed to me the keys for the purpose of making an inventory. Mademoiselle was altogether correct in so doing. For until the funeral had taken place the terms of the will were not disclosed."

"But afterwards, when you took the inventory you must have unlocked them."

"I have not yet begun the inventory, Monsieur Hanaud. There were the arrangements for the funeral, a list of the properties to be made for valuation, and the vineyards to be administered."

"Oho," cried Hanaud alertly. "Then these wardrobes and cupboards and drawers should hold exactly what they held on the night of the twenty-seventh of

April." He ran quickly about the room trying a door here, a drawer there, and came to a stop beside a cupboard fashioned in the thickness of the wall. "The trouble is that a child with a bent wire could unlock any one of them. Do you know what Madame Harlowe kept in this, Monsieur Bex?" and Hanaud rapped with his knuckles upon the cupboard door.

"No, I have no idea. Shall I open it?" and Bex produced a bunch of keys from his pocket.

"Not for the moment, I think," said Hanaud.

He had been dawdling over the locks and the drawers, as though time meant nothing to him at all. He now swung briskly back into the centre of the room, making notes, it seemed to Frobisher, of its geography. The door opening from the corridor faced, across the length of the floor, the two tall windows above the garden. If one stood in the doorway facing these two windows, the bed was on the left hand. On the corridor side of the bed, a second smaller door, which was half open, led to a white-tiled bath-room. On the window side of the bed was the cupboard in the wall about the height of a woman's shoulders. A dressing-table stood between the windows, a great fire-place broke the right-hand wall, and in that same wall, close to the right-hand window, there was yet another door. Hanaud moved to it.

"This is the door of the dressing-room?" he asked of Ann Upcott, and without waiting for an answer pushed it open.

Monsieur Bex followed upon his heels with his keys rattling. "Everything here has been locked up too," he said.

Hanaud paid not the slightest attention. He opened the shutters.

It was a narrow room without any fire-place at all, and with a door exactly opposite to the door by which Hanaud had entered. He went at once to this door.

"And this must be the communicating door which leads into what is called the treasure-room," he said, and

148

he paused with his hand upon the knob and his eyes ranging alertly over the faces of the company.

"Yes," said Ann Upcott.

Jim was conscious of a queer thrill. He thought of the opening of some newly-discovered tomb of a Pharaoh in a hill-side of the Valley of Kings. Suspense passed from one to the other as they waited, but Hanaud did not move. He stood there impassive and still like some guardian image at the door of the tomb. Jim felt that he was never going to move, and in a voice of exasperation he cried:

"Is the door locked?"

Hanaud replied in a quiet but a singular voice. No doubt he, too, felt that strange current of emotion and expectancy which bound all in the room under a spell, and even gave to their diverse faces for a moment a kind of family similitude.

"I don't know yet whether it's locked or not," he said. "But since this room is now the private sitting-room of Mademoiselle Harlowe, I think that we ought to wait until she rejoins us."

Monsieur Bex just had time to remark with approval, "That is very correct," before Betty's fresh, clear voice rang out from the doorway leading to Mrs. Harlowe's bedroom:

"I am here."

Hanaud turned the handle. The door was not locked. It opened at a touch—inwards towards the group of people and upwards towards the corridor. The treasure-room was before them, shrouded in dim light, but here and there a beam of light sparkled upon gold and held out a promise of wonders. Hanaud picked his way daintily to the windows and fastened the shutters back against the outside wall. "I beg that nothing shall be touched," he said as the others filed into the room.

CHAPTER THIRTEEN: *Simon Harlowe's Treasure-room*

L IKE the rest of the reception-rooms along the corridor, it was longer than it was broad and more of a gallery than a room. But it had been arranged for habitation rather than for occasional visits. For it was furnished with a luxurious comfort and not over-crowded. In the fawn-coloured panels of the walls a few exquisite pictures by Fragonard had been framed; on the writing-table of Chinese Chippendale by the window every appointment, ink-stand, pen-tray, candlestick, sand-caster and all were of the pink Battersea enamel and without a flaw. But they were there for use, not for exhibition. Moreover a prominent big fire-place in the middle of the wall on the side of the hall, jutted out into the room and gave it almost the appearance of two rooms in communication. The one feature of the room, indeed, which at a first glimpse betrayed the collector, was the Sedan chair set in a recess of the wall by the fire-place and opposite to the door communicating with Mrs. Harlowe's bedroom. Its body was of a pale French grey in colour, with elaborately carved mouldings in gold round the panels and medallions representing fashionable shepherds and shepherdesses daintily painted in the middle of them. It had glass windows at the sides to show off the occupant, and it was lined with pale grey satin, embroidered in gold to match the colour of the panels. The roof, which could be raised upon a hinge at the back, was ornamented with gold filigree work, and it had a door in front of which the upper part was glass. Altogether it was as pretty a gleaming piece of work as the art of carriage-building could achieve, and a gilt rail very fitly protected it. Even

Hanaud was taken by its daintiness. He stood with his hands upon the rail examining it with a smile of pleasure, until Jim began to think that he had quite forgotten the business which had brought him there. However, he brought himself out of his dream with a start.

"A pretty world for rich people, Monsieur Frobisher," he said. "What pictures of fine ladies in billowy skirts and fine gentlemen in silk stockings! And what splashings of mud for the unhappy devils who had to walk!"

He turned his back to the chair and looked across the room. "That is the clock which marked half-past ten, Mademoiselle, during the moment when you had the light turned up?" he asked of Ann.

"Yes," she answered quickly. Then she looked at it again. "Yes, that's it."

Jim detected or fancied that he detected a tiny change in her intonation, as she repeated her assurance, not an inflexion of doubt—it was not marked enough for that—but of perplexity. It was clearly, however, fancy upon his part, for Hanaud noticed nothing at all. Jim pulled himself up with an unspoken remonstrance. "Take care!" he warned himself. "For once you begin to suspect people, they can say and do nothing which will not provide you with material for suspicion."

Hanaud was without doubt satisfied. The clock was a beautiful small gilt clock of the Louis Quinze period, shaped with a waist like a violin; it had a white face, and it stood upon a marquetry Boulle cabinet, a little more than waist high, in front of a tall Venetian mirror. Hanaud stood directly in front of it and compared it with his watch.

"It is exact to the minute, Mademoiselle," he said to Betty, with a smile as he replaced his watch in his pocket.

He turned about, so that he stood with his back to the clock. He faced the fire-place across the narrow neck of the room. It had an Adam mantelpiece, fashioned from the same fawn-coloured wood as the panels, with slender pillars and some beautiful carving upon the board beneath

the shelf. Above the shelf one of the Fragonards was
framed in the wall and apparently so that nothing should
mask it, there were no high ornaments at all upon the
shelf itself. One or two small boxes of Battersea enamel
and a flat glass case alone decorated it. Hanaud crossed
to the mantelshelf and, after a moment's inspection, lifted,
with a low whistle of admiration, the flat glass case.

"You will pardon me, Mademoiselle," he said to Betty.
"But I shall probably never in my life have the luck to
see anything so incomparable again. And the mantelshelf is a little high for me to see it properly."

Without waiting for the girl's consent he carried it
towards the window.

"Do you see this, Monsieur Frobisher?" he called out,
and Jim went forward to his side.

The case held a pendant wrought in gold and chalced-
ony and translucent enamels by Benvenuto Cellini. Jim
acknowledged that he had never seen craftsmanship so
exquisite and delicate, but he chafed none the less at
Hanaud's diversion from his business.

"One could spend a long day in this room," the detective exclaimed, "admiring these treasures."

"No doubt," Jim replied dryly. "But I had a notion
that we were going to spend an afternoon looking for an
arrow."

Hanaud laughed.

"My friend, you recall me to my duty." He looked at
the jewel again and sighed. "Yes, as you say, we are
not visitors here to enjoy ourselves."

He carried the case back again to the mantelshelf and
replaced it. Then all at once his manner changed. He
was leaning forward with his hands still about the glass
case. But he was looking down. The fire-grate was
hidden from the room by a low screen of blue lacquer;
and Hanaud, from the position in which he stood, could
see over the screen into the grate itself.

"What is all this?" he asked.

He lifted the screen from the hearth and put it care-

fully aside. All now could see what had disturbed him—
a heap of white ashes in the grate.

Hanaud went down upon his knees and picking up the
shovel from the fender he thrust it between the bars and
drew it out again with a little layer of the ashes upon it.
They were white and had been pulverised into atoms.
There was not one flake which would cover a finger-nail.
Hanaud touched them gingerly, as though he had expected to find them hot.

"This room was sealed up on Sunday morning and
to-day is Thursday afternoon," said Jim Frobisher with
heavy sarcasm. "Ashes do not as a rule keep hot more
than three days, Monsieur Hanaud."

Maurice Thevenet looked at Frobisher with indignation. He was daring to make fun of Hanaud! He
treated the Sûreté with no more respect than one might
treat—well, say Scotland Yard.

Even Monsieur Bex had an air of disapproval. For a
partner of the firm of Frobisher & Haslitt this gentleman
was certainly not very correct. Hanaud on the contrary
was milk and water.

"I have observed it," he replied mildly, and he sat back
upon his heels with the shovel still poised in his hands.

"Mademoiselle!" he called; and Betty moved forward
and leaned against the mantelshelf at his side. "Who
burnt these papers so very carefully?" he asked.

"I did," Betty replied.

"And when?"

"On Saturday night, a few, and the rest on Sunday
morning, before Monsieur le Commissaire arrived."

"And what were they, Mademoiselle?"

"Letters, Monsieur."

Hanaud looked up into her face quickly.

"Oho!" he said softly. "Letters! Yes! And what
kind of letters, if you please?"

Jim Frobisher was for throwing up his hands in
despair. What in the world had happened to Hanaud?
One moment he forgot altogether the business upon

which he was engaged in his enjoyment of Simon Harlowe's collection. The next he was off on his wild-goose chase after anonymous letters. Jim had not a doubt that he was thinking of them now. One had only to say "letters," and he was side-tracked at once, apparently ready to accuse any one of their authorship.

"They were quite private letters," Betty replied, whilst the colour slowly stained her cheeks. "They will not help you."

"So I see," Hanaud returned, with just a touch of a snarl in his voice as he shook the shovel and flung the ashes back into the grate. "But I am asking you, Mademoiselle, what kind of letters these were."

Betty did not answer. She looked sullenly down at the floor, and then from the floor to the windows; and Jim saw with a stab of pain that her eyes were glistening with tears.

"I think, Monsieur Hanaud, that we have come to a point when Mademoiselle and I should consult together," he interposed.

"Mademoiselle would certainly be within her rights," said Monsieur Bex.

But Mademoiselle waived her rights with a little petulant movement of her shoulders.

"Very well."

She showed her face now to them all, with the tears abrim in her big eyes, and gave Jim a little nod of thanks and recognition.

"You shall be answered, Monsieur Hanaud," she said with a catch in her voice. "It seems that nothing, however sacred, but must be dragged out into the light. But I say again those letters will not help you."

She looked across the group to her notary.

"Monsieur Bex," she said, and he moved forward to the other side of Hanaud.

"In Madame's bedroom between her bed and the door of the bathroom there stood a small chest in which she kept a good many unimportant papers, such as old receipted bills, which it was not yet wise to destroy. This chest I took to my office after Madame's death, of course with Mademoiselle's consent, meaning to go through the papers at my leisure and recommend that all which were not important should be destroyed. My time, however, was occupied, as I have already explained to you, and it was not until the Friday of the sixth of May that I opened the chest at all. On the very top I saw, to my surprise, a bundle of letters in which the writing had already faded, tied together with a ribbon. One glance was enough to assure me that they were very private and sacred things with which Mademoiselle's notary had nothing whatever to do. Accordingly, on the Saturday morning, I brought them back myself to Mademoiselle Betty."

With a bow Monsieur Bex retired and Betty continued the story.

"I put the letters aside so that I might read them quietly after dinner. As it happened I could not in any case have given them attention before. For on that morning Monsieur Boris formulated his charge against me, and in the afternoon I was summoned to the Office of the Examining Magistrate. As you can understand, I was—I don't say frightened—but distressed by this accusation; and it was not until quite late in the evening, and then rather to distract my thoughts than for any other reason, that I looked at the letters. But as soon as I did look at them I understood that they must be destroyed. There were reasons, which"—and her voice faltered, and with an effort again grew steady—"which I feel it rather a sacrilege to explain. They were letters which passed between my uncle Simon and Mrs. Harlowe during the time when she was very unhappily married to Monsieur Raviart and living apart from him—sometimes long letters, sometimes little scraps of notes scribbled off—without reserve—during a moment of freedom. They were the letters of," and again her voice broke and died away into a whisper, so that none could misunderstand her meaning—"of lovers—lovers speaking very

intimate things, and glorying in their love. Oh, there
was no doubt that they ought to be destroyed! But I
made up my mind that I ought to read them, every one,
first of all lest there should be something in them which
I ought to know. I read a good many that night and
burnt them. But it grew late—I left the rest until the
Sunday morning. I finished them on the Sunday morning, and what I had left over I burnt then. It was soon
after I had finished burning them that Monsieur le Commissaire came to affix his seals. The ashes which you
see there, Monsieur Hanaud, are the ashes of the letters
which I burnt upon the Sunday morning."

Betty spoke with a very pretty and simple dignity
which touched her audience to a warm sympathy.
Hanaud gently tilted the ashes back into the grate.

"Mademoiselle, I am always in the wrong with you,"
he said with an accent of remorse. "For I am always
forcing you to statements which make me ashamed and
do you honour."

Jim acknowledged that Hanaud, when he wished, could
do the handsome thing with a very good grace. Unfor-
tunately grace seemed never to be an enduring quality
in him; as, for instance, now. He was still upon his
knees in front of the hearth. Whilst making his apology
he had been raking amongst the ashes with the shovel
without giving, to all appearance, any thought to what
he was doing. But his attention was now arrested. The
shovel had disclosed an unburnt fragment of bluish-white
paper. Hanaud's body stiffened. He bent forward and
picked the scrap of paper out from the grate, whilst
Betty, too, stooped with a little movement of curiosity.

Hanaud sat back again upon his heels.

"So! You burnt more than letters last Sunday morning," he said.

Betty was puzzled and Hanaud held out to her the
fragment of paper.

"Bills too, Mademoiselle."

Betty took the fragment in her hand and shook her

head over it. It was obviously the right-hand top corner of a bill. For an intriguing scrap of a printed address was visible and below a figure or two in a column.

"There must have been a bill or two mixed up with the letters," said Betty. "I don't remember it."

She handed the fragment of paper back to Hanaud, who sat and looked at it. Jim Frobisher standing just behind him read the printed ends of names and words and the figures beneath and happened to remember the very look of them, Hanaud held them so long in his hand; the top bit of name in large capital letters, the words below echelonned in smaller capitals, then the figures in the columns and all enclosed in a rough sort of triangle with the diagonal line browned and made ragged by the fire—thus—

E R O N
STRUCTION
LLES
IS

$$\overline{}$$
375   .05

"Well, it is of no importance luckily," said Hanaud and he tossed the scrap of paper back into the grate. "Did you notice these ashes, Monsieur Girardot, on Sunday morning?" He turned any slur the question might seem to cast upon Betty's truthfulness with an explanation.

"It is always good when it is possible to get a corroboration, Mademoiselle."

Betty nodded, but Girardot was at a loss. He managed to look extremely important, but importance was not required.

"I don't remember," he said.

However, corroboration of a kind at all events did come though from another source.

"If I might speak, Monsieur Hanaud?" said Maurice Thevenet eagerly.

"But by all means," Hanaud replied.

"I came into this room just behind Monsieur Girardot on the Sunday morning. I did not see any ashes in the hearth, that is true. But Mademoiselle Harlowe was in the act of arranging that screen of blue lacquer in front of the fireplace, just as we saw it to-day. She arranged it, and when she saw who her visitors were she stood up with a start of surprise."

"Aha!" said Hanaud cordially. He smiled at Betty. "This evidence is just as valuable as if he had told us that he had seen the ashes themselves."

He rose to his feet and went close to her.

"But there is another letter which you were good enough to promise to me," he said.

"The an——" she began and Hanaud stopped her hurriedly.

"It is better that we hold our tongues," he said with a nod and a grin which recognised that in this matter they were accomplices. "This is to be our exclusive little secret, which, if he is very good, we will share with Monsieur le Commissaire."

He laughed hugely at his joke, whilst Betty unlocked a drawer in the Chippendale secretary. Girardot the Commissaire tittered, not quite sure that he thought very highly of it. Monsieur Bex, on the other hand, by a certain extra primness of his face, made it perfectly clear that in his opinion such a jape was very, very far from correct.

Betty produced a folded sheet of common paper and handed it to Hanaud, who took it aside to the window and read it carefully. Then with a look he beckoned Girardot to his side.

"Monsieur Frobisher can come too. For he is in the secret," he added; and the three men stood apart at the window looking at the sheet of paper. It was dated the 7th of May, signed "The Scourge," like the others of this hideous brood, and it began without any preface.

There were only a few words typed upon it, and some of them were epithets not to be reproduced which made Jim's blood boil that a girl like Betty should ever have had to read them.

> *"Your time is coming now, you——"* and here followed the string of abominable obscenities. *"You are for it, Betty Harlowe. Hanaud the detective from Paris is coming to look after you with his handcuffs in his pocket. You'll look pretty in handcuffs, won't you, Betty? It's your white neck we want! Three cheers for Waberski? The Scourge."*

Girardot stared at the brutal words and settled his glasses on his nose and stared again.

"But—but——" he stammered and he pointed to the date. A warning gesture made by Hanaud brought him to a sudden stop, but Frobisher had little doubt as to the purport of that unfinished exclamation. Girardot was astonished, as Hanaud himself had been, that this item of news had so quickly leaked abroad.

Hanaud folded the letter and turned back into the room.

"Thank you, Mademoiselle," he said to Betty, and Thevenet the secretary took his notebook from his pocket.

"Shall I make you a copy of the letter, Monsieur Hanaud?" he said, sitting down and holding out his hand.

"I wasn't going to give it back," Hanaud answered, "and a copy at the present stage isn't necessary. A little later on I may ask for your assistance."

He put the letter away in his letter-case, and his letter-case away in his breast-pocket. When he looked up again he saw that Betty was holding out to him a key.

"This unlocks the cabinet at the end of the room," she said.

"Yes! Let us look now for the famous arrow, or we shall have Monsieur Frobisher displeased with us again," said Hanaud.

The cabinet stood against the wall at the end of the room opposite to the windows, and close to the door which opened on to the hall. Hanaud took the key, unlocked the door of the cabinet and started back with a "Wow." He was really startled, for facing him upon a shelf were two tiny human heads, perfect in feature, in hair, in eyes, but reduced to the size of big oranges. They were the heads of Indian tribesmen killed upon the banks of the Amazon, and preserved and reduced by their conquerors by the process common amongst those forests.

"If the arrow is anywhere in this room, it is here that we should find it," he said, but though he found many curious oddities in that cabinet, of the perfect specimen of a poison arrow there was never a trace. He turned away with an air of disappointment.

"Well then, Mademoiselle, there is nothing else for it," he said regretfully; and for an hour he searched that room, turning back the carpet, examining the upholstery of the chairs, and the curtains, shaking out every vase, and finally giving his attention to Betty's secretary. He probed every cranny of it; he discovered the simple mechanism of its secret drawers; he turned out every pigeon-hole; working with extraordinary swiftness and replacing everything in its proper place. At the end of the hour the room was as orderly as when he had entered it; yet he had gone through it with a tooth comb.

"No, it is not here," he said and he seated himself in a chair and drew a breath. "But on the other hand, as the two ladies and Monsieur Frobisher are aware, I was prepared not to find it here."

"We have finished then?" said Betty, but Hanaud did not stir.

"For a moment," he replied, "I shall be glad, Monsieur Girardot, if you will remove the seals in the hall from the door at the end of the room."

The Commissary went out by the way of Mrs. Harlowe's bedroom, accompanied by his secretary. After a minute had passed a key grated in the lock and the door was opened. The Commissary and his secretary returned into the room from the hall.

"Good!" said Hanaud.

He rose from this chair and looking around at the little group, now grown puzzled and anxious, he said very gravely:

"In the interest of justice I now ask that none of you shall interrupt me by either word or gesture, for I have an experiment to make."

In a complete silence he walked to the fireplace and rang the bell.

CHAPTER FOURTEEN: *An Experiment and a Discovery*

G ASTON answered the bell.

"Will you please send Francine Rollard here," said Hanaud.

Gaston, however, stood his ground. He looked beyond Hanaud to Betty.

"If Mademoiselle gives me the order," he said respectfully.

"At once then, Gaston," Betty replied, and she sat down in a chair.

Francine Rollard was apparently difficult to persuade. For the minutes passed, and when at last she did come into the treasure room she was scared and reluctant. She was a girl hardly over twenty, very neat and trim and pretty, and rather like some wild shy creature out of the woods. She looked round the group which awaited her with restless eyes and a sullen air of suspicion. But it was the suspicion of wild people for townsfolk.

"Rollard," said Hanaud gently, "I sent for you, for I want another woman to help me in acting a little scene."

He turned towards Ann Upcott.

"Now, Mademoiselle, will you please repeat exactly your movements here on the night when Madame Harlowe died? You came into the room—so. You stood by the electric-light switch there. You turned it on, you noticed the time, and you turned it off quickly. For this communicating door stood wide open—so!—and a strong light poured out of Madame Harlowe's bedroom through the doorway."

Hanaud was very busy, placing himself first by the side of Ann to make sure that she stood in the exact place which she had described, and then running across the room to set wide open the communicating door.

"You could just see the light gleaming on the ornaments and panels of the Sedan chair, on the other side of the fireplace on your right. So! And there, Mademoiselle, you stood in the darkness and," his words lengthened out now with tiny intervals between each one —"you heard the sound of the struggle in the bedroom and caught some words spoken in a clear whisper."

"Yes," Ann replied with a shiver. The solemn manner of authority with which he spoke obviously alarmed her. She looked at him with troubled eyes.

"Then will you stand there once more," he continued, "and once more listen as you listened on that night. I thank you!" He went away to Betty. "Now, Mademoiselle, and you, Francine Rollard, will you both please come with me."

He walked towards the communicating door but Betty did not even attempt to rise from her chair.

"Monsieur Hanaud," she said with her cheeks very white and her voice shaking, "I can guess what you propose to do. But it is horrible and rather cruel to us. And I cannot see how it will help."

Ann Upcott broke in before Hanaud could reply. She was more troubled even than Betty, though without doubt hers was to be the easier part.

"It cannot help at all," she said. "Why must we pretend now the dreadful thing which was lived then?"

Hanaud turned about in the doorway.

"Ladies, I beg you to let me have my way. I think that when I have finished, you will yourselves understand that my experiment has not been without its use. I understand of course that moments like these bring their distress. But—you will pardon me—I am not thinking of you"—and there was so much quietude and gravity in the detective's voice that his words, harsh though they were, carried with them no offence. "No, I am thinking of a woman more than double the age of either of you,

163

whose unhappy life came to an end here on the night of the 27th of April. I am remembering two photographs which you, Mademoiselle Harlowe, showed me this morning—I am moved by them. Yes, that is the truth."

He closed his eyes as if he saw those two portraits with their dreadful contrast impressed upon his eyelids. "I am her advocate," he cried aloud in a stirring voice. "The tragic woman, I stand for her! If she was done to death, I mean to know and I mean to punish!"

Never had Frobisher believed that Hanaud could have been so transfigured, could have felt or spoken with so much passion. He stood before them an erect and menacing figure, all his grossness melted out of him, a man with a flaming sword.

"As for you two ladies, you are young. What does a little distress matter to you? A few shivers of discomfort? How long will they last? I beg you not to hinder me!"

Betty rose up from her chair without another word. But she did not rise without an effort, and when she stood up at last she swayed upon her feet and her face was as white as chalk.

"Come, Francine!" she said, pronouncing her words like a person with an impediment of speech. "We must show Monsieur Hanaud that we are not the cowards he takes us for."

But Francine still held back.

"I don't understand at all. I am only a poor girl and this frightens me. The police! They set traps—the police."

Hanaud laughed.

"And how often do they catch the innocent in them? Tell me that, Mademoiselle Francine!"

He turned almost contemptuously towards Mrs. Harlowe's bedroom. Betty and Francine followed upon his heels, the others trooped in behind, with Frobisher last of all. He indeed was as reluctant to witness Hanaud's experiment as the girls were to take a part in it. It savoured of the theatrical. There was to be some sort of imagined reproduction of the scene which Ann Upcott had described, no doubt with the object of testing her sincerity. It would really be a test of nerves more than a test of honesty and to Jim was therefore neither reliable nor fair play. He paused in the doorway to say a word of encouragement to Ann, but she was gazing again with that curious air of perplexity at the clock upon the marquetry cabinet.

"There is nothing to fear, Ann," he said, and she withdrew her eyes from the clock. They were dancing now as she turned them upon Frobisher.

"I wondered whether I should ever hear you call me by my name," she said with a smile. "Thank you, Jim!" She hesitated and then the blood suddenly mounted into her face. "I'll tell you, I was a little jealous," she added in a low voice and with a little laugh at herself as though she was a trifle ashamed of the confession.

Jim was luckily spared the awkwardness of an answer by the appearance of Hanaud in the doorway.

"I hate to interrupt, Monsieur Frobisher," he said with a smile; "but it is of a real importance that Mademoiselle should listen without anything to distract her."

Jim followed Hanaud into the bedroom, and was startled. The Commissary and his secretary and Monsieur Bex were in a group apart near to one of the windows. Betty Harlowe was stretched upon Mrs. Harlowe's bed; Francine Rollard stood against the wall, near to the door, clearly frightened out of her wits and glancing from side to side with the furtive restless eyes of the half-tamed. But it was not this curious spectacle which so surprised Jim Frobisher, but something strange, something which almost shocked, in the aspect of Betty herself. She was leaning up on an elbow with her eyes fixed upon the doorway and the queerest, most inscrutable fierce look in them that he had ever seen. She was quite lost to her environment. The experiment from which Francine shrank had no meaning for her. She was possessed—the old phrase leapt into Jim's thoughts—though her face was as still as a mass, a mask of frozen passion. It was only for a second, however, that the strange seizure lasted. Betty's face relaxed; she dropped back upon the bed with her eyes upon Hanaud like one waiting for instructions.

Hanaud, by pointing a finger, directed Jim to take his place amongst the group at the window. He placed himself upon one side of the bed, and beckoned to Francine. Very slowly she approached the end of the bed. Hanaud directed her in the same silent way to come opposite to him on the other side of the bed. For a little while Francine refused. She stood stubbornly shaking her head at the very foot of the bed. She was terrified of some trick, and when at last at a sign from Betty she took up the position assigned to her, she minced to it gingerly as though she feared the floor would open beneath her feet. Hanaud made her another sign and she looked at a scrap of paper on which Hanaud had written some words. The paper and her orders had obviously been given to her whilst Jim was talking to Ann Upcott. Francine knew what she was to do, but her suspicious peasant nature utterly rebelled against it. Hanaud beckoned to her with his eyes riveted upon her compelling her, and against her will she bent forwards over the bed and across Betty Harlowe's body.

A nod from Hanaud now, and she spoke in a low, clear whisper:

"That—will—do—now."

And hardly had she spoken those few words which Ann Upcott said she had heard on the night of Mrs. Harlowe's death, but Hanaud himself must repeat them and also in a whisper.

Having whispered, he cried aloud towards the doorway in his natural voice:

"Did you hear, Mademoiselle? Was that the whisper which reached your ears on the night when Madame died?"

All those in the bedroom waited for the answer in suspense. Francine Rollard, indeed, with her eyes fixed upon Hanaud in a very agony of doubt. And the answer came.

"Yes, but whoever whispered, whispered twice this afternoon. On the night when I came down in the dark to the treasure room, the words were only whispered once."

"It was the same voice which whispered them twice, Mademoiselle?"

"Yes . . . I think so . . . I noticed no difference . . . Yes."

And Hanaud flung out his arms with a comic gesture of despair, and addressed the room.

"You understand now my little experiment. A voice that whispers! How shall one tell it from another voice that whispers! There is no intonation, no depth, no lightness. There is not even sex in a voice which whispers. We have no clue, no, not the slightest to the identity of the person who whispered, 'That will do now,' on the night when Madame Harlowe died." He waved his hand towards Monsieur Bex. "I will be glad if you will open now these cupboards, and Mademoiselle Harlowe will tell us, to the best of her knowledge, whether anything has been taken or anything disturbed."

Hanaud returned to the treasure room, leaving Monsieur Bex and Betty at their work, with the Commissary and his secretary to supervise them. Jim Frobisher followed him. He was very far from believing that Hanaud had truthfully explained the intention of his experiment. The impossibility of identifying a voice which whispers! Here was something with which Hanaud must have been familiar from a hundred cases! No, that interpretation would certainly not work. There was quite another true reason for this melodramatic little scene which he had staged. He was following Hanaud in the hope of finding out that reason, when he heard him speaking in a low voice, and he stopped inside the dressing-room close to the communicating door where he could hear every word and yet not be seen himself.

"Mademoiselle," Hanaud was saying to Ann Upcott, "there is something about this clock here which troubles you."

"Yes—of course it's nonsense. . . . I must be wrong. . . . For here is the cabinet and on it stands the clock."

Jim could gather from the two voices that they were both standing together close to the marquetry cabinet.

"Yes, yes," Hanaud urged. "Still you are troubled."

There was a moment's silence. Jim could imagine the girl looking from the clock to the door by which she had stood, and back again from the door to the clock. Surely that scene in the bedroom had been staged to extort some admission from Ann Upcott of the falsity of her story. Was he now, since the experiment had failed, resorting to another trick, setting a fresh trap?

"Well?" he asked insistently. "Why are you troubled?"

"It seems to me," Ann replied in a voice of doubt, "that the clock is lower now than it was. Of course it can't be . . . and I had only one swift glimpse of it. . . . Yet my recollection is so vivid—the room standing out revealed in the moment of bright light, and then vanishing into darkness again. . . . Yes, the clock seemed to me to be placed higher . . ." and suddenly she stopped as if a warning hand had been laid upon her arm. Would she resume? Jim was still wondering when silently, like a swift animal, Hanaud was in the doorway and confronting him.

"Yes, Monsieur Frobisher," he said with an odd note of relief in his voice, "we shall have to enlist you in the *Sûreté* very soon. That I can see. Come in!"

He took Jim by the arm and led him into the room.

"As for that matter of the clock, Mademoiselle, the light goes up and goes out—it would have been a marvel if you had within that flash of vision seen every detail precisely true. No, there is nothing there!" He flung himself into a chair and sat for a little while silent in an attitude of dejection.

"You said this morning to me, Monsieur, that I had nothing to go upon, that I was guessing here, and guessing there, stirring up old troubles which had better be left quietly in their graves, and at the end discovering nothing. Upon my word, I believe you are right! My little experiment! Was there ever a failure more abject?"

Hanaud sat up alertly.

"What is the matter?" he asked.

Jim Frobisher had had a brain wave. The utter disappointment upon Hanaud's face and in his attitude had enlightened him. Yes, his experiment had failed. For it was aimed at Francine Rollard. He had summoned her without warning, he had bidden her upon the instant to act a scene, nay, to take the chief part in it, in the hope that it would work upon her and break her down to a confession of guilt. He suspected Ann. Well, then, Ann must have had an accomplice. To discover the accomplice—there was the object of the experiment. And it had failed abjectly, as Hanaud himself confessed. Francine had shrunk from the ordeal, no doubt, but the reason of the shrinking was manifest—fear of the police, suspicion of a trap, the furtive helplessness of the ignorant. She had not delivered herself into Hanaud's toils. But not a word of this conjecture did Jim reveal to Hanaud. To his question what was the matter, he answered simply:

"Nothing."

Hanaud beat with the palms of his hands upon the arms of his chair.

"Nothing, eh? nothing! That's the only answer in this case. To every question! To every search! Nothing, nothing, nothing;" and as he ended in a sinking voice, a startled cry rang out in the bedroom.

"Betty!" Ann exclaimed.

Hanaud threw off his dejection like an overcoat. Jim fancied that he was out of his chair and across the dressing-room before the sound of the cry had ceased. Certainly Betty could not have moved. She was standing in front of the dressing-table, looking down at a big jewel-case of dark blue morocco leather, and she was lifting up and down the open lid of it with an expression of utter incredulity.

"Aha!" said Hanaud. "It is unlocked. We have something, after all, Monsieur Frobisher. Here is a jewel-case unlocked, and jewel-cases do not unlock themselves. It was here?"

He looked towards the cupboard in the wall, of which the door stood open.

"Yes," said Betty. "I opened the door, and took the case out by the side handles. The lid came open when I touched it."

"Will you look through it, please, and see whether anything is missing?"

While Betty began to examine the contents of the jewel-case, Hanaud went to Francine, who stood apart. He took her by the arm and led her to the door.

"I am sorry if I frightened you, Francine," he said. "But, after all, we are not such alarming people, the Police, eh? No, so long as good little maids hold their good little tongues, we can be very good friends. Of course, if there is chatter, little Francine, and gossip, little Francine, and that good-looking baker's boy is to-morrow spreading over Dijon the story of Hanaud's little experiment, Hanaud will know where to look for the chatterers."

"Monsieur, I shall not say one word," cried Francine.

"And how wise that will be, little Francine!" Hanaud rejoined in a horribly smooth and silky voice. "For Hanaud can be the wickedest of wicked Uncles to naughty little chatterers. Ohhoho, yes! He seizes them tight—so—and it will be ever so long before he says to them 'That—will—do—now!'"

He rounded off his threats with a quite friendly laugh

and gently pushed Francine Rollard from the room. Then he returned to Betty, who had lifted the tray out of the box and was opening some smaller cases which had been lying at the bottom. The light danced upon pendant and bracelet, buckle and ring, but Betty still searched.

"You miss something, Mademoiselle?"

"Yes."

"It was, after all, certain that you would," Hanaud continued. "If murders are committed, there will be some reason. I will even venture to guess that the jewel which you miss is of great value."

"It is," Betty admitted. "But I expect it has only been mislaid. No doubt we shall find it somewhere, tucked away in a drawer." She spoke with very great eagerness, and a note of supplication that the matter should rest there. "In any case, what has disappeared is mine, isn't it? And I am not going to imitate Monsieur Boris. I make no complaint."

Hanaud shook his head.

"You are very kind, Mademoiselle. But we cannot, alas! say here 'That will do now.'" It was strange to Jim to notice how he kept harping upon the words of that whisper. "We are not dealing with a case of theft, but with a case of murder. We must go on. What is it that you miss?"

"A pearl necklace," Betty answered reluctantly.

"A big one?"

It was noticeable that as Betty's reluctance increased Hanaud became more peremptory and abrupt.

"Not so very."

"Describe it to me, Mademoiselle!"

Betty hesitated. She stood with a troubled face looking out upon the garden. Then with a shrug of resignation she obeyed.

"There were thirty-five pearls—not so very large, but they were perfectly matched and of a beautiful pink. My uncle took a great deal of trouble and some years to collect them. Madame told me herself that they actually cost him nearly a hundred thousand pounds. They would be worth even more now."

"A fortune, then," cried Hanaud.

Not a person in that room had any belief that the necklace would be found, laid aside somewhere by chance. Here was Hanaud's case building itself up steadily. Another storey was added to it this afternoon. This or that experiment might fail. What did that matter? A motive for the murder came to light now. Jim had an intuition that nothing now could prevent a definite result; that the truth, like a beam of light that travels for a million of years, would in the end strike upon a dark spot, and that some one would stand helpless and dazzled in a glare—the criminal.

"Who knew of this necklace of yours, Mademoiselle, beside yourself?" Hanaud asked.

"Every one in the house, Monsieur. Madame wore it nearly always."

"She wore it, then, on the day of her death?"

"Yes, I——" Betty began, and she turned towards Ann for confirmation, and then swiftly turned away again. "I think so."

"I am sure of it," said Ann steadily, though her face had grown rather white and her eyes anxious.

"How long has Francine Rollard been with you?" Hanaud asked of Betty.

"Three years. No—a little more. She is the only maid I have ever had," Betty answered with a laugh.

"I see," Hanaud said thoughtfully; and what he saw, it seemed to Jim Frobisher that every one else in that room saw too. For no one looked at Ann Upcott. Old servants do not steal valuable necklaces: Ann Upcott and Jeanne Baudin, the nurse, were the only new-comers to the Maison Grenelle these many years; and Jeanne Baudin had the best of characters. Thus the argument seemed to run though no one expressed it in words.

Hanaud turned his attention to the lock of the cupboard, and shook his head over it. Then he crossed to the dressing-table and the morocco case.

"Aha!" he said with a lively interest. "This is a different affair;" and he bent down closely over it.

The case was not locked with a key at all. There were three small gilt knobs in the front of the case, and the lock was set by the number of revolutions given to each knob. These, of course, could be varied with each knob, and all must be known before the case could be opened—Mrs. Harlowe's jewels had been guarded by a formula.

"There has been no violence used here," said Hanaud, standing up again.

"Of course my aunt may have forgotten to lock the case," said Betty.

"Of course that's possible," Hanaud agreed.

"And of course this room was open to any one between the time of my aunt's funeral and Sunday morning, when the doors were sealed."

"A week, in fact—with Boris Waberski in the house," said Hanaud.

"Yes . . . yes," said Betty. "Only . . . but I expect it is just mislaid and we shall find it. You see Monsieur Boris expected to get some money from my lawyers in London. No doubt he meant to make a bargain with me. It doesn't look as if he had stolen it. He wouldn't want a thousand pounds if he had."

Jim had left Boris out of his speculations. He had recollected him with a thrill of hope that he would be discovered to be the thief when Hanaud mentioned his name. But the hope died away again before the reluctant and deadly reasoning of Betty Harlowe. On the other hand, if Boris and Ann were really accomplices in the murder, because he wanted his legacy, the necklace might well have been Ann's share. More and more, whichever way one looked at it, the facts pointed damningly towards Ann.

"Well, we will see if it has been mislaid," said Hanaud. "But meanwhile, Mademoiselle, it would be well for you to lock that case up and to take it some time this afternoon to your bankers."

Betty shut down the lid and spun the knobs one after the other. Three times a swift succession of sharp little clicks was heard in the room.

"You have not used, I hope, the combination which Madame Harlowe used," said Hanaud.

"I never knew the combination she used," said Betty. She lifted the jewel-case back into its cupboard; and the search of the drawers and the cupboards began. But it was as barren of result as had been the search of the treasure-room for the arrow.

"We can do no more," said Hanaud.

"Yes. One thing more."

The correction came quietly from Ann Upcott. She was standing by herself, very pale and defiant. She knew now that she was suspected. The very care with which every one had avoided even looking at her had left her in no doubt.

Hanaud looked about the room.

"What more can we do?" he asked.

"You can search my rooms."

"No!" cried Betty violently. "I won't have it!"

"If you please," said Ann. "It is only fair to me." Monsieur Bex nodded violently.

"Mademoiselle could not be more correct," said he.

Ann addressed herself to Hanaud.

"I shall not go with you. There is nothing locked in my room except a small leather dispatch-case. You will find the key to that in the left-hand drawer of my dressing-table. I will wait for you in the library."

Hanaud bowed, and before he could move from his position Betty did a thing for which Jim could have hugged her there and then before them all. She went straight to Ann and set her arm about her waist.

"I'll wait with you, Ann," she said. "Of course it's ridiculous," and she led Ann out of the room.

CHAPTER FIFTEEN: *The Finding of the Arrow*

ANN'S rooms were upon the second floor with the windows upon the garden, a bedroom and a sitting-room communicating directly with one another. They were low in the roof, but spacious, and Hanaud, as he looked around the bedroom, said in a tone of doubt:

"Yes . . . after all, if one were frightened suddenly out of one's wits, one might stumble about this room in the dark and lose one's way to the light switch. There isn't one over the bed." Then he shrugged his shoulders. "But, to be sure, one would be careful that one's details could be verified. So——" and the doubt passed out of his voice.

The words were all Greek to the Commissary of Police and his secretary and Monsieur Bex. Maurice Thevenet, indeed, looked sharply at Hanaud, as if he was on the point of asking one of those questions which he had been invited to ask. But Girardot, the Commissary who was panting heavily with his ascent of two flights of stairs, spoke first.

"We shall find nothing to interest us here," he said. "That pretty girl would never have asked us to pry about amongst her dainty belongings if there had been anything to discover."

"One never knows," replied Hanaud. "Let us see!"

Jim walked away into the sitting-room. He had no wish to follow step by step Hanaud and the Commissary in their search; and he had noticed on the table in the middle of the room a blotting-pad and some notepaper and the materials for writing. He wanted to get all this whirl of conjecture and fact and lies, in which during the last two days he had lived, sorted and separated and set in order

175

in his mind; and he knew no better way of doing so than by putting it all down shortly in the "for" and "against" style of Robinson Crusoe on his desert island. He would have a quiet hour or so whilst Hanaud indefatigably searched. He took a sheet of paper, selected a pen at random from the tray and began. It cost Ann Upcott, however, a good many sheets of notepaper, and more than once the nib dropped out of his pen-holder and was forced back into it before he had finished. But he had his problem reduced at last to these terms:

For	*Against*
(1) Although suspicion that murder had been committed arose in the first instance only from the return to its shelf of the "Treatise on Sporanthus Hispidus," subsequent developments, e.g., the disappearance of the Poison Arrow, the introduction into the case of the ill-famed Jean Cladel, Ann Upcott's story of her visit to the Treasure Room, and now the mystery of Mrs. Harlowe's pearl necklace, make out a prima facie case for inquiry.	But in the absence of any trace of poison in the dead woman's body, it is difficult to see how the criminal can be brought to justice, except by (a) A confession. (b) The commission of another crime of a similar kind. Hanaud's theory—once a poisoner always a poisoner.
(2) If murder was committed, it is probable that it was committed at half-past ten at night when Ann Upcott in the Treasure Room heard the sound of a struggle and the whisper, "That will do now."	Ann Upcott's story may be partly or wholly false. She knew that Mrs. Harlowe's bedroom was to be opened and examined. If she also knew that the pearl necklace had disappeared, she must have realised that it would be advisable for her to tell some story before its disappearance was discovered, which would divert suspicion from her.
(3) It is clear that whoever committed the murder, if murder was committed, Betty Harlowe had nothing to do with it. She had an ample allowance. She was at M. Pouillac's Ball on	It is possible that the disappearance of the necklace is in no way connected with the murder, if murder there was.

The Finding of the Arrow

For	Against
the night. Moreover, once Mrs. Harlowe was dead, the necklace became Betty Harlowe's property. Had she committed the murder, the necklace would not have disappeared.	
(4) Who then are possibly guilty?	
(i) The servants.	(i) All of them have many years of service to their credit. It is not possible that any of them would have understood enough of the "Treatise on Sporanthus Hispidus" to make use of it. If any of them were concerned it can only be as an accessory or assistant working under the direction of another.
(ii) Jeanne Baudin the nurse. More attention might be given to her. It is too easily accepted that she has nothing to do with it.	No one suspects her. Her record is good.
(iii) Francine Rollard. She was certainly frightened this afternoon. The necklace would be a temptation. Was it she who bent over Ann Upcott in the darkness?	She was frightened of the police as a class, rather than of being accused of a crime. She acted her part in the reconstruction scene without breaking down. If she were concerned, it could only be for the reason given above, as an assistant.
(iv) Ann Upcott. Her introduction into the Maison Grenelle took place through Waberski and under dubious circumstances. She is poor, a paid companion, and the necklace is worth a considerable fortune.	Her introductions may be explicable on favourable grounds. Until we know more of her history it is impossible to judge.
She was in the house on the night of Mrs. Harlowe's death. She told Gaston he could turn out the lights and go to bed early that evening. She could easily have admitted Waberski and received the necklace as the price of her complicity.	Her account of the night of the 27th April may be true from beginning to end.

The House of the Arrow

For	Against
The story she told us in the garden may have been the true story of what occurred adapted. It may have been she who whispered "That will do now." She may have whispered it to Waberski.	In that case the theory of a murder is enormously strengthened. But who whispered, "That will do now"? And who was bending over Ann Upcott when she waked up?
Her connection with Waberski was sufficiently close to make him count upon Ann's support in his charge against Betty.	
(v) Waberski. He is a scoundrel, a would-be blackmailer.	
He was in straits for money and he expected a thumping legacy from Mrs. Harlowe.	
He may have brought Ann Upcott into the house with the thought of murder in his mind.	
Having failed to obtain any profit from his crime, he accuses Betty of the same crime as a blackmailing proposition.	
As soon as he knew that Mrs. Harlowe had been exhumed and an autopsy made he collapsed. He knew, if he had used himself the poison arrow, that no trace of poison would be found.	But he would have collapsed equally if he had believed that no murder had been committed at all.
He knew of Jean Cladel, and according to his own story was in the Rue Gambetta close to Jean Cladel's shop. It is possible that he himself had been visiting Cladel to pay for the solution of Strophanthus.	

If murder was committed the two people most obviously suspect are Ann Upcott and Waberski working in collusion.

To this conclusion Jim Frobisher was reluctantly brought, but even whilst writing it down there were certain questions racing through his mind to which he could find no answer. He was well aware that he was an utter novice in such matters as the investigation of crimes; and

he recognised that were the answers to these questions
known to him, some other direction might be given to
his thoughts.

Accordingly he wrote those troublesome questions
beneath his memorandum—thus:

But

(1) Why does Hanaud attach no importance to the
return of the "Treatise on Sporanthus Hispidus" to
its place in the library?

(2) What was it which so startled him upon the
top of the Terrace Tower?

(3) What was it that he had in his mind to say to
me at the Café in the Place D'Armes and in the end
did not say?

(4) Why did Hanaud search every corner of the
treasure room for the missing poison arrow—except
the interior of the Sedan chair?

The noise of a door gently closing aroused him from
his speculations. He looked across the room. Hanaud
had just entered it from the bedroom, shutting the communicating door behind him. He stood with his hand
upon the door-knob gazing at Frobisher with a curious
startled stare. He moved swiftly to the end of the table
at which Jim was sitting.

"How you help me!" he said in a low voice and smiling. "How you do help me!"

Alert though Jim's ears were to a note of ridicule, he
could discover not a hint of it. Hanaud was speaking
with the utmost sincerity, his eyes very bright and his
heavy face quite changed by that uncannily sharp expression which Jim had learned to associate with some new
find in the development of the case.

"May I see what you have written?" Hanaud asked.

"It could be of no value to you," Jim replied modestly,
but Hanaud would have none of it.

"It is always of value to know what the other man
thinks, and even more what the other man sees. What
did I say to you in Paris? The last thing one sees one's

self is the thing exactly under one's nose"; and he began to laugh lightly but continuously and with a great deal of enjoyment, which Jim did not understand. He gave in, however, over his memorandum and pushed it along to Hanaud, ashamed of it as something schoolboyish, but hopeful that some of these written questions might be answered.

Hanaud sat down at the end of the table close to Jim and read the items and the questions very slowly with an occasional grunt, and a still more occasional "Aha!" but with a quite unchanging face. Jim was in two minds whether to snatch it from his hands and tear it up or dwell upon its recollected phrases with a good deal of pride. One thing was clear. Hanaud took it seriously.

He sat musing over it for a moment or two.

"Yes, here are questions, and dilemmas." He looked at Frobisher with friendliness. "I shall make you an allegory. I have a friend who is a matador in Spain. He told me about the bull and how foolish those people are who think the bull not clever. Yes, but do not jump and look the offence with your eyes and tell me how very vulgar I am and how execrable my taste. All that I know very well. But listen to my friend the matador! He says all that the bull wants, to kill without fail all the bull-fighters in Spain, is a little experience. And very little, he learns so quick. Look! Between the entrance of the bull into the arena and his death there are reckoned twenty minutes. And there should not be more, if the matador is wise. The bull—he learns so quick the war-fare of the ring. Well, I am an old bull who has fought in the arena many times. This is your first *corrida*. But only ten minutes of the twenty have passed. Already you have learned much. Yes, here are some shrewd questions which I had not expected you to ask. When the twenty are gone, you will answer them all for yourself. Meanwhile"—he took up another pen and made a tiny addition to item one—"I carry this on one step farther. See!"

He replaced the memorandum under Jim's eyes. Jim read:

"—subsequent developments, e.g., the disappearance of the Poison Arrow, the introduction into the case of the ill-famed Jean Cladel, Ann Upcott's story of her visit to the treasure-room, and now the mystery of Mrs. Harlowe's pearl necklace, *and the finding of the arrow,* make out a prima facie case for inquiry."

Jim sprang to his feet in excitement.

"You have found the arrow, then?" he cried, glancing towards the door of Ann Upcott's bedroom.

"Not I, my friend," replied Hanaud with a grin.

"The Commissaire, then?"

"No, not the Commissaire."

"His secretary, then?"

Jim sat down again in his chair.

"I am sorry. He wears cheap rings. I don't like him."

Hanaud broke into a laugh of delight.

"Console yourself! I, too, don't like that young gentleman of whom they are all so proud. Maurice Thevenet has found nothing."

Jim looked at Hanaud in a perplexity.

"Here is a riddle," he said.

Hanaud rubbed his hands together.

"Prove to me that you have been ten minutes in the bull-ring," he said.

"I think that I have only been five," Jim replied with a smile. "Let me see! The arrow had not been discovered when we first entered these rooms?"

"No."

"And it is discovered now?"

"Yes."

"And it was not discovered by you?"

"No."

"Nor the Commissaire?"

"No."

"Nor Maurice Thevenet?"

"No."

Jim stared and shook his head.

"I have not been one minute in the bull-ring. I don't understand."

Hanaud's face was all alight with enjoyment.

"Then I take your memorandum and I write again."

He hid the paper from Jim Frobisher's eyes with the palm of his left hand, whilst he wrote with his right. Then with a triumphant gesture he laid it again before Jim. The last question of all had been answered in Hanaud's neat, small handwriting.

Jim read:

(4) Why did Hanaud search every corner of the treasure-room for the missing Poison Arrow—except the interior of the Sedan chair?

Underneath the question Hanaud had written as if it was Jim Frobisher himself who answered the question:

"It was wrong of Hanaud to forget to examine the Sedan chair, but fortunately no harm has resulted from that lamentable omission. For Life, the incorrigible Dramatist, had arranged that the head of the arrow-shaft should be the pen-holder with which I have written this memorandum."

Jim looked at the pen-holder and dropped it with a startled cry.

There it was—the slender, pencil-like shaft expanding into a slight bulb where the fingers held it, and the nib inserted into the tiny cleft made for the stem of the iron dart! Jim remembered that the nib had once or twice become loose and spluttered on the page, until he had jammed it in violently.

Then came a terrible thought. His jaw dropped; he stared at Hanaud in awe.

The Finding of the Arrow

"I wonder if I sucked the end of it, whilst I was thinking out my sentences," he stammered.

"O Lord!" cried Hanaud, and he snatched up the penholder and rubbed it hard with his pocket handkerchief. Then he spread out the handkerchief upon the table, and fetching a small magnifying glass from his pocket, examined it minutely. He looked up with relief.

"There is not the least little trace of that reddish-brown clay which made the poison paste. The arrow was scraped clean before it was put on that tray of pens. I am enchanted. I cannot now afford to lose my junior colleague."

Frobisher drew a long breath and lit a cigarette, and gave another proof that he was a very novice of a bull.

"What a mad thing to put the head of that arrow-shaft, which a glance at the plates in the Treatise would enable a child to identify, into an open tray of pens without the slightest concealment!" he exclaimed.

It looked as if Ann Upcott was wilfully pushing her neck into the wooden ring of the guillotine.

Hanaud shook his head.

"Not so mad, my friend! The old rules are the best. Hide a thing in some out-of-the-way corner, and it will surely be found. Put it to lie carelessly under every one's nose and no one will see it at all. No, no! This was cleverly done. Who could have foreseen that instead of looking on at our search you were going to plump yourself down in a chair and write your memorandum so valuable on Mademoiselle Ann's notepaper? And even then you did not notice your pen. Why should you?"

Jim, however, was not satisfied.

"It is a fortnight since Mrs. Harlowe was murdered, if she was murdered," he cried. "What I don't understand is why the arrow wasn't destroyed altogether!"

"But until this morning there was never any question of the arrow," Hanaud returned. "It was a curiosity, an item in a collection—why should one trouble to destroy it? But this morning the arrow becomes a dangerous

183

thing to possess. So it must be hidden away in a hurry. For there is not much time. An hour whilst you and I admired Mont Blanc from the top of the Terrace Tower."

"And while Betty was out of the house," Jim added quickly.

"Yes—that is true," said Hanaud. "I had not thought of it. You can add that point, Monsieur Frobisher, to the reasons which put Mademoiselle Harlowe out of our considerations. Yes."

He sat lost in thought for a little while and speaking now and then a phrase rather to himself than to his companion: "To run up here—to cut the arrow down—to round off the end as well as one can in a hurry—to stain it with some varnish—to mix it with the other pens in the tray. Not so bad!" He nodded his head in appreciation of the trick. "But nevertheless things begin to look black for that exquisite Mademoiselle Ann with her delicate colour and her pretty ways."

A noise of the shifting of furniture in the bedroom next door attracted his attention. He removed the nib from the arrow-head.

"We will keep this little matter to ourselves just for the moment," he said quickly, and he wrapped the improvised pen-holder in a sheet of the notepaper. "Just you and I shall know of it. No one else. This is my case, not Girardot's. We will not inflict a great deal of pain and trouble until we are sure."

"I agree," said Jim eagerly. "That's right, I am sure."

Hanaud tucked the arrow-head carefully away in his pocket.

"This, too," he said, and he took up Jim Frobisher's memorandum. "It is not a good thing to carry about, and perhaps lose. I will put it away at the Prefecture with the other little things I have collected."

He put the memorandum into his letter-case and got up from his chair.

"The rest of the arrow-shaft will be somewhere in this room, no doubt, and quite easy to see. But we shall not have time to look for it, and, after all, we have the important part of it."

He turned towards the mantelshelf, where some cards of invitation were stuck in the frame of the mirror, just as the door was opened and the Commissary with his secretary came out from the bedroom.

"The necklace is not in that room," said Monsieur Girardot in a voice of finality.

"Nor is it here," Hanaud replied with an unblushing assurance. "Let us go downstairs."

Jim was utterly staggered. This room had not been searched for the necklace at all. First the Sedan chair, then this sitting-room was neglected. Hanaud actually led the way out to the stairs without so much as a glance behind him. No wonder that in Paris he had styled himself and his brethren the Servants of Chance.

CHAPTER SIXTEEN: *Hanaud Laughs*

A T the bottom of the stairs Hanaud thanked the Commissary of Police for his assistance.

"As for the necklace, we shall of course search the baggage of every one in the house," he said. "But we shall find nothing. Of that we may be sure. For if the necklace has been stolen, too much time has passed since it was stolen for us to hope to find it here."

He bowed Girardot with much respect out of the house, whilst Monsieur Bex took Jim Frobisher a little aside.

"I have been thinking that Mademoiselle Ann should have some legal help," he said. "Now both you and I are attached to the affairs of Mademoiselle Harlowe. And—it is a little difficult to put it delicately—it may be that the interests of those two young ladies are not identical. It would not therefore be at all correct for me, at all events, to offer her my services. But I can recommend a very good lawyer in Dijon, a friend of mine. You see, it may be important."

Frobisher agreed.

"It may be, indeed. Will you give me your friend's address?" he said.

Whilst he was writing the address down Hanaud startled him by breaking unexpectedly into a loud laugh. The curious thing was that there was nothing whatever to account for it. Hanaud was standing by himself between them and the front door. In the courtyard outside there was no one within view. Within the hall Jim and Monsieur Bex were talking very seriously in a low voice. Hanaud was laughing at the empty air and his laughter betokened a very strong sense of relief.

"That I should have lived all these years and never noticed that before," he cried aloud in a sort of amazement that there could be anything capable of notice which he, Hanaud, had not noticed.

"What is it?" asked Jim.

But Hanaud did not answer at all. He dashed back through the hall past Frobisher and his companion, vanished into the treasure-room, closed the door behind him and actually locked it.

Monsieur Bex jerked his chin high in the air.

"He is an eccentric, that one. He would not do for Dijon."

Jim was for defending Hanaud.

"He must act. That is true," he replied. "Whatever he does and however keenly he does it, he sees a row of footlights in front of him."

"There are men like that," Monsieur Bex agreed. Like all Frenchmen, he was easy in his mind if he could place a man in a category.

"But he is doing something which is quite important," Jim continued, swelling a little with pride. He felt that he had been quite fifteen minutes in the bull-ring. "He is searching for something somewhere. I told him about it. He had overlooked it altogether. I reproached him this morning with his reluctance to take suggestions from people only too anxious to help him. But I did him obviously some injustice. He is quite willing."

Monsieur Bex was impressed and a little envious.

"I must think of some suggestions to make to Hanaud," he said. "Yes, yes! Was there not once a pearl necklace in England which was dropped in a match-box into the gutter when the pursuit became too hot? I have read of it, I am sure. I must tell Hanaud that he should spend a day or two picking up the match-boxes in the gutters. He may be very likely to come across that necklace of Madame Harlowe's. Yes, certainly."

Monsieur Bex was considerably elated by the bright idea which had come to him. He felt that he was again upon a level with his English colleague. He saw Hanaud pouncing his way along the streets of Dijon and explaining to all who questioned him: "This is the idea of Monsieur Bex, the notary. You know, Monsieur Bex, of the Place Etienne Dolet." Until somewhere near— but Monsieur Bex had not actually located the particular gutter in which Hanaud should discover the match-box with the priceless beads, when the library door opened and Betty came out into the hall.

She looked at the two men in surprise.

"And Monsieur Hanaud?" she asked. "I didn't see him go."

"He is in your treasure-room," said Jim.

"Oh!" Betty exclaimed in a voice which showed her interest. "He has gone back there!"

She walked quickly to the door and tried the handle.

"Locked!" she cried with a little start of surprise. She spoke without turning round. "He has locked himself in! Why?"

"Because of the footlights," Monsieur Bex answered, and Betty turned about and stared at him. "Yes, we came to that conclusion, Monsieur Frobisher and I. Everything he does must ring a curtain down;" and once more the key turned in the lock.

Betty swung round again as the sound reached her ears and came face to face with Hanaud. Hanaud looked over her shoulder at Frobisher and shook his head ruefully.

"You did not find it, then?" Jim asked.

"No."

Hanaud looked away from Jim to Betty Harlowe.

"Monsieur Frobisher put an idea into my head, Mademoiselle. I had not looked into that exquisite Sedan chair. It might well be that the necklace had been hidden behind the cushions. But it is not there."

"And you locked the door, Monsieur," said Betty stiffly. "The door of my room, I ask you to notice."

Hanaud drew himself erect.

"I did, Mademoiselle," he replied. "And then?"

Betty hesitated with some sharp rejoinder on the tip

of her tongue. But she did not speak it. She shrugged her shoulders and said coldly as she turned from him:

"You are within your rights, no doubt, Monsieur."

Hanaud smiled at her good-humouredly. He had offended her again. She was showing him once more the petulant, mutinous child in her which he had seen the morning before. But the smile did remain upon his face. In the doorway of the library Ann Upcott was standing, her face still very pale, and fires smouldering in her eyes.

"You searched my rooms, I hope, Monsieur," she said in a challenging voice.

"Thoroughly, Mademoiselle."

"And you did not find the necklace?"

"No!" and he walked straight across the hall to her with a look suddenly grown stern.

"Mademoiselle, I should like you to answer me a question. But you need not. I wish you to understand that. You have a right to reserve your answers for the Office of the Examining Magistrate and then give them only in the presence of and with the consent of your legal adviser. Monsieur Bex will assure you that is so."

The girl's defiance weakened.

"What do you wish to ask me?" she asked.

"Exactly how you came to the Maison Grenelle."

The fire died out of her eyes; Ann's eyelids fluttered down. She stretched out a hand against the jamb of the door to steady herself. Jim wondered whether she guessed that the head of Simon Harlowe's arrow was now hidden in Hanaud's pocket.

"I was at Monte Carlo," she began and stopped.

"And quite alone?" Hanaud continued relentlessly.

"Yes."

"And without money?"

"With a little money," Ann corrected.

"Which you lost," Hanaud rejoined.

"Yes."

"And at Monte Carlo you made the acquaintance of Boris Waberski?"

"Yes."

"And so you came to the Maison Grenelle?"

"Yes."

"It is all very curious, Mademoiselle," said Hanaud gravely, and "If it were only curious!" Jim Frobisher wished with all his heart. For Ann Upcott quailed before the detective's glance. It seemed to him that with another question from him, an actual confession would falter and stumble from her lips. A confession of complicity with Boris Waberski! And then? Jim caught a dreadful glimpse of the future which awaited her. The guillotine? Probably a fate much worse. For that would be over soon and she at rest. A few poignant weeks, an agony of waiting, now in an intoxication of hope, now in the lowest hell of terror; some dreadful minutes at the breaking of a dawn—and an end! That would be better after all than the endless years of sordid heart-breaking labour, coarse food and clothes, amongst the criminals of a convict prison in France.

Jim turned his eyes away from her with a shiver of discomfort and saw with a queer little shock that Betty was watching him with a singular intentness; as if what interested her was not so much Ann's peril as his feeling about it.

Meanwhile Ann had made up her mind.

"I shall tell you at once the little there is to tell," she declared. The words were brave enough, but the bravery ended with the words. She had provoked the short interrogatory with a clear challenge. She ended it in a hardly audible whisper. However, she managed to tell her story, leaning there against the post of the door. Indeed her voice strengthened as she went on and once a smile of real amusement flickered about her lips and in her eyes and set the dimples playing in her cheeks.

Up to eighteen months ago she had lived with her mother, a widow, in Dorsetshire, a few miles behind Weymouth. The pair of them lived with difficulty. For Mrs. Upcott found herself in as desperate a position as

England provides for gentlewomen. She was a small
landowner taxed up to her ears, and then rated over the
top of her head. Ann for her part was thought in the
neighbourhood to have promise as an artist. On the
death of her mother the estate was sold as a toy to a
manufacturer, and Ann with a small purse and a sack-
load of ambitions set out for London.

"It took me a year to understand that I was and should
remain an amateur. I counted over my money. I had
three hundred pounds left. What was I going to do with
it? It wasn't enough to set me up in a shop. On the
other hand, I hated the idea of dependence. So I made
up my mind to have ten wild gorgeous days at Monte
Carlo and make a fortune, or lose the lot."

It was then that the smile set her eyes dancing.

"I should do the same again," she cried quite unrepent-
antly. "I had never been out of England in my life, but I
knew a good deal of schoolgirl's French. I bought a few
frocks and hats and off I went. I had the most glorious
time. I was nineteen. Everything from the sleeping-
cars to the croupiers enchanted me. I stayed at one of the
smaller hotels up the hill. I met one or two people whom
I knew and they introduced me into the Sporting Club.
Oh, and lots and lots of people wanted to be kind to me!"
she cried.

"That is thoroughly intelligible," said Hanaud dryly.

"Oh, but quite nice people too," Ann rejoined. Her
face was glowing with the recollections of that short
joyous time. She had forgotten, for the moment,
altogether the predicament in which she stood, or she
was acting with an artfulness which Hanaud could hardly
have seen surpassed in all his experience of criminals.

"There was a croupier, for instance, at the trente-et-
quarante table in the big room of the Sporting Club. I
always tried to sit next to him. For he saw that no one
stole my money and that when I was winning I insured
my stake and clawed a little off the heap from time to
time. I was there for five weeks and I had made four

hundred pounds—and then came three dreadful nights
and I lost everything except thirty pounds which I had
stowed away in the hotel safe." She nodded across the
hall towards Jim. "Monsieur Frobisher can tell you
about the last night. For he sat beside me and very
prettily tried to make me a present of a thousand francs."

Hanaud, however, was not to be diverted.

"Afterwards he shall tell me," he said, and resumed
his questions. "You had met Waberski before that
night?"

"Yes, a fortnight before. But I can't remember who
introduced me."

"And Mademoiselle Harlowe?"

"Monsieur Boris introduced me a day or two later to
Betty at tea-time in the lounge of the Hôtel de Paris."

"Aha!" said Hanaud. He glanced at Jim with an
almost imperceptible shrug of the shoulders. It was,
indeed, becoming more and more obvious that Waberski
had brought Ann Upcott into that household deliberately,
as part of a plan carefully conceived and in due time to
be fulfilled.

"When did Waberski first suggest that you should join
Mademoiselle Harlowe?" he asked.

"That last night," Ann replied. "He had been standing opposite to me on the other side of the trente-et-
quarante table. He saw that I had been losing."

"Yes," said Hanaud, nodding his head. "He thought
that the opportune moment had come."

He extended his arms and let his hands fall against his
thighs. He was like a doctor presented with a hopeless
case. He turned half aside from Ann with his shoulders
bent and his troubled eyes fixed upon the marble squares
of the floor. Jim could not but believe that he was at
this moment debating whether he should take the girl
into custody. But Betty intervened.

"You must not be misled, Monsieur Hanaud," she said
quickly. "It is true no doubt that Monsieur Boris mentioned the subject to Ann for the first time that night.

But I had already told both my aunt and Monsieur Boris that I should like a friend of my own age to live with me and I had mentioned Ann."

Hanaud looked up at her doubtfully.

"On so short an acquaintance, Mademoiselle?"

Betty, however, stuck to her guns.

"Yes. I liked her very much from the beginning. She was alone. It was quite clear that she was of our own world. There was every good reason why I should wish for her. And the four months she has been with me have proved to me that I was right."

She crossed over to Ann with a defiant little nod at Hanaud, who responded with a cordial grin and dropped into English.

"So I can push that into my pipe and puff it, as my dear Ricardo would say. That is what you mean? Well, against loyalty, the whole world is powerless." As he made Betty a friendly bow. He could hardly have told Betty in plainer phrase that her intervention had averted Ann's arrest; or Ann herself that he believed her guilty.

Every one in the hall understood him in that sense. They stood foolishly looking here and looking there and not knowing where to look; and in the midst of their discomfort occurred an incongruous little incident which added a touch of the bizarre. Up the two steps to the open door came a girl carrying a big oblong cardboard milliner's box. Her finger was on the bell, when Hanaud stepped forward.

"There is no need to ring," he said. "What have you there?"

The girl stepped into the hall and looked at Ann.

"It is Mademoiselle's dress for the Ball to-morrow night. Mademoiselle was to call for a final fitting but did not come. But Madame Grolin thinks that it will be all right." She laid the box upon a chest at the side of the hall and went out again.

"I had forgotten all about it," said Ann. "It was ordered just before Madame died and tried on once."

193

Hanaud nodded.

"For Madame Le Vay's masked ball, no doubt," he said. "I noticed the invitation card on the chimney-piece of Mademoiselle's sitting-room. And in what character did Mademoiselle propose to go?"

Ann startled them all. She flung up her head, whilst the blood rushed into her cheeks and her eyes shone.

"Not Madame de Brinvilliers, Monsieur, at all events," she cried.

Even Hanaud was brought up with a start.

"I did not suggest it," he replied coldly. "But let me see!" and in a moment whilst his face was flushed with anger his hands were busily untying the tapes of the box.

Betty stepped forward.

"We talked over that little dress, together, Monsieur, more than a month ago. It is meant to represent a water-lily."

"What could be more charming?" Hanaud asked, but his fingers did not pause in their work.

"Could suspicion betray itself more brutally?" Jim Frobisher wondered. What could he expect to find in that box? Did he imagine that this Madame Grolin, the milliner, was an accomplice of Waberski's too? The episode was ludicrous with a touch of the horrible. Hanaud lifted off the lid and turned back the tissue-paper. Underneath was seen a short *crêpe de Chine* frock of a tender vivid green with a girdle of gold and a great gold rosette at the side. The skirt was stiffened to stand out at the hips, and it was bordered with a row of white satin rosettes with golden hearts. To complete the dress there were a pair of white silk stockings with fine gold clocks and white satin shoes with single straps across the insteps and little tassels of brilliants where the straps buttoned, and four gold stripes at the back round the heels.

Hanaud felt under the frock and around the sides, replaced the lid, and stood up again. He never looked at Ann Upcott. He went straight across to Betty Harlowe.

"I regret infinitely, Mademoiselle, that I have put you to so much trouble and occupied so many hours of your day," he said with a good deal of feeling. He made her a courteous bow, took up his hat and stick from the table on which he had laid it, and made straight for the hall door. His business in the Maison Grenelle was to all appearances finished.

But Monsieur Bex was not content. He had been nursing his suggestion for nearly half an hour. Like a poem it demanded utterance.

"Monsieur Hanaud!" he called; "Monsieur Hanaud! I have to tell you about a box of matches."

"Aha!" Hanaud answered, stopping alertly. "A box of matches! I will walk with you towards your office, and you shall tell me as you go."

Monsieur Bex secured his hat and his stick in a great hurry. But he had time to throw a glance of pride towards his English colleague. "Your suggestion about the treasure room was of no value, my friend. Let us see what I can do!" The pride and the airy wave of the hand spoke the unspoken words. Monsieur Bex was at Hanaud's side in a moment, and talked volubly as they passed out of the gates into the street of Charles-Robert.

Betty turned to Jim Frobisher.

"To-morrow, now that I am once allowed to use my motor-car, I shall take you for a drive and show you something of our neighbourhood. This afternoon—you will understand, I know—I belong to Ann."

She took Ann Upcott by the arm and the two girls went out into the garden. Jim was left alone in the hall—as at that moment he wanted to be. It was very still here now and very silent. The piping of birds, the drone of bees outside the open doors were rather an accompaniment than an interruption of the silence. Jim placed himself where Hanaud had stood at that moment when he had laughed so strangely—half-way between the foot of the stairs where Monsieur Bex and he himself had been standing and the open porch. But Jim could detect nothing whatever to provoke any laughter, any excitement. "That I should have lived all these years and never noticed it before," he had exclaimed. Notice what? There was nothing to notice. A table, a chair or two, a barometer hanging upon the wall on one side and a mirror hanging upon the wall on the other—No, there was nothing. Of course, Jim reflected, there was a strain of the mountebank in Hanaud. The whole of that little scene might have been invented by him maliciously, just to annoy and worry and cause discomfort to Monsieur Bex and himself. Hanaud was very capable of a trick like that! A strain of the mountebank indeed! He had a great deal of the mountebank. More than half of him was probably mountebank. Possibly quite two-thirds!

"Oh, damn the fellow! What in the world did he notice?" cried Jim. "What did he notice from the top of the Tower? What did he notice in this hall? Why must he be always noticing something?" and he jammed his hat on in a rage and stalked out of the house.

A T nine o'clock that night Jim Frobisher walked past
the cashier's desk and into the hall of the Grande
Taverne. High above his head the cinematograph
machine whirred and clicked and a blade of silver light
cut the darkness. At the opposite end of the hall the
square screen was flooded with radiance and the pictures
melted upon it one into the other.

For a little while Jim could see nothing but that screen.
Then the hall swam gradually within his vision. He saw
the heads of people like great bullets and a wider central
corridor where waitresses with white aprons moved. Jim
walked up the corridor and turned off to the left between
the tables. When he reached the wall he went forward
again towards the top of the hall. On his left the hall
fell back, and in the recess were two large cubicles in
which billiard tables were placed. Against the wall of the
first of these a young man was leaning with his eyes fixed
upon the screen. Jim fancied that he recognised Maurice
Thevenet, and nodded to him as he passed. A little
further on a big man with a soft felt hat was seated
alone, with a Bock in front of him—Hanaud. Jim
slipped into a seat at his side.

"You?" Hanaud exclaimed in surprise.

"Why not? You told me this is where you would be
at this hour," replied Jim, and some note of discouragement in his voice attracted Hanaud's attention.

"I didn't think that those two young ladies would let
you go," he said.

"On the contrary," Jim replied with a short laugh.
"They didn't want me at all."

He began to say something more, but thought better of
it, and called to a waitress.

"Two Bocks, if you please," he ordered, and he offered Hanaud a cigar.

When the Bocks were brought, Hanaud said to him:

"It will be well to pay at once, so that we can slip away when we want."

"We have something to do to-night?" Jim asked.

"Yes."

He said no more until Jim had paid and the waitress had turned the two little saucers on which she had brought the Bocks upside down and had gone away. Then he leaned towards Jim and lowered his voice.

"I am glad that you came here. For I have a hope that we shall get the truth to-night, and you ought to be present when we do get it."

Jim lit his own cigar.

"From whom do you hope to get it?"

"Jean Cladel," Hanaud answered in a whisper. "A little later when all the town is quiet we will pay a visit to the street of Gambetta."

"You think he'll talk?"

Hanaud nodded.

"There is no charge against Cladel in this affair. To make a solution of that poison paste is not an offence. And he has so much against him that he will want to be on our side if he can. Yes, he will talk I have no doubt."

There would be an end of the affair then, to-night. Jim Frobisher was glad with an unutterable gladness. Betty would be free to order her life as she liked, and where she liked, to give to her youth its due scope and range, to forget the terror and horror of these last weeks, as one forgets old things behind locked doors.

"I hope, however," he said earnestly to Hanaud, "and I believe, that you will be found wrong, that if there was a murder Ann Upcott had nothing to do with it. Yes, I believe that." He repeated his assertion as much to convince himself as to persuade Hanaud.

Hanaud touched his elbow.

"Don't raise your voice too much, my friend," he said. "I think there is some one against the wall who is honouring us with his attention."

Jim shook his head.

"It is only Maurice Thevenet," he said.

"Oho?" answered Hanaud in a voice of relief. "Is that all? For a moment I was anxious. It seemed that there was a sentinel standing guard over us." He added in a whisper, "I, too, hope from the bottom of my heart that I may be proved wrong. But what of that arrow head in the pen tray? Eh? Don't forget that!" Then he fell into a muse.

"What happened on that night in the Maison Grenelle?" he said. "Why was that communicating door thrown open? Who was to be stripped to the skin by that violent woman? Who whispered 'That will do now'? Is Ann Upcott speaking the truth, and was there some terrible scene taking place before she entered so unexpectedly the treasure room—some terrible scene which ended in that dreadful whisper? Or is Ann Upcott lying from beginning to end? Ah, my friend, you wrote some questions down upon your memorandum this afternoon. But these are the questions I want answered, and where shall I find the answers?"

Jim had never seen Hanaud so moved. His hands were clenched, and the veins prominent upon his forehead, and though he whispered his voice shook.

"Jean Cladel may help," said Jim.

"Yes, yes, he may tell us something."

They sat through an episode of the film, and saw the lights go up and out again, and then Hanaud looked eagerly at his watch and put it back again into his pocket with a gesture of annoyance.

"It is still too early?" Jim asked.

"Yes. Cladel has no servant and takes his meals abroad. He has not yet returned home."

A little before ten o'clock a man strolled in, and seating

himself at a table behind Hanaud twice scraped a match upon a match-box without getting a light. Hanaud, without moving, said quietly to Frobisher:

"He is at home now. In a minute I shall go. Give me five minutes and follow."

Jim nodded.

"Where shall we meet?"

"Walk straight along the Rue de la Liberté, and I will see to that," said Hanaud.

He pulled his packet of cigarettes from his pocket, put one between his lips, and took his time in lighting it. Then he got up, but to his annoyance Maurice Thevenet recognised him and came forward.

"When Monsieur Frobisher wished me good-evening and joined you I thought it was you, Monsieur Hanaud. But I had not the presumption to recall myself to your notice."

"Presumption! Monsieur, we are of the same service, only you have the advantage of youth," said Hanaud politely, as he turned.

"But you are going, Monsieur Hanaud?" Thevenet asked in distress. "I am desolated. I have broken into a conversation like a clumsy fellow."

"Not at all," Hanaud replied. To Frobisher his patience was as remarkable as Maurice Thevenet's impudence. "We were idly watching a film which I think is a little tedious."

"Then, since you are not busy I beg for your indulgence. One little moment that is all. I should so dearly love to be able to say to my friends, 'I sat in the cinema with Monsieur Hanaud—yes, actually I'—and asked for his advice."

Hanaud sat down again upon his chair.

"And upon what subject can you, of whom Monsieur Girardot speaks so highly, want my advice?" Hanaud asked with a laugh.

The eternal ambition of the provincial was tormenting the eager youth. To get to Paris—all was in that!

Fortune, reputation, a life of colour. A word from Monsieur Hanaud and a way would open. He would work night and day to justify that word.

"Monsieur, all I can promise is that when the time comes I shall remember you. But that promise I make now with my whole heart," said Hanaud warmly, and with a bow he moved away.

Maurice Thevenet watched him go.

"What a man!" Maurice Thevenet went on enthusiastically. "I would not like to try to keep any secrets from him. No, indeed!" Jim had heard that sentiment before on other lips and with a greater sympathy. "I did not understand at all what he had in his mind when he staged that little scene with Francine Rollard. But something, Monsieur. Oh, you may be sure. Something wise. And that search through the treasure room! How quick and complete! No doubt while we searched Mademoiselle Upcott's bedroom, he was just as quick and complete in going through her sitting-room. But he found nothing. No, nothing."

He waited for Jim to corroborate him, but Jim only said "Oho!"

But Thevenet was not to be extinguished.

"I shall tell you what struck me, Monsieur. He was following out no suspicions; isn't that so? He was detached. He was gathering up every trifle, on the chance that each one might sometime fit in with another and at last a whole picture be composed. An artist! There was a letter, for instance, which Mademoiselle Harlowe handed to him, one of those deplorable letters which have disgraced us here—you remember that letter, Monsieur?"

"Aha!" said Frobisher, quite in the style of Hanaud. "But I see that this film is coming to its wedding bells. So I shall wish you a good evening."

Frobisher bowed and left Maurice Thevenet to dream of success in Paris. He strolled between the groups of spectators to the entrance and thence into the street. He walked to the arch of the Porte Guillaume and turned into the Rue de la Liberté. The provincial towns go to bed early and the street so busy throughout the day was like the street of a deserted city. A couple of hundred yards on, he was startled to find Hanaud, sprung from nowhere, walking at his side.

"So my young friend, the secretary engaged you when I had gone?" he said.

"Maurice Thevenet," said Jim, "may be as the Commissary says a young man of a surprising intelligence, but to tell you the truth, I find him a very intrusive fellow. First of all he wanted to know if you had discovered anything in Ann Upcott's sitting-room, and then what Miss Harlowe's anonymous letter was about."

Hanaud looked at Jim with interest.

"Yes, he is anxious to learn, that young man, Girardot is right. He will go far. And how did you answer him?"

"I said 'Oho'! first, and then I said 'Aha'! just like a troublesome friend of mine when I ask him a simple question which he does not mean to answer."

Hanaud laughed heartily.

"And you did very well," he said. "Come, let us turn into this little street upon the right. It will take us to our destination."

"Wait!" whispered Jim eagerly. "Don't cross the road for a moment. Listen!"

Hanaud obeyed at once; and both men stood and listened in the empty street.

"Not a sound," said Hanaud.

"No! That is what troubles me!" Jim whispered importantly. "A minute ago there were footsteps behind us. Now that we have stopped they have stopped too. Let us go on quite straight for a moment or two."

"But certainly my friend," said Hanaud.

"And let us not talk either," Jim urged.

"Not a single word," said Hanaud.

They moved forward again and behind them once more footsteps rang upon the pavement.

"What did I tell you?" asked Jim, taking Hanaud by the arm.

"That we would neither of us speak," Hanaud replied. "And lo! you have spoken!"

"But why? Why have I spoken? Be serious, Monsieur," Jim shook his arm indignantly. "We are being followed."

Hanaud stopped dead and gazed in steady admiration at his junior colleague.

"Oh!" he whispered. "You have discovered that? Yes, it is true. We are being followed by one of my men who sees to it that we are not followed."

Frobisher shook Hanaud's arm off indignantly. He drew himself up stiffly. Then he saw Hanaud's mouth twitching and he understood that he was looking "proper."

"Oh, let us go and find Jean Cladel," he said with a laugh and he crossed the road. They passed into a network of small, mean streets. There was not a soul abroad. The houses were shrouded in darkness. The only sounds they heard were the clatter of their own footsteps on the pavement and the fainter noise of the man who followed them. Hanaud turned to the left into a short passage and stopped before a little house with a shuttered shop front.

"This is the place," he said in a low voice and he pressed the button in the pillar of the door. The bell rang with a shrill sharp whirr just the other side of the panels.

"We may have to wait a moment if he has gone to bed," said Hanaud, "since he has no servant in the house."

A minute or two passed. The clocks struck the half hour. Hanaud leaned his ear against the panels of the door. He could not hear one sound within the house. He rang again; and after a few seconds shutters were thrown back and a window opened on the floor above. From behind the window some one whispered:

"Who is there?"

"The police," Hanaud answered, and at the window above there was silence.

"No one is going to do you any harm," Hanaud continued, raising his voice impatiently. "We want some information from you. That's all."

"Very well." The whisper came from the same spot. The man standing within the darkness of the room had not moved. "Wait! I will slip on some things and come down."

The window and the shutter were closed again. Then through the chinks a few beams of light strayed out. Hanaud uttered a little grunt of satisfaction.

"That animal is getting up at last. He must have some strange clients amongst the good people of Dijon if he is so careful to answer them in a whisper."

He turned about and took a step or two along the pavement and another step or two back like a man upon a quarter deck. Jim Frobisher had never known him so restless and impatient during these two days.

"I can't help it," he said in a low voice to Jim. "I think that in five minutes we shall touch the truth of this affair. We shall know who brought the arrow to him from the Maison Grenelle."

"If any one brought the arrow to him at all," Jim Frobisher added.

But Hanaud was not in the mood to consider ifs and possibilities.

"Oh, that!" he said with a shrug of the shoulders. Then he tapped his forehead. "I am like Waberski. I have it here that some one did bring the arrow to Jean Cladel."

He started once more his quarter-deck pacing. Only it was now a trot rather than a walk. Jim was a little nettled by the indifference to his suggestion. He was still convinced that Hanaud had taken the wrong starting point in all his inquiry. He said tartly:

"Well, if some one did bring the arrow here, it will

be the same person who replaced the treatise on Sporanthus on its book shelf."

Hanaud came to a stop in front of Jim Frobisher. Then he burst into a low laugh.

"I will bet you all the money in the world that that is not true, and then Madame Harlowe's pearl necklace on the top of it. For after all it was not I who brought the arrow to Jean Cladel, whereas it was undoubtedly I who put back the treatise on the shelf."

Jim took a step back. He stared at Hanaud with his mouth open in a stupefaction.

"You?" he exclaimed.

"I," replied Hanaud, standing up on the tips of his toes. "Alone I did it."

Then his manner of burlesque dropped from him. He looked up at the shuttered windows with a sudden anxiety.

"That animal is taking longer than he need," he muttered. "After all, it is not to a court ball of the Duke of Burgundy that we are inviting him."

He rang the bell again with a greater urgency. It returned its shrill reply as though it mocked him.

"I do not like this," said Hanaud.

He seized the door-handle and leaned his shoulder against the panel and drove his weight against it. But the door was strong and did not give. Hanaud put his fingers to his mouth and whistled softly. From the direction whence they had come they heard the sound of a man running swiftly. They saw him pass within the light of the one street lamp at the corner and out of it again; and then he stood at their side. Jim recognised Nicolas Moreau, the little agent who had been sent this very morning by Hanaud to make sure that Jean Cladel existed.

"Nicolas, I want you to wait here," said Hanaud. "If the door is opened, whistle for us and keep it open."

"Very well, sir."

Hanaud said in a low and troubled voice to Frobisher:

"There is something here which alarms me." He dived into a narrow alley at the side of the shop.

"It was in this alley no doubt that Waberski meant us to believe that he hid on the morning of the 7th of May," Jim whispered as he hurried to keep with his companion.

"No doubt."

The alley led into a lane which ran parallel with the street of Gambetta. Hanaud wheeled into it. A wall five feet high, broken at intervals by rickety wooden doors, enclosed the yards at the backs of the houses. Before the first of these breaks in the wall Hanaud stopped. He raised himself upon the tips of his toes and peered over the wall, first downwards into the yard, and then upwards towards the back of the house. There was no lamp in the lane, no light showing from any of the windows. Though the night was clear of mist it was as dark as a cavern in this narrow lane behind the houses. Jim Frobisher, though his eyes were accustomed to the gloom, knew that he could not have seen a man, even if he had moved, ten yards away. Yet Hanaud still stood peering at the back of the house with the tips of his fingers on the top of the wall. Finally he touched Jim on the sleeve.

"I believe the back window on the first floor is open," he whispered, and his voice was more troubled than ever. "We will go in and see."

He touched the wooden door and it swung inwards with a whine of its hinges.

"Open," said Hanaud. "Make no noise."

Silently they crossed the yard. The ground floor of the house was low. Jim looking upwards could see now that the window above their heads yawned wide open.

"You are right," he breathed in Hanaud's ear, and with a touch Hanaud asked for silence.

The room beyond the window was black as pitch. The two men stood below and listened. Not a word came from it. Hanaud drew Jim into the wall of the house. At the end of the wall a door gave admission into the house. Hanaud tried the door, turning the handle first and then gently pressing with his shoulder upon the panel.

"It's locked, but not bolted like the door in front," he whispered. "I can manage this."

Jim Frobisher heard the tiniest possible rattle of a bunch of keys as Hanaud drew it from his pocket, and then not a noise of any kind whilst Hanaud stooped above the lock. Yet within half a minute the door slowly opened. It opened upon a passage as black as that room above their heads. Hanaud stepped noiselessly into the passage. Jim Frobisher followed him with a heart beating high in excitement. What had happened in that lighted room upstairs and in the dark room behind it? Why didn't Jean Cladel come down and open the door upon the street of Gambetta? Why didn't they hear Nicolas Moreau's soft whistle or the sound of his voice? Hanaud stepped back past Jim Frobisher and shut the door behind them and locked it again.

"You haven't an electric torch with you, of course?" Hanaud whispered.

"No," replied Jim.

"Nor I. And I don't want to strike a match. There's something upstairs which frightens me."

You could hardly hear the words. They were spoken as though the mere vibration of the air they caused would carry a message to the rooms above.

"We'll move very carefully. Keep a hand upon my coat," and Hanaud went forward. After he had gone a few paces he stopped.

"There's a staircase here on my right. It turns at once. Mind not to knock your foot on the first step," he whispered over his shoulder; and a moment later, he reached down and, taking hold of Jim's right arm, laid his hand upon a balustrade. Jim lifted his foot, felt for and found the first tread of the stairs, and mounted behind Hanaud. They halted on a little landing just above the door by which they had entered the house.

In front of them the darkness began to thin, to become opaque rather than a black, impenetrable hood drawn over their heads. Jim understood that in front of him was an open door and that the faint glimmer came from that open window on their left hand beyond the door.

Hanaud passed through the doorway into the room. Jim followed and was already upon the threshold, when Hanaud stumbled and uttered a cry. No doubt the cry was low, but coming so abruptly upon their long silence it startled Frobisher like the explosion of a pistol. It seemed that it must clash through Dijon like the striking of a clock.

But nothing followed. No one stirred, no one cried out a question. Silence descended upon the house again, impenetrable, like the darkness a hood upon the senses. Jim was tempted to call out aloud himself, anything, however childish, so that he might hear a voice speaking words, if only his own voice. The words came at last, from Hanaud and from the inner end of the room, but in an accent which Jim did not recognise.

"Don't move! . . . There is something. . . . I told you I was frightened. . . . Oh!" and his voice died away in a sigh.

Jim could hear him moving very cautiously. Then he almost screamed aloud. For the shutters at the window slowly swung to and the room was once more shrouded in black.

"Who's that?" Jim whispered violently, and Hanaud answered:

"It's only me—Hanaud. I don't want to show a light here yet with that window open. God knows what dreadful thing has happened here. Come just inside the room and shut the door behind you."

Jim obeyed, and having moved his position, could see a line of yellow light, straight and fine as if drawn by a pencil, at the other end of the room on the floor. There was a door there, a door into the front room where they had seen the light go up from the street of Gambetta.

Jim Frobisher had hardly realised that before the door was burst open with a crash. In the doorway, outlined against the light beyond, appeared the bulky frame of Hanaud.

"There is nothing here," he said, standing there blocking up the doorway with his hands in his pockets. "The room is quite empty."

That room, the front room—yes! But between Hanaud's legs the light trickled out into the dark room behind, and here, on the floor illuminated by a little lane of light, Jim, with a shiver, saw a clenched hand and a forearm in a crumpled shirt-sleeve.

"Turn round," he cried to Hanaud. "Look!"

Hanaud turned.

"Yes," he said quietly. "That is what I stumbled against."

He found a switch in the wall close to the door and snapped it down. The dark room was flooded with light, and on the floor, in the midst of a scene of disorder, a table pushed back here, a chair overturned there, lay the body of a man. He wore no coat. He was in his waistcoat and his shirt sleeves, and he was crumpled up with a horrible suggestion of agony like a ball, his knees towards his chin, his head forward towards his knees. One arm clutched the body close, the other, the one which Jim had seen, was flung out, his hand clenched in a spasm of intolerable pain. And about the body there was such a pool of blood as Jim Frobisher thought no body could contain.

Jim staggered back with his hands clasped over his eyes. He felt physically sick.

"Then he killed himself on our approach," he cried with a groan.

"Who?" answered Hanaud steadily.

"Jean Cladel. The man who whispered to us from behind the window."

Hanaud stunned him with a question.

"What with?"

Jim drew his hands slowly from before his face and forced his eyes to their service. There was no gleam of a knife, or a pistol, anywhere against the dark background of the carpet.

"You might think that he was a Japanese who had committed *hari-kari*," said Hanaud. "But if he had, the knife would be at his side. And there is no knife."

He stooped over the body and felt it, and drew his hand back.

"It is still warm," he said, and then a gasp, "Look!" He pointed. The man was lying on his side in this dreadful pose of contracted sinews and unendurable pain. And across the sleeve of his shirt there was a broad red mark.

"That's where the knife was wiped clean," said Hanaud.

Jim bent forward.

"By God, that's true," he cried, and a little afterwards, in a voice of awe: "Then it's murder."

Hanaud nodded.

"Not a doubt."

Jim Frobisher stood up. He pointed a shaking finger at the grotesque image of pain crumpled upon the floor, death without dignity, an argument that there was something horribly wrong with the making of the human race—since such things could be.

"Jean Cladel?" he asked.

"We must make sure," answered Hanaud. He went down the stairs to the front door and, unbolting it, called Moreau within the house. From the top of the stairs Jim heard him ask:

"Do you know Jean Cladel by sight?"

"Yes," answered Moreau.

"Then follow me."

Hanaud led him up into the back room. For a moment Moreau stopped upon the threshold with a blank look upon his face.

"Is that the man?" Hanaud asked.

Moreau stepped forward.

"Yes."

"He has been murdered," Hanaud explained. "Will you fetch the Commissary of the district and a doctor? We will wait here."

Moreau turned on his heel and went downstairs. Hanaud dropped into a chair and stared moodily at the dead body.

"Jean Cladel," he said in a voice of discouragement. "Just when he could have been of a little use in the world! Just when he could have helped us to the truth! It's my fault, too. I oughtn't to have waited until to-night. I ought to have foreseen that this might happen."

"Who can have murdered him?" Jim Frobisher exclaimed.

Hanaud roused himself out of his remorse.

"The man who whispered to us from behind the window," answered Hanaud.

Jim Frobisher felt his mind reeling.

"That's impossible!" he cried.

"Why?" Hanaud asked. "It must have been he. Think it out!" And step by step he told the story as he read it, testing it by speaking it aloud.

"At five minutes past ten a man of mine, still a little out of breath from his haste, comes to us in the Grande Taverne and tells us that Jean Cladel has just reached home. He reached home then at five minutes to ten."

"Yes," Jim agreed.

"We were detained for a few minutes by Maurice Thevenet. Yes." He moistened his lips with the tip of his tongue and said softly: "We shall have to consider that very modest and promising young gentleman rather carefully. He detained us. We heard the clock strike half-past ten as we waited in the street."

"Yes."

"And all was over then. For the house was as silent as what, indeed, it is—a grave. And only just over, for the body is still warm. If this—lying here, is Jean Cladel, some one else must have been waiting for him to come home to-night, waiting in the lane behind, since my man didn't see him. And an acquaintance, a friend—for Jean Cladel lets him in and locks the door behind him."

Jim interrupted.

"He might have been here already, waiting for him with his knife bared in this dark room."

Hanaud looked around the room. It was furnished cheaply and stuffily, half office, half living-room. An open bureau stood against the wall near the window. A closed cabinet occupied the greater part of one side.

"I wonder," he said. "It is possible, no doubt—— But if so, why did the murderer stay so long? No search has been made—no drawers are ransacked." He tried the door of the cabinet. "This is still locked. No, I don't think that he was waiting. I think that he was admitted as a friend or a client—I fancy Jean Cladel had not a few clients who preferred to call upon him by the back way in the dark of the night. I think that his visitor came meaning to kill, and waited his time and killed, and that he had hardly killed before we rang the bell at the door." Hanaud drew in his breath sharply. "Imagine that, my friend! He is standing here over the man he has murdered, and unexpectedly the shrill, clear sound of the bell goes through the house—as though God said, 'I saw you!' Imagine it! He turned out the light and stands holding his breath in the dark. The bell rings again. He must answer it or worse may befall. He goes into the front room and throws open the window, and hears it is the police who are at the door." Hanaud nodded his head in a reluctant admiration. "But that man had an iron nerve! He doesn't lose his head. He closes the shutter, he turns on the light, that we may think he is getting up, he runs back into this room. He will not waste time by stumbling down the stairs and fumbling with the lock of the back door. No, he opens these shutters and drops to the ground. It is done in a second. Another second, and he is in the lane; another, and he is safe, his dreadful mission ended. Cladel will not speak. Cladel will not tell us the things we want to know."

Hanaud went over to the cabinet and, using his skeleton keys, again opened its doors. On the shelves were ranged a glass jar or two, a retort, the simplest utensils of a laboratory and a few bottles, one of which, larger than the rest, was half filled with a colourless liquid.

"Alcohol," said Hanaud, pointing to the label.

Jim Frobisher moved carefully round on the outskirts of the room, taking care not to alter the disarrangements of the furniture. He looked the bottles over. Not one of them held a drop of that pale lemon-coloured solution which the Professor, in his Treatise, had described. Hanaud shut and locked the doors of the cabinet again and stepped carefully over to the bureau. It stood open, and a few papers were strewn upon the flap. He sat down at the bureau and began carefully to search it. Jim sat down in a chair. Somehow it had leaked out that, since this morning, Hanaud knew of Jean Cladel. Jean Cladel therefore must be stopped from any revelations; and he had been stopped. Frobisher could no longer doubt that murder had been done on the night of April the 27th, in the Maison Grenelle. Development followed too logically upon development. The case was building itself up—another storey had been added to the edifice with this new crime. Yes, certainly and solidly it was building itself up—this case against some one.

CHAPTER EIGHTEEN: *The White Tablet*

WITHIN the minute that case was to be immeasurably strengthened. An exclamation broke from Hanaud. He sprang to his feet and turned on the light of a green-shaded reading lamp, which stood upon the ledge of the bureau. He was holding now under the light a small drawer, which he had removed from the front of the bureau. Very gingerly he lifted some little thing out of it, something that looked like a badge that men wear in their buttonholes. He laid it down upon the blotting paper; and in that room of death laughed harshly.

He beckoned to Jim.

"Come and look!"

What Jim saw was a thin, small, barbed iron dart, with an iron stem. He had no need to ask its nature, for he had seen its likeness that morning in the Treatise of the Edinburgh Professor. This was the actual head of Simon Harlowe's poison-arrow.

"You have found it!" said Jim in a voice that shook.

"Yes."

Hanaud gave it a little push, and said thoughtfully:

"A negro thousands of miles away sits outside his hut in the Kombé country and pounds up his poison seed and mixes it with red clay, and smears it thick and slab over the shaft of his fine new arrow, and waits for his enemy. But his enemy does not come. So he barters it, or gives it to his white friend the trader on the Shiré river. And the trader brings it home and gives it to Simon Harlowe of the Maison Grenelle. And Simon Harlowe lends it to a professor in Edinburgh, who writes about it in a printed book and sends it back again. And in the end, after all its travels, it comes to the tenement of Jean Cladel in a

214

slum of Dijon, and is made ready in a new way to do its deadly work."

For how much longer Hanaud would have moralised over the arrow in this deplorable way, no man can tell. Happily Jim Frobisher was reprieved from listening to him by the shutting of a door below and the noise of voices in the passage.

"The Commissary!" said Hanaud, and he went quickly down the stairs.

Jim heard him speaking in a low tone for quite a long while, and no doubt was explaining the position of affairs. For when he brought the Commissary and the doctor up into the room he introduced Jim as one about whom they already knew.

"This is that Monsieur Frobisher," he said.

The Commissary, a younger and more vivacious man than Girardot, bowed briskly to Jim and looked towards the contorted figure of Jean Cladel.

Even he could not restrain a little gesture of repulsion. He clacked his tongue against the roof of his mouth.

"He is not pretty, that one!" he said. "Most certainly he is not pretty."

Hanaud crossed again to the bureau and carefully folded the dart around with paper.

"With your permission, Monsieur," he said ceremoniously to the Commissary, "I shall take this with me. I will be responsible for it." He put it away in his pocket and looked at the doctor, who was stooping by the side of Jean Cladel. "I do not wish to interfere, but I should be glad to have a copy of the medical report. I think that it might help me. I think it will be found that this murder was committed in a way peculiar to one man."

"Certainly you shall have a copy of the report, Monsieur Hanaud," replied the young Commissary in a polite and formal voice.

Hanaud laid a hand on Jim's arm.

"We are in the way, my friend. Oh, yes, in spite of Monsieur le Commissaire's friendly protestations. This is not our affair. Let us go!" He conducted Jim to the door and turned about. "I do not wish to interfere," he repeated, "but it is possible that the shutters and the window will bear the traces of the murderer's fingers. I don't think it probable, for that animal had taken his precautions. But it is possible, for he left in a great hurry."

The Commissary was overwhelmed with gratitude.

"Most certainly we will give our attention to the shutters and the window-sill."

"A copy of the finger-prints, if any are found?" Hanaud suggested.

"Shall be at Monsieur Hanaud's disposal as early as possible," the Commissary agreed.

Jim experienced a pang of regret that Monsieur Bex was not present at the little exchange of civilities. The Commissary and Hanaud were so careful not to tread upon one another's toes and so politely determined that their own should not be trodden upon. Monsieur Bex could not but have revelled in the correctness of their deportment.

Hanaud and Frobisher went downstairs into the street. The neighbourhood had not been aroused. A couple of *sergents-de-ville* stood in front of the door. The street of Gambetta was still asleep and indifferent to the crime which had taken place in one of its least respectable houses.

"I shall go to the Prefecture," said Hanaud. "They have given me a little office there with a sofa. I want to put away the arrow head before I go to my hotel."

"I shall come with you," said Jim. "It will be a relief to walk for a little in the fresh air, after that room."

The Prefecture lay the better part of a mile away across the city. Hanaud set off at a great pace, and reaching the building conducted Jim into an office with a safe set against the wall.

"Will you sit down for a moment? And smoke, please," he said.

He was in a mood of such deep dejection; he was so

changed from his mercurial self; that only now did Jim
Frobisher understand the great store he had set upon his
interview with Jean Cladel. He unlocked the safe and
brought over to the table a few envelopes of different
sizes, the copy of the Treatise and his green file. He
seated himself in front of Jim and began to open his
envelopes and range their contents in a row, when the
door was opened and a gendarme saluted and advanced.
He carried a paper in his hand.

"A reply came over the telephone from Paris at nine
o'clock to-night, Monsieur Hanaud. They say that this
may be the name of the firm you want. It was established in the Rue de Batignolles, but it ceased to exist
seven years ago."

"Yes, that would have happened," Hanaud answered
glumly, as he took the paper. He read what was written
upon it. "Yes—yes. That's it. Not a doubt."

He took an envelope from a rack upon the table and
put the paper inside it and stuck down the flap. On the
front of the envelope, Jim saw him write an illuminating
word. "Address."

Then he looked at Jim with smouldering eyes.

"There is a fatality in all this," he cried. "We become
more and more certain that murder was committed and
how it was committed. We get a glimpse of possible
reasons why. But we are never an inch nearer to evidence
—real convincing evidence—who committed it. Fatality?
I am a fool to use such words. It's keen wits and
audacity and nerve that stop us at the end of each lane and
make an idiot of me!"

He struck a match viciously and lit a cigarette. Frobisher made an effort to console him.

"Yes, but it's the keen wits and the audacity and the
nerve of more than one person."

Hanaud glanced at Frobisher sharply.

"Explain, my friend."

"I have been thinking over it ever since we left the
street of Gambetta. I no longer doubt that Mrs. Har-

lowe was murdered in the Maison Grenelle. It is impossible to doubt it. But her murder was part of the activities of a gang. Else how comes it that Jean Cladel was murdered too to-night?"

A smile drove for a moment the gloom from Hanaud's face.

"Yes. You have been quite fifteen minutes in the bull-ring," he said.

"Then you agree with me?"

"Yes!" But Hanaud's gloom had returned. "But we can't lay our hands upon the gang. We are losing time, and I am afraid that we have no time to lose." Hanaud shivered like a man suddenly chilled. "Yes, I am very troubled now. I am very—frightened."

His fear peered out of him and entered into Frobisher. Frobisher did not understand it, he had no clue to what it was that Hanaud feared, but sitting in that brightly-lit office in the silent building, he was conscious of evil presences thronging about the pair of them, presences grotesque and malevolent such as some old craftsman of Dijon might have carved on the pillars of a cathedral. He, too, shivered.

"Let us see, now!" said Hanaud.

He took the end of the arrow shaft from one envelope, and the barb from his pocket, and fitted them together. The iron barb was loose now because the hole to receive it at the top of the arrow shaft had been widened to take a nib. But the spoke was just about the right length. He laid the arrow down upon the table, and opened his green file. A small square envelope, such as chemists use, attracted Jim's notice. He took it up. It seemed empty, but as he shook it out, a square tablet of some hard white substance rolled on to the table. It was soiled with dust, and there was a smear of green upon it; and as Jim turned it over, he noticed a cut or crack in its surface, as though something sharp had struck it.

"What in the world has this to do with the affair?" he asked.

Hanaud looked up from his file. He reached out his hand swiftly to take the tablet away from Jim, and drew his hand in again.

"A good deal perhaps. Perhaps nothing," he said gravely. "But it is interesting—that tablet. I shall know more about it to-morrow."

Jim could not for the life of him remember any occasion which had brought this tablet into notice. It certainly had not been discovered in Jean Cladel's house, for it was already there in the safe in the office. Jim had noticed the little square envelope as Hanaud fetched it out of the safe. The tablet looked as if it had been picked up from the road like Monsieur Bex's famous match-box. Or—yes, there was that smear of green—from the grass. Jim sat up straight in his chair. They had all been together in the garden this morning. Hanaud, himself, Betty and Ann Upcott. But at that point Frobisher's conjectures halted. Neither his memory nor deduction could connect that tablet with the half-hour the four of them had passed in the shade of the sycamores. The only thing of which he was quite sure was the great importance which Hanaud attached to it. For all the time that he handled and examined it Hanaud's eyes never left him, never once. They followed each little movement of finger tip and thumb with an extraordinary alertness, and when Jim at last tilted it off his palm back into its little envelope, the detective undoubtedly drew a breath of relief.

Jim Frobisher laughed good-humouredly. He was getting to know his man. He did not invite any "Aha's" and "Oho's" by vain questionings. He leaned across the table and took up his own memorandum which Hanaud had just laid aside out of his file. He laid it on the table in front of him and added two new questions to those which he had already written out. Thus:

(5) What was the exact message telephoned from Paris to the Prefecture and hidden away in an envelope marked by Hanaud: "Address"?

(6) When and where and why was the white tablet picked up, and what, in the name of all the saints, does it mean?

With another laugh Frobisher tossed the memorandum back to Hanaud. Hanaud, however, read them slowly and thoughtfully. "I had hoped to answer all your questions to-night," he said dispiritedly. "But you see! We break down at every corner, and the question must wait."

He was fitting methodically the memorandum back into the file when a look of extreme surprise came over Frobisher's face. He pointed a finger at the file.

"That telegram!"

There was a telegram pinned to the three anonymous letters which Hanaud had in the file—the two which Hanaud had shown to Frobisher in Paris and the third which Betty Harlowe had given to him that very afternoon. And the telegram was pieced together by two strips of stamp-paper in a cross.

"That's our telegram. The telegram sent to my firm by Miss Harlowe on Monday—yes, by George, this last Monday."

It quite took Jim's breath away, so crowded had his days been with fears and reliefs, excitements and doubts, discoveries and disappointments, to realise that this was only the Friday night; that at so recent a date as Wednesday he had never seen or spoken with Betty Harlowe. "The telegram announcing to us in London that you were engaged upon the case."

Hanaud nodded in assent.

"Yes. You gave it to me."

"And you tore it up."

"I did. But I picked it out of the waste-paper basket afterwards and stuck it together." Hanaud explained, in no wise disconcerted by Jim Frobisher's attack of perspicacity. "I meant to make some trouble here with the Police for letting out the secret. I am very glad now that I did pick it out. You yourself must have realised its importance the very next morning before I even arrived at the Maison Grenelle, when you told Mademoiselle that you had shown it to me."

Jim cast his memory back. He had a passion for precision and exactness which was very proper in one of his profession.

"It was not until you came that I learnt Miss Harlowe had the news by an anonymous letter," he said.

"Well, that doesn't matter," Hanaud interposed a trifle quickly. "The point of importance to me is that when the case is done with, and I have a little time to devote to these letters, the telegram may be of value."

"Yes, I see," said Jim. "I see that," he repeated, and he shifted uncomfortably in his chair; and opened his mouth and closed it again; and remained suspended between speech and silence, whilst Hanaud read through his file and contemplated his exhibits and found no hope in them.

"They lead me nowhere!" he cried violently; and Jim Frobisher made up his mind.

"Monsieur Hanaud, you do not share your thoughts with me," he said rather formally, "but I will deal with you in a better way; apart from this crime in the Maison Grenelle, you have the mystery of these anonymous letters to solve. I can help you to this extent. Another of them has been received."

"When?"

"To-night, whilst we sat at dinner."

"By whom?"

"Ann Upcott."

"What!"

Hanaud was out of his chair with a cry, towering up, his face white as the walls of the room, his eyes burning upon Frobisher. Never could news have been so unexpected, so startling.

"You are sure?" he asked.

"Quite. It came by the evening post—with others. Gaston brought them into the dining-room. There was one for me from my firm in London, a couple for Betty, and this one for Ann Upcott. She opened it with a frown, as though she did not know from whom it came. I saw it as she unfolded it. It was on the same common paper—typewritten in the same way—with no address at the head of it. She gasped as she looked at it, and then she read it again. And then with a smile she folded it and put it away."

"With a smile?" Hanaud insisted.

"Yes. She was pleased. The colour came into her face. The distress went out of it."

"She didn't show it to you, then?"

"No."

"Nor to Mademoiselle Harlowe?"

"No."

"But she was pleased, eh?" It seemed that to Hanaud this was the most extraordinary feature of the whole business. "Did she say anything?"

"Yes," answered Jim. She said 'He has been always right, hasn't he?'"

"She said that! 'He has been always right, hasn't he?'" Hanaud slowly resumed his seat, and sat like a man turned into stone. He looked up in a little while.

"What happened then?" he asked.

"Nothing until dinner was over. Then she picked up her letter and beckoned with her head to Miss Betty, who said to me: 'We shall have to leave you to take your coffee alone.' They went across the hall to Betty's room. The treasure-room. I was a little nettled. Ever since I have been in Dijon one person after another has pushed me into a corner with orders to keep quiet and not interfere. So I came to find you at the Grande Taverne."

At another moment Jim's eruption of injured vanity would have provoked Hanaud to one of his lamentable exhibitions, but now he did not notice it at all.

"They went away to talk that letter over together," said Hanaud. "And that young lady was pleased, she

222

who was so distressed this afternoon. A way out, then!"
Hanaud was discussing his problem with himself, his eyes
upon the table. "For once the Scourge is kind? I wonder! It baffles me!" He rose to his feet and walked once
or twice across the room. "Yes, I the old bull of a hundred corridas, I, Hanaud, am baffled!"

He was not posturing now. He was frankly and
simply amazed that he could be so utterly at a loss. Then,
with a swift change of mood, he came back to the table.

"Meanwhile, Monsieur, until I can explain this strange
new incident to myself, I beg of you your help," he
pleaded very earnestly and even very humbly. Fear had
returned to his eyes and his voice. He was disturbed
beyond Jim's comprehension. "There is nothing more
important. I want you—how shall I put it so that I may
persuade you? I want you to stay as much as you can in
the Maison Grenelle—to—yes—to keep a little watch on
this pretty Ann Upcott, to——"

He got no further with his proposal. Jim Frobisher
interrupted him in a very passion of anger.

"No, no, I won't," he cried. "You go much too far,
Monsieur. I won't be your spy. I am not here for that.
I am here for my client. As for Ann Upcott, she is my
countrywoman. I will not help you against her. So help
me God, I won't!"

Hanaud looked across the table at the flushed and angry
face of his "junior colleague," who now resigned his
office and, without parley, accepted his defeat.

"I don't blame you," he answered quietly. "I could,
indeed, hope for no other reply. I must be quick, that's
all. I must be very quick!"

Frobisher's anger fell away from him like a cloak one
drops. He saw Hanaud sitting over against him with a
white, desperately troubled face and eyes in which there
shone unmistakeably some gleam of terror.

"Tell me!" he cried in an exasperation. "Be frank
with me for once! Is Ann Upcott guilty? She's not

alone, of course, anyway. There's a gang. We're agreed
upon that. Waberski's one of them, of course? Is Ann
Upcott another? Do you believe it?"

Hanaud slowly put his exhibits together. There was
a struggle going on within him. The strain of the night
had told upon them both, and he was tempted for once to
make a confidant, tempted intolerably. On the other
hand, Jim Frobisher read in him all the traditions of his
service; to wait upon facts, not to utter suspicions; to be
fair. It was not until he had locked everything away
again in the safe that Hanaud yielded to the temptation.
And even then he could not bring himself to be direct.

"You want to know what I believe of Ann Upcott?"
he cried reluctantly, as though the words were torn from
him. "Go to-morrow to the Church of Notre Dame and
look at the façade. There, since you are not blind, you
will see."

He would say no more; that was clear. Nay, he stood
moodily before Frobisher, already regretting that he had
said so much. Frobisher picked up his hat and stick.

"Thank you," he said. "Good night."

Hanaud let him go to the door. Then he said:

"You are free to-morrow. I shall not go to the Maison
Grenelle. Have you any plans?"

"Yes. I am to be taken for a motor-drive round the
neighbourhood."

"Yes. It is worth while," Hanaud answered listlessly.
"But remember to telephone to me before you go. I shall
be here. I will tell you if I have any news. Good night."

Jim Frobisher left him standing in the middle of the
room. Before he had closed the door Hanaud had forgotten his presence. For he was saying to himself over
and over again, almost with an accent of despair: "I must
be quick! I must be very quick!"

Frobisher walked briskly down to the Place Ernest
Renan and the Rue de la Liberté, dwelling upon Hanaud's
injunction to examine the façade of Notre Dame. He

must keep that in mind and obey it in the morning. But that night was not yet over for him.

As he reached the mouth of the little street of Charles-Robert he heard a light, quick step a little way behind him—a step that seemed familiar. So when he turned into the street he sauntered and looked round. He saw a tall man cross the entrance of the street very quickly and disappear between the houses on the opposite side. The man paused for a second under the light of a street lamp at the angle of the street, and Jim could have sworn that it was Hanaud. There were no hotels, no lodgings in this quarter of the city. It was a quarter of private houses. What was Hanaud seeking there?

Speculating upon this new question, he forgot the façade of Notre Dame; and upon his arrival at the Maison Grenelle a little incident occurred which made the probability that he would soon remember it remote. He let himself into the house with a latchkey which had been given to him, and turned on the light in the hall by means of a switch at the side of the door. He crossed the hall to the foot of the stairs, and was about to turn off the light, using the switch there to which Ann Upcott had referred, when the door of the treasure-room opened. Betty appeared in the doorway.

"You are still up?" he said in a low voice, half pleased to find her still afoot and half regretful that she was losing her hours of sleep.

"Yes," and slowly her face softened to a smile. "I waited up for my lodger."

She held the door open, and he followed her back into the room.

"Let me look at you," she said, and having looked, she added: "Jim, something has happened to-night."

Jim nodded.

"What?" she asked.

"Let it wait till to-morrow, Betty!"

Betty smiled no longer. The light died out of her dark, haunting eyes. Lassitude and distress veiled them.

"Something terrible, then?" she said in a whisper.

"Yes," and she stretched out a hand to the back of a chair and steadied herself.

"Please tell me, now, Jim! I shall not sleep to-night unless you do; and oh, I am so tired!"

There was so deep a longing in her voice, so utter a weariness in the pose of her young body that Jim could not but yield.

"I'll tell you, Betty," he said gently. "Hanaud and I went to find Jean Cladel to-night. We found him dead. He had been murdered—cruelly."

Betty moaned and swayed upon her feet. She would have fallen had not Jim caught her in his arms.

"Betty!" he cried.

Betty buried her face upon his shoulder. He could feel the heave of her bosom against his heart.

"It's appalling!" she moaned. "Jean Cladel! . . . No one ever had heard of him till this morning . . . and now he's swept into this horror—like the rest of us! Oh, where will it end?"

Jim placed her in a chair and dropped on his knees beside her.

She was sobbing now, and he tried to lift her face up to his.

"My dear!" he whispered.

But she would not raise her head.

"No," she said in a stifled voice, "no," and she pressed her face deeper into the crook of his shoulder and clung to him with desperate hands.

"Betty!" he repeated, "I am so sorry. . . . But it'll all come right. I'm sure it will. Oh, Betty!" And whilst he spoke he cursed himself for the banality of his words. Why couldn't he find some ideas that were really fine with which to comfort her? Something better than these stupid commonplaces of "I am sorry" and "It will all straighten out"? But he couldn't, and it seemed that there was no necessity that he should. For her arms crept round his neck and held him close.

CHAPTER NINETEEN: *A Plan Frustrated*

THE road curled like a paper ribbon round the shoulder of a hill and dropped into a shallow valley. To the left a little below the level of the road, a stream ran swiftly through a narrow meadow of lush green grass. Beyond the meadow the wall of the valley rose rough with outcroppings of rock, and with every tuft of its herbage already brown from the sun. On the right the northern wall rose almost from the road's edge. The valley was long and curved slowly, and half-way along to the point where it disappeared a secondary road, the sort of road which is indicated in the motorist's hand-books by a dotted line, branched off to the left, crossed the stream by a stone bridge and vanished in a cleft of the southern wall. Beyond this branching road grew trees. The stream disappeared under them as though it ran into a cavern; the slopes on either side were hidden behind trees—trees so thick that here at this end the valley looked bare in the strong sunlight, but low trees, as if they had determined to harmonise with their environment. Indeed, the whole valley had a sort of doll's-house effect—it was so shallow and narrow and stunted. It tried to be a valley and succeeded in being a depression.

When the little two-seater car swooped round the shoulder of the hill and descended, the white ribbon of road was empty but for one tiny speck at the far end, behind which a stream of dust spurted and spread like smoke from the funnel of an engine.

"That motor dust is going to smother us when we pass," said Jim.

"We shall do as much for him," said Betty, looking over her shoulder from the steering wheel. "No, worse!" Behind the car the dust was a screen. "But I don't mind, do you, Jim?" she asked with a laugh, in which for the first time, with a heart of thankfulness, Jim heard a note of gaiety. "To be free of that town if only for an hour! Oh!" and Betty opened her lungs to the sunlight and the air. "This is my first hour of liberty for a week!"

Frobisher was glad, too, to be out upon the slopes of the Côte-d'Or. The city of Dijon was ringing that morning with the murder of Jean Cladel; you could not pass down a street but you heard his name mentioned and some sarcasms about the police. He wished to forget that nightmare of a visit to the street of Gambetta and the dreadful twisted figure on the floor of the back room.

"You'll be leaving it for good very soon, Betty," he said significantly.

Betty made a little grimace at him, and laid her hand upon his sleeve.

"Jim!" she said, and the colour rose into her face, and the car swerved across the road. "You musn't speak like that to the girl at the wheel," she said with a laugh as she switched the car back into its course, "or I shall run down the motor-cyclist and that young lady in the side-car."

"The young lady," said Jim, "happens to be a port-manteau!"

The motor-cyclist, indeed, was slowing down as he came nearer to the branching road, like a tourist un-acquainted with the country, and when he actually reached it he stopped altogether and dismounted. Betty brought her car to a standstill beside him, and glanced at the clock and the speedometer in front of her.

"Can I help you?" she asked.

The man standing beside the motor-cycle was a young man, slim, dark, and of a pleasant countenance. He took off his helmet and bowed politely.

"Madame, I am looking for Dijon," he said in a harsh accent which struck Frobisher as somehow familiar to his ears.

"Monsieur, you can see the tip of it through that gap

across the valley," Betty returned. In the very centre of the cleft the point of the soaring spire of the cathedral stood up like a delicate lance. "But I warn you that that way, though short, is not good."

Through the gradually thinning cloud of dust which hung behind the car they heard the jug-jug of another motor-cycle.

"The road by which we have come is the better one," she continued.

"But how far is it?" the young man asked.

Betty once more consulted her speedometer.

"Forty kilometres, and we have covered them in forty minutes, so that you can see the going is good. We started at eleven punctually, and it is now twenty minutes to twelve."

"Surely we started before eleven?" Jim interposed.

"Yes, but we stopped for a minute or two to tighten the strap of the tool-box on the edge of the town. And we started from there at eleven."

The motor-cyclist consulted his wrist-watch.

"Yes, it's twenty minutes to twelve now," he said. "But forty kilometres! I doubt if I have the essence. I think I must try the nearer road."

The second motor-cycle came out of the dust like a boat out of a sea mist and slowed down in turn at the side of them. The rider jumped out of his saddle, pushed his goggles up on to his forehead and joined in the conversation.

"That little road, Monsieur. It is not one of the national highways. That shows itself at a glance. But it is not so bad. From the stone bridge one can be at the Hôtel de Ville of Dijon in twenty-five minutes."

"I thank you," said the young man. "You will pardon me. I have been here for seven minutes, and I am expected."

He replaced his helmet, mounted his machine, and with a splutter and half a dozen explosions ran down into the bed of the valley.

The second cyclist readjusted his goggles.

"Will you go first, Madame?" he suggested. "Otherwise I give you my dust."

"Thank you!" said Betty with a smile, and she slipped in the clutch and started.

Beyond the little forest and the curve the ground rose and the valley flattened out. Across their road a broad highway set with kilometre stones ran north and south.

"The road to Paris," said Betty as she stopped the car in front of a little inn with a tangled garden at the angle. She looked along the road Pariswards. "Air!" she said, and drew a breath of longing, whilst her eyes kindled and her white strong teeth clicked as though she was biting a sweet fruit.

"Soon, Betty," said Jim. "Very soon!"

Betty drove the car into a little yard at the side of the river.

"We will lunch here, in the garden," she said, "all amongst the earwigs and the roses."

An omelet, a cutlet perfectly cooked and piping hot, with a salad and a bottle of Clos du Prince of the 1904 vintage brought the glowing city of Paris immeasurably nearer to them. They sat in the open under the shade of a tall hedge; they had the tangled garden to themselves; they laughed and made merry in the golden May, and visions of wonder trembled and opened before Jim Frobisher's eyes.

Betty swept them away, however, when he had lit a cigar and she a cigarette; and their coffee steamed from the little cups in front of them.

"Let us be practical, Jim," she said. "I want to talk to you."

The sparkle of gaiety had left her face.

"Yes!" he asked.

"About Ann." Her eyes swept round and rested on Jim's face. "She ought to go."

"Run away!" cried Jim with a start.

"Yes, at once and as secretly as possible."

Jim turned the proposal over in his mind whilst Betty waited in suspense.

"It couldn't be managed," he objected.

"It could."

"Even if it could, would she consent?"

"She does."

"Of course it's pleading guilty," he said slowly.

"Oh, it isn't, Jim. She wants time, that's all. Time for my necklace to be traced, time for the murderer of Jean Cladel to be discovered. You remember what I told you about Hanaud? He must have his victim. You wouldn't believe me, but it's true. He has got to go back to Paris and say, 'You see, they sent from Dijon for me, and five minutes! That's all I needed! Five little minutes and there's your murderess, all tied up and safe!' He tried to fix it on me first."

"No."

"He did, Jim. And now that has failed he has turned on Ann. She'll have to go. Since he can't get me he'll take my friend—yes, and manufacture the evidence into the bargain."

"Betty! Hanaud wouldn't do that!" Frobisher protested.

"But, Jim, he has done it," she said.

"When?"

"When he put that Edinburgh man's book about the arrow poison back upon the bookshelf in the library."

Jim was utterly taken back.

"Did you know that he had done that?"

"I couldn't help knowing," she answered. "The moment he took the book down it was clear to me. He knew it from end to end, as if it was a primer. He could put his finger on the plates, on the history of my uncle's arrow, on the effect of the poison, on the solution that could be made of it in an instant. He pretended that he had learnt all that in the half-hour he waited for us. It wasn't possible. He had found that book the afternoon before somewhere and had taken it away with him secretly and sat up half the night over it. That's what he had done."

Jim Frobisher was sunk in confusion. He had been guessing first this person, then that, and in the end had had to be told the truth; whereas Betty had reached it in a flash by using her wits. He felt that he had been just one minute and a half in the bull-ring.

Betty added in a hot scorn:

"Then when he had learnt it all up by heart he puts it back secretly in the bookshelf and accuses us."

"But he admits he put it back," said Jim slowly.

Betty was startled.

"When did he admit it?"

"Last night. To me," replied Jim, and Betty laughed bitterly. She would hear no good of Hanaud.

"Yes, now that he has something better to go upon."

"Something better?"

"The disappearance of my necklace. Oh, Jim, Ann has got to go. If she could get to England they couldn't bring her back, could they? They haven't evidence enough. It's only suspicion and suspicion and suspicion. But here in France it's different, isn't it? They can hold people on suspicion, keep them shut up by themselves and question them again and again. Oh, yesterday afternoon in the hall—don't you remember, Jim?—I thought Hanaud was going to arrest her there and then."

Jim Frobisher nodded.

"I thought so, too."

He had been a little shocked by Betty's proposal, but the more familiar he became with it, the more it appealed to him. There was an overpowering argument in its favour of which neither he nor Hanaud had told Betty a word. The shaft of the arrow had been discovered in Ann Upcott's room, and the dart in the house of Jean Cladel. These were overpowering facts. On the whole, it was better that Ann should go, now, whilst there was still time—if, that is, Hanaud did undoubtedly believe her to be guilty.

"But it is evident that he does," cried Betty.

Jim answered slowly:

"I suppose he does. We can make sure, anyway. I had a doubt last night. So I asked him point-blank."

"And he answered you?" Betty asked with a gasp.

"Yes and no. He gave me the strangest answer."

"What did he say?"

"He told me to visit the Church of Notre Dame. If I did, I should read upon the façade whether Ann was innocent or not."

Slowly every tinge of colour ebbed out of Betty's face. Her eyes stared at him horror-stricken. She sat, a figure of ice—except for her eyes which blazed.

"That's terrible," she said with a low voice, and again "That's terrible!" Then with a cry she stood erect. "You shall see! Come!" and she ran towards the motor-car.

The sunlit day was spoilt for both of them. Betty drove homewards, bending over the wheel, her eyes fixed ahead. But Frobisher wondered whether she saw anything at all of that white road which the car devoured. Once as they dropped from the highland and the forests to the plains, she said:

"We shall abide by what we see?"

"Yes."

"If Hanaud thinks her innocent, she should stay. If he thinks her guilty, she must go."

"Yes," said Frobisher.

Betty guided the car through the streets of the city, and into a wide square. A great church of the Renaissance type, with octagonal cupolas upon its two towers and another little cupola surmounted by a loggia above its porch, confronted them. Betty stopped the car and led Frobisher into the porch. Above the door was a great bas-relief of the Last Judgment, God amongst the clouds, angels blowing trumpets, and the damned rising from their graves to undergo their torments. Both Betty and Frobisher gazed at the representation for a while in silence. To Frobisher it was a cruel and brutal piece of work which well matched Hanaud's revelation of his true belief.

"Yes, the message is easy to read," he said: and they drove back in a melancholy silence to the Maison Grenelle.

The chauffeur, Georges, came forward from the garage to take charge of the car. Betty ran inside the house and waited for Jim Frobisher to join her.

"I am so sorry," she said in a broken voice. "I kept a hope somewhere that we were all mistaken . . . I mean as to the danger Ann was in. . . . I don't believe for a moment in her guilt, of course. But she must go—that's clear."

She went slowly up the stairs, and Jim saw no more of her until dinner was served long after its usual hour. Ann Upcott he had not seen at all that day, nor did he even see her then. Betty came to him in the library a few minutes before nine.

"We are very late, I am afraid. There are just the two of us, Jim," she said with a smile, and she led the way into the dining-room.

Through the meal she was anxious and preoccupied, nodding her assent to anything that he said, with her thoughts far away and answering him at random, or not answering him at all. She was listening, Frobisher fancied, for some sound in the hall, an expected sound which was overdue. For her eyes went continually to the clock, and a flurry and agitation, very strange in one naturally so still, became more and more evident in her manner. At length, just before ten o'clock, they both heard the horn of a motor-car in the quiet street. The car stopped, as it seemed to Frobisher, just outside the gates, and upon that there followed the sound for which Betty had so anxiously been listening—the closing of a heavy door by some one careful to close it quietly. Betty shot a quick glance at Jim Frobisher and coloured when he intercepted it. A few seconds afterwards the car moved on, and Betty drew a long breath. Jim Frobisher leaned forward to Betty. Though they were alone in the room, he spoke in a low voice of surprise:

"Ann Upcott has gone then?"

"Yes."

"So soon? You had everything already arranged then?"

"It was all arranged yesterday evening. She should be in Paris to-morrow morning, England to-morrow night. If only all goes well!"

Even in the stress of her anxiety Betty had been sensitive to a tiny note of discontent in Jim Frobisher's questions. He had been left out of the counsels of the two girls, their arrangements had been made without his participation, he had only been told of them at the last minute, just as if he was a babbler not to be trusted and an incompetent whose advice would only have been a waste of time. Betty made her excuses.

"It would have been better, of course, if we had got you to help us, Jim. But Ann wouldn't have it. She insisted that you had come out here on my account, and that you mustn't be dragged into such an affair as her flight and escape at all. She made it a condition, so I had to give way. But you can help me now tremendously."

Jim was appeased. Betty at all events had wanted him, was still alarmed lest their plan undertaken without his advice might miscarry.

"How can I help?"

"You can go to that cinema and keep Monsieur Hanaud engaged. It's important that he should know nothing about Ann's flight until late to-morrow."

Jim laughed at the futility of Hanaud's devices to hide himself. It was obviously all over the town that he spent his evenings in the Grande Taverne.

"Yes, I'll go," he returned. "I'll go now."

But Hanaud was not that night in his accustomed place, and Jim sat there alone until half-past ten. Then a man strolled out from one of the billiard-rooms, and standing behind Jim with his eyes upon the screen, said in a whisper:

"Do not look at me, Monsieur! It is Moreau. I go outside. Will you please to follow."

He strolled away. Jim gave him a couple of minutes' grace. He had remembered Hanaud's advice and had paid for his Bock when it had been brought to him. The little saucer was turned upside down to show that he owed nothing. When two minutes had elapsed he sauntered out and, looking neither to the right nor to the left, strolled indolently along the Rue de la Gare. When he reached the Place Darcy Nicolas Moreau passed him without a sign of recognition and struck off to the right along the Rue de la Liberté. Frobisher followed him with a sinking heart. It was folly of course to imagine that Hanaud could be so easily eluded. No doubt that motor-car had been stopped. No doubt Ann Upcott was already under lock and key! Why, the last words he had heard Hanaud speak were "I must be quick!"

Moreau turned off into the Boulevard Sevigné and, doubling back to the station square, slipped into one of the small hotels which cluster in that quarter. The lobby was empty; a staircase narrow and steep led from it to the upper stories. Moreau now ascended it with Frobisher at his heels, and opened a door. Frobisher looked into a small and dingy sitting-room at the back of the house. The windows were open, but the shutters were closed. A single pendant in the centre of the room gave it light, and at a table under the pendant Hanaud sat poring over a map.

The map was marked with red ink in a curious way. A sort of hoop, very much the shape of a tennis racket without its handle, was described upon it and from the butt to the top of the hoop an irregular line was drawn, separating the hoop roughly into two semi-circles. Moreau left Jim Frobisher standing there, and in a moment or two Hanaud looked up.

"Did you know, my friend," he asked very gravely, "that Ann Upcott has gone to-night to Madame Le Vay's fancy dress ball?"

Frobisher was taken completely by surprise.

"No, I see that you didn't," Hanaud went on. He took up his pen and placed a red spot at the edge of the hoop close by the butt.

Jim recovered from his surprise. Madame Le Vay's ball was the spot from which the start was to be made. The plan after all was not so ill-devised, if only Ann could have got to the ball unnoticed. Masked and in fancy dress, amongst a throng of people similarly accoutred, in a house with a garden, no doubt thrown open upon this hot night and lit only by lanterns discreetly dim—she had thus her best chance of escape. But the chance was already lost. For Hanaud laid down his pen again and said in ominous tones:

"The water-lily, eh? That pretty water-lily, my friend, will not dance very gaily to-night."

CHAPTER TWENTY: *A Map and the Necklace*

HANAUD turned his map round and pushed it across the table to Jim Frobisher.

"What do you make of that?" he asked, and Jim drew up a chair and sat down to examine it.

He made first of all a large scale map of Dijon and its environments, the town itself lying at the bottom of the red hoop and constituting the top of the handle of the tennis racket. As to the red circle, it seemed to represent a tour which some one had made out from Dijon, round a good tract of outlying country and back again to the city. But there was more to it than that. The wavy dividing line, for instance, from the top of the circle to the handle, that is to Dijon; and on the left-hand edge of the hoop, as he bent over the map, and just outside Dijon, the red mark, a little red square which Hanaud had just made. Against this square an hour was marked.

"Eleven a.m.," he read.

He followed the red curve with his eyes and just where this dividing line touched the rim of the hoop, another period was inscribed. Here Frobisher read:

"Eleven forty."

Frobisher looked up at Hanaud in astonishment.

"Good God!" he exclaimed, and he bent again over the map. The point where the dividing line branched off was in a valley, as he could see by the contours—yes—he had found the name now—the Val Terzon. Just before eleven o'clock Betty had stopped the car just outside Dijon, opposite a park with a big house standing back, and had asked him to tighten the strap of the tool box. They had started again exactly at eleven. Betty had taken note of the exact time—and they had stopped where the secondary road branched off and doubled back to Dijon, at the top of the hoop, at the injunction of the rim and the dividing line, exactly at eleven forty.

"This is a chart of the expedition we made to-day," he cried. "We were followed then?"

He remembered suddenly the second motor-cyclist who had come up from behind through the screen of their dust and had stopped by the side of their car to join in their conversation with the tourist.

"The motor-cyclist?" he asked, and again he got no answer.

But the motor-cyclist had not followed them all the way round. On their homeward course they had stopped to lunch in the tangled garden. There had been no sign of the man. Jim looked at the map again. He followed the red line from the junction of the two roads, round the curve of the valley, to the angle where the great National road to Paris cut across and where they had lunched. After luncheon they had continued along the National road into Dijon, whereas the red line crossed it and came back by a longer and obviously a less frequented route.

"I can't imagine why you had us followed this morning, Monsieur Hanaud," he exclaimed with some heat. "But I can tell you this. The chase was not very efficiently contrived. We didn't come home that way at all."

"I haven't an idea how you came home," Hanaud answered imperturbably. "The line on that side of the circle has nothing to do with you at all, as you can see for yourself by looking at the time marked where the line begins."

The red hoop at the bottom was not complete; there was a space where the spliced handle of the racket would fit in, the space filled by the town of Dijon, and at the point on the right hand side where the line started Frobisher read in small but quite clear figures:

"Ten twenty-five a.m."

Jim was more bewildered than ever.

"I don't understand one word of it," he cried.

Hanaud reached over and touched the point with the tip of his pen.

"This is where the motor-cyclist started, the cyclist who met you at the branch road at eleven-forty."

"The tourist?" asked Jim. A second ago it had seemed to him impossible that the fog could thicken about his wits any more. And yet it had.

"Let us say the man with the portmanteau on his trailer," Hanaud corrected. "You see that he left his starting point in Dijon thirty-five minutes before you left yours. The whole manœuvre seems to have been admirably planned. For you met precisely at the arranged spot at eleven-forty. Neither the car nor the cycle had to wait one moment."

"Manœuvre! Arranged spot!" Frobisher exclaimed, looking about him in a sort of despair. "Has every one gone crazy? Why in the world should a man start out with a portmanteau in a side-car from Dijon at ten twenty-five, run thirty or forty miles into the country by a roundabout road and then return by a bad straight track? There's no sense in it!"

"No doubt it's perplexing," Hanaud agreed. He nodded to Moreau who went out of the room by a communicating door towards the front of the house. "But I can help you," Hanaud continued. "At the point where you started after tightening the strap of the tool-box, on the edge of the town, a big country house stands back in a park?"

"Yes," said Jim.

"That is the house of Madame Le Vay where this fancy dress ball takes place to-night."

"Madame Le Vay's château!" Frobisher repeated. "Where——" he began a question and caught it back. But Hanaud completed it for him.

"Yes, where Ann Upcott now is. You started from it at precisely eleven in the morning." He looked at his watch. "It is not yet quite eleven at night. So she is still there."

Frobisher started back in his chair. Hanaud's words were like the blade of silver light cutting through the darkness of the cinema hall and breaking into a sheet of radiance upon the screen. The meaning of the red diagram upon Hanaud's map, the unsuspected motive of Betty's expedition this morning were revealed to him.

"It was a rehearsal," he cried.

Hanaud nodded.

"A time-rehearsal."

"Yes, the sort of thing which takes place in theatres, without the principal members of the company," thought Frobisher. But a moment later he was dissatisfied with that explanation.

"Wait a moment!" he said. "That won't do, I fancy."

The motor-cyclist with the side-car had brought his arguments to a standstill. His times were marked upon the map; they were therefore of importance. What had he to do with Ann Upcott's escape? But he visualised the motor-cyclist and his side-car and his connection with the affair became evident. The big portmanteau gave Frobisher the clue. Ann Upcott would be leaving Madame Le Vay's house in her ball-dress, just as if she was returning to the Maison Grenelle—and without any luggage at all. She could not arrive in Paris in the morning like that if she were to avoid probably suspicion and certainly remark. The motor-cyclist was to meet her in the Val Terzon, transfer her luggage rapidly to her car, and then return to Dijon by the straight quick road whilst Ann turned off at the end of the valley to Paris. He remembered now that seven minutes had elapsed between the meeting of the cycle and the motor-car and their separation. Seven minutes then were allowed for the transference of the luggage. Another argument flashed into his thoughts. Betty had told him nothing of this plan. It had been presented to him as a mere excursion on a summer day, her first hours of liberty naturally

employed. Her silence was all of a piece with the deter-
mination of Betty and Ann Upcott to keep him altogether
out of the conspiracy. Every detail fitted like the blocks
in a picture puzzle. Yes, there had been a time-rehearsal.
And Hanaud knew all about it!

That was the disturbing certainty which first overwhelmed Frobisher when he had got the better of his
surprise at the scheme itself. Hanaud knew! and Betty
had so set her heart on Ann's escape.

"Let her go!" he pleaded earnestly. "Let Ann Upcott
get away to Paris and to England!" and Hanaud leaned
back in his chair with a little gasp. The queerest smile
broke over his face.

"I see," he said.

"Oh, I know," Frobisher exclaimed, hotly appealing.
"You are of the *Sûreté* and I am a lawyer, an officer of
the High Court in my country and I have no right to
make such a petition. But I do without a scruple. You
can't get a conviction against Ann Upcott. You haven't
a chance of it. But you can throw such a net of suspicion
about her that she'll never get out of it. You can ruin
her—yes—but that's all you can do."

"You speak very eagerly, my friend," Hanaud interposed.

Jim could not explain that it was Betty's anxiety to
save her friend which inspired his plea. He fell back
upon the scandal which such a trial would cause.

"There has been enough publicity already owing to
Boris Waberski," he continued. "Surely Miss Harlowe
has had distress enough. Why must she stand in the
witness-box and give evidence against her friend in a
trial which can have no result? That's what I want you
to realise, Monsieur Hanaud. I have had some experience of criminal trials"—O shade of Mr. Haslitt! Why
was that punctilious man not there in the flesh to wipe
out with an indignant word the slur upon the firm of
Frobisher and Haslitt?—"And I assure you that no jury
could convict upon such evidence. Why, even the pearl

necklace has not been traced—and it never will be. You can take that from me, Monsieur Hanaud! It never will be!"

Hanaud opened a drawer in the table and took out one of those little cedar-wood boxes made to hold a hundred cigarettes, which the better class of manufacturers use in England for their wares. He pushed this across the table towards Jim. Something which was more substantial than cigarettes rattled inside of it. Jim seized upon it in a panic. He had not a doubt that Betty would far sooner lose her necklace altogether than that her friend Ann Upcott should be destroyed by it. He opened the lid of the box. It was filled with cotton-wool. From the cotton-wool he took a string of pearls perfectly graded in size, and gleaming softly with a pink lustre which, even to his untutored eyes, was indescribably lovely.

"It would have been more correct if I had found them in a matchbox," said Hanaud. "But I shall point out to Monsieur Bex that after all matches and cigarettes are akin."

Jim was still staring at the necklace in utter disappointment when Moreau knocked upon the other side of the communicating door. Hanaud looked again at his watch.

"Yes, it is eleven o'clock. We must go. The car has started from the house of Madame Le Vay."

He rose from his chair, buried the necklace again within the layers of cotton-wool, and locked it up once more in the drawer. The room had faded away from Jim Frobisher's eyes. He was looking at a big, brilliantly illuminated house, and a girl who slipped from a window and, wrapping a dark cloak about her glistening dress, ran down the dark avenue in her dancing slippers to where a car waited hidden under trees.

"The car may not have started," Jim said with sudden hopefulness. "There may have been an accident to it. The chauffeur may be late. Oh, a hundred things may have happened!"

"With a scheme so carefully devised, so meticulously rehearsed? No, my friend."

Hanaud took an automatic pistol from a cabinet against the wall and placed it in his pocket.

"You are going to leave that necklace just like that in a table drawer?" Jim asked. "We ought to take it first to the Prefecture."

"This room is not unwatched," replied Hanaud. "It will be safe."

Jim hopefully tried another line of argument.

"We shall be too late now to intercept Ann Upcott at the branch road," he argued. "It is past eleven, as you say—well past eleven. And thirty-five minutes on a motor-cycle in the daytime means fifty minutes in a car at night, especially with a bad road to travel."

"We don't intend to intercept Ann Upcott at the branch road," Hanaud returned. He folded up the map and put it aside upon the mantelshelf.

"I take a big risk, you know," he said softly. "But I must take it! And—no! I can't be wrong!" But he turned from the mantelshelf with a very anxious and troubled face. Then, as he looked at Jim, a fresh idea came into his mind.

"By the way," he said. "The façade of Notre Dame?" Jim nodded.

"The bas-relief of The Last Judgment. We went to see it. We thought your way of saying what you believed a little brutal."

Hanaud remained silent with his eyes upon the floor for a few seconds. Then he said quietly: "I am sorry." He tacked on a question. "You say 'we'?"

"Mademoiselle Harlowe and I," Jim explained.

"Oh, yes—to be sure. I should have thought of that," and once more his troubled cry broke from him. "It must be that!—No, I can't be wrong. . . . Anyway, it's too late to change now."

A second time Moreau rapped upon the communicating door. Hanaud sprang to alertness.

"That's it," he said. "Take your hat and stick, Monsieur Frobisher! Good! You are ready?" and the room was at once plunged into darkness.

Hanaud opened the communicating door, and they passed into the front room—a bedroom looking out upon the big station square. This room was in darkness too. But the shutters were not closed, and there were patches of light upon the walls from the lamps in the square and the Grande Taverne at the corner. The three men could see one another, and to Jim in this dusk the faces of his companions appeared of a ghastly pallor.

"Daunay took his position when I first knocked," said Moreau. "Patinot has just joined him."

He pointed across the square to the station buildings. Some cabs were waiting for the Paris train, and in front of them two men dressed like artisans were talking. One of them lit a cigarette from the stump of a cigarette held out to him by his companion. The watchers in the room saw the end of the cigarette glow red.

"The way is clear, Monsieur," said Moreau. "We can go." And he turned and went out of the inn to the staircase. Jim started to follow him. Whither they were going Jim had not a notion, not even a conjecture. But he was gravely troubled. All his hopes and Betty's hopes for the swift and complete suppression of the Waberski affair had seemingly fallen to the ground. He was not reassured when Hanaud's hand was laid on his arm and detained him.

"You understand, Monsieur Frobisher," said Hanaud with a quiet authority, his eyes shining very steadily in the darkness, his face glimmering very white, "that now the Law of France takes charge. There must not be a finger raised or a word spoken to hinder officers upon their duty. On the other hand, I make you in return the promise you desire. No one shall be arrested on suspicion. Your own eyes shall bear me out."

The two men followed Moreau down the stairs and into the street.

CHAPTER TWENTY-ONE: *The Secret House*

I T was a dark, clear night, the air very still and warm, and the sky bright with innumerable stars. The small company penetrated into the town by the backways and narrow alleys. Daunay going on ahead, Patinot the last by some thirty yards, and Moreau keeping upon the opposite side of the street. Once they had left behind them the lights of the station square, they walked amongst closed doors and the blind faces of unlit houses. Frobisher's heart raced within his bosom. He strained his eyes and ears for some evidence of spies upon their heels. But no one was concealed in any porch, and not the stealthiest sound of a pursuit was borne to their hearing.

"On a night like this," he said in tones which, strive as he might to steady them, were still a little tremulous, "one could hear a footstep on the stones a quarter of a mile away, and we hear nothing. Yet, if there is a gang, it can hardly be that we are unwatched."

Hanaud disagreed. "This is a night for alibis," he returned, lowering his voice; "good, sound, incontestable alibis. All but those engaged will be publicly with their friends, and those engaged do not know how near we are to their secrets."

They turned into a narrow street and kept on its left-hand side.

"Do you know where we are?" Hanaud asked. "No? Yet we are near to the Maison Grenelle. On the other side of these houses to our left runs the street of Charles-Robert."

Jim Frobisher stopped dead.

"It was here, then, that you came last night after I left you at the Prefecture," he exclaimed.

"Ah, you recognised me, then!" Hanaud returned imperturbably. "I wondered whether you did when you turned at the gates of your house."

On the opposite side of the street the houses were broken by a high wall, in which two great wooden doors were set. Behind the wall, at the end of a courtyard, the upper storey and the roof of a considerable house rose in a steep ridge against the stars.

Hanaud pointed towards it.

"Look at that house, Monsieur! There Madame Raviart came to live whilst she waited to be set free. It belongs to the Maison Grenelle. After she married Simon Harlowe, they would never let it, they kept it just as it was, the shrine of their passion—that strange romantic couple. But there was more romance in that, to be sure. It has been unoccupied ever since."

Jim Frobisher felt a chill close about his heart. Was that house the goal to which Hanaud was leading him with so confident a step? He looked at the gates and the house. Even in the night it had a look of long neglect and decay, the paint peeling from the doors and not a light in any window.

Some one in the street, however, was awake, for just above their heads, a window was raised with the utmost caution and a whisper floated down to them.

"No one has appeared."

Hanaud took no open notice of the whisper. He did not pause in his walk, but he said to Frobisher:

"And, as you hear, it is still unoccupied."

At the end of the street Daunay melted away altogether. Hanaud and Frobisher crossed the road and, with Moreau just ahead, turned down a passage between the houses to the right.

Beyond the passage they turned again to the right into a narrow lane between high walls; and when they had covered thirty yards or so, Frobisher saw the branches of leafy trees over the wall upon his right. It was so dark here under the shade of the boughs that Frobisher could not even see his companions; and he knocked against

Moreau before he understood that they had come to the end of their journey. They were behind the garden of the house in which Madame Raviart had lived and loved.

Hanaud's hand tightened upon Jim Frobisher's arm, constraining him to absolute immobility. Patinot had vanished as completely and noiselessly as Daunay. The three men left stood in the darkness and listened. A sentence which Ann Upcott had spoken in the garden of the Maison Grenelle, when she had been describing the terror with which she had felt the face bending over her in the darkness, came back to him. He had thought it false then. He took back his criticism now. For he too imagined that the beating of his heart must wake all Dijon.

They stood there motionless for the space of a minute, and then, at a touch from Hanaud, Nicolas Moreau stooped. Frobisher heard the palm of his hand sliding over wood and immediately after the tiniest little click as a key was fitted into a lock and turned. A door in the wall swung silently open and let a glimmer of light into the lane. The three men passed into a garden of weeds and rank grass and overgrown bushes. Moreau closed and locked the door behind them. As he locked the door the clocks of the city struck the half hour.

Hanaud whispered in Frobisher's ear:

"They have not yet reached the Val Terzon. Come!"

They crept over the mat of grass and weeds to the back of the house. A short flight of stone steps, patched with mould, descended from a terrace; at the back of the terrace were shuttered windows. But in the corner of the house, on a level with the garden, there was a door. Once more Moreau stooped, and once more a door swung inwards without a sound. But whereas the garden door had let through some gleam of twilight, this door opened upon the blackness of the pit. Jim Frobisher shrank back from it, not in physical fear but in an appalling dread that some other man than he, wearing his clothes and his flesh, would come out of that door again. His heart came to a standstill, and then Hanaud pushed him gently into the passage. The door was closed behind them, an almost inaudible sound told him that now the door was locked.

"Listen!" Hanaud whispered sharply. His trained ear had caught a sound in the house above them. And in a second Frobisher heard it too, a sound regular and continuous and very slight, but in that uninhabited house filled with uttermost blackness, very daunting. Gradually the explanation dawned upon Jim.

"It's a clock ticking," he said under his breath.

"Yes! A clock ticking away in the empty house!" returned Hanaud. And though his answer was rather breathed than whispered, there was a queer thrill in it the sound of which Jim could not mistake. The hunter had picked up his spoor. Just beyond the quarry would come in view.

Suddenly a thread of light gleamed along the passage, lit up a short flight of stairs and a door on the right at the head of them, and went out again. Hanaud slipped his electric torch back into his pocket and, passing Moreau, took the lead. The door at the head of the stairs opened with a startling whine of its hinges. Frobisher stopped with his heart in his throat, though what he feared he could not have told even himself. Again the thread of light shone, and this time it explored. The three found themselves in a stone-flagged hall.

Hanaud crossed it, extinguished his torch and opened a door. A broken shutter, swinging upon a hinge, enabled them dimly to see a gallery which stretched away into the gloom. The faint light penetrating from the window showed them a high double door leading to some room at the back of the house. Hanaud stole over the boards and laid his ear to the panel. In a little while he was satisfied; his hand dropped to the knob and a leaf of the door opened noiselessly. Once more the torch glowed. Its beam played upon the high ceiling, the tall windows shrouded in heavy curtains of red silk brocade, and re-

vealed to Frobisher's amazement a room which had a
look of daily use. All was orderly and clean, the furniture polished and in good repair; there were fresh flowers
in the vases, whose perfume filled the air; and it was
upon the marble chimney-piece of this room that the clock
ticked.

The room was furnished with lightness and elegance,
except for one fine and massive press, with double doors
in marquetry, which occupied a recess near to the fire-
place. Girandoles with mirrors and gilt frames, now
fitted with electric lights, were fixed upon the walls, with
a few pictures in water-colour. A chandelier glittering
with lustres hung from the ceiling, an Empire writing-
table stood near the window, a deep-cushioned divan
stretched along the wall opposite the fire-place. So much
had Frobisher noticed when the light again went out.
Hanaud closed the door upon the room again.

"We shall be hidden in the embrasure of any of these
windows," Hanaud whispered, when they were once more
in the long gallery. "No light will be shown here with
that shutter hanging loose, we may be sure. Meanwhile
let us watch and be very silent."

They took their stations in the deep shadows by the
side of the window with the broken shutter. They could
see dimly the courtyard and the great carriage doors in
the wall at the end of it, and they waited; Jim Frobisher
under such a strain of dread and expectancy that each
second seemed an hour, and he wondered at the immobility of his companions. The only sound of breathing
that he heard came from his own lungs.

In a while Hanaud laid a hand upon his sleeve, and the
clasp of the hand tightened and tightened. Motionless
though he stood like a man in a seizure, Hanaud too was
in the grip of an intense excitement. For one of the
great leaves of the courtyard door was opening silently.
It opened just a little way and as silently closed again.
But some one had slipped in—so vague and swift and
noiseless a figure that Jim would have believed his imag-

ination had misled him but for a thicker blot of darkness at the centre of the great door. There some one stood now who had not stood there a minute before, as silent and still as any of the watchers in the gallery, and more still than one. For Hanaud moved suddenly away on the tips of his toes into the deepest of the gloom and, sinking down upon his heels, drew his watch from his pocket. He drew his coat closely about it and for a fraction of a second flashed his torchlight on the dial. It was now five minutes past twelve.

"It is the time," he breathed as he crept back to his place. "Listen now!"

A minute passed and another. Frobisher found himself shivering as a man shivers at a photographer's when he is told by the operator to keep still. He had a notion that he was going to fall. Then a distant noise caught his ear, and at once his nerves grew steady. It was the throb of a motor-cycle, and it grew louder and louder. He felt Hanaud stiffen at his side. Hanaud had been right, then! The conviction deepened in his mind. When all had been darkness and confusion to him, Hanaud from the first had seen clearly. But what had he seen? Frobisher was still unable to answer that question, and whilst he fumbled amongst conjectures a vast relief swept over him. For the noise of the cycle had ceased altogether. It had roared through some contiguous street and gone upon its way into the open country. Not the faintest pulsation of its engine was any longer audible. That late-faring traveller had taken Dijon in his stride.

In a revulsion of relief he pictured him devouring the road, the glow of his lamp putting the stars to shame, the miles leaping away behind him; and suddenly the pleasant picture was struck from before his vision and his heart fluttered up into his throat. For the leaf of the great coach-door was swung wider, and closed again, and the motor-cycle with its side-car was within the courtyard. The rider had slipped out his clutch and stopped his engine more than a hundred yards away in the other street. His own impetus had been enough and more than enough to swing him round the corner along the road and into the courtyard. The man who had closed the door moved to his side as he dismounted. Between them they lifted something from the side-car and laid it on the ground. The watchman held open the door again, the cyclist wheeled out his machine, the door was closed, a key turned in the lock. Not a word had been spoken, not an unnecessary movement made. It had all happened within the space of a few seconds. The man waited by the gate, and in a little while from some other street the cyclist's engine was heard once more to throb. His work was done.

Jim Frobisher wondered that Hanaud should let him go. But Hanaud had eyes for no one but the man who was left behind and the big package upon the ground under the blank side wall. The man moved to it, stooped, raised it with an appearance of effort, then stood upright holding it in his arms. It was something shapeless and long and heavy. So much the watchers in the gallery could see, but no more.

The man in the courtyard moved towards the door without a sound; and Hanaud drew his companions back from the window of the broken shutter. Quick as they were, they were only just in time to escape from that revealing twilight. Already the intruder with his burden stood within the gallery. The front door was unlatched, that was clear. It had needed but a touch to open it. The intruder moved without a sound to the double door, of which Hanaud had opened one leaf. He stood in front of it, pushed it with his foot and both the leaves swung inwards. He disappeared into the room. But the faint misty light had fallen upon him for a second, and though none could imagine who he was, they all three saw that what he carried was a heavy sack.

Now, at all events, Hanaud would move, thought Frobisher. But he did not. They all heard the man now, but not his footsteps. It was just the brushing of his clothes against furniture: then came a soft, almost inaudible sound, as though he had laid his burden down upon the deep-cushioned couch: then he himself reappeared in the doorway, his arms empty, his hat pressed down upon his forehead, and a dim whiteness where his face should be. But dark as it was, they saw the glitter of his eyes.

"It will be now," Frobisher said to himself, expecting that Hanaud would leap from the gloom and bear the intruder to the ground.

But this man, too, Hanaud let go. He closed the doors again, drawing the two leaves together, and stole from the gallery. No one heard the outer door close, but with a startling loudness some metal thing rang upon stone, and within the house. Even Jim Frobisher understood that the outer door had been locked and the key dropped through the letter slot. The three men crept back to their window. They saw the intruder cross the courtyard, open one leaf of the coach door, peer this way and that and go. Again a key tinkled upon stones. The key of the great door had been pushed or kicked underneath it back into the courtyard. The clocks suddenly chimed the quarter. To Frobisher's amazement it was a quarter-past twelve. Between the moment when the cyclist rode his car in at the doors and now, just five minutes had elapsed. And again, but for the three men, the house was empty.

Or was it empty?

For Hanaud had slipped across to the door of the room and opened it; and a slight sound broke out of that black room, as of some living thing which moved uneasily. At Jim Frobisher's elbow Hanaud breathed a sigh of relief. Something, it seemed, had happened for which he had hardly dared to hope; some great dread he knew with certainty had not been fulfilled. On the heels of that sigh a sharp loud click rang out, the release of a spring, the withdrawal of a bolt. Hanaud drew the door swiftly to and the three men fell back. Some one had somehow entered that room, some one was moving quietly about it. From the corner of the corridor in which they had taken refuge, the three men saw the leaves of the door swing very slowly in upon their hinges. Some one appeared upon the threshold, and stood motionless, listening, and after a few seconds advanced across the gallery to the window. It was a girl—so much they could determine from the contour of her head and the slim neck. To the surprise of those three a second shadow flitted to her side. Both of them peered from the window into the courtyard. There was nothing to tell them there whether the midnight visitors had come and gone or not yet come at all. One of them whispered:

"The key!"

And the other, the shorter one, crept into the hall and returned with the key which had been dropped through the letter slot in her hand. The taller of the two laughed, and the sound of it, so clear, so joyous like the trill of a bird, it was impossible for Jim Frobisher even for a second to mistake. The second girl standing at the window of this dark and secret house, with the key in her hand to tell her that all that had been plotted had been done, was Betty Harlowe. Jim Frobisher had never imagined a sound so sinister, so alarming, as that clear, joyous laughter lilting through the silent gallery. It startled him, it set his whole faith in the world shuddering.

"There must be some good explanation," he argued, but his heart was sinking amidst terrors. Of what dreadful event was that laughter to be the prelude?

The two figures at the window flitted back across the gallery. It seemed that there was no further reason for precautions.

"Shut the door, Francine," said Betty in her ordinary voice. And when this was done, within the room the lights went on. But time and disuse had warped the doors. They did not quite close, and between them a golden strip of light showed like a wand.

"Let us see now!" cried Betty. "Let us see," and again she laughed; and under the cover of her laughter the three men crept forward and looked in: Moreau upon his knees, Frobisher stooping above him, Hanaud at his full height behind them all.

CHAPTER TWENTY-TWO: *The Corona Machine*

THE detective's hand fell softly upon Frobisher's shoulder warning him to silence; and this warning was needed. The lustres of the big glass chandelier were so many flashing jewels; the mirrors of the girandoles multiplied their candle-lamps; the small gay room was ablaze; and in the glare Betty stood and laughed. Her white shoulders rose from a slim evening frock of black velvet; from her carefully dressed copper hair to her black satin shoes she was as trim as if she had just been unpacked from a bandbox; and she was laughing wholeheartedly at a closed sack on the divan, a sack which jerked and flapped grotesquely like a fish on a beach. Some one was imprisoned within that sack. Jim Frobisher could not doubt who that some one was, and it seemed to him that no sound more soulless and cruel had ever been heard in the world than Betty's merriment. She threw her head back: Jim could see her slender white throat working, her shoulders flashing and shaking. She clapped her hands with a horrible glee. Something died within Frobisher's breast as he heard it. Was it in his heart, he wondered? It was, however, to be the last time that Betty Harlowe laughed.

"You can get her out, Francine," she said, and whilst Francine with a pair of scissors cut the end of the sack loose, she sat down with her back to it at the writing-table and unlocked a drawer. The sack was cut away and thrown upon the floor, and now on the divan Ann Upcott lay in her gleaming dancing-dress, her hands bound behind her back, and her ankles tied cruelly together. Her hair was dishevelled, her face flushed, and she had the look of one quite dazed. She drew in deep breaths of air, with her bosom labouring. But she was unaware for the moment of her predicament or surroundings, and her eyes rested upon Francine and travelled from her to Betty's back without a gleam of recognition. She wrenched a little at her wrists, but even that movement was instinctive; and then she closed her eyes and lay still, so still that but for her breathing the watchers at the door would hardly have believed that she still lived.

Betty, meanwhile, lifted from the open drawer, first a small bottle half-filled with a pale yellow liquid, and next a small case of morocco leather. From the case she took a hypodermic syringe and its needle, and screwed the two parts together.

"Is she ready?" Betty asked as she removed the stopper from the bottle.

"Quite, Mademoiselle," answered Francine. She began with a giggle, but she looked at the prisoner as she spoke and she ended with a startled gasp. For Ann was looking straight at her with the strangest, disconcerting stare. It was impossible to say whether she knew Francine or knowing her would not admit her knowledge. But her gaze never faltered, it was actually terrifying by its fixity, and in a sharp, hysterical voice Francine suddenly cried out:

"Turn your eyes away from me, will you?" and she added with a shiver: "It's horrible, Mademoiselle! It's like a dead person watching you as you move about the room."

Betty turned curiously towards the divan and Ann's eyes wandered off to her. It seemed as though it needed just that interchange of glances to awaken her. For as Betty resumed her work of filling the hypodermic syringe from the bottle, a look of perplexity crept into Ann Upcott's face. She tried to sit up, and finding that she could not, tore at the cords which bound her wrists. Her feet kicked upon the divan. A moan of pain broke from her lips, and with that consciousness returned to her.

"Betty!" she whispered, and Betty turned with the

needle ready in her hand. She did not speak, but her face spoke for her. Her upper lip was drawn back a little from her teeth, and there was a look in her great eyes which appalled Jim Frobisher outside the door. Once before he had seen just that look—when Betty was lying on Mrs. Harlowe's bed for Hanaud's experiment and he had lingered in the treasure-room with Ann Upcott. It had been inscrutable to him then, but it was as plain as print now. It meant murder. And so Ann Upcott understood it. Helpless as she was, she shrank back upon the divan; in a panic she spoke with faltering lips and her eyes fixed upon Betty with a dreadful fascination.

"Betty! You had me taken and brought here! You sent me to Madame Le Vay's—on purpose. Oh! The letter, then! The anonymous letter!"—and a new light broke in upon Ann's mind, a new terror shook her. "You wrote it! Betty, you! You—the Scourge!"

She sank back and again struggled vainly with her bonds. Betty rose from her chair and crossed the room towards her, the needle shining bright in her hand. Her hapless prisoner saw it.

"What's that?" she cried, and she screamed aloud. The extremity of her horror lent to her an unnatural strength. Somehow she dragged herself up and got her feet to the ground. Somehow she stood upright, swaying as she stood.

"You are going to——" she began, and broke off. "Oh, no! You couldn't! You couldn't!"

Betty put out a hand and laid it on Ann's shoulder and held her so for a moment, savouring her vengeance.

"Whose face was it bending so close down over yours in the darkness?" she asked in a soft and dreadful voice. "Whose face, Ann? Guess!" She shook her swaying prisoner with a gentleness as dreadful as her quiet voice. "You talk too much. Your tongue's dangerous, Ann. You are too curious, Ann! What were you doing in the treasure-room yesterday evening with your watch in your

hand? Eh? Can't you answer, you pretty fool?" Then
Betty's voice changed. It remained low and quiet, but
hatred crept into it, a deep, whole-hearted hatred.

"You have been interfering with me too, haven't you,
Ann? Oh, we both understand very well!" And
Hanaud's hand tightened upon Frobisher's shoulder.
Here was the real key and explanation of Betty's hatred.
Ann Upcott knew too much, was getting to know more,
might at any moment light upon the whole truth. Yes!
Ann Upcott's disappearance would look like a panic-
stricken flight, would have the effect of a confession—
no doubt! But above all these considerations, paramount
in Betty Harlowe's mind was the resolve at once to punish
and rid herself of a rival.

"All this week, you have been thrusting yourself in my
way!" she said. "And here's your reward for it, Ann.
Yes. I had you bound hand and foot and brought here.
The water-lily!" She looked her victim over as she stood
in her delicate bright frock, her white silk stockings and
satin slippers, swaying in terror. "Fifteen minutes, Ann!
That fool of a detective was right! Fifteen minutes!
That's all the time the arrow-poison takes!"

Ann's eyes opened wide. The blood rushed into her
white face and ebbed, leaving it whiter than it was before.

"Arrow-poison!" she cried. "Betty! It was you, then!
Oh!" she would have fallen forward, but Betty Harlowe
pushed her shoulder gently and she fell back upon the
divan. That Betty had been guilty of that last infamy
—the murder of her benefactress—not until this moment had Ann Upcott for one moment suspected. It was
clear to her, too, that there was not the slightest hope
for her. She burst suddenly into a storm of tears.

Betty Harlowe sat down on the divan beside her and
watched her closely and curiously with a devilish enjoyment. The sound of the girl's sobbing was music in her
ears. She would not let it flag.

"You shall lie here in the dark all night, Ann, and
alone," she said in a low voice, bending over her. "To-

morrow Espinosa will put you under one of the stone flags in the kitchen. But to-night you shall lie just as you are. Come!"

She bent over Ann Upcott, gathering the flesh of her arm with one hand and advancing the needle with the other; and a piercing scream burst from Francine Rollard.

"Look!" she cried, and she pointed to the door. It was open and Hanaud stood upon the threshold.

Betty looked up at the cry and the blood receded from her face. She sat like an image of wax, staring at the open doorway, and a moment afterwards with a gesture swift as lightning she drove the needle into the flesh of her own arm and emptied it.

Frobisher with a cry of horror started forward to prevent her, but Hanaud roughly thrust him back.

"I warned you, Monsieur, not to interfere," he said with a savage note in his voice, which Jim had not heard before; and Betty Harlowe dropped the needle on to the couch, whence it rolled to the floor.

She sprang up now to her full height, her heels together, her arms outstretched from her sides.

"Fifteen minutes, Monsieur Hanaud," she cried with bravado. "I am safe from you."

Hanaud laughed and wagged his forefinger contemptuously in her face.

"Coloured water, Mademoiselle, doesn't kill."

Betty swayed upon her feet and steadied herself.

"Bluff, Monsieur Hanaud!" she said.

"We shall see."

The confidence of his tone convinced her. She flashed across the room to her writing-table. Swift as she was, Hanaud met her there.

"Ah, no!" he cried. "That's quite a different thing!" He seized her wrists. "Moreau!" he called, with a nod towards Francine. "And you, Monsieur Frobisher, will you release that young lady, if you please!"

Moreau dragged Francine Rollard from the room and locked her safely away. Jim seized upon the big scissors and cut the cords about Ann's wrists and ankles, and unwound them. He was aware that Hanaud had flung the chair from the writing-table into an open space, that Betty was struggling and then was still, that Hanaud had forced her into the chair and snatched up one of the cords which Frobisher had dropped upon the floor. When he had finished his work, he saw that Betty was sitting with her hands in handcuffs and her ankles tied to one of the legs of the chair; and Hanaud was staunching with his handkerchief a wound in his hand which bled. Betty had bitten him like a wild animal caught in a trap.

"Yes, you warned me, Mademoiselle, the first morning I met you," Hanaud said with a savage irony, "that you didn't wear a wrist-watch, because you hated things on your wrists. My apologies! I had forgotten!"

He went back to the writing-table and thrust his hand into the drawer. He drew out a small cardboard box and removed the lid.

"Five!" he said. "Yes! Five!"

He carried the box across the room to Frobisher, who was standing against the wall with a face like death.

"Look!"

There were five white tablets in the box.

"We know where the sixth is. Or, rather, we know where it was. For I had it analysed to-day. Cyanide of potassium, my friend! Crunch one of them between your teeth and—fifteen minutes? Not a bit of it! A fraction of a second! That's all!"

Frobisher leaned forward and whispered in Hanaud's ear. "Leave them within her reach!"

His first instinctive thought had been to hinder Betty from destroying herself. Now he prayed that she might, and with so desperate a longing that a deep pity softened Hanaud's eyes.

"I must not, Monsieur," he said gently. He turned to Moreau. "There is a cab waiting at the corner of the Maison Grenelle," and Moreau went in search of it. Hanaud went over to Ann Upcott, who was sitting upon the divan her head bowed, her body shivering. Every now and then she handled and eased one of her tortured wrists.

"Mademoiselle," he said, standing in front of her, "I owe you an explanation and an apology. I never from the beginning—no, not for one moment—believed that you were guilty of the murder of Madame Harlowe. I was sure that you had never touched the necklace of pink pearls—oh, at once I was sure, long before I found it. I believed every word of the story you told us in the garden. But none of this dared I shew you. For only by pretending that I was convinced of your guilt, could I protect you during this last week in the Maison Grenelle."

"Thank you, Monsieur," she replied with a wan effort at a smile.

"But, for to-night, I owe you an apology," he continued. "I make it with shame. That you were to be brought back here to the tender mercies of Mademoiselle Betty, I hadn't a doubt. And I was here to make sure you should be spared them. But I have never in my life had a more difficult case to deal with, so clear a conviction in my own mind, so little proof to put before a court. I had to have the evidence which I was certain to find in this room to-night. But I ask you to believe me that if I had imagined for a moment the cruelty with which you were to be handled, I should have sacrificed this evidence. I beg you to forgive me."

Ann Upcott held out her hand.

"Monsieur Hanaud," she replied simply, "but for you I should not be now alive. I should be lying here in the dark and alone, as it was promised to me, waiting for Espinosa—and his spade." Her voice broke and she shuddered violently so that the divan shook on which she sat.

"You must forget these miseries," he said gently. "You have youth, as I told you once before. A little time and——"

The return of Nicolas Moreau interrupted him; and

with Moreau came a couple of gendarmes and Girardot the Commissary.

"You have Francine Rollard?" Hanaud asked.

"You can hear her," Moreau returned dryly.

In the corridor a commotion arose, the scuffling of feet and a woman's voice screaming abuse. It died away.

"Mademoiselle here will not give you so much trouble," said Hanaud.

Betty was sitting huddled in her chair, her face averted and sullen, her lips muttering inaudible words. She had not once looked at Jim Frobisher since he had entered the room; nor did she now.

Moreau stooped and untied her ankles and a big gendarme raised her up. But her knees failed beneath her; she could not stand; her strength and her spirit had left her. The gendarme picked her up as if she had been a child; and as he moved to the door, Jim Frobisher planted himself in front of him.

"Stop!" he cried, and his voice was strong and resonant. "Monsieur Hanaud, you have said just now that you believed every word of Mademoiselle Ann's story."

"It is true."

"You believe then that Madame Harlowe was murdered at half-past ten on the night of the 27th of April. And at half-past ten Mademoiselle here was at Monsieur de Pouillac's ball! You will set her free."

Hanaud did not argue the point.

"And what of to-night?" he asked. "Stand aside, if you please!"

Jim held his ground for a moment or two, and then drew aside. He stood with his eyes closed, and such a look of misery upon his face as Betty was carried out that Hanaud attempted some clumsy word of condolence:

"This has been a bitter experience for you, Monsieur Frobisher," he began.

"Would that you had taken me into your confidence at the first!" Jim cried volubly.

"Would you have believed me if I had?" asked Hanaud, and Jim was silent. "As it was, Monsieur Frobisher, I took a grave risk which I know now I had not the right to take and I told you more than you think."

He turned away towards Moreau.

"Lock the courtyard doors and the door of the house after they have gone and bring the keys here to me."

Girardot had made a bundle of the solution, the hypodermic syringe, the tablets of cyanide, and the pieces of cord.

"There is something here of importance," Hanaud observed and, stooping at the writing-table, he picked up a square, flat-topped black case. "You will recognise this," he remarked to Jim as he handed it to Girardot. It was the case of a Corona typewriting machine; and from its weight, the machine itself was clearly within the case.

"Yes," Hanaud explained, as the door closed upon the Commissary. "This pretty room is the factory where all those abominable letters were prepared. Here the information was filed away for use; here the letters were typed; from here they were issued."

"Blackmailing letters!" cried Jim. "Letters demanding money!"

"Some of them," answered Hanaud.

"But Betty Harlowe had money. All that she needed, and more if she chose to ask for it."

"All that she needed? No," answered Hanaud with a shake of the head. "The blackmailer never has enough money. For no one is so blackmailed."

A sudden and irrational fury seized upon Frobisher. They had agreed, he and Hanaud, that there was a gang involved in all these crimes. It might be that Betty was of them, yes, even led them, but were they all to go scot-free?

"There are others," he exclaimed. "The man who rode this motor-cycle——"

"Young Espinosa," replied Hanaud. "Did you notice his accent when you stopped at the fork of the roads in the Val Terzon? He did not mount his cycle again. No!"

"And the man who carried in the—the sack?"

"Maurice Thevenet," said Hanaud. "That promising young novice. He is now at the Depot. He will never get that good word from me which was to unlock Paris for him."

"And Espinosa himself—who was to come here to-morrow——" he stopped abruptly with his eyes on Ann.

"And who murdered Jean Cladel, eh?" Hanaud went on. "A fool that fellow! Why use the Catalan's knife in the Catalan's way?" Hanaud looked at his watch. "It is over. No doubt Espinosa is under lock and key by now. And there are others, Monsieur, of whom you have never heard. The net has been cast wide to-night. Have no fear of that!"

Moreau returned with the keys and handed them to Hanaud. Hanaud put them into a pocket and went over to Ann Upcott.

"Mademoiselle, I shall not trouble you with any questions to-night. To-morrow you will tell me why you went to Madame Le Vay's ball. It was given out that you meant to run away. That, of course, was not true. You shall give me the real reason to-morrow and an account of what happened to you there."

Ann shivered at the memories of that night, but she answered quietly.

"Yes. I will tell you everything."

"Good. Then we can go," said Hanaud cheerfully.

"Go?" Ann Upcott asked in wonderment. "But you have had us all locked in."

Hanaud laughed. He had a little surprise to spring on the girl, and he loved surprises so long as they were of his own contriving.

"Monsieur Frobisher, I think, must have guessed the truth. This house, Mademoiselle, the Hôtel de Brebizart is very close, as the crow flies, to the Maison Grenelle. There is one row of houses, the houses of the street of Charles-Robert, between. It was built by Etienne Bouchart de Grenelle, President of the Parliament during the reign of Louis the Fifteenth, a very dignified and important figure; and he built it, Mademoiselle—this is the point—at the same time that he built the Maison Grenelle. Having built it, he installed in it a joyous lady of the province from which it takes its name—Madame de Brebizart. There was no scandal. For the President never came visiting Madame de Brebizart. And for the best of reasons. Between this house and the Maison Grenelle he had constructed a secret passage in that age of secret passages."

Frobisher was startled. Hanaud had given credit to him for an astuteness which he did not possess. He had been occupied heart and brain by the events of the evening, so rapidly had they followed one upon the other, so little time had they allowed for speculations.

"How in the world did you discover this?" he asked.

"You shall know in due time. For the moment let us content ourselves with the facts," Hanaud continued. "After the death of Etienne de Grenelle, at some period or another the secret of this passage was lost. It is clear, too, I think that it fell into disrepair and became blocked. At all events at the end of the eighteenth century, the Hôtel de Brebizart passed into other hands than those of the owner of the Maison Grenelle. Simon Harlowe, however, discovered the secret. He bought back the Hôtel de Brebizart, restored the passage and put it to the same use as old Etienne de Grenelle had done. For here Madame Raviart came to live during the years before the death of her husband set her free to marry Simon. There! My little lecture is over. Let us go!"

He bowed low to Ann like a lecturer to his audience and unlatched the double doors of the big buhl cabinet in the recess of the wall. A cry of surprise broke from Ann, who had risen unsteadily to her feet. The cabinet was quite empty. There was not so much as a shelf, and all could see that the floor of it was tilted up against one end and that a flight of steps ran downwards in the thickness of the wall.

"Come," said Hanaud, producing his electric torch. "Will you take this, Monsieur Frobisher, and go first with Mademoiselle. I will turn out the lights and follow."

But Ann with a little frown upon her forehead drew sharply back. She put a hand to Hanaud's sleeve and steadied herself by it. "I will come with you," she said. "I am not very steady on my legs."

She laughed her action off but both men understood it. Jim Frobisher had thought her guilty—guilty of theft and murder. She shrank from him to the man who had had no doubt that she was innocent. And even that was not all. She was wounded by Jim's distrust more deeply than any one else could have wounded her. Frobisher inclined his head in acknowledgment and, pressing the button of the torch, descended five or six of the narrow steps. Moreau followed him.

"You are ready, Mademoiselle? So!" said Hanaud.

He put an arm about her to steady her and pressed up a switch by the open doors of the cabinet. The room was plunged in darkness. Guided by the beam of light, they followed Frobisher on to the steps. Hanaud closed the doors of the cabinet and fastened them together with the bolts.

"Forward," he cried, "and you, Mademoiselle, be careful of your heels on these stone steps."

When his head was just below the level of the first step he called upon Frobisher to halt and raise the torch. Then he slid the floor board of the cabinet back into its place. Beneath this a trap-door hung downwards. Hanaud raised it and bolted it in place.

"We can go on."

Ten more steps brought them to a tiny vaulted hall. From that a passage, bricked and paved, led into darkness. Frobisher led the way along the passage until the foot of another flight of steps was reached.

"Where do these steps lead, my friend?" Hanaud asked of Frobisher, his voice sounding with a strange hollowness in that tunnel. "You shall tell me."

Jim, with memories of that night when he and Ann and Betty had sat in the dark of the perfumed garden and Ann's eyes had searched this way and that amidst the gloom of the sycamores, answered promptly:

"Into the garden of the Maison Grenelle."

Hanaud chuckled.

"And you, Mademoiselle, what do you say?"

Ann's face clouded over.

"I know now," she said gravely. Then she shivered and drew her cloak slowly about her shoulders. "Let us go up and see!"

Hanaud took the lead. He lowered a trap-door at the top of the steps, touched a spring and slid back a panel.

"Wait," said he, and he sprang out and turned on a light.

Ann Upcott, Jim Frobisher and Moreau climbed out of Simon Harlowe's Sedan chair into the treasure room.

CHAPTER TWENTY-THREE: *The Truth About the Clock on the Marquetry Cabinet*

TO the amazement of them all Moreau began to laugh. Up till now he had been alert, competent and without expression. Stolidity had been the mark of him. And now he laughed in great gusts, holding his sides and then wringing his hands, as though the humour of things was altogether unbearable. Once or twice he tried to speak, but laughter leapt upon the words and drowned them.

"What in the world is the matter with you, Nicolas?" Hanaud asked.

"But I beg your pardon," Moreau stammered, and again merriment seized and mastered him. At last two intelligible words were heard. "We, Girardot," he cried, settling an imaginary pair of glasses on the bridge of his nose, and went off into a fit. Gradually the reason of his paroxysms was explained in broken phrases.

"We, Girardot!—We fix the seals upon the doors— And all the time there is a way in and out under our nose! These rooms must not be disturbed—No! The great Monsieur Hanaud is coming from Paris to look at them. So we seal them tight, we, Girardot. My God! but we, Girardot look the fool! So careful and pompous with our linen bands! We, Girardot shall make the laughter at the Assize Court! Yes, yes, yes! I think, we, Girardot shall hand in our resignation before the trial is over?"

Perhaps Moreau's humour was a little too professional for his audience. Perhaps, too, the circumstances of that night had dulled their appreciation; certainly Moreau had all the laughter to himself. Jim Frobisher was driven to the little Louis Quinze clock upon the marquetry cabinet. He never could for a moment forget it. So much hung for Betty Harlowe upon its existence. Whatever wild words she might have used to-night, there was the incontrovertible testimony of the clock to prove that she had had no hand whatever in the murder of Mrs. Harlowe. He drew his own watch from his pocket and compared it with the clock.

"It is exact to the minute," he declared with a little accent of triumph. "It is now twenty-three minutes past one——" and suddenly Hanaud was at his side with a curious air of alertness.

"Is it so?" he asked, and he too made sure by a comparison with his own watch that Frobisher's statement was correct. "Yes. Twenty-three minutes past one. That is very fortunate."

He called Ann Upcott and Moreau to him and they all now stood grouped about the cabinet.

"The key to the mystery about this clock," he remarked, "is to be found in the words which Mademoiselle Ann used, when the seals were removed from the doors and she saw this clock again, in the light of day. She was perplexed. Isn't that so, Mademoiselle?"

"Yes," Ann returned. "It seemed to me—it seems to me still—that the clock was somehow placed higher than it actually is——"

"Exactly. Let us put it to the test!"

He looked at the clock and saw that the hands now reached twenty-six minutes past one.

"I will ask you all to go out of this room and wait in the hall in the dark. For it was in the dark, you will remember, that Mademoiselle descended the stairs. I shall turn the lights out here and call you in. When I do, Mademoiselle will switch the lights on and off swiftly, just as she did it on the night of the 27th of April. Then I think all will be clear to you."

He crossed to the door leading into the hall, and found it locked with the key upon the inside.

"Of course," he said, "when the passage is used to the Hôtel de Brebizart, this door would be locked."

He turned the key and drew the door towards him. The hall gaped before them black and silent. Hanaud stood aside.

"If you please!"

Moreau and Frobisher went out; Ann Upcott hesitated and cast a look of appeal towards Hanaud. Her perplexities were to be set at rest. She did not doubt that. This man had saved her from death when it seemed that nothing could save her. Her trust in him was absolute. But her perplexities were unimportant. Some stroke was to be delivered upon Betty Harlowe from which there could be no recovery. Ann Upcott was not a good hater of Betty's stamp. She shrank from the thought that it was to be her hand which would deliver that stroke.

"Courage, Mademoiselle!"

Hanaud exhorted her with a friendly smile and Ann joined the others in the dark hall. Hanaud closed the door upon them and returned to the clock. It was twenty-eight minutes past one.

"I have two minutes," he said to himself. "That will just do if I am quick."

Outside the three witnesses waited in the darkness. One of the three shivered suddenly so that her teeth rattled in her mouth.

"Ann," Jim Frobisher whispered and he put his hand within her arm. Ann Upcott had come to the end of her strength. She clung to his hand spasmodically.

"Jim!" she answered under her breath. "Oh, but you were cruel to me!"

Hanaud's voice called to them from within the room. "Come!"

Ann stepped forward, felt for and found the handle. She threw open the door with a nervous violence. The treasure-room was pitch dark like the hall. Ann stepped through the doorway and her fingers reached for the switch.

"Now," she warned them in a voice which shook.

Suddenly the treasure-room blazed with light; as suddenly it was black again; and in the darkness rose a clamour of voices.

"Half-past ten! I saw the hour!" cried Jim.

"And again the clock was higher!" exclaimed Ann.

"That is true," Moreau agreed.

Hanaud's voice, from the far corner of the room, joined in.

"Is that exactly what you saw, Mademoiselle, on the night of the twenty-seventh?"

"Exactly, Monsieur."

"Then turn on the lights again and know the truth!"

The injunction was uttered in tones so grave that it sounded like a knell. For a second or two Ann's fingers refused their service. Once more the conviction forced itself into her mind. Some irretrievable calamity waited upon the movement of her hand.

"Courage, Mademoiselle!"

Again the lights shone, and this time they remained burning. The three witnesses advanced into the room, and as they looked again, from close at hand and with a longer gaze, a cry of surprise broke from all of them.

There was no clock upon the marquetry cabinet at all.

But high above it in the long mirror before which it stood there was the reflection of a clock, its white face so clear and bright that even now it was difficult to disbelieve that this was the clock itself. And the position of the hands gave the hour as precisely half-past ten.

"Now turn about and see!" said Hanaud.

The clock itself stood upon the shelf of the Adam mantelpiece and there staring at them, the true hour was marked. It was exactly half-past one; the long minute hand pointing to six, the shorter hour hand on the right-hand side of the figure twelve, half-way between the one and the two. With a simultaneous movement they all turned again to the mirror; and the mystery was explained. The shorter hour-hand seen in the mirror was on the left-hand side of the figure twelve, and just where it would have been if the hour had been half-past ten and the clock actually where its reflection was. The figures on the dial were reversed and difficult at a first glance to read.

"You see," Hanaud explained, "it is the law of nature to save itself from effort even in the smallest things. We live with clocks and watches. They are as customary as our daily bread. And with the instinct to save ourselves from effort, we take our time from the position of the hands. We take the actual figures of the hours for granted. Mademoiselle comes out of the dark. In the one swift flash of light she sees the hands upon the clock's face. Half-past ten! She herself, you will remember, Monsieur Frobisher, was surprised that the hour was so early. She was cold, as though she had slept long in her arm-chair. She had the impression that she had slept long. And Mademoiselle was right. For the time was half-past one, and Betty Harlowe had been twenty minutes home from Monsieur de Pouillac's ball."

Hanaud ended with a note of triumph in his voice which exasperated Frobisher.

"Aren't you going a little too fast?" he asked. "When the seals were removed and we entered this room for the first time, the clock was not upon the mantelshelf but upon the marquetry cabinet."

Hanaud nodded.

"Mademoiselle Upcott told us her story before luncheon. We entered this room after luncheon. During the luncheon hours the position of the clock was changed." He pointed to the Sedan chair. "You know now with what ease that could be done."

" 'Could, could!' " Frobisher repeated impatiently. "It doesn't follow that it *was* done."

"That is true," Hanaud replied. "So I will answer now one of the questions in your memorandum. What was it that I saw from the top of the Terrace Tower? I saw the smoke rising from this chimney into the air. Oh, Monsieur, I had paid attention to this house, its windows, and its doors, and its chimney-stacks. And there at midday, in all the warmth of late May, the smoke was rising from the chimney of the sealed room. There was an entrance then of which we knew nothing! And somebody had just made use of it. Who? Ask yourself that! Who went straight out from the Maison Grenelle the moment I had gone, and went alone? That clock had to be changed. Apparently some letters also had to be burnt."

Jim hardly heard the last sentence. The clock still occupied his thoughts. His great argument had been riddled; his one dream of establishing Betty's innocence in despite of every presumption and fact which could be brought against her had been dispelled. He dropped on to a chair.

"You understood it all so quickly," he said with bitterness.

"Oh, I was not quick!" Hanaud answered. "Ascribe to me no gifts out of the ordinary run, Monsieur. I am trained—that is all. I have been my twenty minutes in the bull-ring. Listen how it came about!" He looked at Frobisher with a comical smile. "It is a pity our eager young friend, Maurice Thevenet, is not here to profit by the lesson. First of all, then! I knew that Mademoiselle Betty was here doing something of great importance. It may be only burning those letters in the hearth. It may be more. I must wait and see. Good! There, standing before the mirror, Mademoiselle Ann makes her little remark that the clock seemed higher. Do I understand yet? No, no! But I am interested. Then I notice a curious thing, a beautiful specimen of Benvenuto Cellini's work set up high and flat on that mantelshelf where no one can see it. So I take it down, and I carry it to the window, and I admire it very much and I carry it back to the mantelshelf; and then I notice four little marks upon the wood which had been concealed by the flat case of the jewel; and those four little marks are just the marks which the feet of that very pretty Louis Quinze clock might have made, had it stood regularly there—in its natural place. Yes, and the top of that marquetry cabinet so much lower than the mantelshelf is too the natural place for the Cellini jewel. Every one can see it there. So I say to myself: 'My good Hanaud, this young lady has been rearranging her ornaments.' But do I guess why? No, my friend. I told you once, and I tell you again very humbly, that we are the servants of Chance. Chance is a good mistress if her servants do not go to sleep; and she treated me well that afternoon. See! I am standing in the hall, in great trouble about this case. For nothing leads me anywhere. There is a big old-fashioned barometer like a frying-pan on the wall behind me and a mirror on the opposite wall in front of me. I raise my eyes from the floor and by chance I see in the mirror the barometer behind me. By chance my attention is arrested. For I see that the indicator in the barometer points to stormy weather—which is ridiculous. I turn me about so. It is to fine weather that the indicator points. And in a flash I see. I look at the position of the hand without looking at the letters. If I look the barometer in the face the hand points to the fair weather. If I turn my back and look into the mirror the hand points to the stormy weather. Now indeed I have it! I run into the treasure-room. I lock the door, for I do not wish to be caught. I do not move the clock. No, no, for nothing in the world will I move that clock. But I take out my watch. I face the mirror. I hold my watch facing the mirror, I open the glass and I move the hands until in the mirror they seem to mark half-past ten. Then I look at my watch itself. It is half-past one. So now I know! Do I want more proof? Monsieur, I get it. For as I unlock the door and open it again, there is Mademoiselle Betty face to face with me! That young girl! Even though already I suspect her I get a shock,

I can tell you. The good God knows that I am hardened enough against surprises. But for a moment the mask had slipped from her face. I felt a trickle of ice down my spine. For out of her beautiful great eyes murder looked."

He stood held in a spell by the memory of that fierce look. "Ugh," he grunted; and he shook himself like a great dog coming up out of the water.

"But you are talking too much, Monsieur Frobisher," he cried in a different voice, "and you are keeping Mademoiselle from her bed, where she should have been an hour ago. Come!"

He drove his companions out into the hall, turned on the lights, locked the door of the treasure-room and pocketed the key.

"Mademoiselle, we will leave these lights burning," he said gently to Ann, "and Moreau will keep watch in the house. You have nothing to fear. He will not be far from your door. Good night."

Ann gave him her hand with a wan smile.

"I shall thank you to-morrow," she said, and she mounted the stairs slowly, her feet dragging, her body swaying with her fatigue.

Hanaud watched her go. Then he turned to Frobisher with a whimsical smile.

"What a pity!" he said. "You—she! No? After all, perhaps——" and he broke off hurriedly. Frobisher was growing red and beginning to look "proper"; and the last thing which Hanaud wished to do was to offend him in this particular.

"I make my apologies," he said. "I am impertinent and a gossip. If I err, it is because I wish you very well. You understand that? Good! Then a further proof. To-morrow Mademoiselle will tell us what happened to her to-night, how she came to go to the house of Madame Le Vay—everything. I wish you to be present. You shall know everything. I shall tell you myself step by step, how my conclusions were reached. All your questions shall be answered. I shall give you every help, every opportunity. I shall see to it that you are not even called as a witness of what you have seen to-night. And when all is over, Monsieur, you will see with me that whatever there may be of pain and distress, the Law must take its course."

It was a new Hanaud whom Frobisher was contemplating now. The tricks, the Gasconnades, the buffooneries had gone. He did not even triumph. A dignity shone out of the man like a strong light, and with it he was gentle and considerate.

"Good night, Monsieur!" he said, and bowed; and Jim on an impulse thrust out his hand.

"Good night!" he returned.

Hanaud took it with a smile of recognition and went away.

Jim Frobisher locked the front door and with a sense of desolation turned back to the hall. He heard the big iron gates swing to. They had been left open, of course, he recognised, in the usual way when one of the household was going to be late. Yes, everything had been planned with the care of a commander planning a battle. Here in this house, the servants were all tucked up in their beds. But for Hanaud, Betty Harlowe might at this very moment have been stealing up these stairs noiselessly to her own room, her dreadful work accomplished. The servants would have waked to-morrow to the knowledge that Ann Upcott had fled rather than face a trial. Sometime in the evening, Espinosa would have called, would have been received in the treasure-room, would have found the spade waiting for him in the great stone-vaulted kitchen of the Hôtel de Brebizart. Oh, yes, all dangers had been foreseen—except Hanaud. Nay, even he in a measure had been foreseen! For a panic-stricken telegram had reached Frobisher and Haslitt before Hanaud had started upon his work.

"I shall be on the stairs, Monsieur, below Mademoiselle's door, if you should want me," said Moreau.

Jim Frobisher roused himself from his reflections.

"Thank you," he answered, and he went up the stairs to his room. A lot of use to Betty that telegram had been, he reflected bitterly! "Where was she to-night?" he asked, and shut up his mind against the question.

He was to know that it was precisely that panic-stricken telegram and nothing else which had brought Betty Harlowe's plans crashing about her ears.

CHAPTER TWENTY-FOUR: *Ann Upcott's Story*

EARLY the next morning Hanaud rang up the Maison Grenelle and made his appointment for the afternoon. Jim accordingly spent the morning with Monsieur Bex, who was quite overwhelmed with the story which was told to him.

"Prisoners have their rights nowadays," he said. "They can claim the presence of their legal adviser when they are being examined by the Judge. I will go round at once to the Prefecture"; with his head erect and his little chest puffed out like a bantam cock, he hurried to do battle for his client. There was no battle to be waged, however. Certainly Monsieur Bex's unhappy client was for the moment *au secret*. She would not come before the Judge for a couple of days. It was the turn of Francine Rollard. Every opportunity was to be given to the defence, and Monsieur Bex would certainly be granted an interview with Betty Harlowe, if she so wished, before she was brought up in the Judge's office.

Monsieur Bex returned to the Place Etienne Dolet to find Jim Frobisher restlessly pacing his office. Jim looked up eagerly, but Monsieur Bex had no words of comfort.

"I don't like it!" he cried. "It displeases me. I am not happy. They are all very polite—yes. But they examine the maid first. That's bad, I tell you," and he tapped upon the table. "That is Hanaud. He knows his affair. The servants. They can be made to talk, and this Francine Rollard——" He shook his head. "I shall get the best advocate in France."

Jim left him to his work and returned to the Maison Grenelle. It was obvious that nothing of these new and terrible developments of the "Affaire Waberski" had yet leaked out. There was not a whisper of it in the streets, not a loiterer about the gates of the Maison Grenelle. The "Affaire Waberski" had, in the general view, become a stale joke. Jim sent up word to Ann Upcott in her room that he was removing his luggage to the hotel in the Place Darcy, and leaving the house to her where he prayed her to remain. Even at that moment Ann's lips twitched a little with humour as she read the embarrassed note.

"He is very correct, as Monsieur Bex would say," she reflected, "and proper enough to make every nerve of Monsieur Hanaud thrill with delight."

Jim returned in the afternoon and once more in the shade of the sycamores whilst the sunlight dappled the lawn and the bees hummed amongst the roses, Ann Upcott told a story of terror and darkness, though to a smaller audience. Certain additions were made to the story by Hanaud.

"I should never have dreamed of going to Madame Le Vay's Ball," she began, "except for the anonymous letter," and Hanaud leaned forward alertly.

The anonymous letter had arrived whilst she, Betty and Jim Frobisher were sitting at dinner. It had been posted therefore in the middle of the day and very soon after Ann had told her first story in the garden. Ann opened the envelope expecting a bill, and was amazed and a little terrified to read the signature, "The Scourge." She was more annoyed than ever when she read the contents, but her terror had decreased. "The Scourge" bade her attend the Ball. He gave her explicit instructions that she should leave the ball-room at half-past ten, follow a particular corridor leading to a wing away from the reception-rooms, and hide behind the curtains in a small library. If she kept very still she would overhear in a little while the truth about the death of Mrs. Harlowe. She was warned to tell no one of her plan.

"I told no one then," Ann declared. "I thought the letter just a malicious joke quite in accord with 'The Scourge's' character. I put it back into its envelope. But

I couldn't forget it. Suppose that by any chance there was something in it—and I didn't go! Why should 'The Scourge' play a trick on me, who had no money and was of no importance? And all the while the sort of hope which no amount of reasoning can crush, kept growing and growing!"

After dinner Ann took the letter up to her sitting-room and believed it and scorned herself for believing it, and believed it again. That afternoon she had almost felt the handcuffs on her wrists. There was no chance which she ought to refuse of clearing herself from suspicion, however wild it seemed!

Ann made up her mind to consult Betty, and ran down to the treasure-room, which was lit up but empty. It was half-past nine o'clock. Ann determined to wait for Betty's return, and was once more perplexed by the low position of the clock upon the marquetry cabinet. She stood in front of it, staring at it. She took her own watch in her hand, with a sort of vague idea that it might help her. And indeed it was very likely to. Had she turned its dial to the mirror behind the clock, the truth would have leapt at her. But she had not the time. For a slight movement in the room behind her arrested her attention.

She turned abruptly. The room was empty. Yet without doubt it was from within the room that the faint noise had come. And there was only one place from which it could have come. Some one was hiding within the elaborate Sedan chair with its shining grey panels, its delicate gold beading. Ann was uneasy rather than frightened. Her first thought was to ring the bell by the fire-place—she could do that well out of view of the Sedan chair—and carry on until Gaston answered it. There were treasures enough in the room to repay a hundred thieves. Then, without arguing at all, she took the bolder line. She went quietly towards the chair, advancing from the back, and then with a rush planted herself in front of the glass doors.

She started back with a cry of surprise. The rail in

front of the doors was down, the doors were open, and leaning back upon the billowy cushions sat Betty Harlowe. She sat quite still, still as an image even after Ann had appeared and uttered a cry of surprise; but she was not asleep. Her great eyes were blazing steadily out of the darkness of the chair in a way which gave Ann a curious shock.

"I have been watching you," said Betty very slowly; and if ever there had been a chance that she would relent, that chance was gone for ever now. She had come up out of the secret passage to find Ann playing with her watch in front of the mirror, seeking for an explanation of the doubt which troubled her and so near to it—so very near to it! Ann heard her own death sentence pronounced in those words, "I have been watching you." And though she did not understand the menace they conveyed, there was something in the slow, steady utterance of them which a little unnerved her.

"Betty," she cried, "I want your advice."

Betty came out of the chair and took the anonymous letter from her hand.

"Ought I to go?" Ann Upcott asked.

"It's your affair," Betty replied. "In your place I should. I shouldn't hesitate. No one knows yet that there's any suspicion upon you."

Ann put forward her objection. To go from this house of mourning might appear an outrage.

"You're not a relation," Betty argued. "You can go privately, just before the time. I have no doubt we can arrange it all. But of course it's your affair."

"Why should the Scourge help me?"

"I don't suppose that he is, except indirectly," Betty reasoned. "I imagine that he's attacking other people, and using you." She read through the letter again. "He has always been right, hasn't he? That's what would determine me in your place. But I don't want to interfere."

Ann spun round on her heel.

"Very well. I shall go."

"Then I should destroy that letter"; and she made as if to tear it.

"No!" cried Ann, and she held out her hand for it. "I don't know Madame Le Vay's house very well. I might easily lose my way without the instructions. I must take it with me."

Betty agreed and handed the letter back.

"You want to go quite quietly," she said, and she threw herself heart and soul into the necessary arrangements.

She would give Francine Rollard a holiday and herself help Ann to dress in her fanciful and glistening frock. She wrote a letter to Michel Le Vay, Madame Le Vay's second son and one of Betty's most indefatigable courtiers. Fortunately for himself, Michel Le Vay kept that letter, and it saved him from any charge of complicity in her plot. For Betty used to him the same argument which had persuaded Jim Frobisher. She wrote frankly that suspicion had centred upon Ann Upcott and that it was necessary that she should get away secretly.

"All the plans have been made, Michel," she wrote. "Ann will come late. She is to meet the friends who will help her—it is best that you should know as little as possible about them—in the little library. If you will keep the corridor clear for a little while, they can get out by the library doors into the park and be in Paris the next morning."

She sealed up this letter without showing it to Ann and said, "I will send this by a messenger to-morrow morning, with orders to deliver it into Michel's own hands. Now how are you to go?"

Over that point the two girls had some discussion. It would be inviting Hanaud's interference if the big limousine were ordered out. What more likely than that he should imagine Ann meant to run away and that Betty was helping her? That plan certainly would not do.

"I know," Betty cried. "Jeanne Leclerc shall call

for you. You will be ready to slip out. She shall stop
her car for a second outside the gates. It will be quite
dark. You'll be away in a flash."

"Jeanne Leclerc!" Ann exclaimed, drawing back.

It had always perplexed Ann that Betty, so exquisite
and fastidious in her own looks and bearing, should have
found her friends amongst the flamboyant and the cheap.
But she would rather throne it amongst her inferiors
than take her place amongst her equals. Under her re-
served demeanour she was insatiable of recognition.
The desire to be courted, admired, looked up to as a
leader and a chief, burned within her like a raging flame.
Jeanne Leclerc was of her company of satellites—a big,
red-haired woman of excessive manners, not without
good looks of a kind, and certainly received in the society
of the town. Ann Upcott not merely disliked, but dis-
trusted her. She had a feeling that there was something
indefinably wrong in her very nature.

"She will do anything for me, Ann," said Betty.
"That's why I named her. I know that she is going to
Madame Le Vay's dance."

Ann Upcott gave in, and a second letter was written to
Jeanne Leclerc. This second letter asked Jeanne to call
at the Maison Grenelle at an early hour in the morning;
and Jeanne Leclerc came and was closeted with Betty for
an hour between nine and ten. Thus all the arrangements
were made.

It was at this point that Frobisher interrupted Hanaud's
explanations.

"No," he said. "There remain Espinosa and the young
brother to be accounted for."

"Mademoiselle has just told us that she heard a slight
noise in the treasure-room and found Betty Harlowe
seated in the Sedan chair," Hanaud replied. "Betty Harlowe had just returned from the Hôtel de Brebizart,
whither Espinosa went that night after it had grown dark
and about the time when dinner was over in the Maison
Grenelle. . . . From the Hôtel de Brebizart Espinosa

went to the Rue Gambetta and waited for Jean Cladel. It
was a busy night, that one, my friends. That old wolf,
the Law, was sniffing at the bottom of the door. They
could hear him. They had no time to waste!"

The next night came. Dinner was very late, Jim remembered. It was because Betty was helping Ann to
dress, Francine having been given her holiday. Jim and
Betty dined alone, and whilst they dined Ann Upcott
stole downstairs, a cloak of white ermine hiding her
pretty dress. She held the front door a little open, and
the moment Jeanne Leclerc's car stopped before the gates,
she flashed across the courtyard. Jeanne had the door of
her car open. It had hardly stopped before it went on
again. Jim, as the story was told, remembered vividly
Betty's preoccupation whilst dinner went on, and the im-
mensity of her relief when the hall door so gently closed
and the car moved forward out of the street of Charles-
Robert. Ann Upcott had gone for good from the Maison
Grenelle. She would not interfere with Betty Harlowe
any more.

Jeanne Leclerc and Ann Upcott reached Madame Le
Vay's house a few minutes after ten. Michel Le Vay
came forward to meet them.

"I am so glad that you came, Mademoiselle," he said
to Ann, "but you are late. Madame my mother has left
her place at the door of the ball-room, but we shall find
her later."

He took them to the cloak-room, and coming away
they were joined by Espinosa.

"You are going to dance now?" Michel Le Vay asked.
"No, not yet! Then Señor Espinosa will take you to
the buffet while I look after others of our guests."

He hurried away towards the ball-room, where a clatter
of high voices competed with the music of the band.
Espinosa conducted the two ladies to the buffet. There
was hardly anybody in the room.

"We are still too early," said Jeanne Leclerc in a low
voice. "We shall take some coffee."

But Ann would not. Her eyes were on the door, her feet danced, her hands could not keep still. Was the letter a trick? Would she, indeed, within the next few minutes learn the truth? At one moment her heart sank into her shoes, at another it soared.

"Mademoiselle, you neglect your coffee," said Espinosa urgently. "And it is good."

"No doubt," Ann replied. She turned to Jeanne Leclerc. "You will send me home, won't you? I shall not wait—afterwards."

"But of course," Jeanne Leclerc agreed. "All that is arranged. The chauffeur has his orders. You will take your coffee, dear?"

Again Ann would not.

"I want nothing," she declared. "It is time that I went." She caught a swift and curious interchange of glances between Jeanne Leclerc and Espinosa, but she was in no mood to seek an interpretation. There could be no doubt that the coffee set before her had had some drug slipped into it by Espinosa when he fetched it from the buffet to the little table at which they sat; a drug which would have half stupefied her and made her easy to manage. But she was not to be persuaded, and she rose to her feet.

"I shall get my cloak," she said, and she fetched it, leaving her two companions together. She did not return to the buffet.

On the far side of the big central hall a long corridor stretched out. At the mouth of the corridor, guarding it, stood Michel Le Vay. He made a sign to her, and when she joined him:

"Turn down to the right into the wing," he said in a low voice. "The small library is in front of you."

Ann slipped past him. She turned into a wing of the house which was quite deserted and silent. At the end of it a shut door confronted her. She opened it softly. It was all dark within. But enough light entered from the corridor to show her the high bookcases ranged against the walls, the position of the furniture, and some dark, heavy curtains at the end. She was the first, then, to come to the tryst. She closed the door behind her and moved slowly and cautiously forwards with her hands outstretched, until she felt the curtains yield. She passed in between them into the recess of a great bow window opening on to the park; and a sound, a strange, creaking sound, brought her heart into her mouth.

Some one was already in the room, then. Somebody had been quietly watching as she came in from the lighted corridor. The sound grew louder. Ann peered between the curtains, holding them apart with shaking hands, and through that chink from behind her a vague twilight flowed into the room. In the far corner, near to the door, high up on a tall bookcase, something was clinging—something was climbing down. Whoever it was, had been hiding behind the ornamental top of the heavy mahogany book-case; was now using the shelves like the rungs of a ladder.

Ann was seized with a panic. A sob broke from her throat. She ran for the door. But she was too late. A black figure dropped from the book-case to the ground and, as Ann reached out her hands to the door, a scarf was whipped about her mouth, stifling her cry. She was jerked back into the room, but her fingers had touched the light switch by the door, and as she stumbled and fell, the room was lighted up. Her assailant fell upon her, driving the breath out of her lungs, and knotted the scarf tightly at the back of her head. Ann tried to lift herself, and recognised with a gasp of amazement that the assailant who pinned her down by the weight of her body and the thrust of her knees was Francine Rollard. Her panic gave place to anger and a burning humiliation. She fought with all the strength of her supple body. But the scarf about her mouth stifled and weakened her, and with a growing dismay she understood that she was no match for the hardy peasant girl. She was the taller of the two, but her height did not avail her; she was like a child

matched with a wildcat. Francine's hands were made of
steel. She snatched Ann's arms behind her back and
bound her wrists, as she lay face downwards, her bosom
labouring, her heart racing so that she felt that it must
burst. Then, as Ann gave up the contest, she turned and
tied her by the ankles.

Francine was upon her feet again in a flash. She ran
to the door, opened it a little way and beckoned. Then
she dragged her prisoner up on to a couch, and Jeanne
Leclerc and Espinosa slipped into the room.

"It's done?" said Espinosa.

Francine laughed.

"Ah, but she fought, the pretty baby! You should
have given her the coffee. Then she would have walked
with us. Now she must be carried. She's wicked, I can
tell you."

Jeanne Leclerc twisted a lace scarf about the girl's face
to hide the gag over her mouth, and, while Francine held
her up, set her white cloak about her shoulders and
fastened it in front. Espinosa then turned out the light
and drew back the curtains.

The room was at the back of the house. In the front
of the window the park stretched away. But it was the
park of a French château, where the cattle feed up to the
windows, and only a strip about the front terrace is de-
voted to pleasure-gardens and fine lawns. Espinosa
looked out upon meadow-land thickly studded with trees,
and cows dimly moving in the dusk of the summer night
like ghosts. He opened the window, and the throb of
the music from the ball-room came faintly to their ears.

"We must be quick," said Espinosa.

He lifted the helpless girl in his arms and passed out
into the park. They left the window open behind them,
and between them they carried their prisoner across the
grass, keeping where it was possible in the gloom of the
trees, and aiming for a point in the drive where a motor-
car waited half-way between the house and the gates. A
blur of light from the terrace and ornamental grounds in

front of it became visible away upon their left, but here all was dark. Once or twice they stopped and set Ann upon her feet, and held her so, while they rested.

"A few more yards," Espinosa whispered and, stifling an oath, he stopped again. They were on the edge of the drive now, and just ahead of him he saw the glimmer of a white dress and close to it the glow of a cigarette. Swiftly he put Ann down again and propped her against a tree. Jeanne Leclerc stood in front of her and, as the truants from the ball-room approached, she began to talk to Ann, nodding her head like one engrossed in a lively story. Espinosa's heart stood still as he heard the man say:

"Why, there are some others here! That is curious. Shall we see?"

But even as he moved across the drive, the girl in the white dress caught him by the arm.

"That would not be very tactful," she said with a laugh. "Let us do as we would be done by," and the couple sauntered past.

Espinosa waited until they had disappeared. "Quick! Let us go!" he whispered in a shaking voice.

A few yards farther on they found Espinosa's closed car hidden in a little alley which led from the main drive. They placed Ann in the car. Jeanne Leclerc got in beside her, and Espinosa took the wheel. As they took the road to the Val Terzon a distant clock struck eleven. Within the car Jeanne Leclerc removed the gag from Ann Upcott's mouth, drew the sack over her and fastened it underneath her feet. At the branch road young Espinosa was waiting with his motor-cycle and side-car.

"I can add a few words to that story, Mademoiselle," said Hanaud when she had ended. "First, Michel Le Vay went later into the library, and bolted the window again, believing you to be well upon your way to Paris. Second, Espinosa and Jeanne Leclerc were taken as they returned to Madame Le Vay's ball."

"WE are not yet quite at the end," said Hanaud, as he sat with Frobisher for awhile upon the lawn after Ann Upcott had gone in. "But we are near to it. There is still my question to be answered. 'Why was the communicating door open between the bedroom of Madame Harlowe and the treasure-room on the night when Ann Upcott came down the stairs in the dark?' When we know that, we shall know why Francine Rollard and Betty Harlowe between them murdered Madame Harlowe."

"Then you believe Francine Rollard had a hand in that crime too?" asked Jim.

"I am sure," returned Hanaud. "Do you remember the experiment I made, the little scene of reconstruction? Betty Harlowe stretched out upon the bed to represent Madame, and Francine whispering 'That will do now'?"

"Yes."

Hanaud lit a cigarette and smiled.

"Francine Rollard would not stand at the side of the bed. No! She would stand at the foot and whisper those simple but appalling words. But nowhere else. That was significant, my friend. She would not stand exactly where she had stood when the murder was committed." He added softly, "I have great hopes of Francine Rollard. A few days of a prison cell and that untamed little tiger-cat will talk."

"And what of Waberski in all this?" Jim exclaimed.

Hanaud laughed and rose from his chair.

"Waberski? He is for nothing in all this. He brought a charge in which he didn't believe, and the charge happened to be true. That is all." He took a step or two away and returned. "But I am wrong. That is not all. Waberski is indeed for something in all this. For when he was pressed to make good his charge and must rake up some excuse for it somehow, by a piece of luck he thinks of a morning when he saw Betty Harlowe in the street of Gambetta near to the shop of Jean Cladel. And so he leads us to the truth. Yes, we owe something to that animal Boris Waberski. Did I not tell you, Monsieur, that we are all the servants of Chance?"

Hanaud went from the garden and for three days Jim Frobisher saw him no more. But the development which Monsieur Bex feared and for which Hanaud hoped took place, and on the third day Hanaud invited Jim to his office in the Prefecture.

He had Jim's memorandum in his hand.

"Do you remember what you wrote?" he asked. "See!" He pushed the memorandum in front of Jim and pointed to a paragraph.

"But in the absence of any trace of poison in the dead woman's body, it is difficult to see how the criminal can be brought to justice except by:

"(*a*) A confession.

"(*b*) The commission of another crime of a similar kind.

"Hanaud's theory—once a poisoner, always a poisoner."

Frobisher read it through.

"Now that is very true," said Hanaud. "Never have I come across a case more difficult. At every step we break down. I think I have my fingers on Jean Cladel. I am five minutes too late. I think that I shall get some useful evidence from a firm in Paris. The firm has ceased to be for the last ten years. All the time I strike at air. So I must take a risk—yes, and a serious one. Shall I tell you what that risk was? I have to assume that Mademoiselle Ann will be brought alive to the Hôtel de Brebizart on that night of Madame Le Vay's ball.

That she would be brought back I had no doubt. For one thing, there could be no safer resting-place for her than under the stone flags of the kitchen there. For another, there was the portmanteau in the side-car. It was not light, the portmanteau. Some friends of mine watched it being put into the side-car before young Espinosa started for his rendezvous. I have no doubt it weighed just as many kilos as Mademoiselle Ann."

"I never understood the reason of that portmanteau," Frobisher interrupted.

"It was a matter of timing. There were twenty-five kilometres of a bad track, with many sharp little twists between the Val Terzon and the Hôtel de Brebizart. And a motor-cycle with an empty side-car would take appreciably longer to cover the distance than a cycle with a side-car weighted, which could take the corners at its top speed. They were anxious to get the exact time the journey would take with Ann Upcott in the side-car, so that there might be no needless hanging about waiting for its arrival. But they were a little too careful. Our friend Boris said a shrewd thing, didn't he? Some crimes are discovered because the alibis are too unnaturally perfect. Oh, there was no doubt they meant to bring back Mademoiselle Ann! But suppose they brought her back dead! It wasn't likely—no! It would be so much easier to finish her off with a dose of the arrow-poison. No struggle, no blood, no trouble at all. I reckoned that they would dope her at Madame Le Vay's ball and bring her back half conscious, as indeed they meant to do. But I shivered all that evening at the risk I had taken, and when that cycle shut off its engine, as we stood in the darkness of the gallery, I was in despair."

He shook his shoulders uncomfortably as though the danger was not yet passed.

"Anyway, I took the risk," he resumed, "and so we got fulfilled your condition (*b*). The commission or, in this case, the attempted commission of another crime of the same kind."

Frobisher nodded.

"But now," said Hanaud, leaning forward, "we have got your condition (*a*) fulfilled—a confession; a clear and complete confession from Francine Rollard, and so many admissions from the Espinosas, and Jeanne Leclerc and Maurice Thevenet, that they amount to confessions. We have put them all together, and here is the new part of the case with which Monsieur Bex and you will have to deal—the charge not of murder attempted but of murder committed—the murder of Madame Harlowe."

Jim Frobisher was upon the point of interrupting, but he thought better of it.

"Go on!" he contented himself with saying.

"Why Betty Harlowe took to writing anonymous letters, Monsieur—who shall say? The dulness of life for a girl young and beautiful and passionate in a provincial town, as our friend Boris suggests? The craving for excitement? Something bad and vicious and abnormal born in her, part of her, and craving more and more expression as she grew in years? The exacting attendance upon Madame? Probably all of these elements combined to suggest the notion to her. And suddenly it became easy for her. She discovered a bill in that box in Madame Harlowe's bedroom, a receipted bill ten years old from the firm of Chapperon, builders, of the Rue de Batignolles in Paris. You, by the way, saw an unburnt fragment of the bill in the ashes upon the hearth of the treasure-room. This bill disclosed to her the existence of the hidden passage between the treasure-room and the Hôtel de Brebizart. For it was the bill of the builders who had repaired it at the order of Simon Harlowe. An old typewriting machine belonging to Simon Harlowe and the absolute privacy of the Hôtel de Brebizart made the game easy and safe. But as the opportunity grew, so did the desire. Betty Harlowe tasted power. She took one or two people into her confidence— her maid Francine, Maurice Thevenet, Jeanne Leclerc, and Jean Cladel, a very useful personage—and once

started the circle grew; blackmail followed. Blackmail of
Betty Harlowe, you understand! She, the little queen,
became the big slave. She must provide Thevenet with
his mistress, Espinosa with his car and his house, Jeanne
Leclerc with her luxuries. So the anonymous letters become themselves blackmailing letters. Maurice Thevenet
knows the police side of Dijon and the province. Jeanne
Leclerc has a—friend, shall we say?—in the Director of
an Insurance Company, and, believe me, for a blackmailer
nothing is more important than to know accurately the
financial resources of one's—let us say, clients. Thus the
game went merrily on until money was wanted and it
couldn't be raised. Betty Harlowe looked around Dijon.
There was no one for the moment to exploit. Yes, one
person! Let us do Betty Harlowe the justice to believe
that the suggestion came from that promising young
novice, Maurice Thevenet! Who was that person, Monsieur Frobisher?"

Even now Jim Frobisher was unable to guess the truth,
led up to it though he had been by Hanaud's exposition.

"Why, Madame Harlowe herself," Hanaud explained,
and, as Jim Frobisher started back in a horror of disbelief, he continued: "Yes, it is so! Madame Harlowe
received a letter at dinner-time, just as Ann Upcott did,
on the night of Monsieur de Pouillac's ball. She took
her dinner in bed, you may remember, that night. That
letter was shown to Jeanne Baudin the nurse, who remembers it very well. It demanded a large sum of money,
and something was said about a number of passionate
letters which Madame Harlowe might not care to have
published—not too much, you understand, but enough to
make it clear that the *liaison* of Madame Raviart and
Simon Harlowe was not a secret from the Scourge. I'll
tell you something else which will astonish you, Monsieur
Frobisher. That letter was shown not only to Jeanne
Baudin, but to Betty Harlowe herself when she came to
say good night and show herself in her new dance frock
of silver tissue and her silver slippers. It was no wonder

that Betty Harlowe lost her head a little when I set my little trap for her in the library and pretended that I did not want to read what Madame had said to Jeanne Baudin after Betty Harlowe had gone off to her ball. I hadn't one idea what a very unpleasant little trap it was!"

"But wait a moment!" Frobisher interrupted. "If Madame Harlowe showed this letter first of all to Jeanne Baudin, and afterwards to Betty Harlowe in Jeanne Baudin's presence, why didn't Jeanne Baudin speak of it at once to the examining magistrate when Waberski brought his accusation? She kept silent! Yes, she kept silent!"

"Why shouldn't she?" returned Hanaud. "Jeanne Baudin is a good and decent girl. For her, Madame Harlowe had died a natural death in her sleep, the very form in which death might be expected to come for her. Jeanne Baudin didn't believe a word of Waberski's accusation. Why should she rake up old scandals? She herself proposed to Betty Harlowe to say nothing about the anonymous letter."

Jim Frobisher thought over the argument and accepted it. "Yes, I see her point of view," he admitted, and Hanaud continued his narrative.

"Well, then, Betty Harlowe is off to her ball on the Boulevard Thiers. Ann Upcott is in her sitting-room. Jeanne Baudin has finished her offices for the night. Madame Harlowe is alone. What does she do? Drink? For that night—no! She sits and thinks. Were there any of the letters which passed between her and Simon Harlowe, before she was Simon Harlowe's wife, still existing? She had thought to have destroyed them all. But she was a woman, she might have clutched some back. If there were any, where would they be? Why in that house at the end of the secret passage. Some such thoughts must have passed through her mind. For she rose from her bed, slipped on her dressing-gown and shoes, unlocked the communicating door between her and the treasure-room and passed by the secret way into the empty Hôtel de Brebizart. And what does she find there, Monsieur? A room in daily use, a bundle of her letters ready in the top drawer of her Empire writing-table, and on the writing-table Simon's Corona machine, and the paper and envelopes of the anonymous letters. Monsieur, there is only one person who can have access to that room, the girl whom she has befriended, whom in her exacting way she no doubt loved. And at eleven o'clock that night Francine Rollard is startled by the entrance of Madame Harlowe into her bedroom. For a moment Francine fancied that Madame had been drinking. She was very quickly better informed. She was told to get up, to watch for Betty Harlowe's return and to bring her immediately to Madame Harlowe's bedroom. At one o'clock Francine Rollard is waiting in the dark hall. As Betty comes in from her party, Francine Rollard gives her the message. Neither of these two girls know as yet how much of their villainies has been discovered. But something at all events. Betty Harlowe bade Francine wait and ran upstairs silently to her room. Betty Harlowe was prepared against discovery. She had been playing with fire, and she didn't mean to be burnt. She had the arrow-poison ready—yes, ready for herself. She filled her hypodermic needle, and with that concealed in the palm of her glove she went to confront her benefactress.

"You can imagine that scene, the outraged woman whose romance and tragedy were to be exploited blurting out her fury in front of Francine Rollard. It wasn't Waberski who was to be stripped to the skin—no, but the girl in the pretty silver frock and the silver slippers. You can imagine the girl, too, her purpose changing under the torrent of abuse. Why should she use the arrow-poison to destroy herself when she can save everything—fortune, liberty, position—by murder? Only she must be quick. Madame's voice is rising in gusts of violence. Even in that house of the old thick walls, Jeanne Baudin, some one, might be wakened by the clamour. And in a moment the brutal thing is done. Madame Harlowe is flung back upon her bed. Her mouth is covered and held by Francine Rollard. The needle does its work. 'That will do now,' whispers Betty Harlowe. But at the door of the treasure-room in the darkness Ann Upcott is standing, unable to identify the voice which whispered, just as you and I were unable, Monsieur, to identify a voice which whispered to us from the window of Jean Cladel's house, but taking deep into her memory the terrible words. And neither of the murderesses knew it.

"They go calmly about their search for the letters. They cannot find them, because Madame had pushed them into the coffer of old bills and papers. They rearrange the bed, they compose their victim in it as if she were asleep, they pass into the treasure-room, and they forget to lock the door behind them. Very likely they visit the Hôtel de Brebizart. Betty Harlowe has the rest of the arrow-poison and the needle to put in some safe place, and where else is safe? In the end when every care has been taken that not a scrap of incriminating evidence is left to shout 'Murder' the next morning, Betty creeps up the stairs to make sure that Ann Upcott is asleep; and Ann Upcott waking, stretches up her hands and touches her face.

"That, Monsieur," and Hanaud rose to his feet, "is what you would call the case for the Crown. It is the case which you and Monsieur Bex have to meet."

Jim Frobisher made up his mind to say the things which he had almost said at the beginning of this interview.

"I shall tell Monsieur Bex exactly what you have told me. I shall give him every assistance that I personally or my firm can give. But I have no longer any formal connection with the defence."

Hanaud looked at Frobisher in perplexity.

"I don't understand, Monsieur. This is not the moment to renounce a client."

"Nor do I," rejoined Frobisher. "It is the other way

about. Monsieur Bex put it to me very—how shall I say?"

Hanaud supplied the missing word with a twitch of his lips.

"Very correctly."

"He told me that Mademoiselle did not wish to see me again."

Hanaud walked over to the window. The humiliation evident in Frobisher's voice and face moved him. He said very gently, "I can understand that, can't you? She has fought for a great stake all this last week, her liberty, her fortune, her good name—and you. Oh, yes," he continued, as Jim stirred at the table. "Let us be frank! And you, Monsieur! You were a little different from her friends. From the earliest moment she set her passions upon you. Do you remember the first morning I came to the Maison Grenelle? You promised Ann Upcott to put up there though you had just refused the same invitation from Betty Harlowe. Such a fury of jealousy blazed in her eyes, that I had to drop my stick with a clatter in the hall lest she should recognise that I could not but have discovered her secret. Well, having fought for this stake and lost, she would not wish to see you. You had seen her, too, in her handcuffs and tied by the legs like a sheep. I understand her very well."

Jim Frobisher remembered that from the moment Hanaud burst into the room at the Hôtel de Brebizart, Betty had never once even looked at him. He got up from his chair and took up his hat and stick.

"I must go back to my partner in London with this story as soon as I have told it to Monsieur Bex," he said. "I should like it complete. When did you first suspect Betty Harlowe?"

Hanaud nodded.

"That, too, I shall tell you. Oh, don't thank me! I am not so sure that I should be so ready with all these confidences, if I was not certain what the verdict in the Assize

Court must be. I shall gather up for you the threads which are still loose, but not here."

He looked at his watch.

"See, it is past noon! We shall once more have Philippe Le Bon's Terrace Tower to ourselves. It may be, too, that we shall see Mont Blanc across all the leagues of France. Come! Let us take your memorandum and go there."

CHAPTER TWENTY-SIX: *The Façade of Notre Dame*

FOR a second time they were fortunate. It was a day without mist or clouds, and the towering silver ridge hung in the blue sky distinct and magical. Hanaud lit one of his black cigarettes and reluctantly turned away from it.

"There were two great mistakes made," he said. "One at the very beginning by Betty Harlowe. One at the very end by me, and of the two mine was the least excusable. Let us begin, therefore, at the beginning. Madame Harlowe has died a natural death. She is buried; Betty Harlowe inherits the Harlowe fortune. Boris Waberski asks her for money and she snaps her the fingers. Why should she not? Ah, but she must have been very sorry a week later that she snapped her the fingers! For suddenly he flings his bomb. Madame Harlowe was poisoned by her niece Betty. Imagine Betty Harlowe's feelings when she heard of that! The charge is preposterous. No doubt! But it is also true. A minute back she is safe. Nothing can touch her. Now suddenly her head is loose upon her neck. She is frightened. She is questioned in the examining magistrate's room. The magistrate has nothing against her. All will be well if she does not make a slip. But there is a good chance she may make a slip. For she has done the murder. Her danger is not any evidence which Waberski can bring, but just herself. In two days she is still more frightened, for she hears that Hanaud is called in from Paris. So she makes her mistake. She sends a telegram to you in London."

"Why was that a mistake?" Frobisher asked quickly.

"Because I begin to ask myself at once: 'How does

Betty Harlowe know that Hanaud has been called in?'
Oh, to be sure, I made a great fluster in my office about
the treachery of my colleagues in Dijon. But I did not
believe a word of that. No! I am at once curious about
Betty Harlowe. That is all. Still, I am curious. Well,
we come to Dijon and you tell her that you have shown
me that telegram."

"Yes," Jim admitted. "I did. I remember, too," he
added slowly, "that she put out her hand on the window
sill—yes, as if to steady herself."

"But she was quick to recover," returned Hanaud with
a nod of appreciation. "She must account for that telegram. She cannot tell me that Maurice Thevenet sent a
hurried word to her. No! So when I ask her if she
has ever received one of these anonymous letters—which,
remember, were my real business in Dijon—she says at
once 'Yes, I received one on the Sunday morning which
told me that Monsieur Hanaud was coming from Paris
to make an end of me.' That was quick, eh? Yes, but I
know it is a lie. For it was not until the Sunday evening
that any question of my being sent for arose at all. You
see Mademoiselle Betty was in a corner. I had asked
her for the letter. She does not say that she has destroyed it, lest I should at once believe that she never
received any such letter at all. On the contrary she says
that it is in the treasure-room which is sealed up, knowing
quite well that she can write it and place it there by way
of the Hôtel de Brebizart before the seals are removed.
But for the letter to be in the treasure-room she must
have received it on the Sunday morning, since it was
on the Sunday morning that the seals were affixed. She
did not know when it was first proposed to call me in.
She draws a bow at a venture, and I know that she is
lying; and I am more curious than ever about Betty
Harlowe."

He stopped. For Jim Frobisher was staring at him
with a look of horror in his eyes.

"It was I then who put you on her track?—I who

came out to defend her!" he cried. "For it was I who showed you the telegram."

"Monsieur Frobisher, that would not have mattered if Betty Harlowe had been, as you believed her, innocent," Hanaud replied gravely; and Frobisher was silent.

"Well, then, after my first interview with Betty Harlowe, I went over the house whilst you and Betty talked together in the library!"

"Yes," said Jim.

"And in Mademoiselle Ann's sitting-room I found something which interested me at the first glance. Now tell me what it was!" and he cocked his head at Jim with the hope that his riddle would divert him from his self-reproaches. And in that to some extent he succeeded.

"That I can guess," Frobisher answered with the ghost of a smile. "It was the treatise on Sporanthus."

"Yes! The arrow-poison! The poison which leaves no trace! Monsieur, that poison has been my nightmare. Who would be the first poisoner to use it? How should I cope with him and prove that it brought no more security than arsenic or prussic-acid? These are questions which have terrified me. And suddenly, unexpectedly, in a house where a death from heart failure has just occurred, I find a dry-as-dust treatise upon the poison tucked away under a pile of magazines in a young lady's sitting-room. I tell you I was staggered. What was it doing there? How did it come there? I see a note upon the cover, indicating a page. I turn to the page and there, staring at me, is an account of Simon Harlowe's perfect specimen of a poison-arrow. The anonymous letters? They are at once forgotten. What if that animal Waberski, without knowing it, were right, and Madame Harlowe was murdered in the Maison Grenelle? I must find that out. I tuck the treatise up my back beneath my waistcoat and I go downstairs again, asking myself some questions. Is Mademoiselle Ann interested in such matters as Sporanthus Hispidus? Or had she anything to hope for from Madame Harlowe's death? Or did she perhaps not know at all that the treatise was under that pile of magazines upon the table at the side? I do not know, and my head is rather in a whirl. Then I catch that wicked look of Betty Harlowe at her friend—Monsieur, a revealing look! I have not the demure and simple young lady of convention to deal with at all. No. I go away from the Maison Grenelle, still more curious about Betty Harlowe."

Jim Frobisher sat quickly down at Hanaud's side.

"Are you sure of that?" he asked suspiciously.

"Quite," Hanaud replied in wonder.

"You have forgotten, haven't you, that immediately after you left the Maison Grenelle that day you had the sergent-de-ville removed from its gates?"

"No, I don't forget that at all," Hanaud answered imperturbably. "The sergent-de-ville in his white trousers was an absurdity—worse than that, an actual hindrance. There is little use in watching people who know that they are being watched. So I remove the sergent-de-ville and now I can begin really to watch those young ladies of the Maison Grenelle. And that afternoon, whilst Monsieur Frobisher is removing his luggage from his hotel, Betty Harlowe goes out for a walk, is discreetly followed by Nicolas Moreau—and vanishes. I don't blame Nicolas. He must not press too close upon her heels. She was in that place of small lanes about the Hôtel de Brebizart. No doubt it was through the little postern in the wall which we ourselves used a few days afterwards that she vanished. There was the anonymous letter to be written, ready for me to receive when the seals of the treasure-room were broken. But I don't know that yet. No! All that I know is that Betty Harlowe goes out for a walk and is lost, and after an hour reappears in another street. Meanwhile I pass my afternoon examining so far as I can how these young ladies pass their lives and who are their friends. An examination not very productive, and not altogether futile. For I find some curious friends in Betty Harlowe's circle. Now, observe this, Monsieur! Young girls with advanced ideas, social, political, literary, what you will—in their case curious friends mean nothing! They are to be expected. But with a young girl who is to all appearance leading the normal life of her class, the case is different. In her case curious friends are—curious. The Espinosas, Maurice Thevenet, Jeanne Leclerc—flashy cheap people of that type—how shall we account for them as friends of that delicate piece of china, Betty Harlowe?"

Jim Frobisher nodded his head. He, too, had been a trifle disconcerted by the familiarity between Espinosa and Betty Harlowe.

"The evening," Hanaud continued, "which you spent so pleasantly in the cool of the garden with the young ladies, I spent with the Edinburgh Professor. And I prepared a little trap. Yes, and the next morning I came early to the Maison Grenelle and I set my little trap. I replace the book about the arrows on the bookshelf in its obvious place."

Hanaud paused in his explanation to take another black cigarette from his eternal blue bundle, and to offer one to Jim.

"Then comes our interview with the animal Waberski; and he tells me that queer story about Betty Harlowe in the street of Gambetta close to the shop of Jean Cladel. He may be lying. He may be speaking the truth and what he saw might be an accident. Yes! But also it fits in with this theory of Madame Harlowe's murder which is now taking hold of me. For if that poison was used, then some one who understood the composition of drugs must have made the solution from the paste upon the arrow. I am more curious than ever about Betty Harlowe! And the moment that animal has left me, I spring my trap; and I have a success beyond all my expectations. I point to the treatise of the Edinburgh Professor. It was not in its place yesterday. It is to-day. Who then replaced it? I ask that question and Mademoiselle Ann is utterly at sea. She knows nothing about that book. That is evident as Mont Blanc over there in the sky. On

The Façade of Notre Dame

the other hand Betty Harlowe knows at once who has replaced that book; and in a most unwise moment of sarcasm, she allows me to see that she knows. She knows that I found it yesterday, that I have studied it since and replaced it. And she is not surprised. No, for she knows where I found it. I am at once like Waberski. I know it in my heart that she put it under those magazines in Ann Upcott's room, although I do not yet know it in my head. Betty Harlowe had prepared to divert suspicion from herself upon Ann Upcott, should suspicion arise. But innocent people do not do that, Monsieur.

"Then we go into the garden and Mademoiselle Ann tells us her story. Monsieur Frobisher, I said to you immediately afterwards that all great criminals who are women are great actresses. But never in my life have I seen one who acted so superbly as Betty Harlowe while that story was being unfolded. Imagine it! A cruel murder has been secretly committed and suddenly the murderess has to listen to a true account of that murder in the presence of the detective who is there to fix the guilt! There was some one at hand all the time—almost an eye-witness—perhaps an actual eye-witness. For she cannot know that she is safe until the last word of the story is told. Picture to yourself Betty Harlowe's feelings during that hour in the pleasant garden, if you can! The questions which must have been racing through her mind! Did Ann Upcott in the end creep forward and peer through the lighted doorway? Does she know the truth—and has she kept it hidden until this moment when Hanaud and Frobisher are present and she can speak it safely? Will her next words be 'And here at my side sits the murderess'? Those must have been terrible moments for Betty Harlowe!"

"Yet she gave no sign of any distress," Frobisher added.

"But she took a precaution," Hanaud remarked. "She ran suddenly and very swiftly into the house."

305

"Yes. You seemed to me on the point of stopping her."

"And I was," continued Hanaud. "But I let her go and she returned——"

"With the photographs of Mrs. Harlowe," Frobisher interrupted.

"Oh, with more than those photographs," Hanaud exclaimed. "She turned her chair towards Mademoiselle Ann. She sat with her handkerchief in her hand and her face against her handkerchief, listening—the tender, sympathetic friend. But when Mademoiselle Ann told us that the hour of the murder was half-past ten, a weakness overtook her—could not but overtake her. And in that moment of weakness she dropped her handkerchief. Oh, she picked it up again at once. Yes, but where the handkerchief had fallen her foot now rested, and when the story was all ended, and we got up from our chairs, she spun round upon her heel with a certain violence so that there was left a hole in that well-watered turf. I was anxious to discover what it was that she had brought out from the house in her handkerchief, and had dropped with her handkerchief and had driven with all the weight of her body into the turf so that no one might see it. In fact I left my gloves behind in order that I might come back and discover it. But she was too quick for me. She fetched my gloves herself, much to my shame that I, Hanaud, should be waited on by so exquisite a young lady. However, I found it afterwards when you and Girardot and the others were all waiting for me in the library. It was that tablet of cyanide of potassium which I showed to you in the Prefecture. She did not know how much Ann Upcott was going to reveal. The arrow-poison had been hidden away in the Hôtel de Brebizart. But she had something else at hand—more rapid—death like a thunderbolt. So she ran into the house for it. I tell you, Monsieur, it wanted nerve to sit there with that tablet close to her mouth. She grew very pale. I do not wonder. What I do wonder is that she did not topple straight off her chair in a dead faint before us all. But no! She sat ready to swallow that tablet at once if there were need, before my hand could stop her. Once more I say to you, people who are innocent do not do that."

Jim had no argument wherewith to answer.

"Yes," he was forced to admit. "She could have got the tablets no doubt from Jean Cladel."

"Very well, then," Hanaud resumed. "We have separated for luncheon and in the afternoon the seals are to be removed. Before that takes place, certain things must be done. The clock must be moved from the mantelshelf in the treasure-room on to the marquetry cabinet. Some letters too must be burnt."

"Yes. Why?" Frobisher asked eagerly.

Hanaud shrugged his shoulders.

"The letters were burned. It is difficult to say. For my part I think those old letters between Simon Harlowe and Madame Raviart alluded too often to the secret passage. But here I am guessing. What I learnt for certain during that luncheon hour is that there is a secret passage and that it runs from the treasure-room to the Hôtel de Brebizart. For this time Nicolas Moreau makes no mistake. He follows her to the Hôtel de Brebizart and I from this tower see the smoke rising from the chimney. Look, Monsieur, there it is! But no smoke rises from it to-day."

He rose to his feet and turned his back upon Mont Blanc. The trees in the garden, the steep yellow-patterned roof, and the chimneys of the Maison Grenelle stood out above the lesser buildings which surrounded them. Only from one of the chimneys did the smoke rise to-day, and that one at the extreme end of the building where the kitchens were.

"We are back then in the afternoon. The seals are removed. We are in Madame Harlowe's bedroom and something I cannot explain occurs."

"The disappearance of the necklace," Frobisher exclaimed confidently; and Hanaud grinned joyfully.

"See, I set a trap for you and at once you are caught!"
he cried. "The necklace? Oh, no, no! I am prepared
for that. The guilt is being transferred to Mademoiselle
Ann. Good! But it is not enough to hide the book
about the arrow in her room. No, we must provide her
also with a motive. Mademoiselle is poor; Mademoiselle
inherits nothing. Therefore the necklace worth a hundred thousand pounds vanishes, and you must draw from
its vanishing what conclusion you will. No, the little
matter I cannot explain is different. Betty Harlowe and
our good Girardot pay a visit to Jeanne Baudin's bedroom
to make sure that a cry from Madame's room could not
be heard there."

"Yes."

"Our good Girardot comes back."

"Yes."

"But he comes alone. That is the little thing I cannot
explain. Where is Betty Harlowe? I ask for her before
I go into the treasure-room, and lo! very modestly and
quietly she has slipped in amongst us again. I am very
curious about that, my friend, and I keep my eyes open
for an explanation, I assure you."

"I remember," said Frobisher. "You stopped with
your hand upon the door and asked for Mademoiselle
Harlowe. I wondered why you stopped. I attached no
importance to her absence."

Hanaud flourished his hand. He was happy. He was
in the artist's mood. The work was over, the long strain
and pain of it. Now let those outside admire!

"Of all that the treasure-room had to tell us, you know,
Monsieur Frobisher. But I answer a question in your
memorandum. The instant I am in the room, I look for
the mouth of that secret passage from the Hôtel de Brebizart. At once I see. There is only one place. The
elegant Sedan chair framed so prettily in a recess of the
wall. So I am very careful not to pry amongst its
cushions for the poison arrow; just as I am very careful

not to ask for the envelope with the post mark in which the anonymous letter was sent. If Betty Harlowe thinks that she has overreached the old fox Hanaud—good! Let her think so. So we go upstairs and I find the explanation of that little matter of Betty Harlowe's absence which has been so troubling me."

Jim Frobisher stared at him.

"No," he said. "I haven't got that. We went into Ann Upcott's sitting-room. I write my memorandum with the shaft of the poison arrow and you notice it. Yes! But the matter of Betty Harlowe's absence! No, I haven't got that."

"But you have," cried Hanaud. "That pen! It was not there in the pen-tray on the day before, when I found the book. There was just one pen—the foolish thing young ladies use, a great goose-quill dyed red—and nothing else. The arrow shaft had been placed there since. When? Why, just now. It is clear, that. Where was that shaft of the poison-arrow before? In one of two places. Either in the treasure-room or in the Hôtel de Brebizart. Betty Harlowe has fetched it away during that hour of freedom; she carries it in her dress; she seizes her moment when we are all in Madame Harlowe's bed-room and—pau, pau!—there it is in the pen-tray of Mademoiselle Ann, to make suspicion still more convincing! Monsieur, I walk away with Monsieur Bex, who has some admirable scheme that I should search the gutters for a match-box full of pearls. I agree—oh yes, that is the only way. Monsieur Bex has found it! On the other hand I get some useful information about the Maison Grenelle and the Hôtel de Brebizart. I carry that information to a very erudite gentleman in the Palace of the Departmental Archives, and the next morning I know all about the severe Etienne de Grenelle and the joyous Madame de Brebizart. So when you and Betty Harlowe are rehearsing in the Val Terzon, Nicolas Moreau and I are very busy in the Hôtel de Brebizart—

with the results which now are clear to you, and one of which I have not told you. For the pearl necklace was in the drawer of the writing-table."

Jim Frobisher took a turn across the terrace. Yes, the story was clear to him now—a story of dark passions and vanity, and greed of power with cruelties for its methods. Was there no spark of hope and cheer in all this desolation? He turned abruptly upon Hanaud. He wished to know the last hidden detail.

"You said that you had made the inexcusable mistake. What was it?"

"I bade you read my estimate of Ann Upcott on the façade of the Church of Notre Dame."

"And I did," cried Jim Frobisher. He was still looking towards the Maison Grenelle, and his arm swept to the left of the house. His fingers pointed at the Renaissance church with its cupolas and its loggia, to which Betty Harlowe had driven him.

"There it is and under its porch is that terrible relief of the Last Judgment."

"Yes," said Hanaud quietly. "But that is the Church of St. Michel, Monsieur."

He turned Frobisher about. Between him and Mont Blanc, close at his feet, rose the slender apse of a Gothic church, delicate in its structure like a jewel.

"That is the Church of Notre Dame. Let us go down and look at the façade."

Hanaud led Frobisher to the wonderful church and pointed to the frieze. There Frobisher saw such images of devils half beast, half human, such grinning hog-men, such tortured creatures with heads twisted round so that they looked backwards, such old and drunken and vicious horrors as imagination could hardly conceive; and amongst them one girl praying, her sweet face tormented, her hands tightly clasped, an image of terror and faith, a prisoner amongst all these monsters imploring the passers-by for their pity and their help.

"That, Monsieur Frobisher, is what I sent you out to

see," said Hanaud gravely. "But you did not see it."

His face changed as he spoke. It shone with kindness. He lifted his hat.

Jim Frobisher, with his eyes fixed in wonder upon that frieze, heard Ann Upcott's voice behind him.

"And how do you interpret that strange work, Monsieur Hanaud?" She stopped beside the two men.

"That, Mademoiselle, I shall leave Monsieur Frobisher to explain to you."

Both Ann Upcott and Jim Frobisher turned hurriedly towards Hanaud. But already he was gone.

THE END

Other Mystery and Suspense Titles
Available from Carroll & Graf

The Third Arm—by Kenneth Royce
An intriguing plot places a band of world-notorious terrorists in a confused and vulnerable London in this literate and astonishing thriller that will enthrall fans of John LeCarre and Graham Greene.

$3.50

Channel Assault—by Kenneth Royce
A treacherous plot to negotiate a secret "peace" treaty with Hitler and assassinate Winston Churchill brings together a British doctor, his mistress and an American OSS agent in this novel which combines the realism of historical fiction with the gut grip of a thriller.

$3.50

Deadline—by Thomas B. Dewey
The Chicago private detective known only as "Mac" in a last minute fight against the corruption of a one-man dominated small town.

$3.50

Murder for Pleasure—by Howard Haycraft
A time-honored history of the mystery genre from A.C. Doyle to Raymond Chandler that will delight the general reader and fan alike.

$10.95

The Red Right Hand—by Joel Townsley Rogers
The chilling story of a young couple on their way to be married who pick up an ominous hitchhiker and are involved in a strange accident is a tale of sheer terror.

$3.50

A Sad Song Singing—by Thomas B. Dewey
Masterful suspense and an unusual mystery set "Mac" against Chicago's shadowy world of entertainers and caberets.

$3.50

The Shrewsdale Exit—by John Buell
Brutal highway terrorism destroys a man's family in this poignant and suspenseful tale of innocence confronted by irrational violence.

$3.50

Fog of Doubt—by Christianna Brand
A mystery in the Christie-Carr-Queen manner. A tour de force in which the last words of the novel name the murderer.

$3.50

Fantasy and Science Fiction Titles
Available from Carroll & Graf

Citadel of Fear—by Francis Stevens
A masterpiece of the fantastic, a classic allegory set in Tlapallan, lost city of an ancient race.

$3.50

Om, The Secret of Ahbor Valley—by Talbot Mundy
Set in India in the 1920's this wonderful tale of adventure and mysticism can be fairly called a cross between *Raiders of the Lost Ark* and *Kim*.

$3.95

The House on the Borderland—by William Hope Hodgson
Renowned as one of the greatest cosmic fantasy tales in the English language, this novel is a work of pure imagination which sustains an overpowering level of wonder and mounting horror. It will appeal equally to fans of fantasy, horror and science-fiction.

$3.25